EXACERBYTE
By Cat Connor

Acknowledgements

I would like to thank the following people:

Rosanne, Megan, and Dionne – for weekend dinners and laughter. (Breathe deeply!)

Lorenza Ponce – musician/songwriter, amazing woman. Heartfelt thanks for your time and energy, in helping me round out a new character and giving me a window into the world of rock stars. (You too are a Soul Shifter.)

Jayne Southern – whose humor is vital to the editing process. Thank you!

With heartfelt thanks to my very supportive publisher, Caroline Addenbrooke.

And last but by no means least – my family for putting up with me.

For Rebekah and Josephine
"Reach for the dream."

Chapter One
Every Intention

My phone chirped like a demented cricket. It was the second call in two minutes. Demented crickets are never good. I pulled over to the shoulder and stopped. Cars whizzed by me. The phone chirped again.

"SSA Conway."

"Ellie, Chrissy here. Just reminding you about the high school visit."

"I hadn't forgotten – there's plenty of time yet." I checked the time on my watch just to be sure. "I'm dropping by Cassie's then I have a few things to do. I don't have to be at the school until later this afternoon."

"Tell her she's invited to my place next weekend. My turn to cook for us all."

"I'll pass it along."

I dropped my phone on the passenger seat and pulled back into the traffic.

Ten minutes later, I parked in the driveway behind Cassie's Subaru. Icy rain splattered from the gray sky as I cleared some mail I noticed poking from the mailbox. Clutching a few letters, I wrapped my jacket tighter against the cold wind and hurried to the front door.

I knocked and waited, shuffling from foot to foot to keep warm. I knocked again. There were no signs of life beyond the stained-glass inset in the door.

"Cassie!" I called.

No reply.

I walked along the porch. The curtains were open. It was difficult to see into the room; even weak winter light caused too much glare. I cupped one hand against the window and placed my eye up to it. No one moved within. I knocked on the window as I peered. For a second I thought I saw something moving by the living room door. "Cassie!"

There was a skittering of paws on wood. Suddenly Roscoe's face appeared, pressed against the window, his huge paws on the windowsill. Tongue lolling.

"Roscoe! Sit!" The large dog dropped to his hairy backside, tongue still hanging from his open mouth. He wasn't the brightest of dogs but he was sweet.

He'd left a large reddish smear across the glass. I craned my neck to see if the dog was bleeding but couldn't see anything. I jogged around the back of the house, letting myself in the back gate. Still no sign of human life.

I pulled out my cell phone and called Cassie's cell. From where I stood, I heard it ring. It had to be in the kitchen. I hung up before it went to voicemail and hammered on the solid back door. The only noise beyond was the dog tearing across the house and sliding into the kitchen cabinets.

It just wasn't right. Cassie never left without her cell. Her car was there. Roscoe was in the house, not in his centrally-heated dog run. I counted rocks in the garden beside the back porch until I found the hollow one and the back door key. I knocked, turned the key and handle and then called out as the door swung open.

Roscoe hit me like a freight train, knocking me back. I scrambled to my feet and wiped my slimy hands down my jeans. "Damn drooling dog."

Roscoe bounced around me, slobber flying.

"Sit!"

He plopped like a stone sending a cloud of fluff into the air. His yellow fur was stained red in patches. His large hairy feet were matted and messy.

"What's on you?" I held his collar and leaned down. There was no mistaking the smell. "Blood."

I couldn't trust the dog to stay, so with a firm grip on his collar and my Glock in the other hand I started searching the house. We were in the laundry. I followed his dark footprints into the kitchen. My eyes scanned the immediate area. My nose prickled at the smell of fresh blood. On the corner of the kitchen counter, there was blood and long strands of dark hair. Blood dripped down the front of the cabinets. I held the dog tightly, stopping him from putting his hairy feet in any more evidence.

Above the dog's panting, I heard a click. I closed my eyes and concentrated. A door clicked shut. Someone was in the house. Dog, gun, no hands left for the phone. I crouched down next to the dog and pried my cell from my belt. This wasn't going to work. I stood up and put a leg over the dog, successfully trapping his head between my knees. I managed to send an emergency call to Delta A. An open line was all I needed. I slipped the phone into my shirt pocket.

"I hope you can hear me. I'm at Cassandra Smith's home in Reston. Possible home invasion. There is blood all over the floor. Can't find Cassie. I need back-up and paramedics."

Voices jumbled in my pocket. Sam's overrode Lee and Chrissy's. "We're on our way Chicky Babe. Notifying local police."

"Good to know."

I adjusted my grip on the panting dog and wound my fingers tightly under his collar. With care I moved my leg, to stand next to him again. "Come on Roscoe let's find Cassie."

We cleared the kitchen. I noted more blood splatter on the walls and smearing on the doorframe. Drag marks on the floor led down the hallway. The blood faded into the carpet fibers.

Another click.

The dog pulled. I pulled back and whispered, "No."

My heart raced and stomach twisted. With trepidation, I opened the guest bathroom door. Nothing. I closed the door: if anyone was hiding, they couldn't use the rooms I'd cleared for cover without alerting me by opening doors.

My attention focused on the guest bedroom. Silently I opened the door. There was nothing obvious. I checked under the bed, in the closet, behind the curtains. No one. No sign that anyone had even been in the room.

Four more doors led from the hallway.

The dog whined softly as I swung open the next door. It was Cassie's home office. I breathed for a moment. The entire room was visible from the doorway. A desk, chair, overstuffed bookcases and her laptop.

Next was another bedroom, used as a storeroom by the look of it. Boxes piled high around the walls. Roscoe and I swept the room keeping an eye on the hallway the whole time. Only two rooms remained. One on the right and one on the left at the front door end of the hallway. One was the living room and one Cassie's bedroom.

The dog and I stepped carefully into the room on the right. The door was open. Nothing out of place at all. No one hiding under the sofas in the living room. No one behind the floor-length drapes.

The only place left was Cassie's room. It had a walk-in closet/dressing room and a separate bathroom. Two rooms within a room. Both with locks. Maybe she was in one of the rooms and was safe. Maybe it wasn't her blood all over the dog. I looked down at Roscoe. He was the dumbest and friendliest dog I'd ever met. This was not a guard dog; this was a seventy-pound lapdog. He was likely to lick someone to death or maybe trip him or her with his over-exuberance but otherwise, he'd never harm anyone. Roscoe whined and pulled me. He wanted to get into the bedroom.

A door slammed. It sounded close.

My stomach flip-flopped sending bile rushing toward my mouth.

I swallowed hard, took a deep breath, held tight to the

dog and twisted the knob of Cassie's bedroom door. I pushed it so hard it hit the wall behind the door. The dog flinched.

Deep blue curtains billowed into the room. I checked behind them. The French doors were open; there was blood on the floor and bloody footprints outside on the porch. In the distance, sirens.

"Cassie!"

Nothing under the bed. I tried the dressing room door. Locked. I banged.

"Cassie!"

I let the dog go. Roscoe scratched at the door. Then ran to the bathroom door and scratched that.

"Cassie! It's Ellie."

I listened. Roscoe scratched and whined. "Roscoe, shush."

He looked at me with his head on one side, ears alert and goofy tongue falling out of his mouth. Then I heard her voice from the bathroom.

"Ellie."

Bathroom locks aren't that secure. I didn't know where Cassie was, so couldn't shoot. I braced myself on the doorjamb and kicked. Wood splintered. The lock groaned. The dog tried to force his way between my legs. I shoved him out of the way. He made another attempt.

"Get out of the way."

I kicked again. The door flew open.

My gun was already in my holster as I pushed Roscoe again to get him out of my way and rushed to Cassie. She was covered in blood and sitting against the bath, wooden long-handled body brush in her hand.

"Jesus. You look like shit."

"Really? But I feel so good." Roscoe dropped his big furry head on her lap. "You are the dumbest dog in the world," Cassie mumbled patting his head. "Completely useless and I wouldn't be without you." The brush clattered to the tiled floor.

I pulled a towel from the rail and pressed it against her head. My pocket was erupting with noise.

"Excuse my pocket; it's been very worried about you." I lifted my phone and spoke into it. "Cassie needs paramedics. Tell police they're going to need dogs; someone left on foot." I dropped my phone back into my pocket and concentrated on Cassie. "Who did this Cas?"

"Never saw his face ... he wore one of those scarf things soldiers wear ... shema ..."

"Shemagh?"

"A brownish color."

After a couple of false starts, she managed to tell me more. "He had same the same color boots, dark blue jeans, a dark jacket. Odd eyes."

Sirens stopped outside. Heavy footsteps ran to the front door.

"I'll let these guys in, or they'll break your pretty door." I hurried away.

I called out and identified myself before opening the door to four uniformed patrolmen. I gave them a description and went back to Cassie.

The towel was soaked in places. I grabbed another and pressed it against her head.

"Odd eyes?"

"Different shades of brown."

"Excellent." I called out to the police and relayed the extra description of the Unsub's eyes, then turned my attention back to Cassie. "You hurt anywhere else?"

"He hit my head against the corner of the kitchen counter a few times; when I fell he kicked me and then dragged me up the hallway."

"I am so glad I left my scarf here last night."

"Me too." Tears escaped her swollen eyes and coursed through the bloodied bruises. "You scared him away. I locked myself in here when he went to investigate."

"Any idea who he was?"

I was aware of police hovering in the bathroom doorway, they were happy enough to let me ask the questions.

"No, he never spoke but he seemed very interested in the pictures on the fridge."

She moved and from a pocket handed me a piece of paper. "He gave me this."

It was a photo of Cassie and me, taken over a year ago, in a heated debate outside the Hoover Building. "That's an old picture."

"When we met."

We both smiled. We came from opposite ends of the same problem and met with an explosion in the middle. Cassie was the social worker assigned to Carla Torres the day her mother was murdered. Within a week of our first meeting, she began trying to convince me Carla Torres was better off with me than in foster care. Cassie and Carla became fixtures in my life. Fixtures in all our lives. We'd all hung out together. Sam, Lee, me, Carla, Cassie, Chrissy, sometimes even Caine. She had pictures stuck on her fridge of all of us, having fun, proving that family is what you make it.

Cassie looked at me. "Dinner your place next week."

"Yeah. Dinner at my place." I wiped tears from her face with my fingers. "We'll talk before then."

"Call me." Her eyes rolled back. She slumped forward. Her hand went limp in mine.

"Cassie!"

Suddenly a paramedic was in the room. He almost threw me out of the way.

"She's unconscious," I said. "She was talking and seemed okay." As okay as someone who's been beaten to a bloody pulp can be.

She was talking.

I grabbed the dog and pulled him out of the way as the paramedics began CPR.

That's where Sam and Lee found me. With my arms wrapped around the stupid dog, sitting on the bedroom floor, while paramedics tried to bring my friend back to life. A few times while sitting there, I felt sinister eyes watching, an unwelcome feeling I knew all too well and one I'd hoped to never experience again. When I looked over my shoulder, there were only police. I scanned everything with expert eyes looking for telltale signs of hidden cameras and saw nothing out of the ordinary.

Through the bathroom door I saw the paramedics. One looked over at me and shook his head. They weren't in the business of giving up. One was bagging her, the other doing CPR. A suited man ran past me into the bathroom. I watched him drop to his knees next to the paramedics and Cassie. His head turned and eyes locked on mine. Supervisory Special Agent Kurt Henderson otherwise known as Doctor Henderson. His head shook ever so slightly as his mouth took on a grim line.

Police crawled all over the house. They found some clear boot prints on the porch.

Sam went to look. He returned with his opinion. "Combat boots. Cassie mentioned a shemagh? Military or a poseur?"

"My money's on poseur," Lee said, watching the paramedics.

"She's not going to make it." I knew the words were mine but they felt foreign. My arms tightened around the dog's hairy neck. "She has a brother in Richmond. We should call him to take Roscoe."

Lee pulled his phone from his belt and made a call. I listened to him talking to Chrissy. He wrote a number in his notebook. "Ellie, do you want Chrissy to reschedule your afternoon?"

I shook my head. "No. I'll carry on. I'd sooner be busy than sitting around waiting to hear from police."

He finished talking to Chrissy.

I heard Kurt call out the time.

Cassie was dead.

A police officer asked that they leave her body where it was. The medical examiner was on his way.

Kurt weaved his way around people to me. "There was nothing that could be done. Autopsy will confirm but it looks like she had a massive brain bleed due to trauma."

"She was talking. I had no idea she was going to die."

"I know." His hand rested on my shoulder. "Head injuries are unpredictable."

"Thank you for coming," I said, hoping my voice didn't crumble.

"Heard your call. Figured I might be able to help." He shrugged. "Sorry."

Kurt walked away. I guessed he'd wait outside for the medical examiner.

Lee turned to me and said, "I'll find the officer in charge and see about notifying Cassie's brother and finding somewhere for Roscoe to stay in the meantime."

"I need to go home and clean up before I visit that high school."

Lee squatted in front of me. "I can do the high school visit. You could stay here with Cassie and Roscoe."

A few deep breaths later I replied, "You know nothing about poetry." In all honestly I knew about the same. I could write it but had no clue about iambic pentameter or any other device I was sure the kids would know and be able to discuss. "I can't stay here without inserting myself into the police investigation and no one wants me telling cops how to do their jobs."

"I could come with ..."

"Not necessary, but thank you."

"Carla?"

"I'll go over to her foster parents' place after school and tell her myself." The last things Cassie said to me rolled around my head. The air was filled with noise and I needed quiet. "I'm just going to go outside. It's a bit claustrophobic in here all of a sudden. I'll take Roscoe and put him in his run."

Lee nodded. I used the dog to help me stand. He stuck close as I walked to the front door. I didn't need to hold him. From the front porch I could see two police cruisers at the end of the driveway, three more sat across the street. Officers were taping off the front lawn and drive.

Roscoe leaned against my leg as I walked him through the back gate and over to his impressive dog run. He walked inside, whined and pushed against me. I patted his head and tried to speak to him calmly. "It'll be okay Roscoe." I knew he knew Cassie wasn't coming back.

The dog dropped to the ground, his head on his paws, brown sad eyes watching me, as if his life-force had drained with Cassie's. I checked he had water and tossed him a few dog biscuits. Cassie kept a small bag of dog snacks in a cupboard inside the run. It also contained his leash and brush. Roscoe took a biscuit into his kennel. He flopped onto his bed. I closed the wire gate and locked it. I expected the sound of dog teeth crunching to follow me from the backyard but there was nothing but a mournful silence. By the time I reached the house the yard was filled with the saddest howl I could've ever imagined.

I leaned back on the wall by the front door and eyed the two chairs sitting on the porch. Serenaded by the dog's grief I thought about the night before. Cassie and I had sat out on the porch. It was a cold night but the sky was clear. We'd watched shooting stars, consumed coffee and righted every wrong in the world. Cassie had again broached the subject of me adopting Carla. She told me she'd written a letter and placed it in Carla's file, her recommendation for Carla's future. Our coffee cups were still on the small table between the chairs.

A mixture of blood and dog fur stuck to my jeans like a macabre patchwork.

Footsteps.

Caine stood in front of me. "Cassie?" Gruff as ever.

I swallowed, hoping the word wouldn't choke me. "Dead." I looked down not wanting to see Caine's eyes. "Did you see Kurt Henderson?"

He nodded. "Who's running this?"

"Not us. Police. I heard someone say Darren Reid was Officer in Charge."

A cop appeared behind Caine. He was tall, broad shouldered and about forty years old. I'd seen him before but couldn't place him. As it happened, I didn't need to.

"SSA Conway, I'm Darren Reid. We met at Mac Connelly's house a few years ago – home invasion."

That's how I knew him. He was the cop Mac knew.

"You found the cat and took it to Bob Connelly's," I replied, shaking his hand then introducing Caine. "This is

SAC Caine Grafton."

They shook. With pleasantries out of the way, work mode resumed.

"What happened here?" Caine asked while he pulled on the shoe coverings and gloves another officer handed him.

"Cassandra Smith, a fifty-one year old social worker with Child Services was murdered. Agent Conway was first on the scene and with her when she died. We don't have a motive yet. Follow me."

I stayed where I was.

"Conway?" Caine said. I got the message and walked behind Darren and Caine into the well-known interior of Cassie's home. Hundreds of photos of kids smiled down at me from the hallway walls. Their eyes followed me. I figured I could handle those eyes watching me as long as I didn't have to acknowledge losing a friend.

I almost walked into Caine, not noticing he'd stopped outside the kitchen. Darren entered the room. Caine and I stood in the wide doorway. Last night the room had been bathed in warm light and the delicious aroma of homemade lasagna. Today it was blood splatter. I shivered.

"Okay?" Caine asked.

"Sure."

I shuddered. My eyes flicked to the refrigerator door. Photos fixed with magnets covered the entire surface. There were photos of me, Cassie and Carla at various outdoor events over summer. Some of us hanging out in

Cassie's backyard, or my backyard. My eyes landed on a picture of Lee, Sam, Carla and Cassie. I remembered taking it.

"Cassie said the Unsub seemed interested in those photographs." I pointed to the refrigerator. "He gave her a picture. This one." I took the picture from my jacket pocket and gave it to Caine.

He showed Darren and the questions began.

"You know the victim well?"

"I know Cassie very well."

"What's your connection with Cassandra Smith?"

"She was the social worker assigned to protect Carla Torres. Carla's mother was murdered." I breathed in to steady my voice. "Cassie was convinced that Carla would be better off with me than in foster care. She was my friend."

"This is where the injuries were sustained. The Unsub then dragged Cassandra down the hallway ..." Darren walked back down the hall and into Cassie's room. He pointed to a bloody patch on the floor by the bed. "We believe she was left here for a few minutes."

"That could've been when I came in the back. Cassie told me I spooked him. She used that time to get to the bathroom."

"When I came in here, that door was open." I pointed to the french doors. "Once I determined the Unsub was gone I found Cassie in the bathroom."

I blinked trying to stem the prickling at the back of my eyes. Cassie's body called to me. I moved carefully, avoiding blood and crouched beside her. Her out-of-focus eyes stared at nothing.

"Oh Cas, who did this?" I wanted a reply but none came. There was a smell of bleach by her hands. I hadn't noticed it earlier. It tickled the back of my nose and triggered a memory. I sniffed. Chlorine. Chlorine bleach. "Caine – she has chlorine on her hands."

The crime scene took on a new meaning. I scanned it for anything else that would go with the chlorine. Familiar poetry. Notes. Bourbon. Possessed by the past, I walked back through the house searching everything again with new eyes. Caine and Reid followed me in silence. The kitchen gave off the strongest smell of chlorine. My nose led me to the sink and a teacup. I sniffed and recoiled. The cup had contained chlorine bleach. I pointed it out. "She must've been soaking it to remove tea stains."

I opened the cabinet under the sink and discovered a large bottle of Clorox. One mystery solved and it wasn't sinister. I'm pretty sure the sigh that escaped me was audible.

"Do you have any suspects?"

"Only you," Darren replied.

Caine bristled. "SSA Conway was not involved in this unfortunate incident."

"I'm not in the habit of killing my friends and I sure as hell wouldn't beat someone to a pulp then call police," I muttered at Darren. "And I don't wear combat boots. You find a shemagh anywhere? Are my eyes different colors?"

He shook his head.

"We only have the description you gave. My officers weren't able to confirm it with the deceased."

"You need to look elsewhere."

"I'm starting with what's in front of me," Darren replied.

It felt as though he wanted me to be involved. My annoyance intensified. "What else do you have or are you content to waste time with me?"

"Did Cassandra have a partner? A boyfriend? Anyone she's been dating?"

Nothing then.

"No one permanent. She dated a guy from Alexandria a few times but said it wasn't going anywhere." My brain started to kick in. "Have you looked for her day planner – his phone number will be in there."

"There was no day planner that we've found."

"It might be in her car. Or maybe she uses her laptop as a day planner. That's in her home office."

My cell phone chirped. I looked at the screen. Chrissy. I looked at my clothes. Blood soaked. Time to go home and shower.

"I have to go. I'll write my statement tonight and email it to you." I took my card from my pocket and handed it to Reid. "You can reach me anytime. Keep me informed."

He shook my hand. "Don't leave the country."

"If I were you I'd start checking for bugs and wireless cameras. Something is not right here," I said, barely keeping a nasty edge from my voice.

"You Fed's think everything is about terrorists and spies," he scoffed.

"I'll walk you out," Caine said, turning me toward the door before I could snap a retort at Reid. My hand strayed to my hip. My fingers brushed the grip of my Glock. It took real will power to shove my hand in my pocket and not decorate the room with Reid's blood.

"Is he for real?" I snarled at Caine as we stood on the driveway. "Don't leave the country; it's all about terrorists and spies. Who the does that fucktard think he's dealing with?"

"I'll handle him."

"Thanks." I looked at him. "Cassie was a federal employee – can Delta B investigate?"

I knew Delta A couldn't. It'd be like investigating a family member's murder. Not good to be so close.

"No reason why we can't run a parallel investigation. I have the impression you are not filled with confidence by Mac's old buddy?"

"Nope."

"You sure you're okay?"

Hell no.

I avoided the question. "I gotta go clean up and visit a high school."

Chapter Two
Joey

"Good afternoon, I'm Supervisory Special Agent Ellie Conway." I glanced around the classroom, bestowing what I hoped was a congenial smile upon the occupants. "You don't have to spit out that entire title every time you speak, SSA or Agent will do just fine."

I rocked back on the heel of my right boot and waited for the room buzz to settle. Slowly the music that filled my head faded to soft background noise. I didn't have time to explore why I could hear Bon Jovi singing 'Joey', so I let it fade. If it were important, it'd be back.

The class teacher, Audrey Walker, stood beside me, an elegant and bright woman in her early fifties. She spoke quietly and the classroom fell into a serious silence as the students all paid close attention. Audrey had extended an invitation to me via our media liaison Special Agent Chrissy McQueen. She'd asked if I would speak to her high school junior English class – she was attempting to show them there was still a place for poetry in today's world. I figured it would provide a much-needed distraction on what had become a bitter Wednesday afternoon.

Earlier I'd felt as though someone was watching me and now twenty-five pairs of eyes were on me. I found it unnerving.

Speaking to the students was easier than I'd expected – time rushed by and almost before I knew it, I'd been talking for thirty-minutes. The kids had a ton of questions for me. It was interesting answering them but observing the classroom dynamic was far more fascinating. A young man at the back of the room slumped in his chair. I picked up a jumbled vibe from him, as if he wanted to take part but didn't know how. He'd been fiddling with a cell phone. Which now resided in Audrey Walker's desk. His fingers now toyed with a pen and his eyes remained firmly fixed on the desk in front of him. He didn't seem to be interested in the class or having a Special Agent visit. Something about the intensity with which he tried to ignore me piqued my curiosity. He doth try too hard.

A girl in the middle of the room waved her arm so violently I thought she'd dislocate her shoulder.

"You – in the blue sweater – what's your name?" I pointed at her, controlling the rising mirth at her enthusiasm.

"Lily, Agent Conway. I'm Lily." Her voice positively bubbled.

"Hi, Lily. What was your question?"

"What's your favorite movie?"

I replied, "*Die Hard 4.0.*"

My trouble radar detected sudden movement from the back of the room. The disinterested boy looked up and a smile flickered across his face. He muttered something under his breath.

"Did you have something to share with the class?" I asked looking straight at him.

"*Live Free or Die Hard.*"

Engaged.

"I have an international copy of the DVD, therefore ..."

He interrupted, "It's a better name anyway. They should've gone with 4.0 here, it makes more sense."

Lily faltered for a moment then took a breath and threw something else out, "Do you still write poetry?"

"No, Lily, I don't."

The kid at the back of the class closed down. Damn.

"Why not? We all have your book; we persuaded Ms. Walker to let us study your poems for extra credit."

A cold ball grew hands and clawed inside my chest. Books appeared from bags and sat upon desks. They all appeared to have my book. My eyes flicked to the back of the room. No book on that desk.

I smiled. "Are they your books or school books?"

"Ours," the class replied.

Immediately I saw a way of deferring the imminent questions about why I no longer wrote. "Anyone want them signed?"

Giggling and squealing broke out from the middle of the class. Lily spoke, "I do!"

I had a bag with me and in it I had a few copies of my dreaded poetry book, *Whispers on the Water*. I figured I would give a few away to anyone who wanted one but only one teen seemed bookless.

"One by one, bring up your books." A line formed. I signed books and chatted briefly with each person. I was there to talk about poetry – of which I knew little to nothing but used to write it once with my husband – and to talk about being a Special Agent with the FBI to whoever wanted to listen. The kid from the back of the class appeared in front of me, empty-handed.

"I don't have your book," he said. His eyes looked sideways rather than at me.

"That's fine," I replied. It was interesting that he came up anyway.

He looked at me. "You really like *Die Hard 4.0*?"

"Yes I do." I grinned. "I liked all the *Die Hard* movies."

He shot a half a smile at me. "Bruce Willis is the man."

"He most certainly is."

"You ever gone die hard on anyone's ass?"

I pulled a copy of the book from my bag and opted to ignore his question. "What's your name?"

"Joey," he replied.

I understood then why I'd heard Bon Jovi as I entered the classroom. I opened the book to the title page and picked up my pen.

"You don't have to do that, I can buy it. I'm not a charity case."

"I never said you were. I would like you to have this." Something about Joey bothered me. He was tough with sharp edges but I saw hurt. It troubled me so much that I wrote a message in the front of the book and added my cell phone number.

"What's that for?" he asked, reading it.

"You ever need me, call," I said.

"Why would you do that? You don't even know me," he

replied, still looking at the page with my phone number on it.

"I don't know you. You don't know me. Sometimes it's easier to talk to a stranger."

"What makes you think I'd need a Fed?"

"I have no reason to think you'd need a Fed, but if you need someone. I'm willing to listen."

"I won't call." He started to walk away then turned back to face me, recognition flying from his eyes like daggers. "I know who you are," he said quietly. "You're that Fed whose husband was gunned down saving Carla."

I am that Fed.

"Anytime Joey, just call."

He shrugged and grasped the signed copy of my book firmly in his left hand. Then he was right in front of me again. Without warning, he thrust his right hand at me. We shook.

"I live in the same building Carla Torres used to. We walked to school together every day. She is my friend, her mom was ... effing nuts."

Carla Torres was the young girl Mac gave his life to protect. Ironic, I was planning to visit Carla to give her bad news and here was an old friend. It's a small world. Too freaking small at times.

"Do you still see her?" I couldn't remember Carla mentioning she'd seen Joey lately but I did know who he was. She'd talked about him a lot early on.

He shook his head. "She's in a foster home and doesn't go to school round here anymore. We text each other."

He shrugged and shuffled his feet. "I'm real sorry about your husband, you know."

Yeah. Me too.

"Do you want to see her?"

He nodded.

I looked at Audrey then back at Joey. "Wait right here," I told him.

Audrey and I walked over to the door. "How much longer before school finishes for the day?"

"Five minutes," she replied.

"Any objections if I hang around and take Joey with me when I go?"

"None; you can try calling his parents and letting them know Joey is with you ... but I doubt they'll answer or care."

No surprises there.

A quick phone call told my team I was visiting Carla and I wouldn't be back in the office until tomorrow. There was a small argument, as both Sam and Lee tried to insist on going with me. It wasn't going to be easy telling Carla about Cassie. I won. It'd take us thirty minutes to get there.

I thanked the class for letting me talk to them and left a pile of Butterfly Foundation and FBI leaflets on the teacher's desk for the students. The bell rang.

"Hey Joey, we're going on a field trip," I said.

He didn't argue. The teacher gave him back his cell phone and we left the school grounds in silence.

"Where are we going?" he asked as I reminded him to

buckle up.

"To see Carla. Is that okay with you?"

One shoulder gave a semi-shrug. "How come you care so much about loser kids?" he asked, pressing the fast forward button repeatedly on his iPod.

As tempted as I was to brush it off and tell him I was just doing my job. I didn't. I could hear my mother's voice rattling like wind in my skull, reminding me that I couldn't save everyone and, if I'd just given up this crusade of a job, I'd still have a husband. Even in death, the woman was a bitch.

"I wasn't so different from Carla," I replied, flicking on the headlights. The weather had closed in; snow was coming. A tingle moved up my spine and I felt invisible eyes on me again. I checked my mirrors. Everything looked fine.

"You weren't no loser kid," he scoffed. "Look at you — loser kids don't turn out like you."

"Ever heard the expression, 'Don't judge a book by its cover'?" I didn't wait for his answer. "I was the kid who had to look after her little brother because their mother was a lunatic. She beat us, locked him in cupboards, disappeared for days on end ..." I glanced at Joey. "Just because life starts out bad doesn't mean it has to stay that way. You choose how to live your life."

He fell into a deep silence. I hoped he was thinking about how he could rise above it too. In the distance, I heard music and recognized the song. 'Joey.'

"Why do you care?" he asked, subdued.

"Because I had a dream," I replied, letting Martin Luther King's voice resound in my head, my own voice didn't do it justice but I felt every word as I said it. "'If you lose hope, somehow you lose the vitality that keeps life moving, you lose that courage to be, that quality that helps you go on in spite of it all. And so today I still have a dream.' Martin Luther King Jr, *The Trumpet of Conscience*. And I have hope."

Hope drifted into oblivion with Mac's death but Carla was slowly resurrecting it. My vitality relied on caffeine and it took what was left of my courage to get out of bed in the morning. At least I was still getting out of bed. I looked for another way to explain it to Joey without sounding like a history lesson.

"Do you know who Christopher Reeve was?"

"The paralyzed guy? Superman?"

"Christopher Reeve once said, 'Once you choose hope, anything's possible.' If it's good enough for Superman, it's good enough for me."

I pulled into the driveway of the foster home where Carla was staying.

"Let's go," I said. I got out of the car and pushed the door shut behind me. Joey caught up on the path to the front door.

"What if she doesn't want to see me?" He chewed on a fingernail.

I knocked on the door and smiled at him. I saw Carla at school about once a month and every two weeks we met for lunch at the mall and went shopping, or hung out with my dad and sometimes my team. Usually Cassie was with us too. I hadn't dropped by her new foster family's house before. Cassie usually picked her up on the weekends. The invisible eyes were watching me again.

We waited.

A woman answered, wiping her hands on a dishtowel. She looked at me then past me. I turned my head expecting to see someone coming up the path. There was no one. I showed my badge and asked to see Carla.

"She's in the kitchen. I'm Sara Dubois." We shook hands. "Is there something wrong?"

I nodded. "I need to talk to Carla." I introduced Joey.

Sara smiled. "You're Carla's friend?"

Joey nodded but said nothing. Sara showed us into the kitchen. From the doorway, I saw Carla; she didn't look any different from the last time I saw her. She looked up at our footsteps. Her smile frozen. Confusion clouded her face.

"How are you Carla?" I said, hoping I was smiling.

She nodded a little as she spoke, "I'm good. Is something wrong?" Panic flashed across her face.

The words froze in my throat. I felt them slipping away. "Carla."

"Ellie?"

"Come here." I held out my arms. With my arms wrapped around her I whispered, "Cassie died today." Tears fell, dripping onto her hair.

"Cassie?"

"Yes."

"Were you there?"

"I was."

"Was it terrible?"

I didn't know what to say for a few minutes. The lump in my throat hurt as much as the hollowness within me echoed. Eventually I managed. "Yeah, it was." I wiped my eyes with one hand. "It's going to be okay though. You and me, we can get through this."

She tried to smile. Her heart wasn't in it. I should've brought Sam and Lee.

"What about Roscoe?"

"He's okay. Cassie's brother is coming up from Richmond to take care of him."

"Can I come to the funeral?"

"Yes."

I hugged her so hard. I didn't want to let her go. I'd forgotten about Joey until he stood next to me.

"Joey, I'm sorry. It wasn't great of me to bring you along for this."

Carla looked at him as if she hadn't seen him enter the room with me. A smile flickered in her eyes. "Joey." Then she looked up at me. "You're the best, you know, Ellie."

I let her go, watching as she propelled herself into Joey's arms.

I moved aside. Joey swung her around then put her down, she clung to him, talking and crying non-stop. Sara poured me a coffee. We sat at the kitchen table far enough away from Carla and Joey that they could talk, without us over their shoulders.

"Cassie was her social worker, yes? She'll miss her terribly. But I've never seen her so animated as she is now with Joey," Sara said. "She doesn't talk much."

That I found a little strange. Despite everything I'd always found Carla to be talkative, maybe that was just with me and everyone I know. I wiped a finger under my eyes, removing smudged mascara.

"She's a tough kid, she'll be fine. I think we have to remember that it's only been a year and a half since her mom's murder and this is her third foster home." I sipped my coffee and let my words sink in.

"Of course," Sara said.

"We're all going to miss Cassie, but Carla will never be alone." I replied, knowing it came out like a not-so-subtle warning and promptly tried to change the subject. "Good coffee."

I finished my coffee. Joey and Carla were sitting talking on a sofa just beyond the kitchen area of the open-plan kitchen, dining and family room. Crying became laughter and lit the room.

My cell phone rang and startled me into answering it quickly. Truthfully, the phone call was a welcome intrusion. My brother's voice said, "Can you swing by the grocery store on your way over for dinner?"

"Dinner?" I didn't remember a dinner. I didn't want to do dinner. I wanted to go home and drink a fifth of bourbon by myself.

"Tonight Ellie. At my place. Dinner with me and Dad."

"Sure, what do you need?"

"Milk."

"Okay. I'll get it."

"You all right?"

"I'm okay, just busy."

I hung up. Dinner. How come I couldn't remember dinner plans? It's been a shitty day.

"I'd better get Joey home," I said. "Hey Joey, come on, I'll drop you home."

"Can't I stay? I can get a bus," he replied.

I threw him my phone, he snatched it one-handed from the air. "Call your caregiver – let them know where you are."

He threw it back. "Dad's a drunk and Mom ... she doesn't know what day it is."

I looked at Sara. She nodded. "We'll run him home after dinner."

"Thanks. Take it easy Joey. Carla, come say goodbye."

Carla leaped off the sofa and ran over to me. She threw her arms around my waist and gave me a huge hug.

"Thank you for bringing Joey."

"You're welcome. I'm sorry about Cas." I am really fuc'n sorry. "I'll let you know when the funeral arrangements have been made. Call me if you need me."

It was hard to believe the kid hugging the stuffing out of me was going to be fourteen in just over three weeks. We met when she was twelve and a half.

"I'm sorry too."

"I'll call you in a few days – but call me anytime if you need me," I replied, hugging her back. "See you soon."

A soft fat snowflake landed on my nose on my way down the path to the car. The feeling of someone watching returned.

Don't forget the milk.

Chapter Three
Another One Bites The Dust

Nothing I like better than waking up confused. My eyes took their own sweet time adjusting to being awake. A wispy aura of mystery shrouded everything. The ceiling above me was not mine; mine was pristine white. This one was watermarked, fly poop-covered and pale tan. I sat up and swung my legs over the edge of the bed. Still had my boots on. Still had my clothes on. Both good things. I let my mind do a quick inventory of my limbs and pockets. I seemed intact but my pockets felt empty and I could tell I wasn't wearing my holster. My dry mouth, the odd taste in the back of my throat and the nausea suggested drugs. Chloroform maybe. Does anyone still use that shit?

Sun filtered through grime-coated windows. The rays felt warm on my face as they slid between roughly nailed boards. Boarded windows are never a good sign. I stood up. From nowhere a hand shoved me, tipping me off balance. I landed with a thump on the bed. A cloud of dust rose.

"What the fuck!"

"You aren't going anywhere, lady." A clean-cut man stepped into view.

He leaned over me. I could not tell exactly how tall he was, but he seemed about six feet as I sat on the bed. I started to stand again. He pushed me back. "Sit down and be still."

"And you are?" I asked, letting the situation settle into some sort of form that made sense. However, nothing made sense. Last thing I remembered was stopping for milk at the 7-Eleven on Blake Lane.

"Doesn't matter who I am," he replied. "I want you to access some files for me."

I recognized his accent. New Jersey.

"That's not going to happen," I said standing up again. He had moved a few feet away. I was out of his reach and remained on my feet.

"Yeah, it really is. You see, I need to get a look at some files the FBI have. And you are FBI."

My mind ran scenarios and none of them were good. I just hoped Aidan or Dad let my team know I was missing. There was a nagging sense that maybe they would not. It is tiring watching the world move on. Sometimes I dodge commitments, turn off my phones and hide – you do that a few times and people get used to it. I knew they could brand me unreliable, instead of missing.

"I don't think so. I'm not about to let you into the FBI system."

"Then we've come to an impasse."

"I'm going to leave now," I said, digging deep for some serious calm and stepping a few decisive feet toward him. He took one-step back. "You can carry on and play your little game alone."

"Lady, that ain't gonna happen." His lips parted. It could have been a small smile. "You just have to find a file for me that am all."

"Not going to happen."

"Just do it lady. I'd hate to have to mess up your pretty face." I saw the knife in his hand. "We could prevent all the nastiness if you would do as I ask."

Knives do not thrill me.

"Now what? We've established I'm not going to help you." I dipped my head slightly at him. "Your move."

"You could run," he said, slouched against the doorframe with one hand on the door handle. The blade glinted in the dusty sunlight as I wondered what happened to the snow-clouded sky. He picked at the flaking paint with the knife. A small patch of light danced on the ceiling, like a fairy flittering about above his head. With a nasty smirk, he said, "Or ... I dunno ... you could do as I ask."

The fairy disappeared.

"Or I could take that freaking knife and slit your throat," I replied. I stared into his eyes and noted the color. One eye was dark brown, the other lighter, more amber in color. Cassie was killed by a man with odd brown eyes. I looked at his boots. Brown. Not any brown. Coyote brown. I stored the information along with his height, weight, hair color, hair length and a good eidetic image of his whole face. Was he Cassie's killer?

A very real possibility hit me with such force I felt my body sway: what if he killed me?

"What's your name?"

He flicked another flake of paint with the point of the blade. It flew through the air and landed on the floor, disappearing into deep dust and more paint flecks. Captivated I watched as a plume of fine sparkling dust spiraled like fireworks from the floor.

"Seems fair that I should tell you. I know who you are, Special Agent Conway."

I felt my breath catching in my throat. It stuck like dry toast as I replied, "Who are you?"

His strange brown eyes met mine. "David Dunn," he said.

The name of my potential killer was David Dunn. Why was that familiar? And why would he give me his name? Either he's not bright or it doesn't matter. Interesting.

"You were stationed around here?" I asked while moving my weight to my back foot.

He smiled or rather his lips moved. It could've been a snarl. Straight, evenly spaced white teeth. It didn't look as though he smoked or drank much coffee. I surmised his parents spent a lot of money to get his teeth that straight. They must be so proud.

My eyes closed. I couldn't smell smoke on his clothing or skin. He wore a familiar deodorant; it wasn't strong enough to be a cologne or spray. I conjectured he used a stick. Supermarket, common, nothing remarkable or memorable.

Military-style short hair. Clean-shaven. His whole appearance reminded me of something I knew well and his coyote brown boots gave a lot away. I felt the chimes of familiarity turn into a carillon.

"What are you doing?" he asked.

"Wondering how long it will be before you show me how big and scary you are," I replied, beckoning to him. "Come on dickhead. God knows I could use the laugh. Or do you prefer unarmed women taken by surprise in their own homes?"

He closed the distance between us in two strides.

The blade pressed against my throat.

"You're awful smart-mouthed for someone who is *my* prisoner," he sneered.

"Don't hold back. Smack me about. Slit my throat." I lowered my voice. "But make it fuc'n good because you do not want me coming after you, *ever*," I said, pushing his hand away. There was no resistance.

He stepped back and smiled again.

I goaded him some more. "I know you killed my friend. Let's get on with it, shall we? How long before NCIS come looking for you?"

His eyes flickered and the smile faded. I watched it leave. How quickly his manner changed. Lines appeared on his forehead. The look in his eyes hardened. He was a Marine. Growing up on naval bases, I knew a Marine when I saw one. Here we go again – kidnapped by a Marine. What is it with the unhealthy interest Marines have in me?

"Why would they?"

"Because you're a Marine. I'm a Fed remember? We're in Virginia, and this could get you the chair. And the woman you killed – Cassandra Smith – was a federal employee." My last memory was Virginia, so I was hoping

I was still there.

"I won't fry for this," he said with more conviction than he should have. "You don't know anything. I didn't kill anyone." There was a lack of resolve in his voice.

I swear I could smell burning flesh in his future.

"Yeah, you did. You think NCIS won't cough you right up?"

Dunn wanted something but it wasn't to kill me. I scanned the room. No other doors, windows partially boarded up, broken furniture piled in one corner, a dilapidated old bed in the other and a flashy laptop sitting at the end of the bed. A vision of Carla came into my head. I saw tears running down her face as she said, 'If you die, I won't have anyone.'

"I'm not going to die today," I said, hearing real certainty in my voice for the first time in a long time.

"Don't be so sure, lady."

Everything came together in my mind and I sifted through the information: he was Cassie's killer.

I stepped back. The movement allowed some room between me and Dunn, the renegade Marine.

"How long have you been at Belvoir?"

His eyes darted from me to the wall behind me. "Who says I'm stationed at the Fort?" Some of his confidence zapped.

"You just did."

He looked slightly confused. "It doesn't make any difference where I'm stationed."

It probably didn't but the last Marine I tangled with

was from Fort Belvoir. A bottle of water lay on the floor reminding me how thirsty I was.

A smile crept onto my face. I couldn't help it. On the screen in my mind, I saw bright colored bunting around tents and heard people calling out and cheering. As I turned, I saw why. With the thunder of hooves on hard-packed ground, two horses charged down a tilt line toward each other. Knights in full battle armor balancing shields and lances, grim determination in their eyes. Splintering wood as the lances hit. One knight slipped sideways in the saddle, knocked askew by a lance strike. The crowd stomped and clapped. Queen's 'We Will Rock You' filled the arena. A knight I recognized as Heath Ledger nodded at a beautiful girl.

Nothing but a cruel reminder that my knight was dead.

In front of me the boy with a stick transformed into a dick with a knife.

My eyes darted around the room.

"The only way out, is through me," Dunn drawled.

"Your Intel must be crap if they didn't warn you about me."

He paused a moment too long before replying, "I know about you, Agent."

"No, you really don't," I said with a smile. "Atta boy for thinking you do, dumbass."

"I know you got your husband killed."

Without blinking I replied, "Then let me go before the same fate befalls you."

He pushed himself off the doorframe and lurched toward me, his knife hand by his side. "Now letting you go would be unhealthy for me."

I rocked back on my right foot, angling my body away from him. I hoped for a scared look and maintained eye contact. He didn't seem to view me as a threat. He was bigger than I am with a longer arm reach. I rocked back again, this time with my left foot, putting another step between us. I now had the room I needed.

He glared. Intimidation?

Enough already.

I fuc'n hate knives. They tend to cut me and make a mess. *He* was in front of a door. *He* was blocking my exit. I could do some kind of Steven Seagal maneuver and turn his arm into a pretzel but I didn't want to get that close.

I focused on his eyes and imagined a point beyond him, below his hips, then kicked right through the moron with a front snap-kick to his groin.

"Goal," I muttered.

The knife dropped as he did. I hooked it closer to me then bent down and picked it up.

Dunn lay crumpled on the floor clutching himself and groaning. There was a moment when I thought the knife would jump from my hand and stab his cowardly gut. He made me feel stabby. With the impulse controlled, I stepped over him and opened the door. I strode straight into Lee's path. A big arm circled me and lifted me aside. Another set of hands caught me and I looked at Sam.

"What kept you?" I asked.

"You seemed to have the situation under control," Sam

replied with a shrug.

"Thanks."

Sam smiled showing his perfect, straight white teeth. "Your buddy over there took your cell phone. And because he's real bright, he never turned it off. Then he had several attacks of genius and made a few calls. We tracked you through your phone."

I did get the impression he wasn't officer material. I nodded my head toward the crumpled figure of Dunn. "He's going to need a few minutes."

Sam grinned and looked at my feet. "I gotta get me some of those steel-capped cowboy boots you like so much."

They really were cool, and you couldn't tell by looking that the toe concealed a protective steel cap. Do I know how to buy decent boots or what?

"Day and time?" I said quickly.

"Thursday, seven fifteen in the a.m.," Sam replied. "You all right?"

"I'll let you know," I replied. "Lee, we want to talk to him about Cassie's death."

Lee hauled Dunn to his feet and stepped sideways as the Marine vomited. Lee gave him a minute to finish then slapped cuffs on him.

"You and me are gonna have a little chat," Lee said and shoved the Marine through the door ahead of him, missing the doorframe by a quarter inch. "Careful now, you don't want to smack your pretty head."

"Notify Special Agent Noel Gerrard at NCIS, they'll

want in on this too. Also, find out if he's really a Marine or if we have another naval corpsman, just like last time."

A random interlude mixed with television in my head and Gerrard became Jethro Gibbs from NCIS. I couldn't decide if life was imitating art or vice versa. The cuffed Marine turned his face toward me and whispered, "Hawk's back. He says, 'Hello, Gabrielle'."

My stomach twisted into a tight knot. I shivered. I didn't want Hawk back.

"Ellie, EMTs need to check you out," Sam said, ushering me to a waiting ambulance.

"I'm okay," I replied, veering off to the right and out of his reach.

A familiar voice spoke from behind me, "I've heard that before, Conway."

"SSA Kurt Henderson," I said, turning to face him. "Or do I have to call you doctor?"

"Call me whatever you like." He took hold of my elbow and steered me back to the ambulance.

"I'm okay. This is a waste of time." My protest fell on deaf ears. Neither Sam nor Kurt was buying it.

Two hours later with a clean bill of health, Sam took me home to clean up. I showered and changed while he made coffee.

The smell of freshly ground Arabica beans and hot coffee followed me as I wandered the house looking for the cat. She wasn't in her usual places.

"Sam, have you seen the cat?"

"Nope," he replied, pouring two coffees. "You sure you

are okay?"

"I'm fine. Doc cleared me, remember?" I sat on one of the stools at the kitchen counter and picked up the coffee mug Sam slid to me.

"Something on your mind?"

"How can I take care of a child? I don't even know where my cat is and I'm always running out of cat food." I played with the ring my cup made on the countertop.

"Teenagers are almost human, they rarely get lost and I think most of them can feed cats," Sam said using his let's-be-reasonable voice.

"You think the cat would like someone who knows how to feed her?"

"Yeah, maybe Carla could even give the poor animal a name."

"I'm sure she had one but I don't remember it. Mac always called her Puss."

"And you call her Cat."

"I'm being silly."

"Human, Ellie. You are being human and contemplating raising another human – that's huge."

"I want what's right for her," I said, drawing squiggles in the condensation from my cup. "Cassie left a letter. She wanted me to adopt Carla."

"See? You are what's right for her."

"But to take her on alone ..."

"You'll never be alone. Lee and I are looking forward to being uncles. Your dad and brother will be right there." He smiled wickedly. "And then there is Mac's family."

Bile rose. "Don't even joke about it."

The cat still hadn't shown up. I filled her bowl with cat biscuits, put the cups in the sink and we headed into the office.

Chapter Four
Goin' Away Baby

On Friday afternoon, I stood in the empty hallway between my office and the stairwell with my cell phone in one hand and a twisted knot of anticipation in my stomach. There was no one around and no noise coming from any of the offices or adjacent meeting rooms. I'd spent most of Thursday afternoon and Friday morning trying to corroborate the message from David Dunn about Hawk. It took my mind off the cold announcement by Cassie's brother that her funeral would be held in Richmond, with family only. Caine was organizing a memorial service sometime over the next two weeks so we could all pay our respects.

I peered inside the dark cavern within my handbag

A brighter colored phone would be a good idea. A black phone in a black bag wasn't the easiest thing to locate. You'd think I would've learned that the first eight times I found myself searching for the damn thing since purchasing it a few months ago. Apparently, I am a slow learner.

With the phone found I turned my attention to locating a business card.

The hallway was still empty – a good thing. I didn't want anyone overhearing my call. I pocketed both the phone and the card and checked the hallway again. Empty.

A horrible feeling brewed and reminded me that I was stepping into the deep end without my trusty water wings.

Excessive paranoia.

A butterfly flittered in front of me. I reached out my hand and my fingers went right through it. Startled, I examined my fingers. No butterfly residue. Another one danced on the stream of light in front of my eyes. "Mac?" I whispered.

It dipped and swooped on delicate orange wings.

"I know I have to do this for you ... but how am I supposed to do it without you?"

The butterfly floated away on a sunbeam. I took a breath, fished a tissue from my bag and wiped my eyes. Took another breath and called Lee.

"Where are you?"

"Office. You?"

"Leaving. Meet me later and bring Sam."

"You all right, Chicky?"

"I'm okay."

"Where do you want to meet?"

"My place." There was a huge temptation to tell him I wasn't okay; that I didn't think I would ever be okay again but I didn't.

"When?"

"I'm on my way, via the Foundation. Gimme two hours."

"Can do," he said.

I ended the call. The next one I made was to the Director's office.

She wasn't in.

I left a voice message on O'Hare's private line then dropped my phone back into my bag. I knew it would instantly migrate to the darkest corner.

My hand fished out another phone. It was a pre-paid phone, this time light in color and easier to see. I held the phone and pulled the business card from my pocket.

I took the stairs down one floor and entered the long number from the business card into the pre-paid phone. It would've been so much easier to use my *own* phone and choose his name from the directory.

The phone rang and rang and I realized I had no idea what time it was in Moscow. I stood on the landing for the second floor and waited. The insistent ringing in my ear filled the void created by zero thought. Finally, a Russian voice answered from thousands of miles away; my brain kicked in and I knew it was four thousand eight hundred miles, plus change.

"*Da!* You are speaking with Misha Praskovya."

"What no formal greeting?" I feigned horror and enjoyed, for a brief moment, him knowing it was a call from America but not from whom. "Too busy to greet an old friend?"

"Special Agent Conway! *Kak požyvajete?*" How are you?

"I'm okay," I replied, and heard his deep throaty laugh.

"My beautiful friend Ellie is okay. I am thinking this is not true," he replied smoothly.

"I am thinking you are a smart man, Misha." Unconsciously, I had mimicked his syntax. "I have a feeling there is something brewing. A Marine grabbed me Wednesday night – he told me a mutual friend was back. I might be coming to Moscow. So far everything points to him still being over your way."

"I will make sure the paper work is in order and file a request for you to join me in a joint investigation," Misha said. The red tape was considerable, unless we were prepared to say we were entering Russia to track a terrorist who had committed acts of terrorism against US Citizens. Terrorism opened our access to foreign countries and guaranteed assistance but I didn't want to use the T word yet.

"Thank you."

"Sam and Lee?"

"They will come with me." My fingers crossed.

"This is about Mac more than the friend, *da?*"

"*Da*, this is about Mac. It's time for me to step up."

He took a moment to process this. "I understand. When do you leave?"

"It's not decided yet. If we come, I'll try for a late night or early morning flight."

"What do you need?"

A lump rose in my throat. I wanted to tell him that every time I stepped outside I thought someone was watching me and that all I needed was Mac. My voice quivered as I said, "I need ..." I tried to steady my voice. "I need you to keep me informed Misha. Any changes in the movements of the whereabouts of our mutual friend

... would be good to weed out trails that lead nowhere. Can you check Interpol for anything that fits our interest group? If I do it, the *friend* may hear about it. We don't know what he's monitoring."

"Of course. If I hear anything you will be first to know," Misha replied. "This time Ellie, we will get him."

"I hope so. If you need to contact me, use this phone number, please."

"I will. I meet you at airport. Tell me when."

"*Spasibo.*" Thank you.

"Safe travels my friend. *Nadejus vskore vstretitsja svami.*" I hope to see you soon.

"*Ja tebe pozvonju. Dosvidanija.*" I'll call you. Goodbye.

I hung up. Part of me was secretly pleased how much Russian I'd picked up working with Misha. Though I suspected he cringed inwardly with every clumsy word I uttered. Misha's first redeeming feature in my eyes was his fabulous accent – then he proved himself. Misha became a much-trusted member of my team, albeit a temporary one. We maintained a close tie between Delta and the FSB in Russia; Misha was our contact and a frequent visitor to the States. Another man I kept at arm's length – for the same reasons I wouldn't let Gerrard get too close. Tall, dark, intelligent and handsome floated my boat but I didn't want to go there. Anyway, he still wore his wedding ring. Misha's wife died before I met him but to me, he still felt like a married man. My fingers sought out the wedding ring on my own hand.

Ironic.

I shoved the pre-paid phone into my pocket; I'd keep it with me in case Misha called. Last time we tangled with Hawk, information seemed to fall into his hands before I could act. I didn't want him to know I was working the case, even though he'd engineered my involvement. If Hawk really was back – I wanted the edge. My priority was to limit all possible ways information could dribble, leak or gush into the wrong hands.

Once bitten, twice shy.

In truth, I wanted to press the edge of a blade against his throat and slice, letting his blood pour from his body. Not bad for someone who really doesn't like knives.

The stairwell door opened. Two agents were talking as they walked entered the stairwell. I heard the tail end of the conversation; it was boy talk about a girl.

Agent One said, "She's stunning. Have you seen her?"

"Don't think so," his friend replied.

"You'd remember. She's blonde, wears long-sleeved black shirts and cowboy boots. They say her right arm is all scarred, from a knife fight with a Marine over a year ago, before I graduated. I've never seen a finer ass in jeans." The agent held the door for me, as I left I heard him say, "That's her."

I spun around and flung the door open. Startled by my reappearance, one jumped and the other smirked nervously. With one step, I was in front of the agent-with-the-most-to-say and looked him in the eye. "I am not now and never will be a topic of conversation to you. Do you understand?"

He nodded.

"I'm sorry," he said and sounded like he meant it.

"Good. In future, don't discuss fellow agents like that. You're not a teenager in a locker room. You're an FBI agent. Act like one."

With that, I stepped back through the door and disappeared into the bustle of the second floor. A smile broke forth.

Ill-mannered they were – but my ass was indeed fine.

Chapter Five
One Step Closer

Friday afternoon was fast becoming late afternoon by the time I pulled up the driveway and parked behind Mac's red Toyota Tacoma truck. For seventeen months, one week and three days, his truck had sat there. A surprisingly strong ray of sunlight bounced off the rear window of the truck, sending beams of light into the cold air. It took a few minutes for me to heap together all the things I needed to take inside. A stack of papers slid from the passenger seat during the stop-start journey from the city. Envelopes and manila folders spilled their contents on the mat. I was still retrieving them when a car pulled up behind mine. I sprang up and had a quick peek out the back window.

Lee and Sam.

I delved under the seat and grasped the last piece of paper, scanned it quickly then shoved it back into the correct folder.

A light shadow fell like early dusk.

My door opened. The shadow closed in.

All sun disappeared. The night was upon me.

"Want a hand?" a deep voice filled the car.

"I got it." I tossed my keys at Sam. "Open up the house for me?"

He snatched them from midair and ambled away, leaving another sun-blocking shadow to oversee my progress.

"You going to be long?" Lee asked. His sizable hands reached in, picked up all the paper work, manila folders, my laptop, cell phone and shoulder bag from my lap.

Freed from clutter, I climbed out the car, straightened my jacket, ran my fingers through my hair and said, "Nope, all set."

Again, I felt a tingle in my spine and the creepy feeling of being watched. I hurried in the front door, leaving the feeling outside in the cold.

Inside, the smell of freshly-ground dark-roasted coffee beans filled the air. I heard the coffeemaker gurgle as water started to drip through the filter. Hearing noises in the kitchen felt peculiar. I reminded myself it was just Sam.

Lee and I went through to the living room. He piled the armful of paperwork on the side table between two big leather chairs. At the risk of declaring loudly that I'd lost my mind, I turned to Lee and said, "Did the police ever sweep Cassie's house for bugs?"

He shook his head. "Caine said they blocked him at every turn and refused to cooperate. That Reid guy persisted with Cassie's death being a home invasion."

"But we know it wasn't."

"Caine's still trying to get our people into the house." Lee took a breath. "What does your gut say?"

"Someone is watching."

He nodded sagely then left the room. The front door closed.

Low winter sun dappled the carpet as it shone through

the bare tree branches beyond the large windows. Spindly shadows drifted across the coffee table in the middle of the room. Their pointed, gnarled tips looked like witches' fingers. There was a temptation to draw the curtains to keep the scary shadows at bay but the sun was so nice, I just couldn't.

Sam called out, "Coffee will be a few more minutes."

"Thanks, Sam," I called back.

The front door opened and Lee reappeared carrying a small silver rectangular object in his hand. "What's wireless in the house?"

"Router, laptops, cell phones, cordless phones, Xbox, remotes, keyboard and mouse in the office, speakers both in here and upstairs, stereo, PS3. Can't think of anything else."

"Let's start turning it all off," Lee said and then he hollered to Sam, "Come on in here."

Sam waltzed in the door grinning. "I fed the cat. You're out of cat food."

Big surprise.

Lee smiled. "Doing a bug check." He held up the little silver box. "It's an RF signal detector. My new little toy to locate bugs and cameras. It's set so that the beep gets louder the closer I get to a signal."

Sam nodded.

We split up and turned off everything in every room then met back in the hallway by the front door. Lee turned on the device in his hand and slowly swept the house. Apart from the occasional beep from something we'd forgotten to turn off, there was nothing. The RF signal detector was capable of detecting digital signals within forty feet and cameras within five feet.

"Clean," Lee announced.

"Good," I replied. We turned our cell phones back on and toured the house switching life back on. Slowly all the appliances were again ready and waiting. My paranoia slipped into the background.

Back in the living room we all sat down. Both men watched me with inquisitive expressions. I chewed my lip and took a few seconds before speaking.

Sam's eyes narrowed, he nudged Lee.

I stopped chewing and said "In one of the manila folders you bought in, Lee, are plane tickets. More accurately e-tickets. I've booked us on a flight to Moscow tonight."

Lee glanced at the pile of folders and envelopes and pieces of paper piled on the coffee table, then back at me.

No jaw dropping, no stunned looks crossed their very calm faces. Slowly their heads nodded.

"I have a question," Sam said.

"Just one?" I replied.

He nodded. "How much does this trip have to do with yesterday? Have you heard from NCIS regarding the Marine?"

"That's two. A lot to do with yesterday – as far as interrogating David Dunn, Gerrard says Dunn is still saying very little. He is of the opinion that he doesn't know much. This would fit with what we know about Hawk's activity." General terror cell operations: each member only knows his or her task, that way one person can't pull down the entire cell. "Dunn originally reckoned Hawk was back on American soil but after some questioning by Noel Gerrard, he said he was contacted from Russia and told to deliver the message. Gerrard is of the opinion Dunn is a pawn and nothing more. Misha is meeting us. I need to let him know the flight number before we leave."

"Did Dunn confess to Cassie's murder?" Lee asked.

"No. His boots had blood on the soles. There were splatters on his pants. Blood type matched. They're running a DNA comparison. A search of his apartment turned up a blood-splattered brown shemagh."

Sam and Lee nodded. Lee's hair fell forward causing him to push it back with one hand. Until that moment I hadn't even noticed he'd let his hair grow. He was starting to look as though he should be playing guitar and living in Nashville. He reminded me of someone but I couldn't place who. He was almost Sylvester Stallone – but that wasn't right. Or was it? Nope, not Stallone. Definitely someone in the music industry.

I hauled my attention back to the situation at hand when I heard Sam's voice.

"How long are we away?" Sam asked.

"As long as it takes or until we run out of leads."

Lee leaned back in the chair, his muscular frame filling it, a small smile on his lips. He didn't need to ask the question I saw in his eyes but he did anyway. "Who are we going after?"

"Hudson Hawk, or whatever his real name is. The Unsub we believe is responsible for child trafficking on a global scale and the Butterfly Murders."

Lee grinned and quietly replied, "We're going after a terrorist?"

"Did we get confirmation that this dick was a terrorist? The information I have says he conspired to have a Federal Agent murdered while on duty within the Commonwealth of Virginia." I'd practiced saying that for months. Staring at myself in the mirror, daring a reaction as the words jumped out of my mouth, because one day I knew I would say them aloud to my team. A 'Federal Agent' sounded so much less personal than saying 'my husband.' "He is also suspected of being responsible for at least four murders of women within Virginia."

"Misha indicated he was a terrorist. The woman he used to take the kids and possibly killed, was a terrorist according to the Russians," Lee said. His tone suggested I had overlooked some important facts.

We believed two people had committed the murders and at least another two people had been involved in the disappearances of the kids during the Butterfly Murders case, over and above the corpsman and the doctor from Fort Belvoir, who were serving time for their crimes. One of the killers was a Russian female, identified as a terrorist. A dead Russian terrorist now. The other, Hawk ... maybe.

I pulled out my best Mae West voice and said, "I'm seeing a big old blurry line here, boys."

"I'm thinking that if we call this guy a terrorist then we

will have less chance of the plug being pulled on the operation," Sam offered.

I reminded them of something. "If we say 'terrorist', we run the risk of this becoming a joint/international task force situation. It'll take much longer, we'll have to bring extras up to speed, maybe even hand the case over to another agency."

The men agreed, grim-faced.

"The other thing you *need* to *know* is this is a need-to-know operation. Misha and we three are the only ones who actually have any real information on what we're doing. Of course Caine and O'Hare know we are going to Russia."

No one could know about this operation. It would melt like a spun sugar house in the rain if anyone found out what we were doing.

"What about Chrissy?" Sam asked running his hand over his bald head.

"As far as the rest of the FBI – and that includes Chrissy – are concerned, we're following a lead on a series of murders. No one needs to know which case."

"Where does she think we are going?"

I smiled and replied, "New Zealand."

Both men shook their heads in wonder.

"Why?" Sam asked. "I mean why New Zealand?"

I stuck a pin in a map?

"It's summer there and it sounded nice."

But really, I stuck a pin in a map.

"How much information have we got on the European

situation?" Sam asked.

I watched Lee thumb through the original case files. I could tell by the expression on his face that he was looking at the photos of the murdered women. I didn't relish the prospect of walking any more crimes scenes like those.

"Re-capping what we know," I said, knowing damn well it was more what we surmised than anything actually known. "We think this guy is Russian or at least Eastern European. It was considered originally that he'd gone home to regroup or continue hunting." Neither of them interrupted as I paused briefly. "He disappeared from our radar here soon after killing his partner. At the time, we rescued six children before he could remove them from the country. If he had a quota to fill, then it would make sense for him to carry on somewhere safer. Home maybe. But that's supposition on our part at the moment."

"Seven kids, Ellie. Carla Torres. He never got her," Lee replied gently.

"True."

"Then there is the European chatter," Lee said as he read the papers in the folder. "Reported disappearances of seventeen young girls aged ten to thirteen over twenty-seven days from Munich, Hamburg, Stuttgart, Frankfurt in Germany, then Brussels in Belgium, Helsinki in Finland and Oslo in Norway. The last reported disappearance was of four girls in Copenhagen in Denmark, exactly eighteen days ago. They're all potentially Hawk's crimes. Police have no leads and consider them mostly runaways from dysfunctional homes. Hawk operating in Europe is a real possibility."

The list Lee read out stuck in my mind. Almost as if I should know something – but I couldn't think what it was I should know.

"Yes, it's conceivable he's there, or that he's gone skulking back to Russia to make the sales. Or still here somewhere," Sam replied. His best efforts didn't keep the skepticism from his voice. "Or heading to the moon on a shuttle."

Lee handed the papers he was reading to me.

"Do either of you think the pattern of cities means something?" I asked, looking over the list again.

Sam nodded. "I don't know what it means but it feels like it's tied to something. This isn't random."

Lee's phone rang. The phone in my pocket rang. I checked the caller ID and saw Misha's name. He was the only person with the number so chances were it had to be him.

"*Privet!*" I said, concentrating on my call and not the sound of Lee talking on his cell phone.

"Hi to you too, Ellie," Misha replied.

"Problem?"

"*Da.*"

"Big?"

"*Da!*"

"What's happened?"

"We have new information and an informer we've been working with came forward." He paused for a split second. "The informer gave an American Marine a directive. He was to pass a message to you."

"I met him," I replied letting the tone in my voice speak volumes.

Misha continued, "The operation has moved offshore again, they have left Europe. My source says that Hudson Hawk left through Vienna, Austria, seven days ago. He flew to Australia then to ..."

"New Zealand," I interrupted. So much for sticking a pin in a map.

"Bingo. He is traveling as Edward Hawkins. The latest information from Interpol is in your inbox."

I picked my laptop up from the floor and fired it up.

"I got it, Misha. *Spasibo*." Thank you.

"*Pozhalujsta*." You are welcome. "Keep me informed. I will send any further information to you." You are welcome.

"Too bad we have to change our plans. I was looking forward to seeing Moscow."

"Another time, my friend."

"Take care, Misha."

I hung up. Sam and Lee were watching me closely.

"Lee?" I asked.

"It was Chrissy. We've had a call from New Zealand police. Interpol suggested they contact us. They have missing kids. She told them we'd meet with detectives as we were already heading to New Zealand."

"Funny how shit happens." I skimmed over the email forwarded from Misha then briefed the boys on what I knew. "In the last three days, four children between the ages of nine and twelve have gone missing. One in Auckland, two in Hamilton with the most recent in Wellington. Police have no concrete leads and investigations are continuing." As I heard myself say 'in the last three days' I knew where I needed to be. The trail would be cold in Europe; Misha would do better working that angle anyway. But New Zealand was fresh and we stood a good chance of finding the girls plus we had an invitation to help.

"Any murders?" Sam asked.

I looked at Sam. "Not yet. So far, no mothers found murdered. They were single parents of only children; as usual the fathers are the prime suspects."

"Isolated? Do they fit our profile?" Lee asked. He sounded almost flustered. "I mean ... shit! Do you really think these fuckers are operating in clean green New Zealand like they did here?"

I grinned. "As opposed to dirty filthy America?"

"I don't think Lee meant it quite like that, Chicky Babe," Sam replied with a wink.

Lee agreed with a nod and said, "I've never associated New Zealand with anything so sordid and despicable. Doesn't sit right in my gut."

"They helped us break a huge child porn ring – some of the low-life scumbags were in New Zealand," Sam reminded him.

Lee grimaced. "It's still fuc'n off."

"Yes it is," I concurred. It was very fuc'n off. "Now on

that note, none of the victims' mothers have known mental illnesses. No link to the Butterfly Foundation is showing up." Hawk had once used the chat rooms at the Butterfly Foundation as his personal hunting ground.

"No known? Could this fucker be using the same old scam?" Lee asked.

Yeah. That had crossed my mind too. But that didn't explain how he was grabbing kids in Europe. If it was him and my instincts told me it was, I believed he'd come up with another way to lure kids away from their parents; I just didn't know what it was yet.

"Possibly, I'm double checking. I've been over to the Foundation offices and have the tech staff running reports on everyone who has registered." It didn't thrill me to be even thinking that Hawk could be up to his old tricks. "My staff are pinging the ISPs. It's precautionary. Just because no New Zealanders are registered doesn't mean they're not there. Same goes for kids from Europe. It's not difficult to say you're from somewhere else, especially if they used a hotmail address to sign up."

"But you verify the postal address – they need a physical address," Lee replied frowning.

"Yes, they do need a physical address. We haven't changed our policy. But there are also ways around that too. How many people have friends in various places throughout the world? We're heading toward being one big global community, or in some cases, one big global smorgasbord."

Lee nodded. "I see what you mean. It's not hard to ask

a friend if you can use their address and have that friend email you the code from the snail-mail sent from the Foundation."

"Why would anyone do that with the Foundation though?" Sam asked.

"Because we're not worldwide but mental illness is ... and the only way to access the chat rooms is to provide us with a United States physical address."

"How long before we get an answer back from the techies?"

"No idea," I replied. "But really, the only thing we have that suggests the missing children in New Zealand are linked to our case against Hawk, is his movements. So far as we know, they're missing kids and will turn up."

Yeah right.

"But you don't believe that ..." Sam said.

"Not so much," I replied.

"New Zealand it is then." Sam said with way more enthusiasm than he'd shown for the Moscow trip.

"New Zealand," I repeated. "Let me pull up a map of New Zealand." It took me a matter of seconds to find a map of the whole country. We crowded around the screen and looked at New Zealand.

"It's not very big, is it?" Lee muttered.

"Nope," I replied. "Kids are missing from Auckland, Hamilton and Wellington." I traced the cities to Cook Strait. "Does it look to you like he's heading down the country?"

Sam agreed. "So the next big city is Christchurch."

"Yep." I tossed the pre-paid cell phone to Lee. He caught it smoothly. "Can you get us new airplane tickets and cancel the Russian trip?" I tossed him a brilliant smile to sweeten the pot.

It was beginning to feel something like summertime.

"SSA Chicky Babe, your wish is my command," he said with a bow. "Wellington or Christchurch?"

"Christchurch," I replied without hesitation.

He fished out the e-tickets from the folder next to him and left the room.

"Where's that coffee, Sam?"

"Sitting in the pot waiting for me to pour it," Sam replied. He hoisted his muscular body from the seat and ambled out to the kitchen.

Lee returned for a pen and notebook then disappeared again.

Sam came back carrying three coffee mugs. I relieved him of two, enabling him to sit back down. The cat prowled the room looking for a warm seat.

"Too late Cat," I told her, and set the two mugs on the coffee table. I scooped up the furry grey animal. She purred softly and settled on my knee. I knew it was a brief thing. She was Mac's cat and she didn't sit on my lap longer than five minutes. Like me, she was still waiting for Mac to walk in the door.

Didn't we all?

The cat stared at the living room doorway, her ears twitched as she listened to movement in the hallway. I watched her with interest as Lee came back. She jumped off my knee and stalked from the room. She was going to sit by the front door and wait, as she did every day.

Lee said, "We're flying out of Reagan tonight to New York then on to Sydney, Australia and finally Auckland; then we'll get an internal flight to Christchurch. We need to get moving."

"We're heading into summer," I said. A smile lay on my lips; the thought of summertime was fabulous. No snow, no slush, no ice, no thermals! A mere twenty-four hours' flying time and a couple of missing days, on account of the International Date Line, stood between summertime and us.

I reached down and pulled the passports from an envelope on the floor. With a quick look at them, I tossed them to the respective men.

I picked up another envelope and removed credit cards from it. "These are linked to my Foundation account. The only person with access to that account is me."

A hard lesson had been learned once before regarding company credit cards and access. Someone tracked me via the credit card and it was not a good situation to be in. I handed out the cards. Lee and Sam looked at the writing on them then at me.

Sam said, "Butterfly Foundation."

"Who's funding this?" Lee asked.

"Me, for now."

Both men looked at each other and shook their heads.

"Obviously work is paying our air travel, visas etc. I'm providing the incidental cash and our accommodation."

"You're claiming this back, right?"

"Yeah." I grinned, "I'm not made of money and I'm not fronting cash for this trip out of the goodness of my heart."

"If we get anywhere near this guy, don't you think he's going to recognize Agent Chicky Babe and her devastatingly handsome cohorts as FBI?" Sam asked with a grin.

"I do. I'm also hoping that if we get that close, we'll have the scumbag in cuffs."

"We could travel as regular folk. That would probably make it easier," Lee offered.

"You want to give up your gun? Spend days trying to get the required documentation to arrive as tourists?" I replied.

Lee grinned. "All good points."

Sam perused the email we'd received from Misha and more information sent from our liaison officer, Chrissy McQueen.

"Apparently they don't have missing children in New Zealand like we do here," he said. "Chrissy says they're rare and end badly."

"Good to know." I replied. "Anything else?"

"So far the only kid never found was Kirsa Jensen. She went missing from Napier while riding her horse along the beach in 1983." He found some more information and shared it. "Each year about eight thousand people are reported missing. More than half didn't tell their families where they were, so they weren't missing to start with. Some don't want to be found. A very small number are victims of foul play."

"Then we stand a good chance of finding these kids."

I had a few calls to make before we left for the airport. We needed an attaché to meet the plane in Auckland, New Zealand, just to make sure we were cleared to carry guns within their borders. I also wanted to make sure police knew we were coming. The last call I made was to Carla's cell phone.

"Hey kiddo, it's Ellie."

"Hi, Ellie. Thanks for bringing Joey by the other day." Her voice was light and airy and held the promise of a beautiful smile. "When is the memorial for Cassie?"

"In a few weeks. Caine is organizing it."

"I can go, right?"

"Of course. I'll take you myself." I paused. "I'm going away for a while, I don't know how long. But you can still reach me on my cell, okay?"

"Sure," she replied, her voice falling flat. "Where are you going?"

"Overseas with work," I said.

"Okay."

"You sure everything's all right?"

"Yep."

"Call me if you need me – or call Caine Grafton at my office if it's an emergency."

"Bring me a present?"

"Absolutely. Any idea what you want for your birthday?"

"Something cool from wherever you go," she said,

perking up. That was such a typical Carla response; she had an amiable and easy-to-please nature.

"Consider it done. Be good. See you soon."

I hung up and put a memo on my phone to remind me to grab something touristy for Carla before we came home.

At the airport, before boarding, we had time for a coffee and quick chat. The three of us sat in a huddle after clearing security. Sam tapped my arm and looked past me. I turned my head to see Kurt Henderson passing through security.

"That's the third time I've seen him lately. What the fuck?" I muttered. He looked over and waved. My cell phone rang.

Caine.

"Is this about Henderson?" I snapped into my phone.

"This is not my doing. O'Hare wants him traveling with you." The boys were all high-fiving one another and doing the man-hug thing. I slipped away to a quiet corner. "Why?"

"Because last time you tangled with Hawk, both you and Sam needed patching up pretty good. Kurt has all your medical records with him and he's a ..."

"... a doctor," I finished for him. Hell, I just saw him yesterday.

"There's something else: he volunteered. O'Hare was looking for a doc to travel with you and he put up his hand."

"That's interesting." I hung up and rejoined my group.

Henderson volunteered. First rule of Delta A: never volunteer.

"We'll bring you up to speed on the case when we arrive in New Zealand," I said. "Welcome to Delta A." I shook Kurt's hand.

"Thanks," he replied. "Just tell me one thing: is this as bad as last time we worked together?"

I smiled.

"You mean body parts strewn all over town and a lunatic out to get me? Nah, shouldn't think so." There was touch of dismissive flippancy to my tone. "New Zealand should be warm at least."

"I can hardly wait," he replied.

"You know what I want?" I said.

"Tell us what you want," Sam said.

Lee interrupted Sam by launching into a Spice Girls' number.

I grinned. "Spice Girls? I think not!"

"What is it, SSA?" Sam said, stifling his amusement at Lee's interlude.

"I want to know who this Hudson Hawk bastard really is. I want his name and a confirmed identity."

Then I'd like to hollow out his head and use it as a planter.

The boarding call sounded.

"We're going to get him, Chicky Babe," Lee said without a trace of doubt.

Chapter Six
We Got it Going On

We passed through customs in Auckland in the middle of the night, met with an American attaché and now carried documentation which allowed us to wear guns. She'd notified police we were in the country and requested that all case information be delivered to our Christchurch hotel as soon as possible. The detective heading the investigation, Detective Faye Jones, was Wellington-based and would meet with us as soon as she could. Meanwhile, a Sergeant Terry would meet us at Christchurch and be our liaison officer. We spent what was left of our night, in an Auckland hotel jetlagged and unable to sleep.

At five minutes to midday on Monday, the four of us stood at the baggage carousel in Christchurch airport, waiting for our bags to bump along conveyor belt. We were ready to collect our bags and tired as hell. We'd lost days in transit, yet hadn't. It was a bizarre feeling being catapulted into the future. There was no sign of our liaison.

People were milling about. Some were waiting like us, others were greeting friends and family, a good percentage were scurrying to check in. Then there were the lucky ones heading off out the doors to their lives. I envied them.

Sam and Lee stood out like dogs' balls. It amused me. Kurt wasn't quite so out of place but he still stood out. We wore jeans. He wore a very nice suit.

Sam nudged me, "Give?"

"Look around. I think we're kinda obvious."

Lee overheard and turned to me. "Hiding in plain sight, damn we are good!"

"Damn, we are American," I replied with a tired laugh. "Although people will probably think you two play football, and I'm your fuc'n groupie." I nodded towards Kurt. "And he's your manager."

Sam's head lifted as he snorted with laughter. "We can only dream, Chicky Babe. Anyway, Special Agent Ridiculously Good Looking is too pretty to play football."

"Pretty? I don't think I'm pretty," Lee scoffed as Sam enjoyed the joke at Lee's expense. "You're full of shit."

"Settle you two." I noticed a number of people had turned to see what was happening. I kept an eye out for the police officer who was supposed to be meeting us. Suddenly two girls screamed and ran for us. Sam and Lee stepped toward them, blocking me.

I love it when they pull stunts like that, as if I can't shoot straight. Kurt moved in closer.

"Whoa little ladies, what's going on here?" Lee asked. He turned on some Southern charm. Any self-respecting girl would swoon in the presence of Lee; his smile could melt ice and his Southern manners made most women weak at the knees. I was immune.

Both girls clutched autograph books.

The tallest girl, a blonde who stood about five foot one in heels, spoke, "You're American." She looked like a five-year-old standing in front of Sam and Lee. I suspected she was about thirteen, maybe not quite.

"Yeah, we are," Sam replied. "Can we help you?"

The blonde spoke again, "Are you with Grange?"

Lee and Sam shook their heads grinning.

Grange equaled stadium rock on a par with Bon Jovi. They were also from New Jersey.

"Sorry to disappoint, girls. I wish we were," Lee replied.

I piped up, "Not as much as I wish you were."

So Grange was in New Zealand. Good timing on our part. We'd seen the aftermath in Auckland of a recent Bon Jovi tour as we waited for our flight to Christchurch. Hundreds of people wearing Bon Jovi tee shirts boarding planes, chattering non-stop about their concert experiences, as we waited for our flight to Christchurch.

"We're sorry," the girls said again and started to leave.

The dark-haired kid spun around and squealed, "You look like Tony! Oh my God ... it's *Tony*!" Her voice hit fever pitch.

I did a double take. Who looked like Tony? Tony who? Tony Sharron. The lead guitarist from Grange, of course.

Sam punched Lee playfully in the shoulder and drawled, "She's gotta be talking about you, boy. You're the pretty one."

Lee's mouth flapped for a few seconds. The kid launched herself at him. He untwined her tightly-clenched fingers from his shirt and lifted her off the floor at arm's length.

"I am *not* Tony," he growled at her then shifted his gaze to me. "I do *not* look like Tony Sharron."

The kid struggled for freedom from Lee's grip. He held her about twelve inches from his face and said with a firm, quiet voice, "I am not Tony."

He set the kid down.

There was a crazed look in her eyes: she didn't believe him.

Sam intervened placing himself between Lee and the kids.

"Shouldn't you two be squealing over that little Beiber kid and not Grange?" he said.

"He's just a *boy*," the blonde scoffed.

I couldn't believe the derision in the kid's voice.

"Hate to break it to you but you're just a *girl*," I replied under my breath.

The dark-haired kid shrieked again. "It *is* Tony!" as she dove past Sam.

Behind me, I heard running feet. Twenty or thirty screaming women and girls were bearing down on us.

I tapped on Sam's shoulder and pointed.

"Christ," he grumbled.

Lee grimaced as he removed the dark-haired kid's arms from his leg. "This is not going well. I'd like to go now." His eyes smoldered and not in a good way.

"We need crowd control," Sam said.

Screaming twenty- and thirty-somethings surrounded us with a few teens peppered through the horde.

The noise vibrated in my head like a jackhammer.

Flashes from cameras lit the area. Cell phones were pointed in our direction, no doubt capturing the whole ugly scene for YouTube with their built-in cameras.

Screaming. Crying. Hysteria. My god, people are stupid.

"Hang on a minute," I said. "This is so wrong on so many levels."

Only Sam heard me. The screaming had intensified.

"Chicky Babe, they don't care. These loons don't know their asses from their elbows."

Lee spoke, "We gotta get out of here."

"No fuc'n kidding. Got a plan, genius?" I asked and watched his hand stray toward his hip. "That doesn't involve drawing on kids?"

"I'm going for our bags," Lee stated with grim resolve. "Even, if I have to step on a few kids to get them."

"I want pepper spray," Sam growled as he shook two girls off his leg.

"Fuck that. I want a Tazer," I replied. All of a sudden, there was a piercing whistle and I realized it came from me. It caused an abrupt break in the noise. I whispered instructions to Lee – he caused the chaos and he needed to fix it.

Lee bellowed, "Listen up!"

The silence overwhelmed us for a second, then Lee calmly said, "You're all wonderful an' all, but if we don't get out of here, there will be no concert." A general drone hummed through the crowd.

Thinking on our feet. That's why we get paid.

He continued once the buzz died down. "I want you all to wait over there. Until we get our bags then I'll sign those books." Lee pointed to a wall about twenty yards away.

With a strange herding instinct in play, the horde of screamers backed off.

Lee beckoned to the pair who began the hellish yet amusing interlude.

They came forward watched closely by the throng. We heard random squeaks, signaling the hysteria of the group was barely controlled.

"What is it with you? Grange are old men compared with you," Sam said.

The darker headed one spoke, madness began to edge its way back into her voice. "Grange are gods ... we love them."

Kurt tapped Lee. He'd spotted our bags. They disappeared to retrieve them before they went round again.

"Can't you love that Beiber kid? At least he's within the right age group," Sam said. "Tony Sharron and Rowan Grange are old enough to be your fathers."

I watched everyone's eyes follow Lee. It was unnerving the way the whole wall seemed to be nothing but eyes.

The other kid sobbed. "You don't understand. We *love* them." The dark-haired kid looked at me. "Are you married to Tony?"

"No. And that's not Tony. His name is Lee. We're cops."

She shook her head. "But you don't look like cops.

'Cept for him." She pointed at Sam. "He looks like one."
To me Sam always looked the least like a cop and the
most like a nightclub bouncer. The bouncer, the rock star
and Kevin Costner. I checked my thoughts. Kevin Costner? Where the hell did that come from? Furtively I
glanced in Kurt's direction. Maybe it was his sandy hair,
or his size. But I saw the resemblance again and I just
knew it would be bad.

Lee and Kurt placed our bags on the ground. All eyes
returned to watch the four of us.

"Can I leave you guys here for one minute?" I asked
quietly. "I'm going to find a bathroom and I'll thank you
not to shoot anyone while I'm gone."

"With these loons around?" Kurt asked.

I shrugged. "No sleep and too much coffee. When you
gotta go ..."

He smiled. "I saw a bathroom sign back the way we
came in, on the left."

"Be right back."

The crowd remained entranced by Lee. I slipped behind the men and sought out a bathroom. Kurt was right.
I found it easily.

I pushed open the door. Glaring lights startled me almost as much as the strong smell of bleach. Underneath
the bleach was the unfortunate odor of pine cleanser, the
smell of public bathrooms worldwide. At least the bathroom was clean. Judging by the strength of the smell, it
had been recently cleaned. A row of cubicles on the left,
mirrors and basins on the right. At the far end of the

room were hand dryers

I chose a stall to the far left of the occupied one. A few minutes later, I was washing my hands. I gave my hands a quick shake over the basin and then plunged them into the hand drier. One of the air curtain type. Not a fan of them at all. Even less of a fan of bleach. I wanted to get out of there as quickly as possible.

One glance in the mirror told me the middle stall was still occupied and all the others free. It also told me I needed a touch of mineral powder to give me some color. I fished out a small compact and a sable brush from my handbag. A bit of a swirl over the mineralized powder and a light dusting was all it took. Welcome to the human race.

The middle cubicle remained closed. Maybe the door was jammed and it wasn't occupied after all. I noticed a photograph stuck to the wall above the drier. How did I not see it before? For a few weird moments, my brain denied the images in front of me.

My throat tightened.

Carla walking into school.

Thump.

I spun around, my hand tightened on the butt of my still-holstered Glock.

The middle stall door remained closed. A hand poked out from underneath. My eyes flicked from the picture to the stall and back. I pulled my phone and called Kurt.

"Conway?"

"Problem. Women's bathroom."

"You okay?"

"Yeah, it ain't me."

I took a deep breath and forced air through the tightness in my throat. I held the phone tightly to stop my hand shaking and sent a text message to Carla. *Arrived safe. All well. Love you.*

Running feet sounded out in the corridor. My phone buzzed in my hand. I read the text from Carla. *Don't forget my present. Goodnight x.* Relief swamped me. She was okay. Kurt, Sam and Lee burst into the room.

"S'up Chicky Babe?" Sam asked attempting to mask panic with a cloud of cool.

"That." I pointed to the hand. "And this ..." I pointed to the photograph.

All three men snapped on latex gloves. Sam was the only one who noticed my questioning look. He threw me a pair of gloves. "Kurt carries gloves in his bag."

Of course. He was traveling with his medical bag. Would be stupid not to have gloves.

Screaming from outside found its way into the bathroom.

"You brought your fan club?" I asked Lee.

"They weren't invited."

Sam took photographs of the bathroom and the picture, then dropped the picture into a small plastic bag. He shook his head. "Not good."

Lee leaned in for a look. "Carla."

Kurt knocked on the stall door.

No reply.

78

He looked underneath.

"She's fallen against the door."

He stood on an adjoining toilet and hoisted himself over the thin wall. There was a thud followed by some hefty lifting noises and the door opened.

"Verdict?" I asked.

"Deceased. Come over here."

I hadn't realized how close to the exit I was. I moved closer to Kurt. At the cubicle door, I could clearly see a bloodied woman wearing a New Zealand Police uniform.

"She's a cop. Any identification?"

Kurt removed a wallet from her pocket. "Sergeant Coral Terry."

"Terry," I repeated. "We were meeting a Sergeant Terry, or rather she was meeting us."

I breathed in. A whiff of chlorine came off her clothes and hit the back of my throat. I could hear Sam talking by the door. He was talking to a uniformed officer.

Carla and a dead cop.

Our arrival had been anticipated.

Sam sidled up to me. "Photo?"

"Not sharing," I whispered. "Not yet."

I showed my badge and credentials then spoke to the officer. "We are here to work with New Zealand Police on a case. This may be connected. We have identified the body as Sergeant Coral Terry. She was supposed to be meeting us."

He blanched. "I saw her half an hour ago at gate eleven."

We came through gate eleven fifteen minutes later.

"Can you cordon off this bathroom?"

The young police officer stood motionless, staring wide-eyed at the body.

"How did she die?"

Kurt moved a little, revealing the woman's bloodied matted hair. He joined me at the door to deliver his assessment of the situation. "Someone smashed her head – either with something or onto something – and then broke her neck."

"Where?"

"In here, I think. A forensic scene examination will be able to confirm that," Kurt said.

I added, "Someone has cleaned up. Can you smell bleach?"

The cop nodded. "There's a bunch of screaming women outside."

"It's okay, they're with him," Sam replied pointing at Lee. "They'll leave with us."

"Who do you need to call?" I asked. I tried to clamp a lid on the *Ghostbusters* theme song that ripped through my head. Stop it! I could feel my body wanting to move. Never could resist that song. I ain't afraid of no ghost. It's real wrath of God stuff.

"My section Sergeant," he replied. The young man pressed a button on his radio and spoke to Comms. Moments later another cop hurried in.

I introduced us all and explained we were in New Zealand at the request of New Zealand Police. One by one, we showed our badges and gave Sergeant Jim Calais a rundown on the events.

He and I took a walk down the corridor a wee ways.

"You got anything to do with that?" he asked, inclining his head toward all the noise.

"A little bit," I confessed. "They all seem a bit high-strung, something to do with Grange apparently."

"They're doing a concert here later in the week. Rumor has it the band is flying in today sometime."

"Lucky us."

The eyes watched intently. I felt the daggers flying at my back.

"Sergeant Terry was here to meet us. It's just a suggestion but you might want to start looking into who knew why she was here. From our end, only three people knew our travel plans; only one knew who was meeting us."

"We can reach you?"

I took a card from my pocket and wrote the name of our hotel on the back. "My cell phone number is on the card. We'll get going to our hotel and we're not planning on leaving the country any time soon."

"I'll be in touch."

"I'm sorry about your colleague," I said and shook his hand. I really was sorry. More than he knew. If we hadn't come, she'd probably still be alive. Sam, Lee and Kurt also expressed their condolences. Then gathered up our bags.

"Thank you." He glanced down the passage and into the terminal. "Are you going to be all right with that crowd?"

"Sure."

"Seems they're interested in your friend," the cop commented.

"Seems they're not the smartest," I replied.

He agreed.

The little blonde girl called over, "Would've been more fun if you were with Grange."

"Be more fun if you were thirty not thirteen," Lee called back, with a wave.

The kid glared at me as if it was my fault.

How sweet.

We headed out of the terminal amidst a chorus of screams, some of which were still recognizable as 'Tony.'

We piled into a taxi and let the whole situation wash over us. I figured it was going to take a double rinse cycle even to begin to clear the terror I felt.

First Cassie and now a cop. And both times pictures most certainly left for me. Not good at all.

The taxicab careened down a long straight road and I started to wonder if there was a city around anywhere at all. The wide-open fields started to feel a little *Twilight Zone* meets *Field of Dreams*; I expected a baseball diamond to appear any second. And what was with the old time warplane standing on the corner of the road that led to the airport?

The fields rimmed with pine trees and hedges led into suburbs that changed to denser neighborhoods and inner suburban streets. There didn't seem to be any hills, or even rises, in the land until a bluish haze in the distance. I found it uncomfortably flat and devoid of landmarks. Foreign soil it really was. From my short time in Christchurch, I considered the possibility I could become lost, a thought which didn't fill me with delight.

There wasn't much time to take notice of the hotel description when I booked it on the way to the airport back home. When you need a place to stay that's central and don't know the town, it really can come down to the first place that seems half-decent.

The taxi pulled up at the front entrance of the hotel. Sam sucked air noisily through his perfect straight teeth as he stood outside and looked up at the faux-medieval castle frontage.

"This is nice," he crooned, closing the taxi door behind him.

Lee and Kurt hoisted our bags from the trunk while I paid the driver.

There it was again, the feeling of eyes watching. I glanced over the top of the taxi, but couldn't see anyone around.

Lee took my bag and his, Sam and Kurt picked up theirs and, as we approached the door, we watched it open, magically, in front of us.

Lee whispered, "They have a doorman, this is nicer than usual."

I whispered back, "Do you have that bug detector toy with you?"

"Yes. You all right?"

"Paranoid." I shrugged it off

The concierge greeted us at the front desk. They were fully booked and there was a mix up with our booking. Sam and Lee were sharing, which meant Kurt and I were also sharing. The concierge promised to notify us once two more rooms became vacant. We followed along behind a porter to our rooms via a long corridor. A knight in armor stood to the right and on the left beyond glass walls was a large Koi pond. A bridge crossed the expanse of water leading to a restaurant and bar. The thick, deep, red patterned carpets absorbed all noise from our feet as we traveled the corridor to elevators, concealed within stone turrets.

Sam hissed at me in the elevator, "We have adjoining rooms?"

"Adjoining suites and it makes life easier."

The elevator stopped and we followed the porter down a spacious well-lit, dark-carpeted and tastefully decorated hallway. Fresh flower arrangements punctuated the hall at regular intervals filling the area with a sweet old-fashioned rose fragrance. And the feeling of eyes watching. I scanned the walls and spotted a security camera. That explained the creepy eyes watching in the hallway. The porter indicated we'd arrived and opened the first door. Lee and Sam ambled in. Kurt and I took the next room. We had a kitchenette which comprised a small countertop, sink and microwave. I opened a cabinet under the sink and took a look. A filter coffee machine and electric kettle.

I opened the bedroom door. One double bed and one single. Great. We'd have to flip for the double. That could wait. I wanted to unpack, freshen up and enjoy the small amount of peace I found while checking out the view. No one watched me. I'd left the eyes outside.

The knight in armor we'd passed in the hallway stuck with me. Hadn't visions of knights filled my head just a few days ago? Was it ironic or a sign? Ironic seemed the obvious choice. That's how my life went.

I just wanted to catch Hawk and go home. Hopefully before he moved any more kids. 'Moved' was easier to cope with than thinking of them as lost victims of a pedophile.

The fantasy threatened to escalate until I was the only possible savior of every missing kid in the world. I stopped it and stared out the window.

About five minutes of view-gazing non-thought was all I enjoyed. A banging on a door jolted me from my abstraction. I reached for my hip, my fingers slipped around the grip of my Glock.

Another bang followed by Kurt's voice. I investigated the ruckus.

It was one of the internal doors. Sam and Lee's room.

Kurt unlocked the door and stepped back. Sam spilled over the threshold.

He frowned at me and said, "This time thing is screwy. What day is it?"

"It's Monday," I replied, dropping my hand from my hip.

He chuckled. "That's crazy shit."

"It's going to take some getting used to," I said nodding in agreement. "Everything else okay?"

"These rooms are mighty fine," Sam said with a pronounced and exaggerated drawl.

"We sure landed on our feet." I scanned the hotel brochure. "There is room service."

"There is room-fuc'n-everything plus a gym and a pool," Sam replied. "The kitchenettes in our suites will be handy. Microwave, sink, haven't looked in the cabinets under the sink yet."

I noticed Kurt's bag still sitting on the floor in the living area. "Take your bag into the bedroom, there is plenty of drawer space and room." I was almost certain we could share a room without a problem. "There's one double and a single – flip for the double."

Sam produced a quarter and spun it in the air.

I called, "Heads."

Sam caught the coin and slapped it on his hand. "Heads it is."

Kurt grimaced. "Single it is."

"Is there coffee somewhere, Sam?"

"There a coffee machine?"

"Yep." I had looked under the sink.

"Then I'll find us coffee to go in it."

I don't know when Sam became the coffee guy but he did. He had a talent for locating and even for making a fine cup of coffee.

Chapter Seven
Pretty Maids All In a Row

I peered groggily through the peephole in the door. You really could have bowled me over with a feather. I swung the door open to be greeted by a familiar voice, "Look at what the cat dragged in."

Charming.

But not Prince Charming.

The steel-grey eyes of Sean O'Hare met mine. He was the twin brother of the Director of the FBI. I hadn't seen him since Mac's funeral and I sure as hell didn't expect him in New Zealand knocking on my door.

"Sean."

"Ellie. Going to invite me in?"

"Sure." I stepped aside, let him in and shut the door behind us. My tired eyes searched the room but Kurt was not there.

"Coffee?" I offered. Someone must've taken the coffee machine out of the cupboard and turned it on while I napped. Guess that meant Sam found coffee. There was a full pot waiting.

"Sure, black no sweetener," he replied inspecting the room. "Nice place."

I set a cup of coffee on the small table by the armchairs in the sitting area and glanced at the closed door leading to Sam and Lee's room.

"Jackson, Davenport and Henderson are giving us a

few minutes," Sean said.

So Kurt was next door.

"Why exactly are you here?" I asked, keeping my tone light.

"Seems some Americans sailed into Christchurch airport this morning like a three-ring goddamn circus," he said with a quick smile. "By all accounts it had something to do with the lead guitarist from Grange and ended in the death of a police officer."

"And you heard about this how?" I asked sipping my coffee. I surmised everyone in the South Island had heard about it by now. I was grateful for the time reference he threw in. I'd managed to nap when we'd settled into our rooms, which had completely muddled my sense of time. Now I knew it was still Monday.

"The sergeant you met," he said leaning back in his chair. "He gave me a call."

"Why would he do that?"

"Because the dead cop was supposed to work with you and now no one else wants to."

Awesome. "New Zealand?"

"Libby and I were in the process of moving back last time I spoke to you. That was my last day in the District."

Convenient. "You were at Mac's funeral."

"Yes, this amazing invention has happened, I think you've even been on one recently. It's called an airplane."

I rolled my eyes.

"Now back to business Ellie. Without putting a too fine a point on it, you *need* my help."

I didn't deny it. If we were after Hawk as we suspected, he was already playing a deadly game. Pretty much how my life goes.

Sean grinned at me. "A little blonde like you flanked by two huge guys like Sam Jackson and Lee Davenport … didn't you think that would draw some attention?"

"I'm not little," I snapped. "I'm five foot nine"

"Compared to Davenport and Jackson you are little."

"I didn't think of it like that."

Stupid!

"I heard there was some mix up and someone thought one of the guys was from Grange." Sean smiled. "I'm figuring it was Lee, he's got some kind of stadium rocker thing happening. You ever stepped back and really looked at your team? Davenport has that rocker thing. Jackson looks like LL Cool J on steroids. And what's with Henderson doing a Kevin Costner impersonation? What was that movie he did with Whitney Houston?"

I'd never noticed the LL Cool J thing and thought the Kevin Costner thing was just me. Seriously, did Sean have to mention *The Bodyguard*? That's exactly who Kurt reminded me of: Kevin Costner in *The Bodyguard*.

"Okay." My mind was shutting down. It was all too weird.

"You want my help?"

"I want your help."

"You better tell me what you're doing here, so I know what you need by way of assistance."

There seemed to be no point withholding anything.

And as he lived there, he'd know a few things about the way the country worked.

"I need someone who can liaise with New Zealand Police and knows how they work. Can you do that? I have the name of the officer who called us in."

He looked at me with a raised eyebrow.

"The detective in charge; not the poor sergeant who was supposed to be our liaison."

"Not a problem."

"Can we salvage our professional reputations and fix this?"

Sean laughed. "Not sure about your reputations as tough FBI agents but Lee has a new one, as an impersonator. What *this* are we talking about?"

"*This* is hopefully finding Hudson Hawk."

"Hudson Hawk?" he grinned. "You're not talking about a copy of the movie, right?"

What a day. First Grange and Kevin Costner, then LL Cool J and now Bruce Willis.

"I'm talking about the maybe-Russian-possible-terrorist who killed Mac."

And now he's responsible for Cassie's death and a cop.

"The Virginia Butterfly Murders: wasn't that the case you were working when Mac was shot?"

"Mac was *murdered*. He was gunned down in the back of my car protecting a kid."

Sean ignored my outrage.

"Same guy as the Butterfly Murders?" he asked again.

"Yeah, we think he did those too. So, can we fix this?"

"I think so," Sean said.

"You want in on this?"

"I do."

"Why?"

"Because when I needed help to protect my little sister, you were there."

He didn't need to remind me and he certainly didn't owe me a debt. I did my job.

Helping protect his 'little sister' sounded rather innocuous. Knowing his little sister was an award-winning novelist changed the statement completely. The family secret I knew changed things even more.

My life is a strange and sometimes wonderful place. Mostly just strange.

"I'll get the boys in here and we'll bring you up to speed on the case."

I knocked on Lee's door. Within a few seconds, all three men were sitting on the sofa in my suite as we ran through the information and case notes with Sean and Kurt. It was timely; Kurt needed briefing and it was the ideal opportunity.

"This is about the three missing kids here?" Sean asked with a certain knowingness to his tone.

"Yep."

"I heard New Zealand Police had requested help from the FBI. I should've made the connection as soon as I heard about the airport disturbance," Sean said with a small smile, which faded quickly. "People are panicked. Kids don't go missing in this country and sure as hell not three within a week. It's all over the news; has been since the first kid disappeared."

"With a bit of luck we can find them."

I called room service and ordered us all some dinner and drinks, while Sam bounced Sean and Kurt through the worst of the crime scenes we'd come across during the case. I didn't need to hear that particular re-hash. I lived it. The nightmares will always be with me.

"I recall another swathe of destruction that followed Conway," Kurt said in a slightly raised voice, to make sure I heard him. "What is it with you?"

"Guess I just piss people off," I replied.

"I think there is more to it than that."

"Can you hear that?" I asked, cupping my ear in my hand. "That's the sound of no one caring what you think."

I leaned on the counter in the small kitchen and watched the guys talking. 'Intense' was the best word I could come up with to describe the way they all leaned into one another. It seemed forever before Sam reclined back on the sofa and began to look semi-relaxed. Lee continued discussing something with Sean. From where I stood, it looked like Sam was done.

That was possible; he did miss a good deal of the investigation due to a liver laceration, courtesy of the Unsub, so he probably didn't have as much to impart as Lee.

Sam caught my attention with a small wave. He stood up, stretched and came over to my side of the room.

"'S'up?"

"Waiting for dinner," I said.

"Everything okay?" he asked then grinned, his perfect white teeth gleamed against the deep brown backdrop of his face and the fading sunlight.

"Yes," I replied. "It's okay."

"You've worked with O'Hare before, yeah?"

"I have."

"What gives?"

"Seems a little too convenient having him here."

"Did O'Hare send him?"

"I don't think so." It smacked of being babysat. I changed the subject. "The sun's setting."

The colors in the sky changed from blues and whites to deep pinks and mauves. It was pretty but the prettiness barely registered in my mind. I could hear Lee explaining how Mac died; no amount of colored clouds could take his words away.

I wished on streaks of red and orange that he'd come back and help me take care of Carla.

Chapter Eight
Story of My Life.

"Wake up! Come on, it's Tuesday morning. Let's go!"

A voice reached into my subconscious and wrenched me from my sleep. My first reaction was uncharitable. "Go to hell." I rolled over away from the intrusion.

"Ellie!"

"Go away," I grumbled and pulled the covers over my head. "Ellie's not in."

There was a whooshing noise and a sudden draught and my blankets disappeared.

"That was not necessary," I said and grabbed the blanket back from Lee's hands. "You're lucky I packed pajamas."

"Nah, Kurt's lucky you packed pajamas. Get up," he said. "We've got a lead."

I jumped out of bed. "I'm up," I said, chasing all remnants of sleep from my brain. One day it'd be nice to get in more than two hours sleep a night. "Where's this lead?"

"This morning three files arrived from the police – we have copies of the investigations regarding the missing kids."

"Lead?" I repeated impatiently.

"Another kid was reported missing this morning – Nicola Gallagher, her mother has bipolar disorder – and your ping results came back from the techie at the Foundation. She's the only kid who has been on the boards. She's missing from Wellington."

I felt the blood drain from my head. That Nicola had been using the Butterfly Foundation had to be a coincidence, because none of the other victims was a member. Coincidence or not, it sucked out loud. I sat on the edge of the bed, hooked up my jeans from the floor and folded them.

"Is the mother dead or alive?" I asked.

"Alive."

"Can we talk to her?" I fished a hairbrush from the bag near the bed and dragged it through my hair a few times then set it carefully on the nightstand.

"Maybe 'alive' is too strong a word. She's in a secure psychiatric facility, here in Christchurch. She was admitted two days ago."

"So we can't talk to her?"

"Kurt's spoken with her doctors and reckons not until she's stable on her medication and coherent. Could be a few days."

Okay, so having a team doctor could be handy.

"He could've got the kid to Christchurch with the promise of visiting her mother," I replied. "If he is moving the kids south, that is." Something else interested me. "Mother was admitted two days ago, yet the kid is only just reported missing?"

"That what's I was thinking too."

"Okay. Give me a few minutes to shower then we'll get started on the files."

"I'll order breakfast," Lee said and left my bedroom.

I hustled into the adjacent bathroom and took a hot shower. By the time I was done and had passed a mascara wand over my eyelashes, I could smell breakfast.

My stomach rumbled.

Lee, Kurt and Sam were eating when I made my entrance. Files were stacked in a neat pile on the coffee table. My cell phone buzzed frantically and danced all over the counter, its red light flashing.

Sam looked over as I picked it up. "It's been going off every few minutes for the last half hour."

"Fifteen missed calls and twelve messages."

"Someone loves you," Sam replied.

"They're mostly from Caine," I said with a sigh. I flipped through the text messages and paraphrased for the team. "He wants to know where we are and if we're okay."

Sam chuckled. "What did he really say?"

Lee said in a gruff Caine-like voice, "You on vacation Conway? You better be okay down there because I want the joy of causing you serious harm when you come back sporting a tan." He finished with an exaggerated double twitch of his mouth.

He knew Caine well.

There were two messages from Carla; both said she thought someone was following her on her way home from school the last two days. Crap!

My call went straight to her voicemail so I left a message. "Hey kiddo. I want you to call Caine Grafton at my office and tell him what's going on. You know Caine, he'll be happy to hear from you. Tell your caregiver and have her call the police. Tell a teacher. Tell everyone you can think of that you think someone is following you. Do not go anywhere alone. Call me when you can. Be good."

I tossed the phone at the sofa and watched it bounce twice before sliding toward a cushion. Lee and Sam were staring at me. I did a quick calculation of the time difference between New Zealand and Virginia. We're a day ahead and it was dinner time back home. Carla would be eating, which would account for the call going to voicemail. Caine would probably be eating as well. Seemed smarter to call him after my breakfast and not to interrupt his meal, and there was nothing he could do until morning anyway.

"Carla thinks she's being followed," I said. "No surprise given the photograph stuck in the airport bathroom." Fear began building, stacking up little blocks of doubt in my gut and creating havoc. "We think Hawk's here, yes? He can't be in two places at once."

Sam nodded. "He's here. You can feel it as well as we can."

"So he left someone stateside to follow Carla."

"There's a plate here for you," Kurt said, indicating a place at the table. "Sit yourself down and eat. Talk to Caine after breakfast, he'll take care of Carla."

"True enough."

Kurt took a sip of his coffee and voiced his burning question. "Who is Carla?"

Sam grinned. "She's family."

Breakfast was fine.

Fine.

I ate. I drank a chilled, freshly squeezed orange juice and it was fine. While Lee and Sam ploughed through a mountain of food and an entire pot of coffee. Kurt and I read the files. Four missing kids now, that wasn't enough. I would've put money on there being more than four kids missing from New Zealand. Didn't seem like a profitable trip for Hawk. I picked up my cell phone and sent a text message to each of the missing girls' phones. It read, 'I am Special Agent Ellie Conway. I can help you. Text me or call me.' If they had their cell phones on, hopefully they would get the message and try to make contact.

But then, if they had cell phones, surely they would've called or texted someone and said what was happening? The file said police had tried making contact with them via their cell phones and had received no response. There were no reports of cell activity from any of the phones.

"You three can finish going over the files. There's something seriously fucked up with this whole situation. A dead cop – which seems unnecessary. The low number of missing kids, which makes me think there are some we don't know about yet. If that's the case, there could be bodies." Feelings of inadequacy writhed in my gut, suggesting I wasn't focused. I needed to get some exercise. "I'd like to get in a workout or maybe a run."

Showering later would've been smarter. Oh well, cleanliness is next to godliness. Deep down I knew there wasn't enough water in the world to make that true.

Lee was the first to react with a slightly suspicious tone as he stated, "You've showered already, now you're going to work out ..."

"I know, I'm wasteful – all that water down the drain." I smiled. "I'll see if the gym's free," I replied, lifting the telephone receiver from its cradle and calling the concierge.

I was in luck and was able to book an hour and a half starting immediately. I turned down the offer of a personal trainer. That was pushing things a little far; all I really wanted was some thinking time.

The decision to workout led to a hunt through my bag, until I found my iPod. Music encouraged thought, so logically thinking, time required music. It was anybody's guess what was actually on my iPod. I changed into my academy sweats and sneakers. As I opened the bedroom door, I heard my phone ringing.

"Toss me the phone?" I asked Sam.

"Catch," he replied, throwing it right into my hands.

I took a breath and flipped the phone open. "Caine?"

"S.S.A. Conway. Do you have an update for me?"

"Not yet."

In that nanosecond, I had a flash of knowledge or maybe it was an instinctive knowing. Something in my gut spoke and I knew Hawk was here. I knew without *any* doubt there were more missing kids and bodies in the country, somewhere. Now we had to find them.

"Caine, I can't talk about the case right now. I need you

to do something for me. Carla left me a message saying she thinks she was followed home from school the last two days. Check on her for me. I gave her a list of instructions – she should be calling you soon."

All my thoughts jumped into linear order but remained my thoughts. Someone knew I was going to Cassie's. Someone also knew I went to Carla's that day and was going to my brother's for dinner. Someone knew who the cop was who was meeting us in Christchurch and what time.

"All right," Caine replied, his tone said he understood it was important.

"This could get real ugly, real quick. I think someone is watching her. I also think we've got an in-house problem."

"Stateside?"

"I don't know."

"Watch your back."

"I'll call you back later today. What's the time difference?" I rapidly calculated the time zones. "Jesus ... I'll call you, hopefully at a reasonable time."

"I'll go visit Carla tomorrow."

"Take care of her."

"As if she were my own."

I hung up.

Halfway to the gym, I changed my mind. What I needed was to run. Far far away, or at least long enough to clear my head. I needed pavement under my feet and the sun's warmth on my back. I pushed my hands through my long hair pulling it back off my face. I didn't have sunglasses or a cap.

Because I was supposed to be in the gym, I mumbled internally. Didn't have cash either but the hotel had a store where I chose a pair of sunglasses and a black cap with a silver fern on it, which I charged to the room.

On my way out of the hotel, I grabbed a brochure with a map on it figuring I might need it to find my way back.

The minute my feet hit the pavement a soothing lull came over me. It annoyed me that I seemed incapable of thinking my way around the investigation. I came up with two possibilities: we weren't getting enough information or maybe my brain was simply on strike. I switched my iPod on and settled into a rhythm.

Christchurch's flat streets made running just as peaceful as back home and felt normal. It was early and there was hardly any traffic. All in all, a pleasant way to spend half an hour.

I found a river and ran along the grassy banks until I came to an inviting willow tree. The music in my ears flowed from country to country rock and back again. The mix ran from Lorenza Ponce to Kevin Costner and Modern West with a large dose of Bon Jovi mixed with Grange in between. The irony of having Kevin Costner on my iPod didn't escape me.

The prying eyes of yesterday were back and I seemed unable to outrun them.

Under a willow tree, I stopped to stretch. Out on the water ducks quacked and swam up to the bank. Guess they wanted breakfast. I moved on to another willow tree in a more peaceful duck-free environment.

The run hadn't worked. My focus needed work. The disjointed feeling from my topsy-turvey life stayed with me. The eyes watched.

A giant wave of fury surged through me. Someone I trusted was responsible for leaking information to Hawk. The desire to scream grew.

Look where my job took me ... there I sat under a willow tree beside the Avon River in Christchurch, New Zealand, and all I wanted to do was scream bloody murder.

The newly-disappearing children, Hawk being back, it all felt so close and personal I reminded myself it wasn't personal when we faced off last time, not to start with anyway. He'd set an elaborate baited trap to work out which Delta team was available and who would lead the team prior to his killing, kidnapping spree.

Go Ellie!

Having some fucktard kill Cassie and send me a message by having me kidnapped. Now that's personal. Killing a cop – my husband – and messing with Carla was personal. The worst part of my thought process was knowing someone I knew, within the FBI, was feeding information to Hawk. I started ticking off names.

Sam.

I picked up a stone and tossed it across the river. It skimmed. Four jumps.

Lee.

I threw another one and counted five jumps, the last

narrowly missing a duck.

Chrissy.

I chose another flat stone. This time I threw it with purpose. My target was the opposite bank.

Caine.

Time to catch that fucker Hawk and go die hard on his ass.

I let another stone loose and watched as it skipped across the river, leaving a shimmering wake in its path.

Kurt.

The willow's trunk provided a comfortable place to lean against while watching the last ripple disappear. Something new entered my world.

Peace.

I gave it a minute to consolidate, in case it was the beginning of a migraine or maybe a transient ischemic attack. I found my rationale disturbing and was fully aware that most people wouldn't think they were having a mini-stroke because they suddenly felt peaceful.

Then again, two significant head injuries in three years weren't normal either. I consoled myself with the idea that my mind embraced the notion of a migraine or transient ischemic attack and not a hemorrhagic stroke, from which I would not recover. Considering the darkness I fought on a daily basis and the current that persistently tried to tow me under, I think that showed promise. So many times I had wanted to just let go, to stop fighting the miseries of life and to sink into the oblivion, in the hope of being with Mac again.

I took a deep breath and set the thoughts free on another stone. A ripple contorted on the surface of the water. In fascination, I watched as it created Mac's face. He smiled, his mouth opened and words glistened in the air becoming audible as they dripped back into the river. "Someone's out to get you, Babe."

"Yeah, but who?" I whispered at the sparkling watery image of Mac.

"You'll figure it out."

"What about Hawk?"

"It's all about the music."

Mac's facial features drifted farther and farther apart until he was just a collection of tiny ripples.

His reference to music confused me. Really, I should've been more concerned about talking to a river and believing it was my dead husband. That seemed insignificant in relation to what he said. In the back of my mind was a looming apprehension regarding my sanity.

The one person I could always trust was dead and someone close was feeding information to Hawk. Carla was in danger and I was on the other side of the world. Not great.

The ground vibrated behind me.

Pounding feet.

With one hand on the ground, I leaned around the tree trunk and peeked to see who was running, expecting to see Doc and maybe Sam. It wasn't any of my team. One of the running men was Rowan Grange, the lead singer of Grange. Knowing they were in the country was one thing but seeing Rowan Grange out running caused a hint of fan girl to rise up within me. I allowed myself to enjoy my first-ever sighting of him in the wild. A new song came on; listening to Lorenza's voice as she sang 'Soul Shifter' and watching the water for signs of Mac, pushed thoughts of Grange from my mind. The combination of music and water were causing ripples of ideas to form about the case.

I stood up, stretched, threw a couple more stones and then turned back toward the hotel. Opting for a slow jog, I headed back along the riverbank, eager to see something recognizable that would show where I'd come from.

At an intersection, I stopped and consulted my brochure. Finding it next to useless I threw it in a trash basket by the cross lights.

It became obvious that I was going to have to rely on my instincts working in a flat southern hemisphere city, just as they did in northern Virginia. Or find someone and hopefully recall the name of the damn hotel.

Autopilot kicked in and I cruised along trusting blind faith. Before long, a door opened for me and then a familiar concierge in the lobby greeted me with a flourish of impeccable camp.

With a smile, I removed my earphones and took the elevator back to our floor. Right then I changed my mind and hit the gym instead. I wasn't done yet and I'd already booked the gym. Ideas were forming but not cementing. At that stage the ideas were like mist or smoke, I could see shapes but not hold them all together. There was a struggle going on as the incorporeal shapes fought to become substantial entities.

Inside the spacious well-lit gym, I found a row of treadmills with a view over the inner city. I pushed the earpieces back in my ears and switched my iPod on and the volume up.

I set myself up at a decent pace.

Focus.

The missing kids swirled with the faces of those we'd rescued last time Hawk came along. Before I knew it, I was whirling out of control with no concrete plans on how to approach the problem. Anger surfaced again.

The damage had already been done. Hawk already knew where we were and where Carla was. I needed to focus on finding the kids and then worry about finding the traitor.

The anger, however well hidden from the world, had to go.

I ran.

If I ran long enough and hard enough, I could outpace the anger. If I ran far enough, maybe I wouldn't remember why I was angry. If I ran until I couldn't stand, maybe then it wouldn't hurt any more.

Five songs into my run a noise beside me penetrated through the ear buds.

A muffled American voice. I looked, expecting to see Doc. It wasn't. My heart pounded in an odd fashion. I knew who it was but my mind wouldn't accept it.

The man smiled at me from the treadmill next to mine;

his mouth moved.

I dropped one ear bud.

"Sorry I didn't catch that," I replied. Music blared from the ear bud dangling on my chest.

"I said 'hi'," he repeated and then continued in a light conversational tone. "I'm not surprised you didn't hear. You always listen to music that loud?"

"Only when I'm on a treadmill," I replied. His New Jersey accent sent a shiver up my spine.

I looked around expecting to find someone behind me, watching. I filed away the feeling of eyes watching me, intending to discuss it with Lee or Sam, if I could find a way of doing so without sounding like a lunatic. I convinced myself there was probably a security camera somewhere.

The only person in the room was right next to me. My eyes flicked to his hands: no knife. Of course there was no knife. He was a rocker not a killer.

He smiled and indicated the iPod and the current song. "I like that one too."

I smiled without commenting, nor did I put the bud back into my ear. It was time to pay attention to life.

"You're a long way from home," he said.

"So are you," I replied and introduced myself. "I'm Ellie."

We dispensed with the whole handshake introduction; it didn't seem appropriate on treadmills.

"Pleased to meet you Ellie, I'm Rowan."

Like I didn't know his name? With introductions

made, it was now seemly to have a conversation.

"You were out running this morning by the river," I said.

I decided that the other guy I'd seen was a personal trainer or maybe a bodyguard. I put my money on bodyguard. A scene from the movie with Kevin Costner played in my head.

"You saw me?" He seemed surprised.

"You ran by with your bodyguard."

He smiled and inclined his head, subtly. "You should've said something."

I'm not some lunatic fan.

The next song started up. My iPod was on shuffle. Rowan smiled and looked out the window. I could see his reflection. Sun streamed in, the temperature rose, I wanted to push my sleeves up but resisted. People who saw the scars on my arm tended to leave quickly.

"You like that record?" he asked.

"Yes," I replied. "I really do. Do you like it?"

He never moved his head but his eyes met mine in the reflection of the glass.

"What's your favorite song?"

Answering a question with a question. How surprising.

" 'Everybody's Broken.' "

He smiled. It was infectious.

A responding smile spanned my face, catching my reflection by surprise.

He asked, "Why?"

"Because it's true."

My mind screamed curses as I considered the implications of what I'd said.

I snapped like a little fuc'n twig. Now I was having some kind of brain episode and I thought I was talking about Bon Jovi with Rowan Grange.

My hallucinations exhibited exponential growth. Part of me started to think having Dr. Kurt along on this trip was a good thing.

He nodded. " 'Lost Highway' is one of their best."

"I like your new album. You're on tour now?"

A smile traced across his lips leading toward his eyes. "Yes," Rowan replied. "You're south eastern ... Virginia?"

I watched his eyes reading the lettering on my sweatshirt in the window. He could read mirror images. Conway, G, was written next to the FBI seal.

"You're a special agent? Like a field agent?"

I nodded. "I'm a Supervisory Special Agent."

He switched off his treadmill and with two smooth strides was standing in front of me.

"Ellie Conway, the FBI poet," he announced. "I friended you on MySpace and on Facebook ... you're *The Poet with a Gun*."

I don't think I hid the shock I felt fast enough. I remembered the 'friend' requests; I'd assumed it was some assistant who added everyone with Grange in their music preferences, no matter how far down the list it was.

I stopped the treadmill before my feet forgot to move. I could not believe *he* knew who *I* was. He was the super-famous lead singer of Grange. Everyone knew who he was.

"You and your husband opened the Butterfly Foundation; I thought that was an amazing thing to do." He continued, "I was at a fund raiser in DC for your Foundation. You read some of your poetry."

Speechless.

Utterly speechless.

"You okay?"

"I'm fine," I croaked. Okay was way too big a stretch. As far as I could tell, I was in the midst of one hell of a hallucination.

He grabbed two bottled waters from the refrigerator by the window and handed one to me. "Maybe we should sit down," Rowan said, holding out his hand to take mine.

I let him help me. It wasn't as if I had a choice. My legs were about to give way. An electric charge passed from my hand to his. He grinned.

As soon as I stepped off the treadmill, I let go his hand.

We walked together to a sitting area. He undid the screw top of the water bottle in my hand and handed the bottle back to me. Our fingers brushed. Static flew.

"That's twice," he said. Several long drinks later, I noticed a sudden *volte face* from angry, to feeling like a complete idiot. He was still talking.

"Tell me about your poetry." He leaned towards me. "Are you still writing? I loved the book." Rowan sat back, then leaned forward again. "The raw energy, the pain, the power and the feeling of hope; some poems filled me with absolute joy and others with despair." His hands punctuated his words. The impact of his words was greater with his expressive movements.

He loved our book.

Shut up!

I gulped down some more water. His voice carried on exalting our praises, terrifying me with direct quotes. I could *feel* Mac cringing from his grave.

Surely I wasn't sitting in a hotel gym about to discuss our pathetic poetry with a rock star? Things like *that* do not happen in real life.

I nodded like a retard and failed several attempts at coherent speech but decided I was in the midst of a psychotic break, which comforted me.

He launched into another poem,

"Stolen …
When the world is done,
lost in time too tired to run,
a safe place came to be …
Feeling your words surround me,
letting tears cascade …
Hoping my dues in life are paid."

Ice formed in my veins.

I stopped him hoping my voice didn't shake as I said, "I'd rather you didn't quote that one."

The last time I'd read that poem was when Hawk scrawled parts of it over bloody crime scenes.

Rowan Grange reciting that poem scared me. Frosty blood clogged my arteries as my mind tossed up lines of poetry ringing the carnage of the crime scenes. I tried to concentrate on the song lyrics I could still hear in my head but somehow they made it worse. He looked around the room.

"Is your husband here with you ...?" His voice trailed off as he looked at me with the slow dawning of someone with both feet in his mouth. "He was killed ... I'm sorry ... I remembered the news broadcasts once I'd opened my mouth. Oh Lord, I'm so sorry."

"Yeah, me too," I replied, forcing air into my stiff lungs. Death is such a conversation stopper. I tried to divert him from the awkwardness. "Did you really like our stuff?"

"Yes," he said with a grin. "I have a copy of your book with me. Would you sign it?"

He was so sincere and so normal that should've been the point at which I woke up. There was no logical explanation for this rift in reality.

Why would someone like him want *my* autograph?

Mac's voice rang in my head, 'Go with it Ellie. It'll be okay. It's all about the music.'

It was almost too much. I was well used to having an extraordinary life but that much crazy was beyond my comprehension.

"Would you? I didn't get a chance to talk to you at the Butterfly Foundation fundraiser, or I would've asked you to sign it then."

"Absolutely." Sure why not? None of this is real.

"I'd like to hang out with you again sometime."

There it was again, the speechless thing. I hoped I smiled but I suspected it was more like a grimace.

"You wanna run some more?" he asked.

I shook my head. I wanted the floor to swallow me whole.

"What room are you in?" he asked, looking around as if searching for something.

"Ten twenty three." I followed his eyes as they stopped on a desk by the door.

"We're on the same floor," he said. "Wait right there."

Rowan sidestepped several pieces of exercise equipment and made his way over to the desk, paused for a few seconds then came back carrying a piece of paper which he gave to me.

Two phone numbers. One New York landline and one cell phone.

Before the floor opened up in time-honored fashion, I pulled a card from the pocket in my sweat pants and passed it to him.

Rowan looked up from the card and in that gap in time, I saw a deep knowledge and an understanding of life in his eyes. I wondered for a brief moment where the hell he found it.

"Your cell is global?"

"Yes," I replied.

"Mine too, makes it easier for everyone."

No doubt it does.

Then he said, "I'd like to get together and discuss a few ideas when we both have more time."

All the words fell out of my head. He'd done it again.

Mac would've laugh so hard if he could've seen how speechless I'd been rendered by this guy.

Sure, I'll get together with Rowan Grange ... just as soon as hell freezes over. I could imagine his management and publicist having a conniption over any involvement with the FBI.

The urge to write brewed and seethed the more I thought about Mac. His ghostly hand reached out from beyond the grave and smacked me upside the head. My life snapped into place so loudly I was sure he'd heard.

"Meanwhile, I have a job to do." I tapped the piece of paper.

With a bottle of water in my hand, I headed out the door.

"Enjoy the rest of your workout," I called over my shoulder.

Chapter Nine
What Happened To You

On my way to my room, words swirled in some sem-
blance of order. I hurried through the door heading right
for the bedroom. It was still early. Not even nine in the
morning yet. I struggled to remember what day it was
and eventually recalled it was Tuesday.

Doc, Sam and Lee were still reading files. I paused for
a second and looked at them. Doc wasn't around before I
was kidnapped. A movie clip ran in slow motion through
my mind, I was wrong. Doc was there when Cassie died.
He was around before I was kidnapped. But he couldn't
have known the name of the cop who was supposed to
meet us – he wasn't Delta A then. But I knew who did –
going there would be worse than anything else I'd ever
done.

Lee called out, "How was the run?"

Spell broken.

"Good. Showering!" I replied and closed the bedroom
door behind me. Not Sam and Lee, they're family.

I scrabbled through the nightstand and retrieved a legal pad and pen. On the paper I wrote,

Gone.

It culminated in the end
Dripping off the edge of life
The ooze that was primordial slime

Is all that's left at the end of time.

Full circle?

Does it matter?

The words glared at me, full of rage and despair. They were not what I wanted to see at all. I slid the pad and pen back into the drawer. I was hoping for something with less darkness and despair and more rainbows. It occurred to me that I might not be ready for rainbows yet, so I set my sights on grayish clouds instead. A bit of lightning would add color. I dropped the piece of paper with Rowan's phone number on my bed. I doubted it was even him I spoke to. The whole thing was too bizarre. Ten minutes later, I emerged from the shower, clean and refreshed. The piece of paper was still there. Rowan Grange knew the poem Hawk used. I stored both his phone numbers in my phone. It'd make it easier to get hold of him should anything else come to light. Mac's voice reiterated his earlier comment, 'It's all about the music.'

The team was still going over files, comparing ours with the New Zealand Police files. Looking for something that would point us to where Hawk was or where he'd strike next or even confirm it was him. This guy was good; I doubted we'd find him by tracking his past but we had to start somewhere. My techies back home sent a list of New Zealand-based servers, which had shown up during the time-consuming ping and traces I had requested.

With a blue marker pen, I wrote the missing girls' names in bold print on a clean piece of paper. Tasha Cravino, Samantha Rowe, Abbey Jenkins and lastly,

Nicola Gallagher. They had to have something in common.

The first three girls didn't have a Foundation link but little Nicola's mom was in a psychiatric facility. Sam handed me coffee and file summaries.

"This is not going as well as we hoped," he said, yawning.

"I gathered that," I replied as I opened the file and simultaneously sipped the hot coffee. "We gotta stop this before the real killing starts."

What we'd seen so far was nothing, compared with how messy and horrific the killing was last time we tangled with Hawk.

"Hey, Sam. There is something linking these kids. We have to find out what it is."

I leaned forward and tapped a few keys on the open laptop on the coffee table.

"What would bring Hawk to Christchurch at this time of year?" I asked, generally.

"Schools are out, summer holidays over here," Sam said.

"Yeah, but schools are out everywhere in New Zealand ... not just Christchurch. Why Christchurch?" I grabbed the files on the first two missing kids. I intended to add them to my mix and give them a good stir. I flipped through the files. "There is no mention here of either girl coming to Christchurch, or going away, at all. But we don't know if those questions were asked."

The problems we faced needed consideration. The girls

were all about the age of the airport mob, within two years at least, which put them smack into tween land. Not quite a teenager but not a little kid. Young teens were an odd bunch, susceptible to major crushes and hysteria. It seemed a bit strange to me that such young girls liked an older band like Grange.

"How to catch a pre-teen girl without too much fuss ...?" I muttered aloud. "Lee would've had no trouble at all convincing any of those airport kids to go somewhere with him."

"How to catch a kid whose main caregiver is bipolar ...?" Lee said. "Try a little kindness. Even without looking this good ... shit, even Sam could convince a kid to go with him."

Sam grinned. "Thanks bro."

"I have a feeling that Foundation link with Nicola is not the whole story. There is something else. She's the only one with a bipolar mother," I said, feeling a nicotine craving insidiously asserting itself.

Some days I still wanted a cigarette. This was one of them.

"You think Hawk is using the concert?" Lee said. His lip curled into a disgusted snarl.

How very Elvis of him.

"It's entirely possible. Shit, if I were him, I would," I replied. "If I was after teens I'd be haunting concerts all over the world or maybe I'd just be a Catholic priest."

Mac's words echoed in my head. 'It's all about the music.'

"Let's hope you never go to the dark side," Lee said.

Doc seemed to be watching me intently, though I couldn't think why. I wiped my hand across my mouth, maybe it was toothpaste residue.

"Not sure about the age range they expect at these things though. Do young teens have the money for stadium concert tickets? Wouldn't they be fairly pricy?" I said. "If I was hunting little girls I'd be chasing that Beiber kid's fans, not Grange ones."

"Now you got me trying to remember how much I paid last time I went to a concert." Lee paused for thought. "I think I paid about a hundred and ten. What's that over here?"

Sam tapped at his laptop keys then said, "That's about a hundred and forty-four NZ dollars."

"So the answer would be ... probably not. Their folks maybe obliging or even taking them along with them," Doc suggested.

I leaned back in my seat and smiled. "How does a band that's been together seventeen or so years have such a diverse fan base?"

Doc got into the swing of things and offered more input, "Here's a thought – these kids have actually grown up with the music. Their parents probably listen to it."

"Okay, so thinking about the crazy airport fans ... and the longevity of the band, it's possible that young teens will be attending the show," I added.

From Christchurch, Hawk could fly direct to the Middle East; we knew from the last time we tango'd this guy traveled regularly to the Middle East. That seemed to be a plausible reason for picking Christchurch last, so maybe it wasn't concert related.

"Phone!" I demanded. Sam dropped my cell into my hand. I called Misha.

"*Privet!* Ellie."

This time he beat me to it.

"How strong is Hawk's connection with the Middle East?"

"I think very. My feeling is his mother is Russian. We think his father is Arab but we have no proof. He has Syrian ties also."

"Can you find out where his father is from and if Hawk still has close Arab ties? It might help us stop the girls leaving this country." I paused to think then said, "Has there been any activity at the orphanages?" Hawk had used orphanages in Russia to hide kidnapped children. We suspected he was also conducting the sale of children via the orphanages.

"I have surveillance in place. No one is reporting anything, no unusual activity so far."

"It may not be unusual, Misha. That could be why it's so hard to spot."

"*Da*, you have a point. I'll take a trip out there myself and I will call on the other matter as soon as I know. Where are you now?"

"We're in Christchurch, New Zealand."

"Last known destination for Hawk was Christchurch, New Zealand, but we do not know if that is reliable."

"I think it is. I have the techs at the Foundation compiling a list for you of all ISPs that have logged onto the Foundation servers from Europe; they might match up with those seventeen missing kids. You should have it soon but I don't think it will help. I think he's using music – concerts to be more accurate – I just don't know yet how he's making first contact with the kids."

"*Dosvidanija.*"

I hung up. Sam and Lee waited for me to speak.

"Why would young girls like those at the airport follow an established band like Grange?"

"By 'established' you mean 'old', right?" Sam replied.

"Yeah. They're not exactly a boy band or what I would've considered a band tweens would like."

"True," Lee said.

"Maybe they're looking for sugar daddies," I said with a smile. "Or just daddies. These kids have no fathers in their lives."

Doc shook his head slowly. "You astound me, Conway."

I moved on. Plans were forming; ideas were flowing. "Now, let's get this show on the road. Do they do Amber Alerts here? Are they in place? If not, find out what they do instead and do it! We need to blanket the media with pictures. I want pictures at the airport – posters would be good too. I want it so you can't turn around in this town without seeing these kids' photos with a big freaking caption that reads 'missing child.' Get me an interview time with that mother. I don't give a shit how bad a state she's in, I need to talk to that woman. I want to know what music these kids listen to. Who their friends are. Where they spend every second of every day. National media should be encouraged to run stories on these children: on the off chance they're not in Christchurch but en route. Get onto Twitter, Facebook, MySpace, Bebo, any other networking site that kids hang out on. This isn't a big country: our odds are good for finding four missing teens."

I paused and looked at Lee. "We need Sean O'Hare; he knows more about the system here." Initially I wasn't entirely comfortable with Sean O'Hare showing up and offering his assistance. There were things about Sean my team thought were rumors but I knew were true.

He was ex-CIA. Sean O'Hare took part in assassinations, renditions and anti-terror operations all over the world. We'd worked together before. Believing someone within the FBI was feeding Hawk, I knew Sean was someone I wanted on my side. We shared a common past but no one, not even Sean, knew it. I had firsthand knowledge of what we called renditions. The act of removing someone from one country and relocating them to another, without anyone knowing, was not a foreign concept to me. Because of that, I was also quite familiar with black sites – some call them secret prisons – and they're generally outside the U.S. territory. Sometimes people disappear forever. Sometimes people deserve to disappear forever.

I looked at Sam. "Embassy – Sam, notify them of our

position with this investigation. We are going to need logistical support to find these children and the full cooperation of NZ Police. Assure them we will do our darnedest to keep police safe. Officially, I'm calling this situation with the missing kids a probable extension of the Virginia Butterfly murders. Our Unsub is suspected of crossing international borders with minors and as such, Delta A is now fully involved and directing the cases." As I spoke, Captain Picard appeared in front of me, we morphed into one.

There I was on the bridge of the Enterprise looking at Commander Riker as words spun from my mouth, "Make it so, Number One."

Sam was typing on his laptop he looked up and grinned. "Number One? Star Trek interlude, Ellie?"

"I said that aloud, huh?"

"Yep."

A strange thing happened; I felt it stirring in my gut and then creeping across my face. I was smiling.

Lee called Sean and Sam called the Embassy. Doc called the hospital to check on Nicola's mother.

It was time to pick up my phone and dial Caine. No sense waiting until the middle of the night.

I took the call to the bedroom. "Caine, this is our case. This situation in New Zealand is an extension of the Butterfly Murder investigation. Looks to me like our Unsub has set up shop here. He may have a new twist to supplement his supply of children. I suspect he's using rock concerts as a lure. I don't know yet how he is meeting the kids, but it's not through my Foundation."

"That's a relief."

"Yeah it is. He's comfortable online, so I think he is using an online persona to groom the kids. It's just a matter of uncovering where he's using it."

"I've spoken to Carla." He sounded concerned. "She's certain she's being followed. But couldn't give a description; she's never seen the person, just knows someone's there."

"Do you believe her?"

"Yes. Police, however, want more than a gut feeling. Her foster mother tried to tell me Carla was prone to flights of fancy," Caine replied, his voice grating a little more than usual.

"She isn't but police will be swayed by the foster mother's response. I can send you a copy of the photo we found here, if you want to share our evidence with police?"

"Let's keep that up our sleeves for now." He paused. "I'm going to speak to the security at her school, to her teachers and her friends first thing in the morning. I will assign agents to protect her."

"Thank you," I said. "I appreciate it."

"Can't have mini-you in trouble, can we?"

"No, we can't."

"My advice – adopt the kid, Ellie. You'd be a good mother and she needs someone like you." Caine's tone drifted to fatherly.

His advice stunned me. Not because he was wrong but

because, once again, he knew what I was thinking. The more time I spent with Carla, the harder it was to walk away and the more I saw me in her.

"I'm giving that serious consideration," I replied. "One more thing. We have one kid who is a member of the Foundation ... Nicola Gallagher."

Caine interrupted me with a sigh then said, "I'll have someone check up on the American address that was used by her, to make sure everyone is accounted for."

"You need to call me from a secure line tomorrow. And thanks Caine. For everything."

"How bad is it?" he said in his usual brusque manner.

"Very."

"I'm on it."

I hung up.

The second the words 'secure line' left my mouth, they started a chain reaction. When you are standing on the edge, don't look down. Caine would have our offices and the common area we referred to as the bullpen, swept for bugs. He'd also start monitoring communications and the whereabouts of anyone connected to our case.

Someone knocked on the doorframe. I looked up to see Sean filling the doorway. What was it with the men I knew? They all were larger than life in more ways than one.

"What's up?" Sean asked.

"What did you hear?"

"Secure line."

"We're in trouble."

He nodded. "That much I figured." Sean changed tack. "You sure about this case being part of an ongoing case?"

"Yes."

"Good, because you'll need to be. I'm about to notify Interpol that we have an international situation. That's going to put you in the driving seat, until it's over," he said.

A tingle built as the implications of his statement took over. The case was mine. Hawk was mine. I smiled.

"I take it by that honest-to-god smile that you're okay with that?"

"I'm going to get those children back."

"That's what I hoped you'd say. I'm making the call. Do you mind if I use your room? It's noisy out there with Lee and Sam on their phones and Kurt talking medical mumbo jumbo on his."

"Go right ahead. I need to get back out there anyway."

I walked past him as he pulled his phone from his pocket.

It wasn't an obligatory smile on my face. I was happy. Everything had turned to shit yet I felt I was contributing again. There was purpose in my life. In some ways, I'd floated through the last seventeen months devoid of a real reason, trying to figure out what the hell I was supposed to do next. It felt like I'd been treading water, waiting for Hawk to resurface.

Other cases came and went but none of them touched me, because nothing could penetrate the emptiness.

"Where are we at?" I called across the sea of paperwork and coffee cups. Laptops hummed, cell phones buzzed, the smell of coffee filled the room. It felt like the bullpen had uprooted and flown halfway around the world, landing with a bump in Christchurch.

Carla edged into my thoughts. Joey too. They needed me to do this. To find out who Hawk really was. I needed to find the real Hawk and the kids. The person feeding him information could wait – I'd set enough activity in motion and I was sure some of it would cause the mole some panic.

Lee plonked a coffee in front of me.

With that, the investigation changed. Sean received a call from police in Wellington about a murder. A crime scene awaited us.

We headed to the airport.

Chapter Ten
Lie To Me

An air of foreboding tweaked at my gut as we took off from Christchurch airport on Tuesday afternoon. Lee and I were sitting together; Sam and Doc were across the aisle. It wasn't ideal. The little old lady in the window seat next to me delved quickly into a book. She obviously wasn't into small talk.

Fine by me.

There were plenty of better ways to spend early Tuesday afternoon but there I sat, with my fingernails digging into the palms of my hands, as the airplane climbed fast to cruising altitude. It's not that I don't like flying; in fact, I love it. It was knowing where we were headed that caused my anxiety to climb with the aircraft. My past was tapping on the window of my soul and I didn't like it.

"How you doing?" Lee asked, nudging my elbow from the armrest.

"Good," I replied. That was my mistake. Big, loud, glaring, good. I don't do *good*, I do okay. Or lately, fine.

"Not buying it Ellie."

It was time for damage limitation mode. "I'm okay Lee. I am."

He nodded. "So I don't need to switch with Doc then?"

"Please don't." The last thing, the very last thing, I wanted was a fuss.

He leaned across the aisle and spoke quietly to Sam.

I settled into my seat and closed my eyes. There was time for a power nap before our descent to Wellington.

Walking from the arrival gate at Wellington airport conjured memories I didn't want to revisit. A long time ago. Another life. I scanned faces looking for the familiar, the now dead. The anxiety from the plane ebbed as I reminded myself it was a lifetime ago. It was a relief to see our police escort and not to recognize anyone at the airport. After brief introductions, we piled into a police car. I watched out the window of the marked police car, not quite listening to the calls over the radio, mostly looking for buildings I remembered. Wispy faces floated, smiling, above the skyline, as if they knew I was back. As we drove through the streets, I noted what I knew once was gone. My memory of the city lay smothered in concrete and part of the new motorway system. Knowing what I knew, it was probably for the best. Nothing worse than an ugly scar in a beautiful city. I silently acknowledged the past and those who perished protecting our future, knowing, in another incarnation, I was supposedly among the dead. My mind rolled over the list of agents lost that day. The only woman on the list was Demelza. She existed for one deep-cover operation and according to the roll, she died serving her country. There was no one to miss her.

Part of an old poem slipped into mind, obscuring the dead and the me that once was.

'I am an enigma that doesn't exist
A name in the realm of swirling mist
There's nothing to say I was even here

And nothing to remind me that anyone would care.'

Lee's voice penetrated my thoughts. "Ellie?"

"Yes."

"Looks like we're here." It was easy to see the crime scene. Police cars and crime tape marked the house we were going to at the end of a nice street.

A female detective met us at the door. "I'm Detective Faye Jones."

We introduced ourselves and shook hands.

"We've been having issues with cell phone service the last few days." Her eyes rolled. "More like weeks actually. I'm sure you probably sent me messages – I haven't received them yet. And I've been unable to send messages." She handed out bootees and gloves. "I'm in the process of changing phone companies. Ever tried to break an existing contract with a phone company?"

"Actually, yes. I wish you luck."

I needed to say something about the officer who died at the airport but words of condolence always sounded empty.

"I'm very sorry about your colleague. That was one of the voice messages I left for you."

She nodded sagely. "Thank you. She was a good person. I hear no one's too keen on working with you now." She smiled a little. "As for the message, no doubt I'll get it at some stage," she replied, without a trace of hope in her voice. "Probably get fifty text messages three o'clock in the damn morning like last time."

Suitably attired we followed her into the house.

Never did I think I would be walking into something so familiar again. The walls slowly closed in, sucking my breath from my lungs as memories jumbled about. Dark, oppressive and terrifying, with eyes watching.

Entering the kitchen, I was instantly aware of a big difference. Bright, clean, spacious, bathed in warm sunshine. I saw the body of a woman.

"What's her name?"

"Alysia Talbot. Aged thirty-two. One child, Melanie. She's missing."

This time her body lay as she'd fallen, not posed. She was fully clothed, which was a nice change. She lay in a puddle of her own blood. The metallic smell irritated my nerves. I bent down near her head. Her damp blonde hair was fanned across her face; I moved it out of the way. She could've been sleeping; her expression was peaceful. I breathed in: chlorine. She'd been swimming.

At least I knew what was next.

I looked up at the detective. "You need to check her blood for Thorazine and get a list of all the meds she takes. Stomach contents too, please. I'd bet money on the last thing she had being a cup of coffee laced with Thorazine. I can smell chlorine and her hair is damp. I think she went swimming, sometime in the last few hours. Public pools, would be a good place to start a line of inquiry. She may have been swimming with the killer, or even met him at the pool for coffee." He really liked swimming, or maybe he didn't; maybe he liked watching people swim.

Doc crouched on the other side of the body but said

nothing. Even so, I could feel his smart-assed comments surfacing.

There was no empty bottle of booze. No gold ribbon. No scrawled poem. The same but different. It was Hawk. There was no doubt in my mind. I went looking for a note. The relief at not finding one was audible and short-lived.

"We found this on the fridge," Detective Jones said, holding out a paper evidence bag. "Is that you?" I took it and removed a photograph from inside. A nighttime photo of Lee and me crouched on wet ground next to paramedics working on someone. The only color in the picture was the flashing lights from ambulances and police cars.

"It's us," Lee said. He moved closer to me.

I turned the picture over and read the inscription written in what looked like black Sharpie: *Problem solved, Conway.*

"Where was the picture taken?" Detective Jones asked.

"Virginia," I replied. My heart raced. I wanted to say the man on the ground was an agent I didn't know. I needed to distance myself from the image, but the scene grabbed me and squeezed the air from my lungs. "That's Special Agent Mac Connelly on the ground." I swallowed hard. "Lee, photograph both sides of the picture."

All of a sudden, air was in short supply. I handed him the photograph and left the house.

If the murder of Alysia Talbot had been loaded into ViCAP, it wouldn't generate a match to our Butterfly

Murders but I knew it was Hawk's work. The prickling on the back of my neck told me it was him, even without the photograph and the note on the back.

I jumped when Doc spoke. "You all right?"

"I'm fine Doc, just needed some air."

"What's with the chlorine?"

"Hawk and his partner liked to take previous victims swimming before adding Thorazine to their coffee. That was something we never understood about the earlier murders. Why the swimming?"

A few deep breaths and I hurried back into the house and located the detective talking to Sam. "Can I see the child's bedroom?" She nodded and showed me the way.

"Anything in particular you're looking for?"

"I don't know yet," I said with an apologetic shrug.

"This is it," she said leaving me by the door. Glancing down the hallway, I saw Doc with Sam and hoped he'd stay there.

Grange posters covered the walls of Melanie Talbot's bedroom. I swallowed hard. Grange stickers were all over the dressing tables. Posters even covered the ceiling. A laptop sat on a beat-up old desk. I opened it and turned it on. A picture of Rowan smiled at me from the desktop.

Mac's voice was crystal clear in my mind. 'It's all about the music.'

A quick look through recent Messenger conversations revealed she'd been talking to a friend, Emma; they'd made plans to go into the city. Somewhere called Capital E. There was one offline message from her friend; they were meeting at four thirty. I turned off the laptop and unplugged the cord. It was coming with us.

A swift search through Melanie's room netted Emma's name and a cell phone number on a school folder. I looked around again. There was no cell phone charger. A pile of exercise books on the dressing table drew my attention. I flipped through them. She was a good student judging by the comments from her teacher. A few drawers were slightly open. I couldn't tell if clothes were missing but it seemed likely.

I paused to admire the view from the bedroom window. The house sat on a high hill overlooking the harbor. Across the expanse of water, green hills gave way to narrow golden sandy beaches and deep blue water, dotted with sails from small yachts. A jet plane climbed steeply from a narrow band between two sets of hills, leaving behind a white rip in an otherwise pristine sky.

The rip widened and frayed at the edges.

Turning away from the window I called down the hallway, "Lee, Sam, you need to see this room."

"Hell of a view," Lee commented nodding to the large window.

"I want to find this Emma girl," I said. "She might know something."

Outside the house, I briefed the police and called the cell phone number hoping to get Emma. It went to voicemail. I left a message saying I was a family friend looking for Melanie.

My watch said it was just after four. "Where and what

is Capital E?" I asked Detective Jones.

"It's part of the Museum Trust; Capital E has programs for kids. Plays, filmmaking, all sorts of things. It's in Civic Square."

"Can we get a car?"

"I'll drive – we'll use mine. It's unmarked."

She called out to another detective, letting him know she was leaving the scene. Kurt, Sam and Lee crammed themselves into the back of her Holden sedan. It looked like a big car until they all squashed in.

"Your husband was Agent Mac Connelly?" Jones asked as she drove.

"Yeah."

"I met him once."

"Really? Where?"

"Here in Wellington, about six years ago."

Well there was the mistake. Mac wasn't FBI six years ago. He was a stock trader. To my knowledge, Mac had never traveled to New Zealand. I played it cool.

"Some kind of stock trading conference was it?"

"No, no. He was here working out of the embassy on a case," she said brightly.

A sudden onerous hush from the backseat over-whelmed me. I didn't know what to say. It couldn't have been Mac.

"We're here," Jones said, absolving me from comment.

I pushed everything she said about Mac to the back of my mind. She was obviously confused and it was another Mac Connelly or she had the name wrong.

She parked in a multistory car park and pointed across the road to a large building. "That's the Michael Fowler centre, our town hall. Next door is the library. We're going to walk around the road there," she said. "And enter Civic Square."

The five of us started walking. The square was interesting. The library was on the right and National art gallery on the left. Large paving stones covered the entire area; there were sculptures and seats and it smelled of coffee.

"Any idea what the kid looks like?" Sam asked.

"I saw her Messenger picture," I replied. She looked quite a bit like Carla but paler. "She's blonde, has brown eyes, not much color in her face. But it could've been a winter picture."

Many young people milled about in the middle of the square; they all seemed to be young teens or tweens.

"How many do you think are here?" Lee asked.

Jones replied, "A hundred and fifty or so. It's the holidays; there has probably been some outdoor entertainment, bands and stuff."

I pointed to a stage and tech-type people running cables. "Or maybe it hasn't started yet."

The stage gave me an idea. All the children looked similar. Finding one from a Messenger photo was not going to be easy. I stepped up onto the stage and looked out. The view was better but still not great.

Jones climbed up next to me. "Good idea but it's not helping much," she commented, hands on hips. She peered out at the youngsters below.

A technician approached us. We flashed our badges. I asked, "Is this microphone working?"

He nodded.

"Good," Jones replied.

I stepped closer to the microphone, my stomach twisting violently.

"Attention! I need to find Melanie Talbot's friend Emma. I have a message for her from Melanie."

About forty kids stopped and stared blankly at me. Lee signaled he'd seen something. From the corner of my eye, I saw a man moving quickly away from the stage; he had a kid by the arm.

"Can you stay up here and watch?" I said to Jones. "It might be a father removing a wayward daughter. It might be Emma and the man who abducted her."

She nodded. I jumped down and took off around the stage. Exit stage left.

Lee came from my right, Sam stayed with Jones. I couldn't see Doc. The man shoved the girl he was dragging into Lee's path.

"Get her!" I yelled and kept running. Out the corner of my eye, I saw Lee swoop in on the kid. My gun was in my hand and my heart was beating like a drum.

There was a split second of total confusion on rounding the corner after the man. Initially my mind went into what-the-fuck-is-this mode. I found myself smack in the middle of a celebration of some kind, in a courtyard next to the Michael Fowler center. I glanced around and slipped my gun back into the holster, pulling my jacket over it.

No one appeared to notice. Fifty or so people, all fully focused on a priest wearing rainbow vestments.

I attempted to skirt the gathering, all the while looking for the man I'd chased. From what I could see, there was no way out. A barricade blocked the area from the street beyond. The penny dropped. My guy was hiding among wedding guests. I scanned the crowd looking for a sweaty male. It was hot and humid; he'd be sweating. I edged closer to the crowd and managed a glimpse of the brides.

Oh my, they wore ugly dresses. I'd seen feed sacks with more style. The person I'd chased was trying to blend in on the right side of the gathering. Bride? ... Or bride's side?

Tapping one man on the shoulder, I excused myself before barging through.

"Sir, excuse me."

"Pardon?"

I saw my mistake. It wasn't a man. I'm thinking pink frills are not her thing and I doubt she's ever painted her toenails.

"Ma'am. Sorry, ma'am. I'm a Federal Agent and I just need to get by to arrest a gate-crasher."

She glared at me. I flashed my badge. With a quick smile I scooted by her and several other unbecoming folk. I'd never seen so many obviously inbred people in one place before.

I looked at the brides. Good thing they couldn't combine their gene pool. Something else stuck out: attire. I moved up on the suspect. I've seen casual weddings, on the beach and tastefully done – bare foot, wearing gossamer gowns - but this was casual even by baglady standards. My guy eyed me. He'd started to relax.

Wrong.

Using some large unfortunates as cover, I clamped a hand on his shoulder. The heat and sweat through his thin shirt burned under my hand.

"You're under arrest." He tried to shake off my hand as it slid down his arm to his wrist. My grip tightened and I twisted his arm up behind his back and snapped on handcuffs.

Someone spoke near me. Amidst a defiantly bad stutter I made out an offer of help.

I declined, twisted his other arm behind his back and slid the second cuff shut, nice and tight. As I pushed him forward I apologized to the wedding guests, wished the happy couple a prosperous life with good health and, a comprehensive dental plan.

The guests parted as I led the man by the elbow back to where Lee, Sam, Detective Jones and the kid waited.

A smile hovered about my lips as I encouraged my prisoner toward Sam.

"You don't have any jurisdiction here," the man snapped, immediately alerting us to his non-Kiwi accent.

"Oh, but we do," I replied. "Name?"

"Bo Weinberg," he replied. His accent could've come from almost any Eastern Bloc country.

Sam took hold of him. I motioned to Jones. We

stepped away.

"Is that Emma?" I said.

"Yes, she identified herself as Emma Lincoln. She's a friend of Melanie Talbot's. Doesn't know where Melanie is, but knows she had an online boyfriend."

"Hang on a second," I said to Faye while I looked around for Doc. He was talking to a group of kids. An ear-piercing whistle left my mouth. "Over here!" I called when he looked up. Doc ran over.

"Will you take care of Emma – ask the right questions and find out if she's okay?"

He didn't reply but walked over and introduced himself to Emma.

I turned back to Faye and our conversation. "How'd she find herself in the company of Bo, here?"

"Seems Bo knew Emma was supposed to be meeting Melanie and what she looked like. Had a message for her to go with him to meet Melanie somewhere else."

"Awesome. Now Hawk's grabbing two at a time."

"What do you want to do with the girl?" Jones asked. She talked to Doc and used Lee to block Bo Weinberg from her line of sight.

"Make sure she hasn't been in contact with anyone she doesn't know in real life on the Internet, or made any plans to meet anyone. Talk to her parents – give them some information on child safety online. Reassure her that we're looking really hard to find Melanie." I handed Jones two of my business cards. "Give one to her and keep one yourself."

"I'll take her home. Let's get an interview room for you to use to talk to Mr. Weinberg." She looked around while lifting the radio from her hip and talking briefly.

Jones smiled at me. "There is a room at Wellington Central waiting for you."

"Fabulous. Thank you. How do we get there?"

"It's so close you can almost spit on it. Come on, I'll show you, then take Emma home."

Lee marched Weinberg in front of him on the short walk down Victoria Street to the police station. We settled in the interview room and Jones took Emma. I followed her out to have a word with the child.

"Emma." She turned around. "Hi, I'm Special Agent Ellie Conway." I smiled. "Do you mind if I have a look at your cell phone?"

She shrugged and handed it to me. I scrolled quickly through her outbox and then her inbox. There were no recent text messages from Melanie. The last one was two days old. In fact, there were no messages received at all for at least twelve hours and I know how much kids use cell phones. That wasn't right, it didn't add up.

"Nothing from your best friend saying where she was?" I asked, handing the phone back. "Is that why you left an instant message for her using MSN arranging to meet her?"

"Our cell phones don't work properly. We're both on the same plan."

I looked at Faye. "Cell phone service not working?"

"It's the new fancy network with the biggest provider

here. Don't get me started! It's the reason I have been missing messages and losing calls."

"Brilliant." No, I didn't mean that. It was potentially putting lives at risk. Kids' lives in this case.

"Emma, Detective Jones will take you home now. Call one of us if you hear anything from Melanie or remember anything, okay?" As a parting aside I said, "Call from a landline. They still work, right?"

She nodded. I went back into the interview room.

True to form, Weinberg had nothing to say. His passport indicated he was here on a tourist visa from Bulgaria. He'd arrived a week ago and wasn't due to leave for another month. After an hour of listening to his silence, Jones returned. I notified our Embassy and had Weinberg moved there while we carried out a thorough background check. There was no intention on my part to let him resume his so-called vacation. Deportation, or an arrest for attempted kidnapping, seemed the logical next move.

I left a request with Detective Jones to find out where Weinberg was staying and to conduct a search, with finding a laptop computer and cell phone a priority. He had to have some means of contacting Emmet Smith and possibly Hawk. Although I doubted Hawk would risk direct contact.

It was almost ten that night before we were on a plane on the way back to Christchurch. We discussed the findings.

Doc spoke first. "Emma wasn't harmed, other than being quite shaken."

"Seems we got her in time," I replied.

"You think she could have taken off to see Grange?" Lee asked, referring to Melanie. "Not missing so much as run away. The murder maybe coincidental?"

"I doubt very much that a girl of her age had the ability to get from Wellington to Christchurch without help. The attempted kidnapping of her best friend by Bo Weinberg suggests that something sinister is going on."

Sam agreed. He had spent time in Wellington investigating the ways to get to Christchurch: Interisland Ferry to Picton then train or bus. Or fly direct from Wellington. The Interisland Ferry did not take unaccompanied minors. No airline would take an unaccompanied minor without correct documentation from a parent.

"Someone else is involved in her disappearance," Lee said.

"Yeah. Hawk," I replied. "When we get back I want you to go over that laptop and see if you can pull information from her history. We might get lucky and find out how he's hunting."

Sam smiled. "The fucker is playing with us, Chicky Babe."

"Yes he is. We are once again playthings for an evil fucktard."

The urge to laugh maniacally almost overwhelmed me. Uh huh, I'm sane. It bugged me that the fucker was still alive, that he'd engaged me again. Was I that much fun?

'Fun' wasn't exactly how I saw myself. I had a feeling I

was well on the way to cold-hearted bitch. Although I had previously failed at that, I was willing to give it another go.

Maybe he just wanted me to have a nice holiday in the sun.

Lee nudged me. "You know you laughed then?"

Nope, I had no clue.

"Of course. Something I thought is all."

"Something evil perhaps?"

Somewhere fingers snapped and The Addams Family theme song rose from a misty grave.

"Just call me Morticia," I replied.

"I don't wanna be Lurch," Lee said quickly. "Sam should be Lurch."

We both laughed. Sam caught up.

"Is the world ready for a black Lurch?" he asked.

"Hell, yes it is," I replied.

Lee grinned widely. "Yes you can!"

Doc remained silent. I suspected he was dumbstruck.

The flight attendant handed out sweets.

"Anyone else find that Bo guy's name to be sort of familiar?" Sam asked as the plane landed.

"Nope," I replied.

"I think I've heard it before," Lee replied. "But it was on his passport so there is a chance it's his real name."

I looked at Lee. "We need to have that passport examined."

As soon as we landed, I called Detective Jones and left another message on her voicemail. "It's Ellie ... will you have Weinberg's passport examined for us please. Possibly a fake document."

As soon as I'd left the message, I remembered the trouble the country was having with a major cell service provider and called her office landline, leaving the same message. I knew there was a Document Examination Section of New Zealand Police based in Wellington. It would be much quicker than sending the passport back to the FBI Questioned Documents Lab in Quantico, Virginia.

Back at the hotel, the receptionist handed me a plain white envelope with my name written across the front in broad cursive script. Not writing I recognized. Sam and Lee looked over my shoulders as I felt the envelope: there were no edges to suggest a photograph. Doc watched quietly from beside me, he could've looked over my shoulder too, he had the height but there wasn't much room.

"Open it," Sam said.

"Later," I replied folding the envelope and stuffing it into my bag.

Doc headed into the bedroom leaving me alone in the living room. I sat on the couch and opened the letter. Unfolding the paper, the first thing I noticed was the hotel letterhead.

It was a note from Rowan Grange asking if I'd like to have dinner Wednesday night. He would call for me at eight.

Dinner with a super rock star who looked like an ashblond Adonis? Oh, the hardships I must endure. I couldn't imagine what he saw in me or why he wanted to take me to dinner. I picked up the hotel phone and called his room before realizing how late it was.

A groggy voice mumbled, "Hello."

"Rowan. It's Ellie. Sorry about calling so late. I was already committed by the time I noted the hour." Midnight fast approached.

"Everything all right?"

"Absolutely, just got back into town. I got your note, thank you. Dinner on Wednesday sounds great."

"You know that's tomorrow right?"

"Sure," I replied but truly, had no idea. The days were one befuddled mess since stepping foot off the plane in New Zealand.

"I'll see you then," he replied, more awake now. I heard the smile in his voice, which made me smile.

"Yes. Good night."

A noise by the door caught my attention. I hung up and went to investigate. A piece of paper was poking out from under the door. When I picked it up, I saw it was a photograph.

Bile and rage competed violently. It was of Carla talking to Caine outside her school.

"Doc!" I yelled. With the photo in my hand, I flung open the door and checked the hallway. The elevator dinged. I ran toward it, pausing only to bang on Lee's door as I passed. I stuffed the picture in my pocket and drew my gun. The elevator doors shut. Going down. The stairwell door was at the other end of the long hallway. I ran back. Lee emerged from his room, weapon in hand.

"What?" he called as I sprinted down the hall.

"Someone left a picture – the person got in the elevator, they're going down."

Lee joined in the chase.

Sam poked his head out to see what the commotion was.

"Elevator Sam ... go down ... check the lobby," I called. "Where is Doc?"

"On it boss," he replied. His heavy running footsteps moved away from us.

Doc ran to meet Sam, "Sorry, indisposed."

I reached the stairs and bounded down them two at a time. Pausing at each floor to check for elevator dings. He could've gone anywhere. Lee was close behind me as we hit the ground floor.

Sam and Doc were at the front desk with the night manager. He swore no one had come down in the elevator except for Sam and Doc.

My heart pounded and my lungs hurt. I leaned on the desk. "Porters? Who is working tonight?"

The manager handed me the roster. There were four porters on overnight.

"Where are they?" Lee asked.

"They have a lounge in the basement."

"Does the elevator go to the basement?"

He shook his head. "The stairs do."

My head shook slowly from side to side. "We ran down the stairs, they stopped here."

"There are service stairs. Staff use a key card to access

them."

"Lee, you and Doc stay here with ..." I leaned closer to the manager and read his name badge. "... Frank. Sam and I will go visit the porters' lounge."

"Yes, SSA."

"Frank – how do we get there?" I was all smiles and sweetness despite the picture in my pocket that made me want to vomit.

"I'll give you my key card, yes that's what I'll do ..." Frank flapped about looking quite flustered. He took a card from a drawer and handed it to me. "The stairs you are looking for are on your right at the end of the building."

"Thanks."

Sam and I jogged down the full length of the indoor Koi pond, passing several knights in armor. A doorway loomed, marked 'Staff Only.'

"Must be it," I commented. The key card worked. Beyond the door was a staircase. We descended the stairs. At the bottom were several doors off a dimly lit corridor: Laundry, Staff Kitchen and one marked Porters. The key card worked its magic and we stepped into a lounge. Three couches lined walls. A large television was on the fourth wall. There were several coffee tables laden with magazines and newspapers. Four men looked up from the newspapers they were reading. One appeared sweatier than the others did. I singled him out.

"Come here," I said, beckoning to him.

He rose with trepidation oozing from every pore and

walked toward us. "How can I help?

I pulled the picture from my pocket and showed it to him.

"Seen this before? Before you start lying ... I'm FBI. We're experts in uncovering liars," I said using my sweetest, friendliest voice.

"Yeah, sure I have."

"Who told you to deliver it?"

"I don't know who it was. I never met him."

"Then how'd you get the picture?"

"Someone left an envelope for me at the front desk. It had a hundred bucks in it and that picture with instructions," he replied.

"When?" Sam asked.

"The envelope was there when I started work, at 10 p.m."

"Someone who knew you worked for the hotel and that you were on night shift," I said. "Where would a person find that information?"

"Maybe it's a guest," he replied. "It's not a friend of mine or family. Guests get to know who is on when, especially if they're here for a week or more."

Sam and I looked at each other.

That would explain why I feel I'm being watched inside the hotel.

"You don't still have the envelope do you?"

He shook his head. "I threw it in one of the rubbish skips out back. You can look if you want."

"Was it handwritten?" Because if it was, I was definitely going dumpster diving in New Zealand.

"Nah ma'am, was typed or computered, whatever you call it these days."

"What's your name?"

"Raymond Huia."

"Thanks for your help Raymond. Let me know if you get any other letters with photographs, please." I flicked him one of my cards. "Or you can drop by my room ... you obviously know which it is."

Never leave home without business cards, tissues, clean underpants and a gun.

Sam and I left the porters to their reading. I doubted there would be much reading happening now.

I called Caine on our way back to the desk.

"Problem?" he asked, without saying hello.

"Just received a second picture of Carla, someone is watching. I have a photo of you and her talking outside her school. It was delivered to my room."

He thought for a minute; I could feel a disruption in the force. "I'm putting her in a safe house under armed guard. I'll have someone escort her to school and back each day. There will be police doing regular patrols of the school."

"Sounds good. Make sure she knows she can't go anywhere without an escort, this is serious shit."

"I'll make sure she gets it. You want your dad read in?"

"Yes, that'd be great. Tell dad I want him to keep an eye on her ... you know ... if she needs to go out and do girly things, have him take her."

"Simon will love that," Caine replied. We both knew he really would.

"I'll keep in touch."

I put my phone back in my pocket.

Chapter Eleven
Smells Like Teen Spirit

Lee spent almost all Wednesday morning searching through Melanie Talbot's laptop. There were untold pictures of Rowan and the band, gathered from internet sources all over the world. A lot of music. Overall, we found her tastes to be eclectic even though her recent play lists were devoted to Grange. Conveniently, she had all her passwords to social network sites, email and many other frequently visited sites, saved. I reasoned she had no need to worry about snooping, being an only child.

It wasn't easy but I kept telling myself Carla was well taken care of and got on with the business of finding kids.

Time to call Sean. "Sean, it's Ellie. Will you look into the issues with the cell network and see if you can find out which of our missing girls are with the same provider?"

"Yes."

"Thanks. I'm thinking some of them might have tried to call or even text for help but the messages weren't received. I sent a text to each phone yesterday. There have been no replies. But I don't know if the phones are on or off, or connected to a network that is failing."

"I'm on it."

I hung up.

"Ellie. What do you make of this?" Lee asked, beckoning me over. I crouched next to him and looked at the

Gmail screen open on the laptop.

"I think we need to find out who Emmet Smith is," I said reaching over Lee's arm and scrolling down some more.

Lee whistled through his teeth as another part of the email conversation became apparent. "According to this he's a fourteen year old boy who loves Grange."

"Then why do I feel like he's a forty-year old pedophile grooming this kid?"

"That'll be because you've become cynical due to this job," Lee replied, sarcasm resounded in his voice as he read aloud the next part of the email. " 'What's your cell number? I wanna text you. Then we can talk, just us.' "

"Even his name sounds dodgy as hell," I said. "See if you can find anything that suggests she has ever met him."

Sam spoke from the table. "Emmet Smith is fourteen?" I heard keys tapping. "Send me the link to Melanie's Facebook and Twitter accounts will ya, Lee?"

"That's what he said," Lee replied. "Sent already. Her passwords are in the email I sent you. Ellie, I sent you the log-in information for the kid's Yahoo and Hotmail accounts."

I sat back on the couch and dragged my laptop across the coffee table. While Sam searched for signs of Emmet Smith and Lee read the contents of the Gmail account, I went looking through her other email accounts.

Yahoo netted over a thousand emails. She belonged to a group devoted to Grange. The whole Grange obsession worried me.

The coincidence of her disappearing and Grange being in town didn't feel like a coincidence to me. It could be something as simple as her being desperate to go to the concert and running away. It could've been, if her mom wasn't dead.

Forty minutes later, I showed the team an email from her Hotmail account. Same sender as the Gmail emails. Emmet Smith.

"Check it out. They were meeting yesterday morning at the ferry terminal. He gave her an itinerary of sorts. He says he has ferry tickets and that his parents will drive them to Christchurch. He promises to take her to the racecourse market on Wednesday afternoon and the Grange concert on Thursday night."

Sam was on the phone before I finished talking, trying to get a ship's manifest to locate the person who purchased the ferry ticket for Melanie Talbot. Five minutes later, he threw his phone at the wall.

We waited.

"Any fuc'n moron can purchase tickets on the ferries. No ID required. You can do it online. You can use any name you fuc'n well like. No one checks to see if names match as passengers board, or leave, the vessel. There is no record of any ticket purchased for Melanie Talbot or Emmet Smith. But minors cannot travel alone. Either he's an adult as we suspected, or looks a hell of a lot older than fourteen; know any fourteen year olds that look eighteen?"

"Not so many." I looked over the email again.

Lee blew air out his mouth. I looked over to see him staring at the screen. "What?"

"Emmett Smith was a character played by Bruce Willis in a movie called *In Country*."

"And we're looking for Hudson Hawk ..." Sam added. "This doesn't feel coincidental."

"No it fuc'n doesn't. But right now, all we have is an email saying they were on the 10:00 a.m. sailing, no confirmation and a loose itinerary. Let's work it. Find out where this market is. We're going for an afternoon wander."

"Just for shits and giggles I looked up Bo Weinberg. You gonna love this, Ellie," Lee said with a crooked smile.

"Thrill me."

"When I put in Bo Weinberg and Bruce Willis I got the 1991 movie *Billy Bathgate*."

"Curious how Willis movies keep occurring," Doc commented. "What do you think it means?"

"That someone is a fan," I replied. "Just maybe there is something to this Willis thing, fucked if I know what, yet." It also meant that it was probable the passport Weinberg carried was indeed fake. I was anxious to hear back from the forensic examiner. "Let's do this market thing. We might get lucky."

Three quarters of an hour later I watched heat rise from the pavement. Ahead of me on the road I saw waves of hot air undulating, distorting the white lines and blurring my vision. I could smell hot tar as it melted and anticipated tar stuck to my boots.

My tee shirt plastered itself to me. Sweat trickled down my brow. I wiped it away impatiently with the back of my hand. We hadn't even got to the market yet, we were still walking down the car-filled lane. Exhaust fumes added to the discomfort. I could see the sense in leaving our cars out on the main street but, in the heat and fumes, I'd have preferred to be in air-conditioned comfort.

My arm brushed my side occasionally, bumping the holster I wore on my hip under my tee shirt. It was a comfort thing. I felt more relaxed knowing I was armed and dangerous.

Some would say I never ceased being dangerous, armed or not.

Some would be right.

A digital camera swung from a lanyard around my neck. We all carried photos of the missing girl we hoped to find. Despite searching her laptop, we couldn't find any pictures of Emmet. His Facebook page had pictures of friends but not of him, or at least none we could find. He wasn't tagged in any photos on 'friends' pages. True to form, the friends all seemed to be young girls; males were conspicuous by their absence. Knowing what we knew about his name, we were expecting a forty-year-old male.

We avoided tripping over people while making like tourists, the entire time scanning faces of kids, searching for anyone we might have seen recently. Lee and Doc scanned the cars that rolled by us. Sam eyeballed foot traffic while I kept my eyes firmly on the movement of people ahead of us. I started out looking for men with young girls and then for families that didn't seem quite right. By the time we reached the actual entrance I had committed several groups of people to memory and was set to get as close as possible to hear any conversation and hopefully determine how legitimate they were.

A scream.

I spun around looking for the origin and saw a kid pointing at us.

Another scream rang out followed by a young girl's voice. The kid squealed, "Tony!"

"Oh, for fuck's sake!" I bitched at Sam. "Does this shit have to follow us all over the city?"

Lee's lip curled in a horrified snarl. A guy his size had nowhere to hide and the screaming was coming closer.

"We gotta get him outta here," I muttered to Sam. Special Agent Ridiculously Good Looking was a liability.

Lee was pissed. He griped, "How am I supposed to do my job with this bullshit happening?"

"Come on," I said and grabbed his arm. I began searching for a way out without screaming girlies blocking our path. "This way ..."

The four of us ran away from the screaming, ducking behind stalls. We moved as fast as possible and stayed as low as possible.

Screeching followed but not quickly. Every time it started to die down someone would shout and the screaming would climb to reach fever pitch again. I flipped my phone open and called Sean.

"We're at the market at the racecourse ... Lee's causing a scene. There is hysteria and we need a way out."

I hoped like hell there was only one market and one racecourse, because I was sadly lacking in directional information.

Sean sucked in air noisily and I pictured him trying not to laugh.

Dust rose up above the stalls on our left. The horde was coming.

"Now!" I said. I looked over to a row of stalls behind us; beyond them was a gravel road and beyond that a grassy field with cars parked on it.

Stall owners were watching us with way too much interest. They were about to give our position away to the pack.

"Never mind, we'll get out." I shut my phone, tapped my gun for good luck, and pointed to the field full of cars. "That way, stay low."

We moved as fast as we could without creating a telltale dust cloud and without causing undue attention by regular market-going folk. It was quite a feat, keeping people's attention away from us.

Past the edge of the last rows of stalls and over the gravel road, there were rows and rows of parked cars. I scanned the area for signs of the screamers.

All clear.

We crossed several rows and found a spot among a group of large four-wheel drive SUV's. As long as the boys kept their heads down no one would spot us.

"We're going to stay here until the screamers disperse or find someone else to throw themselves at," I said.

"This is not making our jobs any easier," Lee grumbled.

There was a smile on my face that just wouldn't quit. What could I do? This whole hysteria over Lee thing was starting to really float my boat.

He glared at me. "You better not be finding this amusing!"

It's not as if I could help how I found it. An idea sprouted.

"Stay here," I told them. "Sit down and stay put. I'll be back."

"What are you doing?" Lee whispered.

"With the intention of finding a way out, I'm heading back to the market to see what I can find by way of a disguise," I replied. "We need to get you out so the rest of us can get to work."

It wasn't Lee's fault he was the pre-teen target of the moment but short of calling in the real Tony to parade about in front of the screamers I needed a disguise to get Lee out, safely. My safety concerns were more for the screaming kids than Lee. I saw a murderous look in his eye.

"Hurry," Lee replied, with a dismissive wave.

"You want company?" Doc asked. I looked at him in his now-dusty charcoal suit. Who wears a suit to a market?

"Nope."

I skulked back toward the rows of stalls. It wasn't going to be easy. The first stall contained backpacks and cowboy hats. Cowboy hats were a definite no-no, unless the object was to intensify the screamers' experience. It would take his Tony Sharron look and turn him straight into Richie Sambora. I suspected the reaction would be the same.

Oh Lordy, he has his hat on.

Four stalls down the row I spotted baseball caps and tee shirts. They would do. I brought four shirts and four caps. At the next stall, I saw sunglasses. Perfect. I needed to replace, temporarily, Lee's aviators with something slightly more run of the mill.

On a whim, I bought us all new sunglasses. It seemed like a good idea for us all to look a little different.

My phone rang; it was Carla. "Everything okay kiddo?" I clutched the bags of clothing and glasses while I did a quick reconnoiter to determine the whereabouts of the screamers. They'd broken into two packs and were scouring the large stall area. The area was vast and it would take them a while to find me.

"Yeah. Caine is cool. He's okay to hang with"

Cool? Don't think I'd ever heard him described as 'cool' before.

The hordes weren't covering much ground and appeared to stop for scream breaks.

"Good. Sweetheart, I have to go – I'm sort of in the middle of something here. I promise as soon as I get home I'll tell you all about it."

"K, just wanted to say I was okay and that Caine is watching out for me."

I made my way back to the car park area.

"Be good, stay safe. And I'll see you soon as I can."

Then she blurted out something that took me by surprise. "I want you to be my mom, that's what I want for my birthday."

Well, that ain't a laptop. I took a breath. "I've been thinking about that too. We'll see what we can do about it when I get home."

"Really?"

"Really. I love you. Now be good!"

A smile nudged at the sadness that still dwelled on the edges, ready to take over my life. Now I just had to convince the court that I was fit to raise a teenager. I shoved my phone into my pocket and crept along the rows of cars trying desperately to remember where I left my team. The cars all looked the same and there were at least six rows filled predominately with SUV's and trucks.

My phone rang again. I hooked it from my pocket with my free hand and flipped it open. "Yep."

"Where are you?" Sean.

"In a field filled with cars, you?"

"Front entrance of the market."

"I think we're way way at the back."

"Stay put, I'll come to you. There's a road that goes all the way around there."

"Okay. I've gotta find where I left the boys."

"You've lost them?" The incredulity in Sean's voice

rang clearly in my ear.

"Not lost ... misplaced temporarily." If one or other of them would just stand up, I wouldn't have a problem.

Sean laughed.

"Hurry up," I told him and hung up.

I text messaged Sam's phone and stood quietly until I heard his phone go off. As Mr.T bellowed, "Pity the fool that texts me!" I pinpointed the direction to somewhere on my left.

I waited. A hand rose above the roof of a car and waved.

Sam.

After a check for screamers, I quickly covered the distance between me and the cars concealing my team.

"Got stuff," I said and sat on the grass in front of them. The plastic shopping bag rustled as I pulled out tee shirts, caps and glasses.

I pulled my tee shirt over the one I was already wearing. Sam and Lee did the same. "Doc, lose the suit jacket and button down shirt," I said handing him a tee shirt.

He folded his jacket inside out with his shirt and shoved them into one of the plastic bags. He pulled on the tee shirt. Lee swapped his glasses for the cheap pair I gave him. We jammed blue baseball caps on our heads. I looked at Lee. The cap and glasses combination made it worse. I didn't even need to squint to see the resemblance.

"Take the glasses off," I said.

He did. It didn't make a difference.

"Put 'em back on." I sighed. "We're too easy to spot together. They're looking for you, but bad-ass Sam, Doc and I are making you stand out even more."

Sam chuckled. "You're right. A big black dude like me, the suit and a little blonde thing like you, we're like a neon signpost for Tony here."

Lee shot him a filthy look and got a sparkling grin for his trouble.

"Sean's on his way to us," I said.

Sam nodded. "You go with Lee; me and Doc will go with Sean. We'll separate. Meet back at the hotel."

"It's like you can read my mind."

My phone jangled.

"Someone wave or something. I'm standing out here looking like an idiot," Sean said.

I shoved my phone into my pocket then stood up and waved. He cut through the rows of cars, nodding politely to a few older folk who were leaving.

Sean scrutinized the party. "Touristy, the NYC caps are a nice touch." Our tee shirts sported an outline of New Zealand with a big star where Christchurch was. "Always struck me as odd that people would buy NYC caps at a New Zealand market. Now I know people who have."

"Are we off?" I asked.

"Yes." Sean replied. He even managed to keep the smirk from his voice. Impressive. "Kurt, Sam and I are walking through the middle of the market. Hopefully we'll draw some attention." Sean looked at Lee and me. "You two, follow the road that skirts the whole thing. It goes behind buildings and hedges. You'll be mostly covered until you get to the road you came in on. When you see that coming, jump the hedge you'll have on your left and cut through the race course."

"Got it," I replied.

"We'll be fine," Lee added.

"On your way out, try to spot anyone who could be one of our missing kids," I said to them.

Lee and I were the first to leave. We skirted around the parked cars until we were further away from the market, then headed to the road that was somewhere in front of us, waiting to be discovered.

Lee grabbed my arm as I moved ahead of him.

"I want a bottle of Jack," he hissed.

"Straight up?"

"The whole fuc'n bottle," Lee growled. "I'm over this shit."

I hid my smile and walked next to him. From the market, I heard a faint yell, then a shriek, then a scream followed by a wail.

So close I could taste it.

"Come on," I said to Lee. "Let's get out of here."

We increased our speed as the road appeared in front of us, then dove over the hedge and ran through the racecourse, pulling twigs from our hair and brushing off leaves as we went. Before we hit the main road, I had the car keys in my hand. Lee wasn't seeing the absurdity of the situation as I was, which heightened my amusement. Maybe the heat was getting to me, or maybe the thought of little girls losing the plot over Lee really was funny.

Lee and I jumped in the car and locked the doors.

"Is there anyone in this country who doesn't think you're Tony-freaking-Sharron?" I said and slumped in the passenger seat. Giggling became laughter.

It wasn't funny. It was ruining our investigation.

I couldn't stop.

"Bite me," Lee snapped.

Tears poured. Snot bubbled. Breathing hurt.

So alluring.

Lee sat there looking more and more pissed off.

This voice in my head kept telling me how unprofessional I was. Another voice, a familiar deep, male Virginian voice laughed along with me.

I was going straight to hell.

Do not pass go, do not collect two hundred dollars.

Lee was in the driver's seat, so I dropped the keys in his lap, thinking he may as well drive.

I sure as hell was incapable.

He placed a box of Kleenex on my knee.

I would've thanked him if I'd been able to speak.

Chapter Twelve
Gimme The Prize

While Lee waited for me to get a grip, we watched foot traffic in the wing mirrors.

I had an idea but didn't feel able to look at Lee while I vocalized it. With the laughter subsiding to mere strangulated giggles I knew speaking was still out of the question so I texted my cunning plan to everyone.

What I needed to do was turn Lee from a liability to an asset.

The replies came quickly. Lee's quicker than all the others. He just looked at me with a twisted smile on his face and nodded.

A car pulled up in front of ours. I recognized the hulking form of Sam in the passenger seat.

The decision was unanimous. We were using Lee as bait and while the girls fell around him in hysteria, I hoped we'd have the opportunity to take pictures of them and maybe recognize one or two. If we were very lucky, Melanie would be there. She didn't seem the type to be able to resist a Grange band member.

Throughout my meltdown, I kept thinking the guy wanted these kids to go willingly. This meant he was going to take them places, buy them things and make promises. He could steer them away from screaming hordes, which in itself would be telling as long as we were watching. Or he could allow them to take part ... gaining trust. Making the kids think they were free to do whatever they want.

I opened the car door as Sean and Sam came over. "We need to set this up for a fairly open area," I said.

Sean nodded. "There's a grassy area with a bouncy castle on it. That'll work. We can watch everyone approaching Lee there.

"We need to get him there without causing a frenzy," Sam added. "We don't want to set the crowd off before we're ready to snap some pics or grab a kid."

Agreed.

Sean appeared thoughtful and then hurried back to his car for a few minutes. When he reappeared, he smiled and said, "We'll drive him in with a police escort."

"We will?" I asked.

"Yes," Sean said. "I'll drive Lee and Kurt; the police car will be in front of me, with you and Sam behind us. We'll do a motorcade deal and cruise up that side road to the back few rows of market stalls. Once there the police will draw a small amount of attention, then back off. It's only a hundred feet or so to the grassed area from that point."

My brief followed, "So we're going to pose as Lee's security team and station ourselves close enough to get a good look at the kids. Remember people, the ones that don't come over are *as* important. The more pictures the better."

I had a camera around my neck. But the other two needed cameras too. Sam leaned into the car through Lee's window and released the trunk. He hunted round in his backpack for a few seconds then came back to the window with three digital cameras.

He grinned at Lee. "The more kids you can pose with the better the pictures. Give us a whistle and I'll come on over and take the shots. Make it look like a publicity thing."

Doc put his shirt and jacket back on. "Would look better if I took the photographs."

"You're right, "Sam conceded. "You look like his manager or agent, I look like his bodyguard."

Lee nodded.

My turn again. "Now let's get you looking more like Tony."

I took off his cap and replaced it backwards. Removed his cheap sunglasses and gave him back his aviators.

"That'll have to do," I said. I was beginning to see what caused hysterics wherever we went.

"Have you got radio mikes?" Sean asked.

Not that I expected we'd need them at that point but I did have radio mikes in my backpack in the back of the car. I reached over and hauled the bag onto my knee.

Inside a small sturdy box lined with molded foam, I counted ten. I removed five earpiece receivers and five tiny microphones. I handed out the equipment. We pinned the small microphones to our shirts, between the shoulder and the neck front. They looked like sports club pins, nothing out of the ordinary. The small earpieces were almost invisible inside the ear canal.

"This is one peculiar honey trap," Sam muttered as a

police cruiser pulled up and one of the officers yelled out to Sean. Sean indicated for me to go with him.

"Jay Cosgrove," he said, introducing me to the officers in the car, and pointed to the driver, who winked at me with a cheesy grin. "... and Turner Quarrie. This is SSA Ellie Conway, FBI Delta team."

"Welcome to New Zealand," Turner said.

"Thanks. Be nice to come back and have a vacation. I've vacationed Marlborough Sounds but not for quite a few years. Christchurch is quite different from Marlborough."

"Our sergeant said there's a task force being pulled together," Jay said. "We'd like to volunteer."

Sean nodded. "One second," he said. His hand rested lightly on my arm and he motioned for us to step away for a conversation.

"Are they good?" I asked.

"I've worked with both of them a few times. They're dedicated," he replied.

"Thought no one wanted to work with us?"

"Maybe they're not the brightest crayons in the box." He grinned at me.

"Great."

"You don't mean that."

I smiled at him. "Give them the nod then." Sam's voice was in my ear, "Poor bastards don't know what they're volunteering for, SSA."

Sean replied, "Never volunteer. They'll learn."

We stepped back to the car. "Thanks for your offer of

help. We'd be pleased to have you work with us on this." I smiled and shook both their hands. "After this I'll set up a meeting and bring you up to speed on the case. I'll need to see your firearms proficiency tests."

"We're good to go," Sean said. "Lee, Kurt – jump in my car, let's get this circus moving. Over."

"Message understood," they replied.

We now knew the radio signal was loud and clear.

Sam and Lee switched places. Our escort employed rolling lights and led the way.

As the cars bumped along the road, I couldn't quite believe what we were doing. We set the trap. The police car's lights caught the attention of several young girls. I could see them starting to follow us.

I felt sorry for Lee. It was an odd sensation and not something I normally experienced.

So much for cold-hearted bitch. Failed again.

Lee and Doc sauntered into the grassy picnic area trying to look nonchalant. He wasn't having the best day so far and judging by the noise I could hear building around us, it was only going to get worse.

"Have fun with it. The more you play the rocker the better this will go," I whispered.

"Copy that. I'll try. How long do you want to keep up this charade? Over."

"As you long as you can stand it. The minute you start reaching for your weapon, I'll call it off. Over."

Sean's voice broke in, "Good to know SSA. Over."

It was hot. I was uncomfortable and still wearing two

tee shirts. On one side of the area were several hotdog stands, all offering cold drinks. They looked inviting. A cold drink would be heaven.

"Heads up people, we have screamers at three o'clock. Over," Sam said.

Time to take some pictures. I lifted my camera, switched it on and started clicking. Lee smiled, waved and repeatedly executed brilliant rock star poses. I listened to the comments from Doc as he snapped pictures. Sam and I watched for stragglers.

A man escorted a young girl around the edge of the grass. He was attempting to steer her toward the car park area; she was watching Lee with open adoration.

"Sam, on your five, guy in dark-blue jeans and a brown blazer with a military hair cut. Get a look at the kid with him. I don't think its Melanie but she seems out of place. And he's definitely worth another look. Over."

Who wears a blazer in this heat unless they're hiding something?

"Copy. On it. Over."

Sam moved off. Sean was snapping photographs. Turning in full circles to get as many kids and bystanders as possible.

"SSA, could be one of the missing kids. Over," Sam said. That's all I needed to hear.

"Copy that. Pull her and have him cuffed," I replied. "Sean, are our police friends still close? Over."

"Affirmative. Over."

"Copy. Let's get them involved in this. Over," I said.

Doc was still snapping pictures of girls posing with Lee.

Sean disappeared behind the crowd. I could hear him and Sam talking to the male and questioning the girl before Jay and Turner arrived on the scene to give them both a free ride in a police car. Neither had been able to produce identification.

My mouth was dry.

I carried on snapping pictures of the surrounding crowd for another five minutes before Lee tapped out and I heard his voice in my ear.

"Get me out of here. Over," he said, while still smiling at the screaming horde.

Sam's voice came back clearly, "Copy that. Coming for you now. Walk toward the road. Over."

Lee and I linked arms; Doc took his other arm. It was mainly so we were inseparable as we forged our way through the seething mass of sweaty screamy teenagers. The smell of teen spirit burned the back of my nose. Twice I checked my gun as we waded through the bodies to Sam.

Once Sam met us, we moved faster toward the cars. Sean was waiting with the engine running. The police car sat with lights rolling, lead car again. I could see the man and girl in the back. Not ideal. I would have preferred the girl to be in a different car from the get go.

Lee and Doc scrambled into Sean's car, Sam and I ran to the other car. We all met down the road from the market and switched the kid over to Sean's car with Lee and

Doc.

"Sean, I need an interview room, with digital taping facilities. What have you got?"

"Use your hotel. It has several excellent conference rooms with all the gear you could possibly need."

"Awesome. Thanks."

A quick call through to the hotel had a room made available, with two security guards posted outside it.

Sean let the police know we'd be using the hotel as our cars pulled out in convoy. I started scrolling through the photos on my camera. So many red, tear-streaked screaming faces. It was going to be a long tiresome task.

My body cried out for a drink of water but thoughts of bourbon squeezed their way into my mind, the ice clinking against the edges of my skull. "Good job Lee. I'll get you that bottle of Jack A-sap. Over." I enjoyed being able to talk to everyone without picking up the phone. As long as the cars weren't too far apart, we were all in constant communication.

"Copy. You going to help me drink it? Over." It was nearing three in the afternoon. We had an interview to conduct, photographs to wade through, plus two new team members to brief.

"Depends how long it takes to get through this ..." I replied. "Over."

Silence fell like a thick blanket as we negotiated streets laden with midweek traffic. There was a small opportunity to enjoy the scenery. Sam concentrated on the driving. Being on the wrong side of the road took some getting used to. At one point, he narrowly avoided a cyclist only to find another bunch right ahead of us. They drew my attention to a church that seemed to be on the pointy end of a corner. Grave markers flanked the old stone building. I said, "Hey Sean, there's this cool stone church ..."

He interrupted me and said, "Church Corner. You're in Upper Riccarton. And yes, it's worth taking a stroll around the graveyard if you get a chance. Over."

"Wicked!"

The church on the corner thing tickled me pink. I'd come to realize this country said it like it is – Cathedral Square, Church Corner, Bridge 1 and Bridge 2, River Road. The examples were endless. Sam cussed under his breath at every cyclist we came across. I saw some more interesting old buildings I decided I'd like to explore, given half a chance. I didn't expect to find old stone buildings in Christchurch. I don't know what I expected but obviously, it wasn't pretty gardens, large parks and old buildings. Before long, we were back at the hotel.

I spoke to Sean and Lee and Doc before leaving the car. "Give me a few minutes to set the room up and then bring in the kid first. Use the entrance from the underground car park. I don't want too many people seeing uniformed police and a suspect. Over."

At the hotel, I asked the fabulously efficient concierge if we could use our key cards in the boardroom lock. Computers are a wonderful thing. Within minutes, the only access to the boardroom was via our key cards and a spare for Sean.

Sam got busy in the boardroom setting up the chairs the way we wanted them.

Chapter Thirteen
She's A Mystery

Leaving Sam in the boardroom, I hurried up to my room. Something niggled at me. A new part of the poem I'd begun earlier.

Rain pounding
Mud squelching
One by one they leave
Surrounded by flowers
Alone in the earth
The moments before, did they count?
What was special about the day?
Did you measure up in a universal way?

Would I measure up when the bell tolled for me? The jury was still out.

While I was in the room, I gathered laptops and other equipment we had scattered across the small table. I piled the files on top of the four laptops, wound up power cords and added them to the pile. I scouted around for anything else we might need. Paper and pens. I slid a bunch of legal notebooks under the power cords and shoved a handful of pens into my pocket.

Done.

I scooped up everything and managed to get out the door. I hooked the door with my foot but couldn't quite shut it. There was no way I could release a hand from the precariously stacked pile.

Shit!

A voice from down the hall said, "Wanna hand?"

Rowan was opening a door about five doors down.

"Will you shut this door for me, please?" I asked.

He grinned and came over. "Sure."

Sam's voice in my ear said, "I'm on my way."

"Not necessary," I replied. "Taken care of."

Rowan frowned. "But I just—"

"Sorry, the voices in my head needed an answer." I turned my head to the right and tilted it slightly. "Look in my ear."

He shook his head but looked anyway. "That's got to be one of the strangest requests I've had today."

"You obviously need to get out more," I replied.

"Is that a wireless receiver in your ear?"

"Yep."

The voice in my ear spoke again, "Who are you talking too?"

"Rowan Grange," I replied in a semi-whisper.

Rowan looked at me with an enquiring look on his face. I smiled and shook my head.

He scrutinized the part of my shirt that he could see.

"And the microphone ... the pin you're wearing?"

"Yep."

"Cool. Give me that pile, I'll carry it."

"I'm fine," I replied. "There is no need to go out of your way."

"Let me help."

I started to walk to the elevator. Rowan walked with me.

"It's not necessary."

"Up or down?" he asked, his hand hovering over the arrows.

"Down, thank you," I replied.

The elevator pinged a few seconds later and the doors opened. Rowan ushered me in, stepped in himself and with one hand stopping the door from shutting, asked which floor.

"One, please."

He pressed the button then jumped out of the elevator. As the doors started to close he said, "At eight o'clock I'll be knocking at your door."

"Thought you said Wednesday night?"

Just as the door shut properly he said, "It is Wednesday."

Upon exiting the elevator, the gears in my mind shifted to work mode.

Outside the boardroom I said, "Sam, can you get the door?"

The door opened. He took the pile from my arms and spread everything on the large table in the middle of the room.

"I think I'm over having everyone hear my conversations," I said and took the microphone off my shirt. I turned it over in my hand and flipped the tiny switch to 'off.' I left the receiver on and in my ear. Listening to Sean talk to the cops was interesting.

"Too much jibber-jabber for one day, SSA," Sam said with a wide grin.

Sam and I set up our computers. We set two laptops side by side at one end of the table and the third at the far end. I looked around for the CCTV cameras. There were four covering the entire room. Doors at the end of the room lead to a smaller air-conditioned room containing the monitoring stations for the cameras. I checked out the panel and four TV screens, making sure we could record everything that happened in the room to DVD.

Out in the room I spoke to Sam, "Can you configure one of the laptops so that we can start and stop the recording from in here?"

"Shit like this makes the hole left by Mac seem huge," he replied more or less under his breath. "I'll probably screw it up."

I'm not entirely sure what the expression was on my face but I think Sam forgot I still had a receiver in my ear.

He backpedaled. "I'll get on with it, might take me a few minutes."

"Do what you can; I need to get this interview under way."

You could drive a truck through the hole Mac left.

"Call the rest of the team in," I said and started looking over the files, paying particular attention to the three missing girls' information. The kid we grabbed looked very like the first missing kid, the one from Auckland.

There was a quiet knock at the door and Lee, Sean and Doc entered.

"That guy hasn't said a word, not one word," Sean announced. He carried a black attaché case, which he set down on the table. "Turner is with the kid."

"Well, either he has nothing to say, or an accent he doesn't want us to hear," I said.

"That's what I was thinking. Most people would be yelling for lawyers and demanding to know what was going on. He's said zip. The kid isn't talking either."

"I want the girl in first."

"I'll call Turner and have him escort her to the front desk," Sean replied.

"I'll meet her," I said and headed out the door.

Turner handed her over at the front desk.

"Thanks. Can you two sit with the male for a bit longer? I'll try to make this as quick as possible. If you are okay with it, I'll have you sit in on his interview and see how we work."

"Yes ma'am. Call us when you are ready for him."

"Thank you."

I took the silent girl by the arm and led her to the elevator, from where it was a short walk down a wide, well-lit hallway to our temporary and very stylish office.

She wore wide fabric bands around her wrists. They were black with red smiley faces on them.

She said nothing.

She made no eye contact.

She walked willingly.

She kept her head down.

I sat her in a chair between the computer stations we'd

set up. Sam was sitting at one, with Sean next to him.

I joined Lee and Doc at the far end.

I smiled at the girl and introduced myself but not the team; she didn't need to know who was in the room.

"I am Special Agent Ellie Conway."

She didn't respond.

"What's your name?"

No response.

"Your name?"

Nothing.

"Stand please."

She stood but didn't look at me; her gaze remained fixed on a single spot on the table.

"Turn out your pockets. All of them," I instructed, firm but pleasant.

She hesitated.

"Either you do it, or I do it for you." I started to rise from my chair.

That was enough to mobilize her. She dropped everything from her jeans' pockets onto the table, plus the contents from the front pocket of the sleeveless hoodie she wore. In front of her lay an assortment of things. The most interesting one for me was the cell phone.

The girl sat back down.

"Do we have gloves?" I whispered to Lee.

Sean heard and rose from his chair. Guess that meant they were all still wearing mikes and receivers. He picked up the attaché case he'd brought in earlier and opened it, walked down to me and handed me a pair of latex gloves and a pile of evidence bags.

He went back to his chair. I smiled at him. He grinned back.

As I pulled the gloves on, the rubber snapped against my wrists. There was a subtle change in the kid as I did.

I snapped the gloves again, this time watching her closely. She flinched. It was almost undetectable, as if she'd trained herself not to react.

Interesting.

Slowly I walked over to her and stopped on her right. She stared at the same spot.

I picked up the cell phone from the table. Her head never moved and her eyes remained locked on the table.

The phone was on. No text messages received in over three days, not even mine. Prior to that messages were sparse and all from the same number. They were instructions. 'Get dressed', 'Eat', 'Go to bed'. I checked each message; they were days apart. I wrote down the number and gave it to Sam to look up. Her outbox was empty. I suspected she'd deleted the messages if there were any. I searched for phone numbers for her parents.

"Check that," I said. I found a phone number filed under 'mom.' Nothing filed under 'dad.'

From my phone, I called the number. The call dropped out before it was answered. I tried again from the hotel phone that sat upon the table. No answer. Nor was there voicemail attached to the phone number. I scanned the rest of the objects on the table. There was a school identity card. I picked it up, looked at the name then slid it down the table to Lee.

"Seems your mom isn't home," I said.

She said nothing.

"Does she go out a lot, Abbey?"

She blinked slowly. "I'm not Abbey," she said.

My eyes cut to Sam's. He nodded his head.

"Yeah, you are. You are Abbey Jenkins and you've been missing for five days."

I heard Sam whisper in my ear. "She's eleven years old, Ellie."

"*No!* I am not Abbey," she replied.

Uh-oh.

"Who are you?" I asked.

I was starting to smell a big problem. It smelt like Post Traumatic Stress or some kind of dissociation at work. I looked at Doc for confirmation. He nodded.

"I don't know," she replied. "I don't know."

"We think you're Abbey," I said softly. "Who gave you the wrist bands?"

She didn't reply but shoved her hands back into the kangaroo pocket of her hoodie.

"Show me?"

I waited.

"Please?"

She slowly withdrew her hands and removed one wristband. I could see red welts circling her wrist.

"Show me the other one," I said, taking the band she gave me.

She closed her eyes and handed over the second band.

Both wrists bore the same painful-looking welts.

Someone had handcuffed the kid. Angled welts, not straight, ran around her wrists, in some places, almost raw. I felt sick. The little kid in front of me had been handcuffed to something – and she'd struggled.

"Doc, you need to see this and we need to get a medical team in here."

Sam picked up his phone then looked at Sean who took the phone and made a call.

We could hear him talking to emergency medical personnel. Doc joined me.

"Is it okay if I have a look at your wrists?" he asked quietly. "My name is Kurt. I'm a doctor."

Abbey said, "I'm not sick. I'm not her."

"I won't touch, I just want to see," Doc said.

She shook her head and held her arms across her body where he couldn't see.

I touched her arm below the shoulder but above the elbow, the safe zone. She flinched, this time it wasn't subtle. Doc raised his eyebrows at me.

"We're going to get you some help. You will be taken to the hospital and you will be safe," I told her as I crouched next to her. "One of us will go with you and make sure you are safe." I looked over the rest of the contents of her pockets. She had gum, sugar-free mints and a lip-gloss.

"Who is the man you were with?" I asked, not wanting to push her but not wanting to lose the opportunity to gather information.

"I wasn't with a man," she replied.

"Do you know Melanie Talbot?" I asked, showing her the picture I had in my pocket.

Slight surprise registered in her eyes before she shook her head.

I repeated the question, "Do you know Melanie Talbot?"

"No."

"Have you heard her name before?"

She looked down and didn't answer.

"Have you taken anything, maybe someone gave you a pill or something?"

"... No," she replied.

"You hesitated. Did you take a Tylenol tablet or aspirin?"

"I don't know what the first one is."

Sean spoke, "Panadol? Disprin? Nurophen? Any pill for a headache or anything like that?"

She shrugged. "I don't remember taking anything."

"Did he give you anything to eat or drink?"

"Water in a bottle."

"Like you buy in the store?"

"No, a drink bottle."

There was a knock on the door. Sean let the paramedics in. He ushered them straight to the girl. I rose to my feet and tapped Doc. Together we took a paramedic aside.

"I am SSA Conway with the FBI. This is Doctor Kurt Henderson also an SSA with the FBI."

Doc took over, "We have reason to believe this child

was drugged. I also suspect there was sexual abuse and she maybe in a dissociative state. She is denying her name but can't offer an alternative."

Lee joined us with the paramedic and handed over the police missing person's sheet on the girl.

"Thank you," the medic replied as he read the sheet.

"We are trying to locate her family," I said. Lee went back to his computer. "Someone will ride with you, this kid is pivotal to an international investigation regarding a child trafficking ring."

The medic nodded; I appointed Sean to the task. Sending Doc was moot, as he wasn't licensed to practice medicine in New Zealand. As the only female on the team, I felt I should've gone, but I was also the agent responsible for the investigation. Even Special Agent Chicky Babe couldn't be in two places at once.

"Let's get this show on the road," Sean said. "I'll give the boys a call on my way down. Let's hope you can get more out of the male."

Doc and the first paramedic helped the kid to her feet.

Sean came forward.

"Abbey, this is Sean. He works for me and he's going with you. He will keep you safe until we can get your family here for you."

She blanked out. Her reactions went back to zero.

I watched them leave with mixed feelings. She was safe but I had a horrible feeling we were too late. The door was shut. I turned to talk to Lee.

The door flew open with a crash and Abbey stood

wide-eyed in the doorway.

She said, "Tom Mix."

"Is that his name?" I asked.

She nodded. Sean led her away.

Lee typed the name into Google.

"Wanna know which movie that name is from?"

"Sure, make my day," I replied.

"Bruce Willis played Tom Mix in the 1988 movie *Sunset*." He typed again. "This is interesting, probably not to the case but triviawise. The character Tom Mix was based on Thomas Edwin Mix who was an American film actor and the first real Western movie star we had. He was born January 6, 1880 and died October 12, 1940."

"Thank you for that Lee, I can't wait to be able to toss that cowboy movie fact into my conversations." I grinned at him. "When Turner and ... Hooch, or whatever his name is, get in here ... have one of them notify the police that we found Abbey and need to contact the family."

The missed call log on the kid's phone said no one had called her cell phone in over a week. There were no text messages from her mother or anyone else except that one number. Oddly, there weren't many entries in her contacts list: three people including her mother. I fiddled with her phone for a minute and attempted to send a text message. Moments later *Message not sent* appeared on the screen. I looked at the screen; the icon that showed cell service bore a cross through the middle. I cleared the kid's possessions off the table, dropping everything into evidence bags and storing it all in Sean's attaché case. I

187

pulled off my gloves and threw them in the waste paper bin by the door.

Lee said, "I think his name is Jay, Ellie."

Jay not Hooch.

"I wanna know what that prick gave that kid," I said. "She had a fuc'n cell phone ... but it's not connected to the network. Or the network is down. Guess that's why didn't she call her mom at some stage. And why didn't she call for help?"

Neither of them responded.

The rant just wouldn't stop. I tried. But it wouldn't. "There is no record of my text being received on this phone either. I don't know why I'm surprised: a major cell network that has serious outages and failures was bound to cause life-threatening situations. Where is her mother?"

Doc's hand touched my arm. "Breathe."

"I am," I spat, shaking off his arm. I felt my blood pressure soar. I reread the missing child report. No one cared about this kid. No one missed her except one teacher, who had called the police when the child failed to show at a holiday program and she'd been unable to contact a parent. I wondered if the mother was even alive. I read more about the teacher. She was running a school holiday program for kids with nowhere to go.

I didn't have enough answers.

"Where is the freaking mother? Why couldn't police find her?" I looked at Sam. "Someone needs to visit her home – can we make that happen? Who was it who did send those messages to her fuc'n phone?"

"Yes, SSA." Sam checked his screen then typed quickly. He looked at me. "The number that did contact her – it was her mom. It's a pre-paid cell phone but she registered it." Sam called Sean and imparted my request. "He'll have local police go around there now."

I crossed Abbey Jenkins off my missing list.

We waited in silence for the knock at the door. It seemed to take an awful long time to come.

Sam opened the door and let in the officers and the handcuffed Unsub. He indicated seats for the officers and one in the middle of the long table for the Unsub. Jay and Turner smiled at me.

He was calm. He didn't react, nor did he resist.

With everyone seated, I introduced myself, "I am Special Agent Conway. And you are?"

I waited and let him have his minute's silence.

"Name, rank, serial number?"

He said nothing.

Unlike the girl he didn't fix his gaze on the table, he chose a spot on the wall, which meant he sat straight and his head was up.

"Big fan of Bruce Willis, or is it just cowboy movies that you like, Mr. Mix?"

My comment garnered a slight smirk.

"Country of origin?"

Nothing.

"The girl will be returned to her parents."

He shrugged.

"We're going to need a DNA sample from you."

His gaze remained fixed.

Lee went to the other side of the table with one of the digital cameras. He snapped a clear head shot of the Unsub then uploaded it to our database.

"While we wait for your name to spit out ... how do you like New Zealand so far?"

He didn't react.

"I think it's a lovely place. I'm really looking forward to spending some quality time sightseeing," I carried on as if he was taking parting in the conversation. "Might give the Antarctic center a try. The Casino looks good too."

The Unsub was not a great conversationalist.

Lee eventually spoke a name, "Harvey Bauer."

A small glimmer of amusement flickered across our guest's eyes.

"Harvey Bauer, born Harvey Wilhelm Beckenbauer in Hamburg, Germany. Date of birth May 12, 1970. A current resident and citizen of The United States of America," Lee said. "You are a long way from home buddy."

He remained silent.

"Well, it's a relief to know he's not a deceased cowboy actor or Bruce Willis," I said.

I leveled a cold stare at Harvey Bauer. "We're going to turn out your pockets, Harvey."

He remained stationary. His eyes moved from the wall to his handcuffed hands.

"If there is anything you need to tell us, now is the

time," I said.

He stared at the wall again.

Lee's computer beeped. I looked over at his screen. The incoming beep alert was from the Department of Defense. Our photograph of Harvey had caused a ripple effect. Someone else wanted him.

"Dammit," I mumbled and immediately decided to ignore the alert. A few minutes wouldn't hurt.

Harvey sat motionless.

"Sam, do the honors," I said.

Sam eased himself from his chair, fished some large latex gloves from the attaché case and pulled them on. They were tight. His fingers looked like cooked sausages. We needed to carry extra-large gloves.

He reached Harvey in three strides.

"Anything you want to tell me about before I search you?"

Nothing.

"If anything sticks me, I am not going to be happy ... you don't want me unhappy."

Sam did an awesome Mr. T impersonation.

Sam hauled Harvey to his feet and turned out his pockets, then conducted a quick body search. To the table of clutter he added a military knife and a Beretta M9.

It's fuc'n amateur hour.

I looked over at Jay and Turner and shook my head. "Good thing he was cuffed."

They looked sheepish.

I turned my attention to Harvey.

"Oh dear, possession of a firearm and a dangerous weapon. What else have we got there, Sam?"

Sam slid his hand across the tabletop sliding the contents toward me. I peered at the jumble of objects and pieces of paper. "No wallet?"

Harvey sat motionless.

"Who wanders about a market without a wallet?" I asked the men at the table. "Funny. The girl didn't have one either."

He had to have money or credit cards and probably ID somewhere.

"Sam – take off his shoes."

Sam did as he was asked and found what I expected: a military ID card, two credit cards and NZ dollars.

With that mystery solved, I scrutinized the table contents again. No cell phone, no hotel room key, or key of any sort.

"Want to tell me what's in the little baggie?" I flicked the bag out from the other things with the end of my pen. It contained two small white pills that looked like aspirin tablets, scored across the center.

He said nothing.

This was growing old fast.

Sam flipped the packet over and recognized a far-too-familiar brand name – Roche – with a small circle with a number two inside it. He threw it to Doc who confirmed they were two-milligram Rohypnol tablets.

"Is Sean still in range?" I asked Sam quietly.

He shook his head.

"Call him then. I want the hospital to check for Fluni-trazepam use."

He moved away, removed his gloves and called Sean's cell phone.

Bauer had the benefit of my full attention. "You kidnapped a little girl, fed her Roofies and raped her. It shouldn't be too hard to get some hefty charges to stick to you."

He smirked.

I wanted to pull his fingers off one by one with a pair of rusty pliers then make him watch as I fed them to piranha. Fingerless, bleeding, with his consciousness waning I'd stake him out next to an ant colony and then feed him methamphetamine so he was fully awake when the soldier ants started eating him. I could feel my pulse pounding in my temples.

"Any plans to leave the country with her?"

He stared at the wall.

"Where's your friend? You know, the one they call Hawk?"

My head spun in slow circles, dark holes appeared in my vision.

"Seen this kid before?" I showed him a photograph of Melanie Talbot. "She has been hanging out with Emmet Smith, another person who seems to like Bruce Willis movies."

He blinked slowly. I saw the barest of reactions concealed by the blink. Emmet Smith meant something to him.

"Wanna tell me where these three kids are?" Lee slid photographs over to me. I held them up one at a time. "Samantha Rowe, age twelve; Tasha Cravino, age eleven; Nicola Gallagher, age nine. Names ring a bell do they?" I added Melanie Talbot's and Abbey Jenkins' pictures to the mix.

His smirk returned but he remained silent.

My head spun.

Spun and spun.

I couldn't stop it.

The walls swayed.

Bauer blurred. I closed my right eye in an effort to see better.

Fuck!

I recognized the beginning of a major migraine. I leaned toward Lee slightly and hoped like hell I didn't fall onto him. I whispered, "There's a problem."

He whispered his reply, "Yeah a big one, NCIS have emailed me directly and asked us to turn over the suspect. They want him for sexually assaulting an officer." Another alert sounded. "Gets worse. We have received a joint request from Army and Navy to turn him over to NCIS."

Damn. He was the second person involved in the case NCIS had an interest in and now Army wanted in as well. At least the NCIS interest was easily dealt with, a quick phone call or email to Special Agent Noel Gerrard would take care of that. It wouldn't be bad working with him again.

"That's not good. I'll email Gerrard myself and make sure he's in on the loop," I said trying desperately to shake the dizzy fog from my mind without moving my head. I felt sick. My left arm prickled then went numb.

His head turned toward me, words drifted in the air as they came out of his mouth, "Shit, Ellie, not good at all."

"Take over," I whispered unable to open my right eye.

Lee found my microphone, turned it back on and pinned it to my shirt.

"We need to monitor you," he said.

I didn't care.

Doc's voice was suddenly in my head, a quiet whisper, "What's the matter?"

I ignored him.

My focus was on the door. If I was careful, I knew I could get there without letting Bauer know something was wrong. I stood up, walked behind Bauer's chair and crossed the room without incident. The door handle turned by itself. A blue sleeve flashed past my face. Doc's voice rolled over me.

"Hey Conway, let's go get you some meds," he said.

I looked at him then, at the blue sleeve. It wasn't his. It was Hooch's.

"Don't leave Lee," I said. The words danced across the air to Doc. He caught and swallowed them.

Wrong.

I said it again.

This time he caught them and shoved them in his ears. He nodded and spoke to Sam. I saw the words fly through the air like little arrows. They stuck in Sam. He pulled them out and threw them at Lee. Lee caught them, unfurled the arrows and nodded.

"Lee's fine with Sam," Doc said, his words sparkled and twinkled.

Hooch barked then took my arm. Doc was somewhere close; I could smell him.

The dog didn't even drool. He must've finally been housebroken.

Thank god!

Chapter Fourteen
Remedy

I was sufficiently aware of my surroundings to know we were in the elevator and that Hooch was close by. Police dogs are okay in hotels. The movement sucked. My brain spun out of control. It bounced off the sides of my skull and hurt like hell. I wanted to cover my right eye with my hand to stop the pain but I knew Doc would start going all doctor on me if I did. My heart fell to my boots with a sickening thud when the elevator stopped.

I heard Sean's voice in my head but I couldn't figure out how he got in there. "I'm on my way back. We have confirmation of rape and Rohypnol use."

Sam joined him and said, "Ellie's taking a break. Join us A-sap."

Oh, I was taking a break ... and that was why I was in my room?

Hooch spoke to me, "Can I do something for you?"

Wow, they train their police dogs well here.

Doc replied, "Yes, we're out of coffee for the filter machine, can you order a pot of coffee please?"

I watched Hooch make a call from the room then he left. I was in awe of his ability to do things without opposable thumbs. Pain shot through my head, nausea rose and my left arm wouldn't move properly.

Words floated in the air as though someone had typed them. "Here, take these."

Doc held out two capsules and a glass of water. I took them, gagging a few times as I swallowed. There was something behind me. I leaned on it. A couch.

Lee kept talking to me.

Shut up.

I couldn't see him anywhere.

"This is not a stroke," I said to Doc. Watching my words take flight and leave a trail of sparkly dust. At least I don't think it is. "This is a migraine from hell."

Lee was still talking. Maybe Mac would know where he was and why I couldn't see him. I pulled my cell from my pocket and called home.

The ringing stopped after a few minutes and Mac's voice filled the void his absence left in my heart. "We can't take your call right now, probably didn't hear the phone ring. Leave your number and a brief message we'll get back to you as soon as we can."

It was the middle of the night in Virginia, why wasn't he home?

Damn.

Doc kept talking. The words made no sense.

His voice distracted me from finding Mac's mobile number. I could only see out of my left eye and everything was slightly blurry. I hit M but that was only our home and work numbers, then I remembered and scrolled forward. His mobile was under G. Galileo.

I hit call. Someone answered it within a couple of rings, "Hello."

The 'hello' confused me.

"Mac?"

Mac didn't say 'hello' when I rang. He said 'babe' to which my reply was always 'dude.'

"No, you got the wrong number," the voice said.

I started to close my phone when the voice spoke again, "Wait, I know you."

I lifted the phone back to my ear.

"You do?"

"Yes I do. Are you in your room?"

"I think so."

I looked around slowly through the fireworks exploding and the black holes, I deduced it didn't look like my bedroom. I didn't have a couch or a table in my bedroom.

Creepy.

I shut my phone.

Why didn't Mac answer his cell? Who did answer his phone?

Too many voices competed in my mind. Doc said, "She's trying to reach Mac."

"I can't see you," I replied, pressing my hand to my ear to try to stop the intrusion.

He came closer, "Can you see me now?"

"Yes, I'm fine."

Nothing he said made any sense.

A door shut. I think it shut.

I could hear Sam and Lee talking to someone else. Everybody needed to get the hell out of my head. "Shut up!"

Gingerly, I lay on the couch and pulled a cushion over

my head. Violent pain sliced through my skull bringing a huge wave of nausea with it.

"There's too much noise! Shut up!" Everything swam and I hated swimming. All that fuc'n chlorine. The dark from under the cushion was soothing.

My eyes closed. I just might want to die.

The noise in my head started up again. How the hell am I supposed to work with shrunken giants in my head?

It's not right.

A flash of something important came to me. If I could hear them, they could hear me. "He knew Emmet Smith and he could know where he is now. Find out where Bauer is staying. I want his laptop and cell phone. He has to be communicating with someone else from the cell, probably Emmet." The effort involved in speaking used up all available coherence.

My head pounded in a disjointed rhythm; I knew the opening bars but couldn't grasp the name of the song. Someone was knocking.

The voice was familiar but softer than usual, and muffled. Words with no meaning.

Sounds. I took the pillow off my head and listened.

Someone knocked. Then I heard the voice again.

It was a struggle to get vertical and stagger toward the door.

The voices in my head were loud and insufferable and I wished they would shut up. A louder, more insistent voice behind me said, "Conway – sit back down! I'll get the door."

"Shut up!" I covered my ears with my hands. All that did was remove the external noise.

The door was slipping away; it blurred and wavered. The noise on top of the blurring was too much.

A tunnel opened, the edges swirled and faces emerged from the middle, peering at me like bobble-headed freakish toys. I smacked my hand into the side of my head, a wave of pain crashed down and the noise stopped.

It stopped.

Dodging faces coming at me, I stepped back. Something crunched under my foot.

My eyes closed involuntarily, hoping to stop the rapid movement around me. Everything swayed and swirled. I opened them again. An out-of-focus face closed in on me. "Conway, do you have to be contrary all the time?" Doc said reaching out for me.

I succumbed to a falling, sinking, feeling. It wanted me.

There was a floating weightlessness for a few moments then I felt something solid behind me. My eyes opened but everything moved too fast. A voice cracked my peace and split it wide open.

My cell phone rang. Doc answered it.

Then I heard the other voice again.

As he talked, he turned around and took something from another person. Then the door shut. I heard the click. It echoed in my head for a split second. Silence followed and left a big gap where once were loud obnoxious voices. He was talking to someone but the words were lost. I couldn't see them. His voice faded then came back. Still the words were lost. They were such faded words that when they hit the air, their colors merged into nothing.

Doc spoke again, "Conway?"

A coffee cup hovered in front of me; I couldn't see a hand holding the cup. It smelled delicious yet made me nauseous.

The cup floated then finally settled on the coffee table. The cup itself seemed to move in and out, as if it were breathing. I fought the temptation to throw it. Cups shouldn't breathe.

He was on the phone talking to someone. Not that I cared, no one was in my head any more. It was almost peaceful.

My phone was back on the table. I saw it when I reached to pick up the cup. It'd stopped breathing and felt safe to hold.

I turned to look for Doc but there didn't seem to be anyone there.

"Hey," said a voice from the chair to the right of mine. "We have a dinner date."

The insanity in my head was gone, replaced by a soothing fuzziness. I tested my vision and with relief found the black holes were gone. I no longer had to look around them but still needed my right eye closed to stop the pain.

Words were words again, invisible and spoken. All the pretty pictures faded. Then I realized who he was and what he'd witnessed.

Way to look like a retard, Ellie.

"It's okay." I felt like a complete imbecile. "You don't have to hang around. I'm feeling better."

"I can tell." He grinned. "*We*," he pointed to me then himself, "have a dinner date ... did you forget?"

"No, I didn't," I replied with care, trying to placate the confusion in my mind. "It's Wednesday then?"

Why didn't Mac answer his phone? He's always there when I need him. Then it occurred to me he was probably taking care of Carla. So I guess I can go out with Rowan for dinner.

It started slowly and quietly and took a few bars before I recognized the song I could hear. Mac spoke so softly under the words I almost missed it. "It's all about the music. Caine is watching Carla." The music grew louder. I hummed along to Bon Jovi's '*Always*.' Mac used to love to sing along to it in the car.

Rowan spoke as I slipped lazily back to the present. "You still with me?"

"Yes."

"We have a date."

"You still want to take me out?"

He smiled. It still really bugged me that someone else answered Mac's phone.

"Hard day?" Rowan asked.

"I've had better." I was feeling more and more like me as the minutes passed. I stood up slowly. I wasn't quite as steady as I thought. "Where's Doc?"

Rowan jumped to his feet, his hands held me at the elbows until I stopped swaying. "All right?"

"Doc?" I said again.

"I'm here," Kurt replied from behind me.

"I need to take this off." I tried to unclip my holster.

"Let me." Doc's fingers slid along the inside of my waist band. He pried the holster off my belt with his thumb and laid it gently on the table.

Rowan looked down at the holster. There was an element of surprise in his voice when he said, "I never noticed you were armed."

"I was working, not out jogging."

"Sit back down, please," Doc said, holding my arm at the elbow. Without argument, I sat down a little too heavily. My legs felt like a strange mixture of Jell-O and pudding. My mind was a soft comforting pillow, no pain just puffy fluff – the familiar buzz from Demerol. "Dammit Conway, you really are in a bad way. No contrariness."

"I'm okay." I tried desperately to make it so.

"Do you need anything?" Doc's fingers rested on the inside of my wrist. I knew he was taking my pulse.

"More coffee would be freaking awesome, please."

Doc looked over to Rowan. "You heard the lady."

"I've got a suspect downstairs." I said and started to stand up.

Doc's hands pressed my shoulders back down. "No, Conway. You have the evening off. Doctor's orders. You're loaded on Demerol and not going anywhere."

Rowan set a cup of coffee on the table for me then spoke to Doc. "Is she allowed to eat dinner?"

"I'm right fuc'n here," I muttered.

"Sure, dinner is a good idea," he replied. "I want Conway to rest first."

"I'm fine, Doc." I downed the coffee and held the empty cup out to Rowan. "See, I drank coffee and kept it down and everything."

"You're smashed, Conway. Rest first, dinner later."

There was an element of guilt crawling around about having the night off. Sam and Lee were perfectly capable of finishing the interview and even thinking about Bauer made my head throb more than it did already. Vitriol rose as the image of the kid filled my mind. I did need a break. I could go back down there and push myself until my head exploded, or be sensible and take the offered break.

"Dinner it is then."

I watched Rowan walk over to the small kitchenette where the coffee pot waited. He bent down and carefully picked up small pieces of something. He inspected the contents of his hand.

"You weren't hearing voices in your head were you?"

My hand touched my ear releasing a large ah-ha moment. "My receiver is gone."

The voices in my head were my team trying to work.

"I think one of us stood on it," Rowan said and tipped the broken pieces onto the table.

"Damn."

Doc looked at my shirt. "You are still wearing the microphone."

I took it off and held it closer to my mouth while I whispered, "Thanks guys. Feeling okay. Am switching this thing off. I'll send Doc back to you soon."

"All right, that's better. I'm officially off duty." I smiled at Rowan. "If that were something that was actually possible, I would be anyway." Someone forgot to tether my mind to my skull. I felt a bit spacey. Okay, a lot spacey.

Doc was close. His eyes missed nothing. "Conway, you need to relax. Chill. Go with the Demerol and stop trying to fight it. Some sleep would help."

I pulled my legs up under me in the chair and rested my head on the padded arm.

"Maybe you should learn to take the occasional night off," Doc said. I wasn't sure if it was his professional opinion or just him being considerate.

"Maybe so," I said as my eyes closed.

Chapter Fifteen
Now I'm Here

An hour later, I woke to find Doc sitting in an armchair opposite me.

"How're you feeling?" he asked.

"Better."

"You up for dinner?"

"I'm not sure." I opted for honesty.

"This is quite a breakthrough, Conway – no smartassed comment. He seems like a nice guy. Dinner won't kill you."

Me? Smartassed?

"I'll go, a girl needs to eat." I mustered as much enthusiasm as I could but even I knew it was a lame attempt.

"Try not to enjoy yourself. I have Rowan's number. I'll call and tell him you can go to dinner. Go get ready."

I stood up slowly.

"Take it easy. It's not a race," Doc said, as I staggered a little before finding my footing. I was in front of a full-length mirror by the bedroom door. My reflection was unbelievable. I was still wearing two tee shirts, jeans covered in dust and dirty boots. My hair hung down my back in a messy ponytail. I picked a wayward leaf from my hair. There was a mascara line across my cheek and a matching smudge on the side of my face.

It looked like I'd had a hard day on the range – wrestling steers.

"Do you know where are we eating?" I asked, attempting to brush some wayward hair off my face. It was a futile attempt to tidy myself up.

"He mentioned the Casino."

"This is a good look ..." I waved a hand down my body.

He laughed. "If anyone can pull off the lived-in look, you can."

"Yeah, no! I'll be in the shower."

"Don't lock the door," Doc said.

"I'm okay, I just need a shower."

"Just once, do as I ask. Don't lock the door."

My middle finger took on a life of its own.

I'm not a door locker anyway. So there. Thankfully, I stopped short of blurting that out.

A while later, I wiped steam from the bathroom mirror with a hand towel and stared into my own blue eyes. There was a need to give myself a strict talking to.

"You screwed up today, don't let it happen again, dumb ass. No one's going to let you take care of Carla if you can't even look after yourself."

I stared. My eyes stared back harder.

"Now get ready, go to dinner and make like a normal person."

Watching myself staring was creepy.

The steam vanished from around me, sucked from the room by the exhaust fan on the ceiling. I took a deep breath and started with moisturizer then minimal make-up. Because I was actually going out like a regular person, for the first time in a long time, I opted for dark eyeliner along my bottom lashes and a silvery eye shadow along my top lashes. A little extra mascara wouldn't hurt. I towel-dried my wet hair, brushed it and then attacked it with the blow dryer. I surveyed myself in the mirror. Everything above my neck looked okay; everything below could take care of itself. My eyes sparkled, my hair shone, makeup covered the washed-out pasty look I'd worn earlier. All I needed was clothes.

I wrapped myself in a large white bathrobe, tied it securely and padded out to the living area. Rowan looked up from a notebook he was writing in as I opened my bedroom door. A smile spread across his face. Doc was sitting on the couch pretending to watch television.

"Hi Rowan, can I wear jeans, or is there some kind of dress code?"

"Honey, you could wear that robe if you wanted."

"Jeans then?"

"Jeans are fine."

I padded back to the room shutting the door behind me. I lifted my bag onto the bed, emptied the contents and spread my clothes out so I could better see what I'd brought with me.

It was not good.

My coolest jeans were a dark denim and velvet pair with a lace-up fly which I found and pulled them on under my robe.

"Good Ellie, you've got your ass on," I whispered to no one. "And if anyone cares it's a mighty fine ass."

Rowan's voice called out from the living room, "You

gonna be much longer in there?"

I searched frantically for something to wear on my top half. A long-sleeved black button-down shirt sprang into view, because all I have is black. I put it on and did up half the buttons. I leaned forward in the mirror, then did up one more button. Quickly I shoved essential girl items into a little black bag. A mirror check, my hair covered the scar on my forehead, long sleeves covered messy scarring on the inside of my right forearm.

"Coming," I called back.

Feet.

My new black cowboy boots. One was by the door. I stuffed my foot in one and limped around looking for the other.

"Ellie?"

"One sec."

Under the edge of the valance of the bed, I saw black. Yes, my missing boot was missing no longer. I tossed the long strap of the little black bag over my head and shoulder and tugged the boot on while hopping for the door.

There was a knock and the door opened.

I fell through it head first.

Arms grabbed me but the falling continued. I landed hard.

Way to go genius.

A moan exhaled on a long breath from under me.

I couldn't move. I was unsure as to where my limbs had landed and didn't want to inflict any more pain or possible injury on my dinner date.

"Don't move," he said. "Roll with me. On two, roll; go with my body," he said.

I'm sure that at least two million women would've loved to hear him say that.

We rolled. I lay for a moment and took stock; my head hadn't exploded on impact, which was reassuring.

"Okay?" I managed one word.

He grinned. "Little winded but otherwise fine. You?"

"Same, I'm okay," I replied.

He stood up, brushed himself off then reached down and took my hand to help me up. I felt a small shock as his hand met mine.

I'm fine, just fine. Part of me wondered what the hell had got into me. I was going to dinner with Rowan Grange, higher than a freaking kite.

Doc's laughter blanketed the entire escapade. I didn't have the energy to either silence him or join him.

'Fine' still doesn't flow as nicely as 'okay.' I probably needed to try it out more often and get used to it.

Rowan's body was imprinted upon my rib cage and my head was not happy about falling.

What was he made of? Solid steel?

The thought stalled my brain. Man of steel. So now, he's Superman. This hallucination keeps getting better.

Just enjoy it Ellie, no telling what fresh hell lies around the corner.

"Ellie?" Rowan touched my shoulder.

"I'm ready. If you're okay, let's go to dinner," I said and adjusted the strap from my bag. It had tried to strangle me in the fall. He smiled and offered me his arm, which I accepted.

"You kids have a good time now!" Doc sang out, flipping channels.

"You going back down with Sam and Lee?" I asked.

"Yes. Be careful, Conway. Alcohol could trigger another migraine."

"Thanks." It was more likely to trigger a sizable hangover.

Rowan opened the door and something white fell to the ground. He stooped and picked up two pieces of white paper then handed them to me without looking at them first. I turned them over as he closed the door.

The first was a photograph of Rowan and me in the hotel gym, the second a photo of Lee and me at the market. There was no writing on either picture. I pushed them into my bag before Rowan saw them.

"What was it?" he asked.

"A note. Nothing important." I turned on a dazzling smile.

A soupy mix of dread and fear was forming deep in my gut, which I let brew. I wondered what it meant but didn't have time to brood over the new photographs for long.

We walked out of the elevator into a lobby full of people.

His hand took mine as we crossed the lobby then, with a wistful glint in his eye, he said, "I think I saw you once before in a hotel lobby."

Color rose in my cheeks. The Marriot in DC.

It served to make him smile wider.

He continued, "Think it was in DC, about four years ago?"

My face felt hot.

"It *was* about four years ago, and it *was* DC," I replied.

A car waited for us at the front entrance.

It was so quiet outside. I don't know quite what I expected. Fifty or so screaming girls seemed to be the norm when Lee stepped foot outside, so I rather expected Rowan to attract more than a quiet, still evening.

I felt eyes peering from the dark, making my spine tingle and me shiver.

"It's so quiet." I slid into the back seat of the car and moved over for him.

"No one knows where we are staying." He looked out the window at the hotel as the car pulled away

Bauer crawled to the forefront of my mind. Abbey came too. I hoped she'd be okay. Him, I wanted to fry or liquefy. I gave myself permission to consider how it would feel to blow off his head and plant daisies in his neck.

"How'd you know it was me in DC?"

"What can I say? ... You made an impression."

Damn!

"You know that's ever so slightly scary." I didn't know if I should be flattered or worried.

"I've never seen another attractive woman in a bloody tee shirt and socks without boots, wearing a handgun jammed in the waist band of her jeans."

Another reminder of what a great first impression I make.

My cheeks flushed again as my mind stumbled over the attractive thing. "I'm not that memorable."

He leaned closer and said, "You are." I knew by his tone of voice that he was only trying to make me feel better.

Nothing felt right.

How many women in the world would give their first born to trade places with me?

In the back of my mind was concern over Carla's safety; knowing I couldn't get to her at speed sent tendrils of panic through my being.

Leaning my head back, I tried to think calming thoughts. It involved reminding myself over and over that Caine was taking care of her. No one could do a better job. By the time the car pulled into the underground car park at the Casino, I'd begun to relax.

There was still the lingering feeling that I had eaten a large dollop of stupid with my breakfast.

Must've been the long-acting stuff because it kept coming back. The Demerol enhanced it, giving my stupidity super powers.

I stole backward glances over my shoulder several times trying to place the feeling of eyes watching me. I expected Rowan to command a few stares but this felt sinister like all the other eyes I'd felt on me recently.

Our escort took us upstairs in a private elevator and

down a long hallway above the two floors of gaming tables. One-way glass in the private dining room gave us a view of the tables and afforded privacy.

Rowan was 'cool' personified and I let myself bask in the shade of his cool. Tired of feeling broken and the irony of needing a break didn't escape me.

The case edged into my thoughts. Bauer made my skin crawl and, apparently, my head ache to the extreme. That I didn't need again. Sam, Lee and Doc could handle Bauer; they didn't need me tonight.

Rowan leaned back in his chair, looking relaxed and comfortable. "I thought it might be fun to do something together."

Totally unexpected. "Really, like what?"

"I'd like it if we collaborated on a project or two. Are you up for it?" he said with a grin.

Stunned. Speechless.

Oh, this is the *best* hallucination ever. He made a gesture and suddenly there was a wine waiter at the table. Champagne arrived.

Oh, what the hell. "I'll give it a go. Once this case is closed."

"You serious?" Rowan sounded surprised.

"Yep. I'm seriously suffering from FiTH syndrome but what the hell, let's do it."

"Fith?"

Laughter rose. "Fucked in the Head."

The conversation meandered; I listened as he told me how their latest record came about. I enjoyed his stories.

As he talked, life exploded from his being.

It felt good to bathe in the light.

By the time the entrée arrived, I was feeling okay about everything. Maybe he was Superman.

Then the conversation turned to *my* work.

"What is the case that brought you to New Zealand?"

"A case linked to one back home."

"Get far?"

"Today we did." I had another drink. "We found a missing girl."

"Good job," Rowan raised his glass.

A big mouthful of champagne almost choked me as the bubbles tickled my throat and I coughed.

I really wished I hadn't. Pain shot through my head and semi-paralyzed me for a moment.

"Is the girl okay?" Rowan asked.

"It's hard to say. She was kidnapped, drugged and raped." As soon as I realized what I'd said, I knew I should censor myself before opening my mouth. He's not one of us.

The color blanched from Rowan's face. He swallowed a large amount of champagne.

"Is your job always like that?"

"Pretty much."

"How old is she?"

"Let's not go there. She's a kid and she should've been out shopping in the mall with her girlfriends and squealing over Billy Ray Cyrus's kid or that Beiber boy, like every other little girl. There are four more missing."

Rowan's face paled more. "This is not dinner conversation."

He's not one of us.

His eyes met mine. Mac came to mind and I wondered what he'd make of this new lunacy. This delusion was a real repeater, it kept coming back and got better every time and was so vivid.

"Tell me about you," I said.

He scratched his neck and refilled our glasses. "I sing. I'm a lucky bastard. I get to do what I love doing."

I suspected the luck part was minimal considering his enormous talent.

My foot was going to sleep. I lifted my glass for another drink. A few more of those and I wouldn't be feeling any pain.

Dinner arrived.

His banter and the lightness in his voice were uplifting. I was drifting.

Mac's voice resounded within me, 'Don't go too far, Babe.'

Rowan's body language made interesting reading. He was leaning back, the ankle of his right leg rested upon the knee of his left, his right arm draped over the back of the chair he sat on; he rested his left elbow on the table, his fingers touching his chin. Relaxed.

The waiter appeared and filled our glasses. I could hear Doc warning me about the dangers of alcohol, how it could trigger another migraine. I flipped him off in my head.

Rowan leaned over the table. "Enough about me, tell me about you?"

"Nothing much to tell. I work for the FBI. I love music and I inherited a cat and a lunatic brother-in-law from Mac," I replied. "I live a quiet life." Mac's laughter filled my head as he echoed the words, 'I live a quiet life.'

"I have a feeling there is a lot more to you than you're sharing," he said lifting his glass.

I have a feeling I'm too drunk to walk straight. See? We all have feelings. Our glasses touched with a fine tinkle and then I swallowed more bubbles, this time without the unflattering choking.

My eyes drifted down to the gaming tables. The roulette wheel spun. There were three people playing the table. Two men and one woman.

I shifted my focus from gazing at no one in particular, to watching one of the men intently. I could only see his left profile and was looking almost at the top of his head, but still, I found I had a nagging feeling that I'd seen him before.

My hand delved into my bag and removed my phone from under the photographs without Rowan seeing them. "Just need to check something."

I called Lee while paying close attention to the guy below me.

"Everything going okay?" I asked when he answered his phone.

"SSA, it's all good."

"Send me the file photograph of Hawk?"

"To your phone?"

"Yes."

"Misha couldn't confirm it was Hawk."

"I know."

"I've sent it."

As he said that, a picture message arrived. I opened it and held it up by the window, next to where his head was.

The man tilted his head up to look at a screen on the wall in front of him. I saw what was playing. It amused me to think he'd given me a good look at his face so he could see an old Grange video clip.

I showed Rowan. "Look at this and him."

"Could be the same person," he replied, leaning on both his elbows now. He followed his gaze too and smiled. "Damn that's an old clip. What on earth were we wearing?"

"The tightest jeans I've ever seen. Frightening isn't it?" I held the phone to my ear again and said, "We may have a chance to find out if that picture is Hawk. There is a guy at the roulette wheel in the casino who is remarkably similar."

"Can you take him?" Lee asked.

Bless him for asking. "I've been drinking. I'm not even certain my eyes are seeing straight," I told him. "I am off tonight, remember? The boss is taking some personal time ... Doc's orders."

I don't trust myself.

"Describe him."

Feeling very clever, I went one better, snapped a picture with my phone and sent it to Lee.

"He's winning," I told him. "I doubt he'll be in a hurry to leave."

"Sam and I are coming."

"Where's Bauer?"

"Kurt and Sean took him to Christchurch central police station. They're waiting for a Marine escort to arrive from the embassy in Wellington."

"Be safe," I said and hung up.

Rowan was watching with me. "Who is Hawk?"

"There's a thought that he's a terrorist and his cell operates to make money for more militant cells. He's also a murderous scumbag."

"Do I even want to know how they make their money?"

I shook my head.

My brain sloshed. It was a most unpleasant feeling.

"One more call, then I'll let this go," I said with promise in my voice. I flipped through the recent contacts list in my phone. Before I found Misha's number, I noticed Rowan's cell number. I didn't call Rowan. I was sure I didn't call Rowan.

"Did someone call you from my phone?"

He nodded and said, "Yeah, you did, you weren't feeling very well. I think you hit the wrong number."

"I was calling Mac."

The words hung in the air like a giant neon 'loco' sign. They flashed a few times too, in case Rowan missed them.

So I didn't look like a complete nutcase I opened my contact list and showed him the entries for G. His name was right below Galileo. There were no other G's in the list just Galileo and Grange. I must've flicked too far and hit the wrong entry. It didn't explain why I was calling my dead husband. I doubted I could successfully explain that act of lunacy, so I left it alone.

"Galileo?"

"It was his screen name."

He handed me back my phone. "Calling me was an accident," he said with a grin.

I called Misha and in my clumsy Russian asked if Hawk was a gambler. Misha pulled up files and trawled through documents. I could hear paper turning and file drawers opening. There was no reference to him gambling. No bookies, no illegal gambling activity that anyone knew of. But then no one knew who he really was, so unless he used Hudson Hawk or Eddie Hawkins at casinos and during related pursuits, there would be no record.

I closed my phone. Rowan was smiling at me. He had a surprised yet pleased expression on his face as if he'd discovered something that no one else had.

"What was that? Russian?"

"*Da. Ja nemnogo govorju po-russki,*" I replied with a smile.

"I love it and I have no idea what you said."

"Yes. I only speak a little Russian," I translated quickly then added, "And it sucks but Misha seems to appreciate the effort."

Rowan laughed. His eyes drifted back to the gaming

tables.

"Do you need to go down there and do some Special Agent stuff?"

"Ah no. Special Agent stuff isn't very smart when the agent in question would fail a breathalyzer test and a toxicology screen." Although the effects of the Demerol were all but gone.

He nodded and filled up my glass. I hadn't even noticed the arrival of a fresh bottle of champagne.

There was a moment earlier in the evening, when I considered drinking at all after a migraine was plain stupid. It vanished somewhere in the middle of the second glass.

"Look," I said and pointed to Sam as he crossed the room downstairs. I couldn't see Lee until he was standing next to the person in question. He'd come up from directly under us. The woman caught my eye again. She looked uncomfortable.

Time to call Lee back. "I think he was here to meet that woman."

"Yes, SSA."

We hung up.

When I looked over at Rowan, he was watching me.

"How did you know?"

"I dunno, sometimes I *know* stuff." My honesty didn't make me look any more normal. With a minimal shoulder shrug, I said, "Guess I pick up subtle clues no one else sees or something."

There was a theory I'd toyed with on that and it

seemed to hold true for Carla as well. My ability to see things/know things about people was a survival mechanism from living with an insane mother. I noticed early signals that things were going to turn to custard and could react accordingly. Carla had exhibited similar ability. She had a similar background.

I settled back to walk Rowan through the events that would now take place.

We watched the scene unfold. The suspect's winning streak began to fail. He remained calm and didn't seem bothered by the turn of fate.

For whatever reason, the man looked up. If he'd known I was there, we would be staring into each other's eyes. I'd seen those eyes before. Watching.

I called Sam. "I've seen him before. We need to pull the crowd photographs of all the crime scenes from the Butterfly Murders. I'm sure I saw him at several of the scenes." I was sure it wasn't Hawk but he was somehow involved and he wasn't a New Zealander, of that I was certain.

Those scenes had had eyes. The Unsub had rigged cameras and was streaming video of us working the scenes, until I worked it out and had all the scenes searched for cameras and bugs.

"He doesn't look like the picture of Hawk in person."

"It's someone connected to what happened back home."

"We're on him."

"I'm watching." I hung up.

Rowan filled my glass again. This was going to end in a mess.

"I hope that prick had a nice day," I hissed as we watched Lee slap his hand down on the Hawk's wrist. With one twist, he was face down on the roulette table, cuffed and patted down.

Lee raised the man's head by grabbing a handful of hair and pulling.

Sam spoke to the woman. I saw the gold of his badge flash in the light as he moved. A few seconds later, he opened his cell and mine rang.

"We'll take him back to the hotel office and call in Sean. Do you want her?"

"It's your call. We've got nothing and no reason to hold her. My feeling is she's a New Zealander, so tread carefully. But get her details and check her player's card for her name. I bet she has one." I chuckled to myself. "A card I mean, not a name. Although she would have one of those too ..."

Really, I should stop talking.

"Will do."

"Good job, guys. I'll be here toasting you with champagne." I couldn't tell but I think I slurred a few words.

Sam laughed. "Take it easy, Chicky Babe." And hung up.

As I watched them leave, our target brushed against the woman purposely by pulling back as the guys steered him toward the door. They hauled the uncooperative man out of the Casino. The woman disappeared in the other direction.

I flipped my phone open again and called Sam back.

"He gave her something."

"Thanks SSA."

This time I closed my phone and put it away. Enough interruptions for one evening.

If there is a God, he'll stop me making any more of a dick of myself tonight too.

Chapter Sixteen
Bitter Wine

I leaned with a little too much reliance on the wall by my door as Rowan swiped my key card. White papers stuck out from the doorjamb. As the door swung open, I slid my hand over the edge of the paper and grasped it in my fingers. At a quick glance, I determined they were two more photographs. I shoved them into my bag while convincing my legs to walk through the doorway.

We stumbled into the room. That might have been my fault. Neither of my feet knew what they were doing and the photographs blew my limited concentration.

"Okay?" he asked, steadying himself against the small kitchen counter.

"... sure ..." I replied watching the floor undulate. My right foot hovered in midair while I waited for solid ground. I could see it coming.

"It's been quite a night," he said.

"That's rarely a good thing. Why won't the floor stand still?" I put my foot down expecting a solid surface to be closer than it was.

An arm encircled my waist and caught my fall.

"The floor's not moving, it's you."

"It's annoying whatever it is."

"Let's get you to bed," he said. His arm moved a little, the floor disappeared altogether as I felt a slight pressure on the back of my legs.

"I can walk," I protested. It was minimal at best.

"Cannot. You suck at walking."

"Well you suck at … at …"

Damn I had nothing.

"… at … *something.*"

I felt his muscles ripple as he laughed. "Do that again."

"What?"

"Laugh," I said. My head bumped on his shoulder. He smelled good.

"Shush," he replied. He was humming; his choice of song amused me. 'Put the boy back in cowboy.'

Words filled my swimming head and fell out my mouth, "Drinking champagne is stupid – if we'd been drinking Jack, I'd be fine now …"

The room over his shoulder spun. Concentric circles of light swirled around Doc's face.

Rowan's voice met my ears, "Honey, you haven't got the body mass to drink Jack."

"Wanna bet?"

Rowan carried me through the bedroom doorway. I saw colored circles cartwheeling out of control across the ceiling. They moved in time to the song in my head.

"Not good," I mumbled or maybe I just thought it.

He deposited me on the bed.

The room rocked back and forth, alternating the rocking with a twisted spin, music wafted on each movement. I was at a loss to tell if the song was real or in my head.

"What's not good?"

Oh so I did speak. The lights spiraled. "Spinning."

He laughed. "Don't lie down yet." Rowan moved pillows, piling them up for me to lean back on.

"When's your concert?" My words were so clear and coherent in my head, even though I had a sneaking suspicion I was slurring up a storm.

"Tomorrow night."

My eyes closed. My whole body swayed and started to twirl. My eyes pinged open. The swaying was at odds with the bed spinning.

"Whoa."

"Too much movement?" The enquiry came with genuine amusement.

"Not for a roller coaster."

Doc appeared. "Thanks for bringing her back safe," he muttered to Rowan. "I can take it from here." He didn't seem amused.

"See you tomorrow, Ellie." Rowan said. His lips brushed my cheek. "Thank you for a fun night."

"Goodnight," I replied. I'm sure it was fun but I doubted I'd remember much of it.

I don't know if I smiled or if I thought I did. I was living another one of those moments I'd bet forty million women would give their right arm for, except it wasn't like that at all.

"You need sleep," Doc said. "How do you feel?"

"Tired, drunk, okay."

"Drink some water," he said, lifting a glass from the nightstand and handing it to me.

I downed the entire contents of the glass.

There was something disjointed happening. The glass floated in midair then hovered over the nightstand before bumping down.

Way too much champagne. I felt nothing but unpleasant spinning.

Drunk. Not numb enough to feel nothing.

I scrunched down a little on the pillows and settled into a more comfortable position.

"Goodnight, Doc."

"Goodnight Conway."

If I hadn't been so drunk, it would've been a perfect moment. I could cope with the accompaniment of a quiet serenade while I drifted off to sleep, even if it was in my head, even if it was another Bon Jovi song.

A strange twist of conscience saw me try to determine if it was cheating to have Bon Jovi in my head while eating dinner with Rowan Grange.

My alcohol intake probably prohibited reasonable thought.

Laughter bubbled up and suddenly it wasn't laughter, it was an overpowering urge to vomit.

What a perfect end to a fabulously screwed day.

My feet hit the floor and I rushed to the bathroom. The darkness was almost as soothing as the cold porcelain.

I heard Doc say he'd get me a glass of water. He flipped the light switch. Light flooded the bathroom. "That's always going to be wrong, having the switch upside down like that," he said.

My head was in the toilet and cared little for the position of light switches!

This was the night that kept on giving.

Doc disappeared, came back and set a glass next to the sink. He crouched beside me and held my hair. I wanted to fall into the fuc'n toilet.

Somehow, my life had become a sitcom and mostly it wasn't even funny. It pretty much blew. As a matter of fact, it blew chunks. Surreal didn't even begin to cover the madness. The only thing I could come up with at that moment was that expensive champagne didn't make puke taste any better.

I sat back on the floor, pulled a facecloth off the sink and wiped my face. Part of me wanted to hold the cloth over my mouth and nose until I suffocated.

"Bed," Doc said as he stood up. His hand reached for mine, it was much nicer using his hand rather than the toilet bowl to haul myself to my feet. A wave of 'what a fuc'n idiot' hit me with a vengeance.

Wouldn't it be great if you could get a do-over when days turned to absolute shite?

Really, it's all fine. Because it was all so insane, that it had to be one of my more colorful hallucination interludes. I've gone from seeing things as parts of TV shows, to getting messages from songs, to living a full-on psychotic break involving a rock star of mega proportions, and he liked me enough to hang around. Absolutely fuc'n nuts.

At least I'm not a boring two-dimensional person. I have at least four dimensions or is that personalities?

The breathing in the room grew slower.
My eyes closed.

Chapter Seventeen
Wasted Time

Morning brought with it one hell of a headache. At least it was a hangover and not another migraine.

There was a reluctance to move on my part. I was warm and comfortable. Movement seemed like a painful thing to do. My head pounded as if a herd of elephants was stomping around in it and then there was the lingering feeling of idiocy, caused by recalling the night before.

It didn't get much worse than that.

"Morning," Doc said from the other side of the room. He was sitting, fully clothed on the edge of his bed, watching me.

"Morning," I replied finding my voice a little husky. "What day is it?"

"Thursday. How do you feel?" he asked.

"Crappy," I replied.

"To be expected. Food will help."

Why did he care? It was self-inflicted.

It didn't seem that important, the questions in my head faded, there was something else brewing.

Hope. Maybe I wasn't as lost as I thought.

Big fuc'n maybe.

"You awake?" he asked.

"Yes," I replied.

"You're quiet."

"Thinking."

"About?"

"The case."

I looked at my watch and I knew it wouldn't be long before Sam and Lee bashed on our door to brief me regarding the night's interviewing.

"Breakfast should be here already," Doc said.

"When did you organize that?"

"Last night when I saw the mess you were in when you got home," he replied.

I let it slide and sat up, immediately wishing I hadn't. My *everything* hurt.

"I need something stronger than Tylenol this morning," I muttered, swinging my legs over the edge of the bed. I didn't stand right away. I let the walls stop moving and the floor cease undulating first. "Something between Tylenol and Demerol."

He watched me. I felt his eyes. I heard his unspoken questions. My mind flicked on an internal sound track and a Bon Jovi song blared 'Something for the Pain.'

"I'll get you something for your headache."

I grinned at him. "I'm fine, honestly."

"Famous last words?"

"Maybe," I replied as I shut the bathroom door.

"I'm going to see if breakfast is here," he called.

I turned on the shower hoping to drown out the remnants of the night lurking in my head. Red-rimmed blue eyes stared blankly at me from the mirror as steam edged in. I looked like crap, which was good because that was exactly how I felt. It's comforting when things match up.

After a few minutes standing under hot water, I began to feel better. I tipped my head back and let the water tumble over my throat and shoulders.

Cleansing, soothing water washed away the night. The aches in my body dissipated barring the one slightly sore area over two ribs. I tried to see but couldn't quite.

Clean and revived I stepped out and dried off. I wiped the large mirror with the towel and checked my ribs again. A light bruise spread about three inches around my side. He must be made of steel. Body armor was called for if I intended on falling through a doorway and landing on Rowan again.

I sighed and pulled on the white robe and tied it low around my waist. My wet hair hung dripping down my back. It didn't matter if the robe got wet.

Once dressed, I chose to put the robe back on to keep my clothes dry. My head wasn't up to the noise associated with blow-drying my hair. On the nightstand were two small white pills and two slightly larger white pills with a note and a glass of water. "Two Codeine and two Ibuprofen, take them all. Your headache will thank you." I put them all in my mouth and swallowed them with a large mouthful of water.

Doc called out, "Breakfast!"

Breakfast was laid out at a small table. Doc was gone. Rowan pulled out a chair for me. "Thank you, where'd you come from and where's Doc?"

He shrugged. "I came by to check on you. Doc said I should stay for breakfast. He said to tell you, he's gone for a run."

I smiled. "Awesome."

"You coming tonight?"

"Don't have a ticket." I picked up my fork.

Scrambled eggs, just like mom used to make.

"I'm sure I could arrange that," he replied, lifting his fork laden with eggs.

I swallowed my mouthful. "It's okay, I have a badge ..."

He laughed. The atmosphere during breakfast was comfortable. Neither of us mentioned the more stupid events of the night.

Banter, verbal sparring and good coffee punctuated the first meal of the day. Laughter peppered the conversation.

"I've seen a few of your movies," I said.

"Read your book," he countered.

"Got three of your records."

"I've got your phone number." He grinned. "That one didn't work, huh?"

"Not so much."

"Okay, what about this then ... I've read your blog."

I leaned forward, napkin in hand and wiped his lip. "You have a little smudge ... Oh ... it's a tiny bit of bullshit stuck to your lip."

He laughed.

"I read it." There was pure sincerity in his expression.

"You've got better things to do than read my blog."

"Apparently not." Rowan laughed and then quickly began to précis my last three blog entries.

Instantly suspicious, I looked around the room and discovered my laptop open on the couch.

"How much are you willing to bet that I'll find a recent entry in my online history indicating someone accessed my blog this morning?"

Rowan grinned. "I never said when I read it, just that I had."

Damn!

"You should update that by the way. You have a lot of comments asking where you are."

"I'll get right to it."

A generous knocking at the internal door halted the conversation.

"Work beckons," I said.

He stood up. "I'll see you later."

"Maybe. Good luck tonight."

He let himself out as I opened the adjoining doors and let in Sam, Lee and Sean.

"There's coffee," I told them and disappeared to ditch the robe.

Their voices followed me. "Coffee and breakfast for two," Sean commented. "Where's Doc?" I heard a cupboard open and close. "She didn't stuff him in the cupboard."

Then Sam said, "Guess we know who the other person was – and it wasn't Doc."

I joined them a few minutes later, swinging my handbag from my fingers. Lee's expression indicated he had something on his mind and I figured we should get it out of the way before I shared the contents of my bag.

"Come on, spit it out." I gave his leg a shove.

His tongue flicked nervously over his lips. Nerves? From Lee? Color me surprised.

"What?" I asked.

"Give him a chance Ellie," Lee said, inclining his head back toward the hallway.

"Him?" I couldn't think of a 'him' except Rowan Grange. "You mean Grange?"

He nodded. "He's not like us; it's not a bad thing."

"A chance?"

Lee sighed loudly and whistled through his teeth.

"He likes you. Play nice."

Moi?

"Well, he hasn't given me anything to play with yet." As soon as the words left my mouth, I felt a pang of regret exponentially increase by the widening grin on Lee's face.

"Not even gonna touch that," he replied.

"Me either. It's gonna haunt me though, ain't it?"

"Hell yeah."

"Good to know."

"It won't hurt you to have some fun."

Fun? "He was there while I slurred, stumbled about half blind and fuc'n high. I doubt he thinks I am fun." It embarrassed me just thinking about it.

Lee's posture changed. "He didn't take advantage?"

"No, he didn't. No one in his right mind would've tried anything with me – Queen of the Porcelain Throne. Anyway Doc was here."

He relaxed again. I smelled a rat, not a rat exactly. More a conspiracy. I tested my theory.

"You and Sam discuss me much?"

Sam looked like he wanted to crawl under the chair he sat on.

"You are the center of our universe," he replied.

"Uh huh. Is that close to being the Messiah?"

"Yeah, Chicky Babe."

I could live with that. "Regarding Grange, the best I can promise at this stage, is ... not to shoot him."

"Good enough," Sam replied. Sean and Lee laughed. Doc came in the door a few seconds later.

He grinned. "You look better."

"I feel better, thank you." I actually meant it.

"I'll grab a shower," Doc said. He shut the bedroom door behind him.

"You two getting on okay?" Lee asked.

"Yeah, he's all right," I replied. "Don't get any freaky ideas. I'm not there yet with the whole dating thing. You don't need to vet every man I come across as a potential suitor."

Lee never could pull off innocent. "I didn't mean that at all."

I kicked his leg lightly. "Now, work ..."

From my bag, I withdrew four photographs and dropped them on the table.

Lee swooped on them first. "Where did these come from? Has Doc seen them?"

Separating them into groups of two, I explained,

"These two were in the doorjamb before we went out last night; the other two were in the doorjamb when we got back. Doc hasn't seen them. This is fairly significant – seems the freakozoid we're after likes pictures. Makes a nice change from Post-it notes."

"Doc hasn't seen what?" Doc asked, closing the door behind him. Sam was first to comment. "Jeans? Where's the suit?"

"I'm trying something new. What haven't I seen?" He jumped over an arm of one chair and sat with a plop in the seat.

Lee gave the pictures to Sam. He spent a few minutes staring at them then gave them to Doc who studied them with care, then placed them back on the table.

Sean picked them up one by one. "The gym photograph looks like it came from a security camera, as do the arrival and leaving of the casino photographs. But the one at the market – of you and Lee – someone snapped that."

"Lee, can you find out who has access to hotel security cameras and where exactly the cameras are; also same deal with the casino."

"I'll add it to the to-do list," Lee replied. "What do you think this means?"

"We're definitely not alone." I sat on the couch and lifted my laptop onto my knee.

Sam weighed in, "That porter who delivered the photo of Carla – might pay to have a chat with him. If he didn't deliver these pictures he may well know who did and who has access to the cameras."

I made a note then looked at Sean. "You wanna go dangle the porter over a balcony until he talks? Or maybe introduce him to some fun water sports?"

I don't like being watched.

"With pleasure. Gimme his name."

Sam coughed. "Waterboarding isn't a recognized sport."

I flipped a page in my notebook and concentrated on not smiling. "Raymond Huia, he's a night porter."

Sean excused himself. "I'll be downstairs with that ever-so-helpful concierge. I think he likes me."

Sam poured more coffee and sat down.

"So, tell me how the night went?" I asked.

"He's not Hawk. At least we don't think he's Hawk. It's rather hard for us to tell. This Hawk person is as elusive as the Jackal ever was," Lee said.

I didn't need that inference. It gave my warped mind more fodder for more strangeness. It lead to Bruce Willis disguised as a fat greasy Canadian to appear in my head.

"Do we have an ID on the man?"

Sam piped up with, "Originally he tried to have us believe he was Jimmy Tudeski. He carried identification that said as much."

Lee interrupted, "Just so happens *The Whole Nine Yards* was a movie I've seen a few times. We snapped him and his Bruce Willis character/persona real quick."

If just one of them looked like Bruce Willis this would be more entertaining

"Turns out he is Simon Zubrinich. A Russian national, who works for the Russian diplomatic corps on assignment in New Zealand. His last posting was DC," Sam said.

A diplomat. "Well that is fuc'n great," I bellyached. "And the woman?"

"He declares he'd only met her at the gaming table about an hour before we interrupted them," Lee said. He was as unconvinced as I was.

"We already know he's a liar. They touched. You don't touch someone you don't know," I said. "You don't pass things to someone you don't know either."

"He reckons he never met her before and that he didn't give her anything." Again Lee's tone implied disbelief.

"I saw them, they brushed arms and I'm sure he gave something to her."

Or the champagne may have made it look like that.

"I'll send Turner and Jay to pick her up," Sam said. "They're at our disposal."

I smiled. "Awesome. Did any of you ask to see her player's card?"

Sam nodded. "How'd you know she'd have one?"

Not much escapes me, even when I'm under the influence. "I noticed they foist them on almost everyone who steps foot in the casino."

Sam called Turner and gave them the address for the woman. The nice thing about checking someone's player card was all the information was right there and verified at the time of issue by photo ID. The casino had name, date of birth and current address on their computer system. All we needed was a name and date of birth to run an in-depth background scan. It could also tell us how often she visited the casino, if she swiped her card while playing slot machines.

"We need to know more about her. Run her details and see what comes up." I looked over at the boys. "What is her name?"

"Stephanie Harris."

Sam replied, "Doing it now."

I yawned.

Lee caught it. "Late night?"

"Yeah," I replied and said nothing more about it. They knew enough. Doc caught my eye and smiled. I knew then he'd say nothing. "What do we have on the diplomat?"

"We know he was in the DC region during the Butterfly Murders and he told us he was at one of the crime scenes. Apparently the crime scene on Vale Road was near his home."

Sam, Lee and I exchanged pained looks at the mention of the Vale Road crime scene. That was where Sam was stabbed. That was a day we wanted to forget but none of us could. In an instant, I was transported back a year and a half to a stormy night in Virginia.

Time stood still as the memory enveloped my hotel room and me.

***

The first thing I noticed as we re-entered Marie Kline's home was that the smell hadn't improved in the absence of her body. The rotting garbage brought stinging tears to my eyes as it assaulted my senses.

Lee and Sam looked around the rest of the house while Mac and I checked out the kitchen.

"What do you see?" I watched Mac's face. I saw concentration and brow furrowing.

We were standing next to each other in the middle of the filthy, creepy-crawly infested room. Things scuttled out of sight. Shadows made noises. Dark recesses filled with garbage moved inexplicably. Our shoulders touched and without warning, Tammy Wynette slipped into my head and belted out 'Stand By Your Man'. It was impossible to hold back a smile.

"I'm drawing a blank here, Babe," Mac said and turned his face to mine. "You're smiling."

"I'm standing by my man."

He laughed. "Tammy's joined the party, huh?"

The song stopped. Without warning, heavy footsteps ran from the house.

Lee hollered, "Sam's down!"

Everything faded to gray as I ran toward Lee's voice with my phone open in my hand, stopping abruptly in front of them both near the back door. It was as filthy as the rest of the house. Sam was sitting on the ground clutching his side, Lee was kneeling beside him.

"You get a description?" I asked Sam and Lee.

"Neither of us saw anything," Lee replied.

I had Comms on the line and told them to advise all police to be on the lookout for someone running away from the scene. Without a description there wasn't a lot anyone could do, except hope that someone saw the Unsub leave the premises, or noticed a stranger in the area.

I hung up and turned my attention to Sam.

"Sam?"

"It's nothing – a flesh wound." He winced as Lee opened the jacket Sam was wearing. "He hit me from behind, all I saw was a flash of steel in my peripheral vision."

Gray became red, deep velvet red, as it spilled through Sam's cream shirt.

"Your nothing is bleeding all over," I replied and made a decision to get him the hell out of there. We could make better time than an ambulance. Especially since emergency services were stretched to capacity by the storm. "Can you move?"

The dirt around us was a great motivator; the less time our wounded friend spent in the disgusting house the better.

"With help," Sam replied.

Lee applied pressure to the wound. I saw dark, almost black, blood ooze through Lee's fingers.

***

I looked into Sam's dark brown eyes. "You still with us, Chicky Babe?"

Doc looked at me, his brow furrowed.

"Yep, and so are you," I replied.

"Vale?"

"Vale."

I wiped my face with my hands and quietly thanked God for sparing Sam's life that day.

"You're okay, I'm okay and we're okay." I took a breath. "How'd you go pulling crowd photos and running a facial comparison?"

Doc relaxed again. "Lee was right about being at the Vale scene. He was there and it was definitely him we photographed watching as the house burned down. Found him at the Colts Neck scene in Reston too."

"Reston was the scene where we found the first bugs and wireless cameras. It was pouring with rain that night. I remember being horrified that so many people stood in the rain rubbernecking," I thought aloud. The personal impact from Reston was a lot less than the toll taken by the Vale Road scene.

Lee nodded and added, "And we have him at Tulley Gate from the security footage, showing a military pass to gain access to the Fort. Coincidentally the same day you were jacked."

Tulley Gate wasn't good. I'd chosen to meet an informant there and it ended badly. The Fort became the location of a siege after I was the victim of a carjacking. I had a knife fight with a Marine and a bullet nicked Mac's head. It was like some kind of old style war movie as we escaped through a tunnel to waiting medics. The only thing missing was William Holden or maybe Bruce

Willis.

"What you're saying Lee, is that Zubrinich is definitely involved with the cell, but we don't know his exact role?"

He nodded. "And we can't touch him for anything that happens while he is a diplomat," Lee added.

"We'll see who can touch him," I said. "Given that he was on a military base at the time of the kidnapping and assault of a Special Agent – *that* will give us something we can use."

"Or not," Sean added joining the conversation.

"We'll see," I replied. If I had to, I could put pressure on the Russian diplomatic corps, through the FSB. I was sure Misha could dig up something to help us. He could probably have Zubrinich recalled and delivered to FSB. After all Misha started this hunt for the terror cell.

Sam tapped my shoulder. "Chicky Babe ... the woman Harris. She's in debt for nearly five hundred grand, mostly in personal loans. She's missed the last four payments on her mortgage and hasn't made any credit card payments in four months."

"Not good."

"She's an account manager for a big medical company. Good wage, works hard, makes bonuses every month due to exceeding her targets. But she's broke, her four credit cards are maxed out, she has twenty-five dollars in her checking account and no savings at all."

"And she was at the casino. Not the place you'd expect someone in huge financial crisis. Or is it? Be interesting to see how often she swipes that card of hers at the casino. Lee can you get the casino to print us all her activity?"

"On it."

Sam continued, "Her history suggests she's got a gambling problem. She also has two kids. A female child aged twelve and a male child aged six. No husband. There are no custody orders for the kids."

"Could have a private arrangement with the dad," I said. "Try to find the father, if indeed he's still in the picture; also let's find out what she was given."

Her daughter was within the age range: nine to twelve years.

In the pause amidst discussions and coordinated efforts to locate the woman and child, there was a knock at the door.

I nodded to Sam, who flung it open with more gusto than possibly needed, sending a piece of white paper flying into the room. Sam stepped back, covering it with his size fourteens. Rowan stood in the doorway grinning. I watched the exchange between the pair.

"You always open doors like that?" he said to Sam.

"Some days I don't know my own strength," Sam replied with a wide smile.

"Come on in," I called over and beckoned to Rowan.

Lee dropped a file folder over the photographs on the coffee table. Sam bent down and retrieved the latest offering from the floor. He looked over at me and grinned.

It had to be bad.

Our work, our laptops and our guns lay about the table and other surfaces, with some floor spillage. I glanced over the mess quickly as Rowan picked his way around files and general business to reach me.

"Ready for a break?" he asked.

"We're really busy," I said.

"Lunch?" he offered.

"Any other day, I'd be delighted but now is just not good."

"Half an hour, everyone needs a break," he replied smiling. "Half an hour, Ellie, and then you can get back to catching bad guys."

"We're right in the middle of something ..." I was floundering. I couldn't fathom why he'd want to take me to lunch and work was pressing. Sam and Lee beamed at me like complete morons. Doc spoke, "We can carry on with this. Go to lunch."

"We're in the middle ..."

"Conway, take a break."

It took all my concentration to stop my middle finger flying.

"Half an hour, no more."

One flash from my eyes warned them to keep their collective smart mouths shut.

I picked my jacket off the back of a chair. It was a cotton blazer, not for warmth – it was warm enough – but to conceal what would be on my hip.

Rowan took it from me and held it up for me to put on.

There was a sense of merriment rising in my team. With another killer flash from my eyes, they turned their attention back to the screens in front of them.

I shoved my phone in my jacket pocket then clipped my holster to my belt.

"It's lunch Gabrielle, not Iraq," Rowan commented.

You could've heard a pin drop as the 'G' word hit the air.

"At least in Iraq you know who the enemy is," I replied.

"*Touché*," he replied with a nod. Rowan held his arm out to me and shepherded me toward the door. Over his shoulder he said, "I'll have her back in half an hour."

"SSA, we should have the rest of the info and Turner and Jay will have the Harris woman by then, all being well," Lee said. "Y'all have fun now, ya hear?"

"Security footage Lee, it's important, yeah?"

Lee nodded. "I'm sure Sean will have the information we need very soon."

Rowan lifted his hand in a small wave and grinned.

Sam's laughter followed us all the way to the elevator. I was acutely aware of the familiar sense of eyes watching.

Chapter Eighteen
Wish I Were You

Instead of 'Down' to the restaurant Rowan pressed the 'Up' arrow.

"Thought we were having lunch?"

"We are," he replied as the elevator doors slid open. I stepped into the carpeted coffin.

The elevator door opened again about four seconds later; it seemed a long four seconds. Post migraine and hangover elevator rides were not my favorite; it always felt like the walls were closing in. The notice on the wall proclaiming the lift was from Schindler Lifts did not help. My mind went from lift to list and I wanted out. I found I was a foot or two in front of Rowan and tried to disguise my hasty exodus. He came up behind me and covered my eyes with his hands.

"I don't need to see you, to kill you," I whispered.

"You're not going to kill me. Walk straight ahead ... ten paces then stop."

Curiosity kept him alive.

"Turn right."

He knocked and a door opened.

"Walk another five paces," he said, his mouth so close to my ear that his voice drifted in the breath of his whisper. A shiver ran down my spine.

A door shut behind us.

"Close your eyes."

He moved his hands from my eyes to my shoulders. "Open 'em."

Light flooded into my eyes causing me to blink a few times.

Laid out in front of me in a sun-filled room, I saw a beautifully laid table. White linen, red roses, chilling champagne and sparkling silverware.

If it looks too good to be true, then it probably is.

"Have a seat," he whispered in my ear, holding a chair for me.

From the sidelines, waiters appeared carrying covered plates.

Plates were uncovered in front of us. The champagne uncorked and poured. Then with a poof of theatrics, they were gone. Rowan sat opposite me, smiling. He appeared pleased with himself.

"Thank you," I said.

"You're welcome."

"How was your morning?" I asked. I could hear music but couldn't locate the source. It was faint, slowly increasing in volume. I recognized the song as 'Watch Out For Lucy', and Eric Clapton was definitely singing it.

Distracting.

"Good." He leaned back in the chair. Sun lit his hair. I almost needed sunglasses to look at him. "Went over a few things with the band, sound check and whatnot. Had a workout and organized lunch for a friend." His was an expressive face. Mostly, I noticed, it expressed his good nature. "Yours?"

"Work."

"Should I ask?"

I shook my head and found I was pretty much pain-free. I recalled his reaction during dinner and didn't want to repeat it. There was also the fear that I'd slip up and mention the photographs. I wasn't the only one being watched. And I wasn't sure if he was what he appeared to be.

My ghosts were calling me out.

The song started again. This time I could see the performance on my own private YouTube in my head. I knew it meant something and it would become apparent in time.

Rowan reached into his shirt pocket and placed an envelope on the table. He slid it toward my hand until it touched me.

"In case you can make it."

I opened the envelope and pulled out five tickets and five backstage passes. "This is very generous of you."

"I'd like if you could come." A wicked grin spread across his face. "I thought you might enjoy the show and it didn't seem fair to exclude the other four."

"Thank you."

As I watched his hands moving and listened to his conversation, I had an epiphany. I knew what it was that was so comfortable about him. He was calm.

Calm.

That was a rare commodity. I absently wondered if I could bottle it and take it with me, like smelling salts or something. Maybe hang a little vial around my neck for emergency use. It would have to be fairly concentrated if I was to do that. I toyed with my fork on my plate while I considered the possibility.

The Eric Clapton video started again. He was persistent and exceptionally talented. No wonder his fans sprayed painted 'Clapton is God' on the Islington Underground station all those years ago. My entertainment came to an abrupt stop when Rowan's hand waved in front of my face.

"Hello?"

"Hi."

"Penny for them ..."

"They're probably worth more than that, considering your net worth an' all."

Confusion clouded his face. "What are?"

I confessed to my outlandish earlier thoughts of bottling the calmness he exuded. Seemed better than trying to explain Eric Clapton's private performance. My daydream met with quiet laughter.

His eyes were watching me again, back lit by a smile.

My phone rang. Saved by the bell.

I swapped the glass of champagne for water as I listened to Lee fill me in on the developments downstairs. Sean had ascertained that two different people accessed the security footage from the hotel and the casino; one was a hotel security employee and the other an employee of the casino. Both people were paid by bank transfer to find pictures solicited by a third party. We can see the money going into the accounts but, tracing the deposits wasn't as easy as it should have been. Someone closed the bank account shortly after the money transfer. Everything was arranged online. They never met in person. Envelopes had been left at the front desk addressed to a hotel maid. According to the concierge, she picked them up. He had no idea what was in the envelopes. With a twang of a guitar string, I knew why I'd seen and heard the Eric Clapton song.

I'd bet money on her name being Lucy. I kept my comments to myself and continued listening to the update.

Sam discovered that the Harris woman had been given concert tickets in the casino. We now suspected it was her intention to sell her child to cover gambling debts and it would happen at the concert. All we had were our suspicions. It's not illegal to gamble, be in a casino, accept concert tickets, talk to foreigners, or to be in debt. We cannot legislate against stupidity. There was nothing concrete to say she would sell her child and nothing that gave us reason to hold her. There was still no word when the telecommunications company would have the plagued network back up and running smoothly. It didn't do much for my equilibrium. Those kids may as well not have cell phones. I wondered if that was why Abbey still had hers, because Bauer knew the service was crap. Or was it because no one cared and no one would call?

My phone snapped shut. I smiled at Rowan. "I need to get back. Lee is waiting outside," I said. I searched for words then found them lurking in the back corner of my mind. "We'll be there tonight."

Abbey was also supposed to be going to the concert. News had come back from the hospital. The kid's home life was such a mess, she fell for all the lies Bauer told. Harvey Bauer promised her the concert.

There had to be a reason why the kids were going to the concert, one with her mother, the other with the person who kidnapped her and Melanie with Emmett Smith. Maybe it was the trading point.

Lee was at the door for me. "The maid, her name is Lucy?"

Lee nodded but didn't ask how I knew. Eric Clapton stopped playing.

"We need to find her." As the words left my mouth, I felt we were too late.

I pressed the 'Down' button on the wall by the elevator doors. Lee stood next to me. When I glanced over, I noticed his stance, a dead giveaway of his former years in the military. He faced out into the hallway, his feet twelve inches apart and his hands, palms out and overlapping, behind his back. Parade rest.

The elevator dinged. The doors opened.

"Lee."

"Yep," he said, swiveling on one foot to face the open doors. I'd already stepped in and pressed a button to hold the elevator doors open.

A string hung in the middle of the elevator. A photograph dangled at eye level. I pulled latex gloves from my pocket and held the edge of the photo with them to see the picture. "Was that there when you came up?"

"Nope."

"Hinky."

The picture was of a hotel door with a 'Do Not Disturb' sign on it. I pulled out my phone. "Sam find out who is in room ..." I looked at the number in the picture. "Seven-four-five."

"On it."

I called Kurt. "Use the stairs; we're on level twelve by the elevator. Bring your gear. This could be bad."

Lee photographed the interior of the lift then removed the string and picture. I handed him an evidence bag. I would've made a good boy scout.

From down the hall I heard approaching footsteps. Kurt walked toward us, his backpack slung over one shoulder.

"Let's do it." We all stepped into the lift. I pressed level seven. As the elevator descended, my stomach fell into my boots and flopped about. Most unpleasant.

Kurt touched my elbow as the doors opened. "Bit pale, Conway. Try a few deep breaths."

"I'm okay."

"Don't pass out on us," he whispered.

Lee led the way to room seven-four-five. Sam ran toward us from the other end of the hallway.

"Got a key card. The room is empty. Occupants checked out this morning," Sam said. "Camera?"

Lee nodded and pulled one from his jacket pocket. He

snapped a few shots of the door. "Go."

Kurt and I stood back against the wall. Sam opened the door. He and Lee cleared the room: Sam gun drawn, Lee snapping pictures as he followed him.

"Chicky Babe," Lee called. "You were right, it ain't good."

I found him crouching between two double beds. Lee stood and moved out of the way as Kurt tapped his shoulder. With the changing of the guard, I witnessed the prone body of a young woman. Blood soaked into the carpet near her throat.

"Doc?"

"Someone cut her throat," he replied. He lifted her hand and showed me bloody stumps where fingers should've been. "Tortured before her throat was cut."

"Anything to suggest this is related to the kids?"

Kurt shook his head then looked up. "It's a bit of a co-incidence if it isn't."

"Dammit. A photo left in a lift and a dead housemaid. Tying up loose ends?" Did she look like a Lucy?

"If so, then that porter we interviewed best watch out," Sam said from within the bathroom. "Nothing in here."

It wasn't a good feeling, the crawling terror in my stomach. Sean started asking questions about photographs and envelopes left at the front desk and now we had a dead maid.

"Name badge or anything?"

Doc shook his head.

'Watch Out For Lucy' started up again. "Lucy," I whispered. "I'm sorry we didn't get to you in time."

"You know her?" Doc asked.

"No."

"Then how do you know her name?"

The room seemed suddenly still as words tumbled over each other and fell from my mouth. "I heard Eric Clapton singing; over the last half-hour he's sung the same song about four times. Her name is Lucy."

Someone knocked on the door. Sean stepped in. I indicated I wanted to talk to him and escaped Doc's bewildered stare. We stepped back out into the hall. Immediately I felt creepy eyes watching. Damn cameras.

I knew Sean and because I knew Sean, it seemed pertinent that I ask the hard question, "Did you do this?" I was only partly joking: I'd seen his handiwork in the past. I knew what happened when people withheld information from Sean O'Hare.

"No," he stated, unruffled by the question. "I've been looking for her and Raymond Huia. I believe my interview techniques are illegal in New Zealand."

That made me smile. "And most other countries."

"Most," he agreed.

"Looks to me like someone is tidying up loose ends. And that person wanted to know if Lucy had spoken to anyone about her deliveries."

Sean nodded. "I'll get the local police over here to deal with this. You got everything you need?"

I nodded and told my team we were leaving.

"Sean, meet us back in the room when you're done. We

need to find Huia."

"Will do."

Chapter Nineteen
Watch Out For Lucy

"What was her full name?" I asked.

"Lucy MacKay. Aged twenty-three. She was a student at Canterbury University," Sean replied. "Art major."

It was good to get confirmation that songs were still working for me.

"Huia?"

"Nothing yet."

"He must be somewhere," I said.

"You'd think. Thing is, no one has seen him. Family says he came to work yesterday and never came home."

"Door to door within the hotel." I watched Sean's facial expression for a clue as to how he felt. It was like reading a brick wall. "Have police finished with the crime scene?"

"Yes. The techs finished up a few minutes ago."

"Get Turner and Hooch in here."

"Jay, Ellie. His name is Jay. Although I think he's getting used to the Hooch thing."

Sam, Lee and Doc worked the laptops, looking for anything we may have missed concerning the connection between Lucy and Hawk.

A long thirty minutes later Turner and Hooch hustled into my hotel suite.

Turner spoke, "Raymond Huia showed up for work last night; no one remembers him leaving but he signed out."

"He signed out or someone signed him out?" I asked.

"Looks like his signature. Without sending it to the lab we won't know for sure."

Turner was all business. I liked the change in him.

Hooch piped up, "I have a list of all the guests who called the front desk for anything last night."

"Good work. And?"

"A list of empty rooms and guests who checked out this morning. We can't get a list of rooms with 'do not disturb' signs, yet. Housekeeping is still working."

"I think Raymond falls into the 'loose end' category. We'll split up. Sam and Lee, top floor working down. Turner and Hooch, first floor working up. Sean, the kitchens, restaurants, bars, staff areas."

"Alone?" Turner commented.

"Sean is the only one of us who is perfectly capable alone. He'll be taking the concierge with him to make sure hotel staff cooperate."

Sean grinned. "He might cramp my style."

"He likes you, have fun with it. He's knows more than he's letting on," I said with a smile. "Kurt and I are starting on this floor; we'll do the gym, pool, boardrooms, et cetera."

It seemed feasible that Huia wouldn't be that hard to find. Another dangled photograph would be my guess. But where? Not the elevator again, surely?

Sean stood by the door and issued a light warning. "Maintain regular cell phone contact. We don't know if the killer is still in the hotel or not."

The longer it took to play this stupid game with Hawk, the farther away the kids would be.

I stood outside the door and watched everyone file past. Sam slid his palm across mine, catching my fingers in his. "Be safe."

"You too."

Lee did the same.

Turner and Hooch headed for the stairs. Sam, Lee and Sean took the elevator. I waited for the door to open. Plenty of people would've used it by now.

Ping.

The doors slid open. My hand slipped to the grip of my Glock 17.

Eyes from nowhere watched. It made me jumpy ... my gun soothed me.

They all looked back and grinned. Nothing.

"Let's go."

Kurt fell into step beside me. We headed to the gym, using the stairs. No one was in there.

"I think we're looking for a photograph," I said from the middle of the room. There was nothing obvious taped to any of the large mirrors or suspended from the exercise equipment. A few minutes later Doc declared the room devoid of clues.

"Now where?" he asked, holding the door open for me.

"He likes to leave stuff for me to find." I was thinking aloud. "Rowan's room."

We'd come to a stop by the elevator. The elevator pinged and the door opened. I glanced inside.

Nothing.

Moments later, we bumped to a stop at our floor.

"This way." I led the way to Rowan's suite and knocked twice on his door.

When the door opened a piece of white paper floated to the ground. I bent down to grab it. With a mighty thwack, my head collided with Rowan's. Thick carpet cushioned my cheek.

Doc's voice flowed into my ears. "Up and at 'em, Conway."

Little birds tweeted above my head. A butterfly landed on Rowan's hand then glided to Doc and perched on the bridge of his nose.

"I'm okay," I said, letting Doc help me to my feet while the butterfly soared above his head. Standing wasn't much better than lying. The doorway tilted like a seesaw. My hand grabbed for the doorframe and missed, as it wobbled out of reach. A small butterfly swirled a trail of silver sparkles across my vision. Glittery letters effervesced from Doc's mouth, forming words I could see.

"Rowan, your head okay?" Doc asked.

"Yeah." He laughed. "Bit tender but all good."

Doc grabbed my arm. "Conway, lean back on the wall. You're making me sick with all the swaying."

I leaned.

"Picture," I said, wondering if it was real.

Doc retrieved it. Neither Rowan nor I moved. Doc showed me the photograph. I looked at it. It took a bit longer than normal for my brain to process the image.

A hotel door, the room number obvious and a 'Do Not Disturb' sign hanging from the doorknob. Doc took the picture and called the team.

"Room nine-eleven," he said into his phone then hung up.

"Ominous," I muttered as my legs slid out from under me. "Whoops."

A face peered at me, a light jumped from eye to eye then stopped.

"I'm fine," I said holding my hand out to Doc. "Help me up."

"Easy tiger. You're not as fine as you think you are," Doc replied, helping me stand.

"You worry too much," I replied, instantly aware of slurring.

"That's all I need to hear." He flipped his phone open and pressed three numbers.

I could still count.

"Rowan, take her arm."

I was trying to stand still but everything moved. Then I noticed it moved in time to a song. The walls pulsated to Aerosmith's 'I Don't Want To Miss a Thing.' Sound waves sparkled, morphing into butterflies with silver wings. My legs buckled.

The butterflies pulled at my sleeves, lifting and tugging. Aerosmith rocked an imaginary stadium. Steve Tyler was trying to stay awake so he didn't miss a thing. That was the 'aha' moment. I closed my eyes for a second, dug deep and straightened up.

If Tyler would just stop trying to swallow the microphone as he belted out a full-on stage performance, I'd be fantastic.

Steve Tyler became Mac, "Ellie suck it up, there's no time."

I rolled my neck. Yep, I was good. I looked at Doc and dared him to hear any slurring, "Put the phone away. I'm okay."

Armageddon. The song was from *Armageddon*, yet another Bruce Willis movie. It didn't bode well.

"Conway?" Doc appeared a smidge confused.

"Room nine-eleven, let's go," I replied as the last of the silver butterflies disappeared down the hall.

"I'm watching you," Doc replied.

"Isn't everyone?" I retorted. "Rowan, see you tonight." I stepped away from the wall. Rowan's hand stayed on my arm. "I'm going to need my arm back."

We hurried down one flight of stairs and onto the ninth floor. Reading numbers on doors as we moved fast was dizzying.

Ahead of me, I saw Sam and Lee. They were in position outside a room. Nine-eleven. Sam's forehead furrowed as heavy footsteps sounded behind me. I turned, hand on my gun. Sean pounded down the hallway.

He came to an abrupt stop a few feet from the door.

"All right?" I asked.

"Nine-eleven? That trigger any alarm bells for anyone else?"

I raised my hand. "What would you suggest ... calling

in the bomb squad because the room number is iffy?"

"Wouldn't hurt."

"We'll take a peek and if there's a dirty great big nuke sitting on the bed, we'll call in the bomb squad."

"And how about the trip wire across the door?"

I knocked on the door. There was no answer. "No one's home."

"Trip wires don't answer doors."

I shrugged, pulled my weapon free from the holster and swung the door open. "Nope, isn't one."

Sean let out a long sigh behind me. I sensed gritted teeth were involved.

Lee and Sam followed me into the room. "Watch your feet," I whispered. "Looks like a blood trail," indicating dark stains and shoe prints on the floor.

We searched the room for trip wires and living guests. None.

As the smell of blood assaulted my senses, I knew I had to acknowledge the scene in front of me, beside me, dripping from the walls around me.

"Doc, we got blood. We got brain matter and assorted tissue stuck on walls."

"I'm right here," he said from next to me. A gloved hand pointed to a baseball bat partially concealed by the bedding. "That's the kind of weapon I'd expect to find."

"Okay, so someone beat the snot out of him with a baseball bat and then hacked him into pieces with some-thing sharp."

Lee called from the bathroom. "I gotta head." A few

seconds later he added, "And both feet and his hands."

"Awesome." I turned slowly on the spot taking in the entire room. "Hawk is seriously pissed off or he's not alone."

Sam did a head count. "The cop, the woman in Wellington, the hotel maid and now our porter friend. All killed in different ways."

"Yep, and the only one even coming close to his MO is the Wellington woman. She had that peaceful look to her."

Lee emerged from the bathroom. "Huia's expression is about as far from peaceful as a person can get."

"How did no one hear this? People don't usually sit still and silent while being beaten with a baseball bat." It made no sense to me.

"He was gagged. The gag is still in his mouth. There's tape residue around his wrists and feet," Lee replied.

Doc was poking around the room and found pieces of Duct tape stuck to the arms and legs of a chair. "This explains a lot."

I took a closer look. "Tool marks on the metal of the arms and legs and lots of blood around."

"He could've been still there when he was dismembered," Doc said. "And you don't think Hawk did this?"

I shook my head. A butterfly flew across the room. Weird.

"I think he had this done but didn't partake in person."

Sean was standing nearby and had something to say. "While I was making enquiries in the kitchen, the head chef told me two heavy and very expensive meat cleavers went missing last night."

"Doc? Cleavers?"

He was leaning over a section of leg inspecting the bone. "Could've been a cleaver. It wasn't a saw."

I swallowed as hard as I could but there was no stopping the gagging. My hand clamped over my mouth as I ran for the hallway. On the way past Sean, he thrust an empty paper evidence bag into my hand. Clever.

Between retching, I could hear the beep of cameras and the scratching of pens and pencils on paper. Sam and Lee were photographing and sketching the crime scene.

Sean came out and used his phone. He called police to let them know about the crime scene and requested a forensic team.

There was no way I was going back into that room. So I sat down and waited for my team to finish.

A few minutes later, my phone rang. It was Carla.

"You okay?" I asked.

"Yes. When are you coming home?"

The 'yes' was negated by the question.

"Soon as I can. You sure you're okay?"

"I am. I just ... wish you were here."

"Me too, kiddo. Say 'hi' to Caine. Be good. I'll be home before you know it."

"Someone is still watching me."

"I know. And I wish I were home. Be very careful and don't go anywhere without Caine or my dad. Promise me."

"I promise. Please come home."

"Soon as I can. Now go to bed! It's late over there."

We hung up. I was left feeling crappy. I wanted to be home. The snaking, horrid fear I experienced every time Hawk left a picture of Carla, returned. It was a reminder that I couldn't protect her from New Zealand.

Heavy feet shook the floor as police officers descended on room nine-eleven. It was time for us to go.

Chapter Twenty
Summertime

The noise, the overpowering smell of alcohol, the hyped-up crowd: all plastered on a backdrop of dread. There was no mistaking how much fear I held in check. We knew, from the interview with the casino guy, Zubrinich, the handover of the kid was going to be at the beginning of the sixth set. Zubrinich became quite chatty once faced with the Russian equivalent of the FBI. I'd heard the FSB (Federal'naya Sluzhba Bezopasnosti or Federal Security Service) were capable of effective interrogation. We had Misha to thank for the information. He also told us the woman would identify herself as Sarah H, to a man who would call himself Joe Hallenbeck. Again with the Willis movie characters. It was possible that the woman wouldn't make it out of the concert alive. Hawk wasn't leaving loose ends.

I had a set list from Rowan's tour manager and knew we had fifteen songs to find the woman and the kid. They planned seven sets of three songs each and then a five-song encore. The fifteenth song was 'Hide and Go Seek.' Creepy and apt considering the circumstances.

We arrived early, before the gates opened and briefed the security guards. We asked them to keep an eye out for any adults bringing kids into the stadium. It would slow down the entry but we wanted a list of seats with kids in them, if they could do it. I handed out driver's license pictures of the Harris woman and a photo we'd found on Facebook of Shannon Harris. The guards on the gates also had photos of the missing girls Melanie Talbot, Nicola Gallagher, Tasha Calvino and Samantha Rowe. All we could do was hope the security people called through seating areas and numbers of anyone with a kid under sixteen. I didn't expect miracles, especially as the crowds of people swelled. They expected nearly forty-eight thousand people to swarm through the gates looking for their seats.

We were looking for needles in a haystack.

As everyone settled and the gates closed, the seven of us split up a long list of seats containing kids. I tried not to think about Carla but failed. I wanted to find the New Zealand kids and go home as fast as possible so I knew she was safe.

It was stunning how many young kids were at the stadium. I drew the short straw and took the highest stand and the Gold seating area. Slowly I began walking down the concrete steps from the top of the stadium looking for the kids in my area. A cold wind whipped around, making me shiver.

I crossed two boys off the list, both under ten, before the crowd erupted, screaming and chanting for the band. I looked down at the stage and saw them run out one by one. Rowan was last.

The music hit me like a freight train as Grange powered from the stage. I staggered just a little. As I looked down at the stage, I wondered if I could jump inside a song.

Concentrate Ellie.

Rowan kept singing and I wanted to dive right in.

Scenery blurred, the stadium below me distorted and all I heard was the music. Lost within the song and Rowan Grange's voice, I remembered why I was freezing my ass off up in the gods.

Sure as shit, it wasn't for the good of my health.

It felt nothing like summertime. Where does anyone get off calling this Antarctic blast summer? For the first time ever I was grateful for my FBI-issued bulletproof vest, keeping my torso warm.

This is one warped place.

My phone vibrating drew my hand instantly to my pocket. My cold fingers fumbled as I flipped it open.

"Ellie?"

Over the rocking stadium, I heard Sam's dulcet tones.

"Where are you now?" he asked.

"Up high, searching the top tier of Gold, you?"

"Up front."

"Lucky bastard! I'm fuc'n freezing up here."

"See anyone?"

"Not yet. Where is the rest of the team?"

"Sean's up in the stands with you somewhere, Lee is on the ground. Doc is up top somewhere; Turner and Hooch are making their way through the standing crowd."

From where I stood I saw a line of police in reflective jackets enter from the left of the stadium.

The noise rose as the song ended. I covered one ear

with my hand to try to hear Sam better.

"I see the police have filed in. They're on the left, by the barricade. Can you get to them and brief them? Pass out the pictures."

Hope hinged on a dreadful driver's license picture.

"I'm heading there now."

"Keep me posted."

I hung up and went back to searching faces in the crowd. If I could get the camera guys to flick up crowd pictures it would be helpful.

It would be even more helpful if they could also show seat numbers and a clear picture of where it was in relation to me. I filed the first part of my idea away as a last resort. The rest was wishful thinking.

The stage seemed miles away. My eyes gravitated to the big screen. Rowan was front and center. The noise died down a little as he spoke. He introduced a song. From the giant screen, he looked out into the crowd. His eyes searched in front of him; I felt he was looking for me.

Who else was looking for me?

I turned away and back to the task of scanning faces near me.

Rowan's voice rang out. For the first time it was clear enough for me to hear every word, "Out there tonight is someone I was lucky enough to spend time with recently and, I hope to count her as a friend." From the giant screen, he grinned and winked. The crowd exploded.

With a direct stare into the camera he said, "Are you

ready to fly?"

Carla would've had such a kick out of that, if she knew it was me he was talking about.

The band launched into a familiar song from the new album. It was weird and slightly scary hearing him talking about me. The screaming was intense and cameras flashed from every direction. I made my way down from my designated area and, in the back of my mind, I wondered if anyone was photographing me. Guess I'd know soon enough. My search continued on the next level. About ten minutes later my cell phone rang again. I pulled it from my pocket and watched the huge screen in front of me, hoping for a telling crowd shot.

Where the hell were they?

The ringing continued so I answered the call. I had to cover my other ear to hear Sean at all.

"Where are you?" Sean asked.

"Upper bowl," I yelled into my phone. The three people closest to me turned and looked. I smiled. They glared. I turned my back on them displaying the big glowing yellow letters on my jacket that read, FBI.

There was muttering around me. I chose to ignore it as I tried to listen to Sean and his account of the search so far. I resisted the temptation to open my jacket and reveal the Glock 17 on my hip.

We were working on information provided by the casino guy and information provided under duress was not the most reliable. Even so, I hoped to find the woman from the casino before she handed over her kid to Hawk and wound up dead somewhere. Trying to fathom why a mother would sell her offspring was near impossible for me. I knew that catching her mid-transaction would make everything gel and give police reason to charge the woman.

Okay, we knew that gambling addictions were as destructive as drugs. Maybe Sam was right and she couldn't see another way out. If selling kids gave this woman a way out of debt then she needed another option. Jail was a good alternative in my book.

"What section did he say the tickets were for?"

"He said Gold … but both you and I have been here for forty-five minutes now and haven't seen anyone matching the description."

"I'm moving down," I told him.

"Me too," Sean said and we hung up.

The huge screen above the stage captured my attention. I dragged my eyes off Rowan and descended the concrete stairs to the next section.

My phone rang again. I cursed aloud; no one around me could hear me above the band anyway.

"Ellie, we got a …" Sam yelled in my ear but I could barely hear him over the noise around me.

I clamped a hand over my other ear. "We got *what*?"

"Bomb threat! Some idiot called the police and said they'll detonate a bomb in the crowd at nine-thirty tonight."

"Clear the stadium. Take control of the situation." The news tweaked my internal suspicion button because I knew that Hawk had used explosive devices before, and chlorine gas, either of which carried vast destruction potential.

"We have to evacuate," Sam inadvertently yelled in my ear. He must've had police nearby, I heard him say, "I'm in command."

I continued delivering orders via phone, "Brief the police. Get paramedics standing by – Doc can deal with them. We need a bomb disposal unit and explosive-detecting dogs and get Lee and Sean to step up the search. Get the band off that fuc'n stage!"

Sam issued the instructions and I hung up. There went my notion of not interfering with the concert.

No one was watching me. All eyes appeared focused on Grange. I suspected the people around me were too engrossed in the entertainment to listen to my conversation.

It was as it should've been and I would've been enrapt too, given half a chance.

I set an alarm on my phone for five-minute intervals.

Of course, the blame squarely landed on Finagle's Law of Dynamic Negatives. Anything that can go wrong, will. Which is different from Murphy's law which states 'If there are two or more ways to do something and one of those ways can result in a catastrophe, then someone will do it, at the worst possible time.' I wasn't entirely convinced of Murphy's inappropriateness. The jury was still out. Between Finagle and Murphy, anything can, everything could, happen.

I needed to get the hell away from all the people before the nightmare broke loose. From where I stood, the ground seemed like a quick fall away. I didn't look down for fear of falling off the edge as I scurried down the concrete steps to the next level, then ran through the concrete tunnel to the wide-open spaces of the concourse.

A few people milled about. People were coming back from the bar with drinks, or going to and from the toilets. I scanned faces as I moved quickly. Parts of the floor were wet, very wet, as if recently hosed down, maybe to remove vomit. Why would anyone pay a small fortune to see a band like Grange and waste the experience by drinking enough to puke? Somewhere deep in my subconscious I saw a pot call a kettle black. The subtle reminder of a not-so-distant champagne-filled night caused a lapse in attention. I slipped and grabbed the wall to regain my footing.

Someone called out to me, "Hey, where are you going?"

The person was a few yards in front me, wearing a security uniform. I pulled my badge from my pocket and hung it around my neck as I slipped and slid, trying to hurry over to him.

"I'm Supervisory Special Agent Conway. How many of you are there out here?" I pointed to the stadium grounds.

"Six of us."

"Are your radios working?"

He appeared to find my question strange. If I was

Hawk and I'd planted a bomb, I'd be interfering with radio and cell signals just to mess with people.

"Yes."

"In a few minutes the stadium is going to empty. It's going to be total mayhem because *no one* will want to leave. Do you have an evacuation plan?"

He nodded, confused.

Of course they did.

"Then begin to follow your plan."

"Why are we evacuating?"

They should know about it by now!

"Bomb threat," I replied. As if leaving wasn't going to cause panic enough, let's up the ante with a good old-fashioned bomb threat. "Can you handle this area? I've got to keep moving."

"Yes," he said with a sudden burst of authority. He hit the squawk button on his radio and announced to his fellow guards that they were evacuating.

"One other thing," I said, pulling pictures of the missing teens and of the Harris woman from my pocket.

He nodded.

"If you see these people, detain them."

I ran on, following the curved concourse and trying to find a way down. My phone beeped. It was the first reminder. We had fifteen minutes to clear the stadium. Any second I'd be running against the current and unable to get to the stage at all.

That thought terrified me and I couldn't fathom why.

I called Sean while I running. "Turner and Hooch ...

where are they and are they wearing body armor?"

"They're wearing stab-proof vests and they're beside the stage with the band's cars."

"Do we know where this bomb is?"

"In the vicinity of the stage is all we have."

And the Unsub is so trustworthy we should immediately believe him? My internal voice erupted with 'We have no choice.'

"Get a dog to go over those cars." A ghastly feeling of impending doom flowed through my body. "Sean, tell all police to wear ballistic body armor. Stab-proof won't help in this situation."

"On it."

It was hard work convincing myself security never left the cars.

Normally security never left the cars. This wasn't normal.

Another concrete tunnel led me into deafening noise. The stage was still far below me. Rowan called for calm in the crowd.

People rushed toward me. They were anything but calm. I saw angry, panicked and annoyed – but no calm.

I ducked under arms and dodged around people making my way down more steps to another level. This time I chose not to go through the tunnel. I vaulted over the rail and swung into the landing below me. I continued on my new trajectory downward, running down steps, evading the building panic and vaulting over railings onto the landings below.

Rowan was still on stage, so were the rest of the band. Soon I was too low down to see behind the screened-off area, so couldn't tell if the dogs had finished going over the cars. I made it to the grass. The middle was clear because the alarmed crowd of people all jammed themselves into the corners trying to get out.

Police wearing stab-proof vests still lined the barricade as I hurtled toward the stage. A cop stepped in front of me. I came to an abrupt stop.

"Found anything?" I asked, grabbing my badge and shoving it in his face. I was not in a charitable mood. Bombs make me edgy.

"No ma'am," he replied.

"You all need to put on ballistic body armor. Anyone without it is putting themselves at risk."

I vaulted over the barricade and crossed the remaining four feet to the stage edge without replying. Rowan leaned down and held out his hand, which I took as I clambered onto the stage.

"What the *fuck* are you still doing here?" I hissed at him trying to control my breathing and the exasperation I felt at seeing him and the band still on stage.

"Making sure everyone leaves."

"This is not a ship. You are not the captain. Get the fuck out of here!" I looked beyond Rowan at the rest of the band. "Go!"

Turner and Hooch appeared from the right side of the stage behind a black curtain. "They're clear," Turner called.

"Get the band into the cars and gone," I replied.

Rowan still held my hand. I shook it off.

"Are you coming?" he asked.

"Not yet. Now give me some of your calm and get the fuck out of Dodge."

I looked out over the stadium.

Then looked again.

Someone was moving away from the exits. The person was running along the first row of seats and hiding as they went. I tugged my phone from my pocket and made a call. "Hey Sean, heads up ... Someone moving quickly, first row toward the Crusaders' logo on the pitch."

"I'm over that way, I'll intercept."

Hooch called out, "Everyone's in the car except Rowan Grange."

That was because he'd grabbed my hand again. "Go," I said, pulling my hand from his grasp.

"I'll be waiting." His usual easy smile vanished without a trace. "Be careful."

I sent him across the stage to Hooch and he looked back, I felt his eyes. Standing on the stage, I was aware of other eyes, watching.

Police handlers and dogs appeared from the very back of the stage. The crowd slowly dispersed through the exits amidst screaming and crying.

Behind the black curtain, the last car left the area. Road cordons gave them a clear path out. One less thing to worry about.

Dogs sniffed all the equipment and grid-searched the

entire stage. Two more dog teams scoured the stands, starting at the edges, moving slowly in.

Sean ran toward someone.

Lee was visible from my right, moving toward Sean; Sam was heading across the pitch to help. I looked for Doc and spotted him hurtling down the concrete steps not far from where I'd been. I shoved my badge inside my vest so it didn't bounce into my face, jumped off the stage and ran to meet them clutching my phone in one hand.

As I neared the bottom of the stands, something whizzed past my head. I ducked. A familiar sound followed.

The report echoed around the stands. I dove over the low wall separating the stand from the grounds and pulled my gun. Doc disappeared from sight. I pressed the button on the side of my phone and said, "Gunfire."

My fingers scrabbled into my pocket searching for a wireless microphone and receiver.

I depressed the button on the side of my phone again, opening the channel to the rest of my team and said, "Go wireless."

Another shot rang out. I pressed the receiver into my ear then flipped the tiny switch on the microphone and pinned it firmly to my collar.

"Check in," I said.

"Sean, check."

"Lee, check."

"Kurt, check."

Within seconds, I could hear Sam's voice in my ear

with digital clarity.

"Sam, check. Direction of gunfire?"

"Maybe toward the edge by the screened-off area," I replied.

The boys would've all heard the report but sounds distorted in a stadium. We needed another shot to determine direction. Our ears would adapt, calculate and more accurately discern the shots from the echo. We needed one but didn't want another one.

Another shot rang out.

I jammed my phone back in my pocket and said, "Sean, did you get that person? Over."

Sean said, "Copy. It's a kid. Over."

"*The* kid? Over."

"Copy. Her name is Shannon Harris. This is the kid," Sean replied. "I have Shannon Harris. Keep your head down. Lee's moving toward you. Over."

I looked to my right and saw feet running. It wasn't Lee. The shoes belonged to a much younger and smaller person. The feet climbed. I shoved my gun back in my holster and ran, remaining as crouched as I could, following the feet. Four different whispers in my ear demanded to know what I was doing. I whispered back, "Following someone. Over."

The feet went up two rows of seats then stopped. I reached them with minimal breaking of cover. It was a young girl.

I grabbed at the girl's arm and pulled her down behind seats in the nearest row. The rest of her body followed. It was the only cover we had.

"No, No, Stop!" the kid screamed while trying to pull her arm free.

"Shut up," I hissed clamping my hand across her mouth. "I'm a cop."

She was breathing hard and trying to back away but she was up against a seat; there was nowhere to go.

"Calm down. Who are you running from?"

"A man," she puffed. "He bought me here to see the concert. He said I could meet the band."

"This man is where?" I asked, not seeing anyone chasing her.

"I don't know, I ran when the bomb thing happened. He said we were meeting his friend and I'd like him."

I spoke to the kid, "What's your name?"

Another bullet whizzed past us.

"Nicola Gallagher."

"Happy to meet you, Nicola." She slumped into a gap under a chair seat and began to cry. "I'm Special Agent Conway and we've been looking for you and some other girls."

"You're American."

"Yes. FBI." I spoke into my collar. "Lee, did you get that? Over."

"Copy. Nicola is safe. Maybe this shooter wants them too, over."

"Maybe so, over," I replied and dragged the kid further down into the cover provided by the seat backs in front of us. "Are you hurt? Did the man you were running from hurt you?"

She shook her head; her long hair tumbled wildly about her shoulders.

"Doc, negative on injury, over."

"Roger and out," Doc replied.

I directed another question at Nicola. "What's his name?"

"John McClane."

Was our Unsub really a Bruce Willis fan?

"Where've you been all this time?"

"Moving around, we moved a lot. I said I wanted to go home. He said Mom knew where I was and it was okay. He promised I could meet Rowan Grange. I was going to meet a rock star."

This little girl should've been home playing with Bratz dolls, not interested in meeting rock stars and definitely not hiding from a shooter in a stadium.

I whispered into my collar, "Sam ... Do we have a location on the shooter? Over."

"I'm on him like white on rice, Chicky, over."

"Good to know. Do you reckon the other kids are here? Over."

"I reckon so. Sam out."

Nicola tugged at my arm inviting my full attention. "We were going to meet someone with another girl, here somewhere."

"Do you know her name?"

"Samantha, I think that's what he said on the phone."

"Did you all hear that? Over."

Four yesses came back.

I scanned the area, looking for anyone trying to creep up on us.

My legs were starting to cramp crouched the way I was. The temptation to simply stand up was strong. If we stood and moved fast, I reasoned we had a good chance of getting to the nearest tunnel. Moving targets are hard to hit.

Unless of course the shooter is a sniper and using a halfway decent rifle. Not a thought I wanted to entertain because it narrowed the possibility of escape – and my legs hurt.

I grabbed Nicola firmly by the hand and then freed my gun. Her eyes widened.

"You have a gun?"

"I'm FBI. We do guns," I said with a smile. "You and me, we're going to run now." I indicated a tunnel ahead of us, a few rows up. "We're going to run up those stairs over there and into that tunnel."

"He'll shoot us!"

Her panic swelled.

"No he won't," I told her firmly. "He won't because my team *will not* let that happen."

Sam, Sean, Doc and Lee would be scoping our location and listening to everything I said. I needed them to cover us. I pretty much wanted them to open fire on the stadium.

The dogs and handlers from the stands were pulled back for their own safety. All police were now dispersed and in covered positions. I knew some were armed and more armed officers would be on the way.

I let Nicola go for a second and spoke to Lee. "Lee, we need cover fire, but for god's sake don't hit anyone! Over."

"It's too risky, Ellie. Sam and I have narrowed his position and have armed police coming up behind him. Lee out."

Oh, crap.

"Sean, does your kid know anything about a bomb? Over."

"I'll get back to you on that, Sean out."

"Did he mention a bomb?" I whispered to Nicola.

Nicola grabbed my hand. She stumbled over words, "He said it wasn't real. The bomb, I mean."

"And it probably isn't," I replied, as her hand squeezed mine tighter and her fingers dug into my palm.

"Then why is everyone looking for it?"

Everything in front of me spelled the beginning of the end. It was all wrong and there was a sense that it would end badly. I let some of Rowan's faith and calm wash over me.

With composed gentleness, I answered her question, "It's what everyone has to do when a threat is made."

A scream poured from the tunnel. We stared at each other for a beat. Her eyes grew wider and more panicked.

"You can do this," I said and adjusted my grip on Nicola's hand. "Now, run."

We ran up the steps. Gunfire erupted behind us. She

tripped; I dragged her back to her feet and kept moving, clambering quickly up the last steps then along a short flat area and into the tunnel. I pushed Nicola over to the semi-safety of the thick concrete walls and shadows.

"Stay here," I whispered. "I need to see where the screaming came from."

"Don't. Leave. Me. Here." Panic punctuated her small voice. Her words broke apart sending, tumbling into the atmosphere.

Another scream pierced the air. It caught several of the syllables in midair and shot them like arrows across the pitch.

"Wait," I replied firmly. "Sit down and wait."

She sat. I must've hit the right tone. Kids and animals, it's all about tone.

Inching forward, gun in hand, I hugged the wall until the end of the tunnel. No noise. I peered out and looked around.

No one was there. Down the concourse on the left were bathrooms. That was the only place I could see where someone could hide.

I turned back to Nicola. I couldn't let her out of my sight while I sauntered off to check the toilets. Anything could happen.

My mind tried to stop the last image I had of leaving someone alone. There was no way to escape the associated guilt, because I couldn't get past feeling that I had left Mac and Carla alone and the subsequent events were my fault.

That wasn't right. Mac wasn't alone: there were cops everywhere. He was sitting in the back of my car with Carla while I went to view a crime scene and interview a woman possibly responsible for the death of Carla's mother. Yet within minutes, Mac and the suspect were both dead. It left me twisting in the wind trying to figure out what happened.

A gust of cool wind flowed down the tunnel, messing my hair, freezing my ears.

I moved quietly. I listened for any signs of life from the concourse behind me and filtered out the chatter I could hear from the boys as they discussed movement.

Ignore the wind.

It was too quiet.

In my head, the scream echoed on.

Ignore the scream.

My voice croaked as I whispered into my collar before reaching Nicola, "Too quiet, not good. I need backup. Over."

The wind blew a gust into my face. A waft of familiar cologne hit me like an open-handed slap.

My mind was deciphering the discrepancies. If some-one was on the concourse with a kid, where did they go? There was no way out of the stadium.

I hadn't heard any footsteps.

With no one around and nothing to absorb sound, footsteps would've been audible out on the concourse. Echoes should've slipped down the tunnel like the cologne.

Closed and guarded exits. Police working their way through the complex.

Where did they go?

The bathroom.

Radio procedure was foremost in my mind as I issued a priority message. "Break-Break. I need you to come up the front of the stands. I repeat, the front, use external stairs. Over."

Coming up from the inside would put my backup in harm's way, if indeed there were to be someone hiding in a bathroom. The ramps were open and the wide-open concourse provided no cover for us and enabled a shooter to get clear shots from the bathroom areas and access tunnels.

Nicola was crouched, pale, shaking, and studying me.

Innocent eyes.

I signaled to her to stay where she was and moved back a few feet toward the concourse.

Another puff of air filled the tunnel and on it sailed remnants of the same cologne.

"Sean, what's above us? Over."

"A conference room, or something like that. Over," Sean replied.

"Does it overlook the stadium? Over."

"Yes and half the city. Over."

Anyone up there would've seen the police, seen the band leave, seen the kids and seen us. Hell, they would've seen everything.

"He could be up there. Over."

"Yes, but he can't shoot from there, Ellie. Over."

It's worse than someone shooting from up there. Someone up there has a bird's eye view of the entire stadium.

"He can direct a shooter. Over."

"Copy. Jesus," Sean muttered on a hiss of breath.

"I need someone with me. We gotta get these kids to safety. Over."

Knowing I was responsible for children was gnawing at my gut and it was a horrible feeling.

"Copy that. On our way, Chicky Babe. Over," Lee replied.

Shots rang out again, followed by a clear voice somewhere below me, "Armed police. Drop your weapon."

Another shot from below me somewhere.

A single report in reply.

And Sean's voice, "They got the shooter. Over."

One down.

Nicola cried out and ran toward me. Beyond her terrified figure, I saw Sam and Lee block the tunnel entrance. No sign of Doc.

"It's okay," I said, as she hid behind me. "Sam and Lee didn't mean to scare you."

They both sprayed beaming smiles at the kid who cautiously peered around me. She noticed the badges they wore around their necks. "Same as yours," she said quietly.

"They're with me."

She started to smile at Sam and Lee and then let loose

an ear-piercing squeal. "Oh my gosh!"

Lee's smile dropped clean off his face as Nicola launched herself at him.

Oh, for the love of God! Lee caught the kid. She sobbed hysterically into his chest. It'd all been a bit much for the poor kid.

Sean's laughter bounced in my head.

I spoke to him, "Can we take her out the way Sam and Lee came in? Over."

"Copy, all clear out here. Lee, bring her to me. Over." Sean said.

Lee looked at me and nodded. "Off we go," he said and scooped up the kid into his arms.

Sam and I waited until they were out of sight. Our ears filled with the fading sobs through Lee's microphone.

With a little luck, we're all going to get out of here.

"Come on," I said to Sam, leading the way.

We checked for movement before leaving the only cover around and ran quietly along the wall to the first bathroom.

"Who do you think it is?" Sam asked.

"Samantha, Tasha, or Melanie, or maybe all three."

Sam went in first. I followed closely behind.

"FBI," he said softly, his deep voice echoing regardless, in the concrete room. "Samantha? Melanie? Tasha? Anyone here?"

Sam moved down the row of stalls, pushing each door wide open as he did.

"Samantha?"

No one replied.

"Melanie?"

"Tasha?"

The last two doors looked properly shut. Sam flung the first one open.

Empty.

I pushed open the next one.

Jackpot.

Chapter Twenty-One
Wild Horses

Curled beside the toilet in the cramped stall, covered in blood, was a young woman. She wasn't moving.

I stepped closer and felt my breath stick in my throat. I knew right away that she wasn't any of the missing girls. She was older but not old enough to be the Harris woman.

"Hello?"

Her eyes opened.

My heart thumped so hard I thought I was going to vomit. She was alive.

"I'm Special Agent Conway. We're going to help you."

She looked up and started to struggle to her feet. Her hands were pressed tightly to the side of her neck. Blood cascaded through her fingers. My instinct was to get her out to where I could help her. The toilet cubicle was gross and there was no room for me to get close to her, and certainly no room for paramedics. Paramedics need room.

Her voice crackled and emitted a quiet word, "Samantha?"

The movement caused blood to gush from her neck. She moved her hand and I got a faceful of blood. I wiped my eyes and took her arm. She swayed precariously. Blood poured. The floor was slick and hard to stand on.

I clamped a hand over hers on her neck and slowly I backed out of the stall taking the messed-up young woman with me. The full light of the open room gave me a better idea of her injuries. I also took a good look at her face. Her eyes and jawline looked familiar. Sam pointed out the trail of blood she'd left along the wall and floor as she moved out of the cubicle. She started to fall, Sam and I held her, lowering her to the ground with care and resting her back against the wall. I wadded up paper towels and held them to the gash in her neck, hoping to stem the flow of blood. I spoke into my collar, "Break-Break. Doc I need you up here. Over."

Doc replied, "Copy. I'm on my way. Over."

I turned my attention to the woman. The paper towels were soaked in blood. I wadded up more towels and pressed them over the soaked towels against her neck.

"What's your name?"

"Gloria."

Sam spoke, "Doc, we need paramedics. Are we clear for that? Over."

Sean replied to him asking for a location.

"Gloria, hold this on your neck," I said, putting her right hand over the wadded up paper. I waited until I felt her hand apply pressure then moved mine. I wanted to get an idea of the extent of her wounds. The neck seemed the worst but blood seemed to come from all over.

She had defensive wounds on her hands and forearms, several facial cuts, a large neck wound – someone had tried to slit her throat – and cuts to her head.

"Anywhere else?"

"I don't know," she replied, her voice shook. "Where's

Samantha?"

"I'm just going to lift your shirt, and make sure there are no more wounds." Cautiously I lifted her blood-soaked tee shirt. "Sam?" I said turning to look over my shoulder.

"Yeah.".

Sam moved closer to me.

"Gloria, this is Sam Jackson, he works with me," I said. "We've been looking for Samantha and two other girls, Melanie and Tasha." I grabbed more paper towels for her neck, adding them to the sodden wads she already held. "I'm going over to the door to talk to my friend here and to see if our doctor has arrived with the paramedics yet."

Her fear-filled eyes watched me as she spoke, "Samantha is my cousin."

She might be a source of information but there was something more pressing. Sam followed me to the door. I could hear running feet coming up the ramp on the far side of the concourse beyond the bathroom.

"Stop them," I ordered.

Sam turned to me. "What?"

"Stop the paramedics. Gloria is a bomb. Looks like an explosive device attached to her belt. I don't know if I can get it off. There's a cell phone attached to it."

Bet the cell phone wasn't connected to the problematic network we'd heard so much about. Our luck wasn't that good.

"Cell phone," Sam replied and ran out the door; he reached the top of the ramp in time to stop the paramedics from stepping foot on the concourse.

Doc spoke in my ear, "I'm almost there. Over."

"Copy. You can't come in. Stay back with the paramedics. Over."

"Negative. You can't do this by yourself. Over," Doc said.

"Stay back. Over," I warned.

Sean's voice resounded in my head, "Sending a bomb squad to you. Over."

I heard Sam relay a message to the bomb squad about a cell phone RCIED. It meant that the bomb was radio controlled and the cell phone was the set to initiate the firing circuit. All the phone had to do was receive an incoming page or text message and boom.

Sam's voice again, "She needs help, Sean. I'm going back. Over."

Sean's loud veto hurt my ear. "Negative. Sam, Doc, you have to stay with the medics," I whispered. "I've got this. Over."

My eyes closed for a second and took a deep breath. Centered, I went back to the young woman. She was scared and not very old, maybe nineteen. I couldn't leave her. Four voices fought to be heard in my ear.

"Don't make me take the receiver out. Over," I said quietly. "Stand down. All of you. Doc, how do I control this bleeding? Over."

"Let me come in. I have QuikClot in our field kit. Over."

"Negative. Pressure, can I do it with pressure? Over."

"Copy. I believe you could do it with sheer contrariness. Over." Doc said.

I ignored him.

I'm exactly where I'm supposed to be. In my mind, Carla shook her head and said, 'Don't leave me.' I saw Mac slip an arm around Carla and tell her I'd be home soon.

A silver butterfly flittered around a light.

"Okay Gloria?"

"Yes," she rasped. I sat down in front of her with another wad of paper towels and wiped some of the blood off her face; it did no good, more blood just took its place.

I spoke into the microphone on my shirt. "Doc, it's her carotid."

"You need to get in the wound and pinch the artery closed. Over."

I wished I could just let him in to do it for me. Blood is so slippery. I wiped my hands dry on a cleanish patch of my jeans.

"Gloria, I'm going to take these towels away now."

"Okay."

"It's going to be all right," I said quietly, as I removed the sodden towel. Blood spurted. There was so much I couldn't see. I wiped my hand again and stuffed my fingers into the hole in her throat feeling for the severed artery. I found it – it wasn't fully severed. I grasped the edges between my thumb and forefinger and squeezed. The blood flow slowed to a trickle. I grabbed more paper towels with my free hand and wiped some blood away from the wound so I could see. Sitting on the ground with my fingers inside someone's throat was not something I ever thought I would be doing.

Doc was in my ear, "Hold that artery closed, Ellie. How's her airway? Over."

"I got it, Doc. Wasn't fully severed. She's breathing. Over."

"If her chin was down when someone tried to cut her throat then the artery can sometimes be nicked not severed. Over."

Then it wasn't a professional who'd attempted to slit her throat. Unless, of course, the person wanted us to think that and botched it on purpose.

I spoke to Gloria again, "We have to wait a few minutes for some police officers."

She didn't say anything but, "Okay." Her head leaned back on the wall and her pale eyes closed.

So long as you don't explode, everything will be okay.

"Gloria? Don't go to sleep," I said, touching her shoulder. "Can you remember what happened?"

"Sam rang me; she said she was going to the concert and to meet her. She was with some guy and was scared."

"Did he have a name?"

"Dave ..." she whispered.

"Did you hear a last name?"

She tried to nod but my hand inside her throat wound stopped her.

"Addison, I think."

Why was that name familiar?

"Did you see your cousin?"

"Yes, that's the last thing I remember." Tears rolled through the blood on her face.

"I can talk to my team while talking to you. So don't worry if I say things that make no sense," I told her. "Sean – Dave Addison. Over."

Sean commented in my ear, *Moonlighting.* David Addison was Willis's character in *Moonlighting.* Now get out and let the bomb squad help her. Over."

"Negative. Can't do that, Sean. Over." I replied.

"Copy. Then listen to me and listen good ... my sister – your Director – will hang me from the nearest yardarm if I let anything happen to you. Do not go bang! Over."

"I'll do my best. Over," I whispered, the words sticky in my dry throat. "Find the other girls. Over."

Sean kept talking, "The shooter carried an identity card; his name is Art Jeffries. Mean anything to you? Over."

"No. Over." I said in a hoarse murmur. I squeezed the slippery artery tighter. Her own hand fell away. Blood ran down my arm. With my other hand, I reached up and pulled more towels from the dispenser, wadded them up against my leg and added them to the sodden pad I held against the rest of the neck wound. I wished I carried a field first aid kit like SWAT. QuikClot or even some hemostatic sponges would've been damn handy. Deep down I knew they wouldn't have helped: I needed a vascular clamp and a surgeon.

"Doc – give dressings to the ..." I couldn't say bomb

300

squad; I didn't want to panic Gloria.

"Copy. I already have, they should be with you any second. Over."

"Thank you. Over." I was more grateful than could be expressed over our microphones.

"Art Jefferies is another Willis character," Doc said. "Doc out."

"Unsub is quite a fan," I muttered.

Or, for some reason the characters meant something to him. I knew I needed to work out what ... but not right now. Now I needed to concentrate on breathing so I didn't scream.

Two men abruptly appeared next to me.

"Agent Conway, this is Bobby and I'm Mike. How's the girl?" Mike dropped two sterile packages on my knee. "Dressings and clamp."

Words were difficult to use, clearing my throat didn't help. "She's still in one piece. See if you can keep her that way ..." I touched her arm. "Gloria wake up."

She didn't move. I ripped the first package open with my teeth and pulled out a vascular clamp with my left hand as the packet fell. I held the artery and tried to attach the clamp using my left hand. It wasn't going to work; I needed to keep the pressure on with my right hand and couldn't coordinate the scissor action with my left.

"Leave it and go," Bobby said. Mike crouched beside us; he had already opened his case and was inspecting the bomb under the bloody shirt at her waist.

"It's attached to her belt at the buckle and extends most of the way around the back," Mike said. A few seconds later he said, "I'm going to try to remove the belt."

"Do what you do. I'm staying." I moved to the side, maintained pressure on the artery I dropped the clamp and held Gloria's hand with my free hand. Her fingers closed around mine.

My team all yelled at once; my head nearly burst with the noise. I think even the bomb disposal guys heard it.

As a concession, I moved as far out of their way as I could, while still holding her hand and maintaining as much pressure as possible on the artery, which wasn't as much as was needed. "Hang in there; we'll have you in hospital real soon."

My legs were freezing as I sat cross-legged on the bloodied wet concrete; my fingers ached from applying pressure to her neck. In front of me, Mike and Bobby worked as quickly as they could.

Blood dripped from the various wounds. I could see and feel the blood seeping through the wound; at least it wasn't pouring. I hoped what I was doing would at least buy us some time. Gloria remained unconscious.

A blessing.

Mike opened up a large yellow blanket.

"This is a ballistic blanket," he said.

A heavy, padded, fleecy-lined blanket was put over me and some of Gloria; it covered her head and shoulders. They got down to the nitty-gritty of defusing or removing the bomb. All I could see was the inside of the blanket and some of Gloria. The weight was stifling.

Maybe it was better not to see.

There was an aroma under the blood. I closed my eyes. A faint residue of a scent came off her clothing. The cologne. I remembered it from the tunnel.

My mind wandered and I considered I could soon be sitting on a seat next to Mac. The thought of Mac right beside me made me smile.

Mike spoke, "Got it, don't move."

I felt another heavy blanket land on us, blocking all light. I heard footsteps sliding on the wet floor and eventually a muffled boom, which I experienced as a dull noise beyond the ballistic blankets covering me.

Where was it?

It was suffocating under the blankets and I couldn't move. There were too many voices in my head; everyone seemed to be scrambling for information all at once. It was hot and air felt in short supply.

Sam asked someone something but I couldn't hear who he was talking to.

The words I needed stuck like cotton wool in my dry mouth, "Get me out of here. Over."

"Copy, Chicky Babe!" Sam said. "I'm coming. Over."

Gloria let my hand go. Her arm fell with a thud. I tried to shuffle closer to make sure she was breathing, pushing the blanket up as I moved.

"Where did the bomb explode? Over," I asked.

Doc's voice came back clearly in my ear. "They put it under a heap of ballistic blankets down the far end of the bathroom. Over." he said. "They explained earlier, that they'd detonate it as safely as possible if they couldn't defuse it. Are you okay? Over."

"I'm fine. Over."

Blankets moved above us.

"I don't think she's breathing. Over." I said, holding my hand in front of her mouth. Weight lifted. I guessed someone lifted the first of the ballistic blankets clear. From the corner of my eye, I saw dust falling. My eyes adjusted to the haze. I saw Sam's hands holding the handles on the side of the first blanket. He was moving backward. I helped push the other blanket back so I could see Gloria. I still didn't know if she was breathing and was ready to do CPR until Doc arrived. She slumped sideways; my fingers searched for a pulse and I started to lay her down.

I turned my head to Sam and said, "No pulse."

Everything changed. A sudden noise burst from behind her. An explosive pressure pushed me backwards. Sam disappeared from view. The air filled with particles of red and stung my eyes. Hands grabbed for me and pulled my body free of the blanket.

Life caught in my throat. I coughed, spluttered and gasped. As the movement stopped, a different hand placed a mask over my mouth and nose.

"Slow breaths." Doc was there.

I breathed and coughed. My ears needed to pop. Everything seemed distant and too quiet, as it was under the heavy blanket. I hooked the earpiece from my right ear. I held my nose, closed my mouth and blew. My ears popped. I could taste blood. Dark blue eyes scrutinized mine.

Doc. "Okay?"

I nodded. "Sam?"

Every time I attempted speech, a coughing fit ensued. Doc crouched in front of me. I was sitting on something. A gurney. Paramedics hovered around Sam. My mind raced over the probable happenings and settled upon another explosive device.

Sam turned to me, "I'm okay. I was still holding the blanket when the charge went off," Sam said. "Took a bit of shrapnel but I'm okay, Chicky Babe."

I looked to Doc for confirmation. "Doc?"

"Sam's okay. A few stitches in his hands and one arm, some antibiotics and Sam'll be good as new," Doc said. "Look at me." I saw the damn little torture light he loved so much in his hand. He flashed his hateful little light into my eyes.

I lifted the oxygen mask. "Shrapnel?"

"That's what a person's skull becomes when it explodes," Doc replied with care. "How's your head?"

I didn't know. I couldn't process the information he gave me.

"I need water."

Doc handed me a bottle of water. I took a huge mouthful and swished it around my mouth vigorously. I spat the water onto the concrete near my feet. There was a lot of red in the water. Maybe I bit my tongue or cheek.

"What happened?" I asked, hoping the reality wasn't what I thought and Sam didn't really have pieces of Gloria's skull stuck in his hands and arm.

"Another device. We missed it."

That sucked out loud. "Everyone else is unhurt?"

His eyes locked on mine. He knew I meant everyone but Gloria. "No one's really hurt, Ellie."

"Gloria?"

Doc shook his head. "Conway, I think she was dead before the bomb exploded, she'd lost a lot of blood. No pulse. Not an encouraging sign."

I swished more water around my mouth and spat it out. Less red that time.

"Where was it?"

"Behind her, maybe in her hair at the back of her head."

"I didn't see anything," I replied and another coughing fit followed. "Her hair was tied back with a barrette." I struggled to talk. "Could that have contained explosives?" I coughed some more.

Doc put the mask back on me.

"Probably."

I thought about the young woman, where she was when we found her, how far we moved her with the explosives attached to her belt. I'd looked for wounds, found the belt and looked no further.

Damn!

"The bomb disposal squad said you don't need much C4 to explode someone's head, so you could be right about the hair thing," Doc said. "We'll know more once the forensic people examine the fragments of the IED. The other two kids are okay. No sign of Melanie, Tasha or Samantha."

Several police officers taped off the toilet area with bright yellow police tape.

"How'd it detonate?"

"We don't know yet Ellie; we should know soon."

I looked into Doc's eyes. "He created a fuc'n decoy. Those kids are gone."

Someone spoke to me from my right, "How you feeling?"

A paramedic was standing next to me. "I'm okay," I replied through the mask.

She smiled.

"Good that you can hear."

"Yes, it is."

"How do you feel?" She was persistent.

"I'm fine, thanks."

Fine: fucked up, insecure, neurotic and evasive. Described me perfectly.

"You may have some injuries and should be checked out."

I shook my head. Blood dripped from somewhere. Blood covered me already, so more didn't seem to be an issue. There was no way I was going anywhere near a hospital. I took another mouthful of water and rinsed my mouth, then spat. I thought maybe I'd aspirated Gloria's blood, which seemed a better option than to be bleeding myself. My blonde ponytail hung over my shoulder, streaked in red with fragments of something trapped in it. I didn't much care for the lumps of sticky matter.

"I'm okay. Thanks – but I'm okay. We have our doctor with us."

She nodded and smiled at Doc and went back to Sam.

The fact was, I was struggling with all the events leading up to me sitting on a gurney, sucking oxygen.

If there is a God, he seriously fucked up this time. He and I were going to be having a difference of opinion, again.

"Doc?"

"Chicky ..." He cleared his throat. "Conway."

"We've got work to do."

I gave the mask to the paramedic.

When I stood up the whole world tilted. It felt peculiar. Doc took my arm and I was grateful for the support. He hoisted his pack onto one shoulder and called Sean over. I hadn't even noticed him standing with two police officers and the two bomb techs. They looked different without the heavy bombproof outer clothing; they were now wearing dark blue overalls.

"Can you take the scene and work with the crime scene unit?" Doc asked.

"Yes," Sean replied. "You okay Ellie?"

A bloody taste churned in my mouth; I swallowed hard.

I smiled. "Yeah, of course I am. Sam needs some stitches; can you take him back to the hotel later?"

"Of course."

Blood dripped onto my arm as I moved my head.

"Doc ..." Sean said.

"I saw," he replied. "Sit back down, Conway." He encouraged me to sit back on the gurney. His pack hit the ground; he opened it quickly, pulled on gloves and carefully worked his way through my hair. A paramedic came to help. She passed him forceps. Moments later, someone was holding a wound dressing to the side of my head.

"What was it?" I asked.

Doc showed me. "A piece of bone, maybe jaw. And a tooth."

Yuck. He cleaned the wound. "This is going to sting," Doc said. "I'm gluing these cuts, otherwise you'll be dripping blood for ages."

I grimaced as he squeezed the edges of the first cut together. Knowing he was going to do it twice was anything but a thrill a minute.

"All right?"

"Yeah. I've had worse."

"All done."

We attempted leaving again. Sean was waiting with Sam.

"Sean, Where are the other kids and Lee?"

"At the police station. We've got a couple of interview rooms there and a psychological trauma specialist on standby."

"Good."

"See you back at the hotel, Sam." There was some sort

of exchange of looks between Sean and Sam. I didn't quite catch it and didn't care.

"Turner and Jay have a car standing by, they'll take you to the hotel," Sean said as we walked away.

It took all my concentration to stop myself thinking about Gloria and just walk.

Chapter Twenty-Two
I Can't Tell You Why

"Where are we going?" Turner asked.

"Hotel," Doc said. "Conway needs to clean up before I see the kids and talk to parents …"

Turner didn't reply.

No one said another thing until after we pulled into the underground car park at the hotel. Turner parked the car right by the elevator door. The plan was to get me in the elevator and into my room, without causing too much attention. I hoped it was late enough that most people would be either out clubbing or already in their rooms, rather than milling about the swanky lobby and bar.

Hooch threw a reflective police jacket over me as I stepped out of the car.

It took a few seconds before I could stand straight. My brain couldn't process information regarding my physical position. Hardly surprising, it had had a lot to process in a short space of time.

"Thanks for the jacket," I said with a smile.

"Keep it," he replied. If it were mine I wouldn't have wanted it back either.

"We'll meet you two at the station," I said. I still tasted blood in my mouth. I swallowed. I could smell it too.

I clutched the bag containing my boots to me.

"Shitty night, huh?" Turner said through his open window.

"Two kids are okay," I replied. That needed to be my focus. "It's a better result than I'd imagined."

Three kids were gone and a young woman dead. I couldn't let myself dwell on that. Doc tapped the roof of the car as we walked away. It was slow going. My head wanted to go one way but my body argued. After a brief discussion, Doc won. He held my arm and walked with me.

The door shut on the police car and the engine started. The elevator pinged. I hoped no one was waiting near the elevator in the lobby. We switched elevators without any fuss and carried on straight to our floor. I tasted blood again.

Doc checked the hallway and gave me the all clear.

He pulled another two pieces of white paper from the doorjamb, swiped the keycard and let me in. Once inside he showed me the first picture. It was a photo of me climbing on to the stage after the evacuation, with Rowan helping me up. I remembered feeling someone watching.

"That had to be taken from above the stand, that conference room, look at the angle. There was no one on the ground or in the stands but us and police."

"Someone likes you."

"Someone's playing with me."

He flipped over the picture read aloud the scrawled words, " 'Special Agent Conway and her valentine'."

"Seems my tormenter has a sense of humor."

Doc showed me the second picture. A recent photograph of Carla in class. Doc read the caption out, " 'Pretty

Carla. My how she's grown'."

"Motherfucker!"

"She's okay Conway. Chrissy and Caine will take good care of her," Doc said.

My boots tumbled out of the bag into the small sink as I held it upside down and shook it.

"What did you say, Doc?" I studied the picture of Carla. "That's some serious camera the photographer used. The shot had to be taken from outside the school grounds. Maybe three hundred yards from the classroom."

"Chrissy and Caine will take good care of her."

"Chrissy ..."

Thursday just got a fuck lot worse.

Doc looked at me as if I had two heads. "You going to be okay?"

"Yeah." What choice did I have? "I gotta get this mess off before anyone sees me like this."

"Go easy in the shower. You're none too steady on your feet."

"I know."

"You have a concussion. It's from the pressure of the blast."

"I know," I replied. And I'm covered in bone fragments, brain matter and blood.

"I'll be out here," he said. "I'll bag these." Doc waved the photographs in his hand. "Don't lock the door."

No argument this time. "I won't."

In the bedroom, I was as alone as I was going to get.

The jacket almost fell off by itself. I folded it so the inside wasn't visible and placed it over a chair. I shoved my hand into the plastic bag I'd carried my boots in and used it to open the bathroom door, then to turn the shower on. As I peeled off my clothing, I noticed my hands. Blood caked under my nails, dried into the creases of my knuckles and palms.

Gross.

The plastic bag came in handy again. I used it like a glove and unclipped my holster and set it carefully on the shelf by the towels, then used it to pull my phone from my pocket and set that beside my gun.

White towels.

White soap.

My pale face reflected back at me, streaked with ruby lines. Stuff was stuck in my blonde hair, red and gloopy, with sticky patches containing sharp white fragments. I tasted more blood and spat red into the white sink then turned on the tap and watched it swirl clockwise down the drain.

Weird.

I opened my mouth and looked for cuts. I found one quickly and it looked like a tooth or two had gone through my cheek quite a way. I didn't give it much consideration. Mouths heal fast.

Slowly my reflection disappeared as steam filled the room.

If I couldn't see me, nor could one else.

I dropped all my clothes into the plastic garbage bag.

Someone would pick it up and deliver it to whatever laboratory the police used. No telling what trace evidence would be on my clothes from the explosion. I stepped under the hot water.

Dilute scarlet drips chased down the white shower walls. Soap turned pink in my hands.

I scrubbed.

The hot water poured over me making small rivers of crimson swirl by my feet. I shampooed my hair twice and still little pink streaks flew as I moved my head.

I scrubbed.

Somewhere beyond the torrents of water, my phone rang.

I didn't care.

Eventually the water and soap and scrubbing removed all the dark dried blood from under my nails and my hands, arms, face and hair. I stepped into the steamy sauna-like room.

With a dizzy head, I reached for a large thick white towel.

The final test.

As I dried off, I paid special attention to my hair then checked the towel. No red or pink. It was just wet.

A fresh white robe sat on the shelf. I pulled it on and tied it tight. The smell from the garbage bag on the floor stung my nose. It was an all-too-familiar metallic blood smell with too many associations.

As I squeezed the bag, the gush of warm bloody air almost choked me as I tied it shut. I checked my hands again.

Clean.

My phone rang again. I peered at it on the shelf as it rocked and vibrated closer and closer to my gun.

Grange.

I looked again.

Checking it said Grange not Galileo.

Not Mac.

I answered the call, "Hey."

"You okay? We heard something exploded."

Something exploded.

"I'm okay."

"Can I see you," he said.

"I'm fine, really, just getting cleaned up."

"Please?"

I left the bag in the bathroom, ended the call and dropped my phone in the pocket of the robe.

"How you feeling now?" Doc asked. He looked comfortable, legs stretched out across the coffee table, laptop on his knee.

"Bit better. Clean at least." I tossed up whether or not to mention the cut in my mouth. It's a mouth, seemed silly. It'd take care of itself.

My bloody boots were in the sink. They would take some cleaning.

There was a knock at the door. "I'll get it," I said. I found walking in a straight line to be somewhat challenging. "It'll be Rowan." It took massive concentration to make it to the door.

"You sure you feel all right?" Doc asked.

"Yep," I replied, using the countertop as support. "Little bit fuzzy around the edges is all."

"Conway, that's not all right."

"Really, it's fine." We'll discuss it later, unless I can avoid it.

I opened the door and found Rowan leaning on the doorjamb. He wore a new facial expression, one people close to me seemed to develop: worry mixed with a hint of fear and utter disbelief.

I shrugged mentally, there wasn't a damn thing I could do about that.

"See?" I said. "Okay."

He stepped inside and shut the door. "You sure?"

"Yes."

I stepped back toward the counter, needing something to lean on and wanting to block the view of the sink. Rowan walked into the main living area.

"Hey, Rowan," Doc said, moving his feet off the coffee table. "Have a seat."

Rowan sat down. "Do I want to know what happened?" he asked.

My hands gripped the back of a chair as the room twirled in sickening circles.

"Someone died in the stadium."

"We were told there was an incident and it was to do with the bomb threat."

"Yep." That's all anyone would be told.

"We can play tomorrow though."

"Awesome." Don't think I'll be in any hurry to attend another concert, ever.

"Ellie?"

"Uh huh," I said and moved around the chair, not letting go until I could sit on it. My head ached in between bouts of sickening dizziness that tilting my head triggered. The cut inside my mouth felt interesting and my tongue wouldn't leave it alone. I knew Doc was scrutinizing me.

"Conway?"

"It's nothing, Doc. I'm good."

Rowan leaned across the coffee table as if he was going to say something but didn't.

He called room service and ordered coffee.

Doc smiled gratefully. "We haven't had a chance to buy more coffee for the filter machine. Life gets crazy around Conway."

I ignored his comment. My mind pored over the events of the night. I couldn't find a way of reconciling what had happened. Names written in blood crawled across the grass at the stadium, Joe Hallenbeck, Jimmy Tudeski, Tom Mix, Bo Weinberg, Emmet Smith, Art Jeffries, Dave Addison, John McClane, David Dunn.

David Dunn. We'd forgotten about him since arriving in New Zealand. The others were characters played by Willis but he confused me. David Dunn.

Without warning music started up in my head.

A line from a song I knew but couldn't quite place. Patiently, I waited as other lyrics joined with music with a lead vocal to die for. I knew then what I was listening to. Someone knocked on the door. Rowan answered it and took a tray of coffee and cups from a porter. He set the tray on the countertop and closed the door.

"Rowan?"

He stood in front of the sink. "What is that on your boots?"

"Blood," I replied with a conjured, nonchalant air. And maybe some brain and a bit of bone.

He came over carrying the tray of coffee and cups, which he set on the table. Rowan sat back in a chair opposite me and picked up his coffee.

"I don't know what to say," Rowan said. His eyes met mine with force.

No one ever does.

"Answer a question for me. 'Unbreakable' – was it on the set list tonight?"

"Yes." His vision seemed drawn to the sink. "It was on our set list for tonight."

"Bon Jovi, yes?"

"Yes."

Doc watched me with interest.

"Can you check to see if Bruce Willis ever played someone called David Dunn ... and did Willis do a movie called *Unbreakable*?"

He tapped on the laptop keys. "He did and he played David Dunn."

"Curious isn't it?" There was blood in my mouth.

"Yes it is," Doc replied.

"Do we know how Sam is?"

"He's good, said he'll head over to the police station and help Lee out. I told him we'd be along soon."

I took a small mouthful of coffee.

Rowan's eyes never left me.

"Ellie, there's blood," he said, wiping a finger across at his own mouth.

I wiped the back of my hand across my mouth. I'm such a good-time girl. Everyone's idea of a fun date.

"And all over your teeth," he said and stood up and went into my room. A few seconds later, he came back with a clean wet facecloth.

Doc opened his medical kit.

"Thought you were okay?" he said. He held a tongue depressor and a small flashlight. He didn't give me a chance to reply. "Let's have a look."

"I think I might need stitches," I replied, as blood dripped from my mouth and ran over my chin. There was too much to swallow this time and it was making me feel sick. I opened my mouth and let the blood cascade down my chin.

"You think?" Doc replied. Heavy irony seemed to be his forte. "You're an amazing agent but useless at accepting help."

I swallowed. "I am not."

"You knew about this, why didn't you say something?" He had a point.

"Because I thought it would fix itself."

He pulled out his phone and made a call, letting Sean

know we'd be a little later than first thought.

Sitting was still interesting. Half my head wanted to drift to the right and I seemed to have little concept of where my body was situated. I checked the robe ties were secure. My sense of decency prevailed, no matter what.

Blood dripped onto the perfectly white robe.

Okay, so maybe the blast was a little stronger than I thought, and maybe it screwed my head a tad.

"I'm going to use a local anesthetic and stitch that cut," Doc said. "Rowan if you don't like blood and needles, now is a good time to leave."

"I'll be fine," Rowan replied. I noticed he moved so he was looking out the window.

Fine my ass.

Chapter Twenty-Three
Unbreakable

Rowan handed me a glass full of ice chips. "Feel okay?"

"Yeah."

Doc laughed. "She *never* says no; you should know that if you intend to spend time with her."

"I don't like to complain."

My tongue paused to fiddle with the stitches inside my cheek. I could feel Mac reaching out from the grave, I heard him say 'three strikes and you're out.'

"Doc."

"Conway, you want something?"

"Three strikes."

"It's not going to happen," he said with a grin. "It's a mild concussion."

Rowan had worry plastered all over his face; I appreciated his concern. "It's okay, Rowan."

He shrugged and by way of an explanation said, "Unchartered waters."

"Ain't it fun hanging out with me?"

His face clouded with something new and scary. He cared.

I stood up too quickly. My rookie mistake hit me, like the floor, as my legs dumped me unceremoniously.

Doc leaped over the couch and landed beside me. "Conway?" His hand reached for mine.

The sheer stupidity of the situation skyrocketed the

'ludicrous' factor.

"Come on," he said with a grin that could melt an Antarctic ice shelf. His hand tightened around mine as he helped me up.

"I fell over."

"You don't say."

"I haven't even had a drink." Laughter bubbled.

"I know." His voice held his amusement in check but I heard it simmering at the edges.

One hand gripped back of the couch. Doc had a decent grasp of my other arm. I turned my head toward him and the room spun out of control. Our eyes locked. I'm not sure they meant to.

"Oh Jesus, you're not all right."

"Pfff, this is nothing. I'm okay." I covered my ass as well as I could. "But I really need to get rid of the blood-stained robe." I'd seen enough blood for one lifetime. "I think I need your help."

"Really?"

"Yes."

His eyes narrowed. "This is an unprecedented moment, Conway."

More irony. I knew he wasn't buying it. "Can you help me find me some clean clothes, please?"

"You're not going back to work?" Rowan said. I'd forgotten he was still there. He hadn't found my falling over as amusing as Doc and I did.

"Yeah, I am. I'm in the middle of a case here, Rowan. Remember?"

He nodded.

"I'll be back in a few minutes."

Doc and I went into the bedroom. I sat down on the bed and watched as he began the arduous task of finding me clothes. He held up tee shirts for my approval. I settled upon a pale blue one. He turned his attention to underwear and found that a lot more entertaining.

"You think you can manage to get this lot on? Without falling over?"

"I'm feeling adventurous, so I guess we'll find out."

Once I'd shooed him from the room I began the struggle into my clothes. Dressing with wonky balance was entertaining. I figured Doc now knew there was something else amiss.

I knew exactly what was going on. I didn't need an MRI or a head CT to confirm it either. I had a mild concussion but the symptoms I was experiencing indicated a strong possibility of BPPV or Benign Paroxysmal Positional Vertigo. I knew this, because it had happened before. I intended to do my best to pretend it was normal. As long as I didn't fall on my ass again all would go smoothly. I reminded myself to move my head slowly, not look up too far and that bending over would be plain stupid. There would be no closing my eyes while I was sitting or standing: that was guaranteed to drop me on my ass.

If Mac were here, he'd remember the exercises that make it go away. Last time it happened I only did them for a few nights and everything was fine again. I couldn't even remember the name of the treatment.

If Mac were here ... Mac's voice crooned within my brain, 'Babe, tell Kurt. He knows what you need.'

My mind hissed like a leaky tire. Everything's okay.

"Okay, I'm decent," I called out as I walked back into the living area.

"What a shame," Rowan replied.

"Oh please!" I gave a generous eye roll. While my head caught up to the rapid eye movement and I suppressed the sudden nausea, the kids at the police station came to mind. "Can I ask you a favor?"

He nodded.

Even though I'd had the thought and the words were about to fall from my mouth, I still wasn't entirely convinced that Grange was completely innocent in this whole child abduction situation.

"We have two children back at the police station. We found them at the stadium; both had been abducted. Will you come meet them?"

I sensed a hesitation.

"You sure?"

"Yes. At least one of them was promised a meeting with Rowan Grange – it was part of the lure one of the scumbags used."

His face clouded with anger. "That's disgusting."

"Yep. Can you do this? Your people, managers and such, won't go ballistic?"

"Want the whole band?"

"That would be awesome. You're sure this is okay?"

He smiled. "If we don't tell management, they won't know. They will assume we are all in our beds. Let's treat this as our little secret."

"Living dangerously," Doc commented. "I ordered some more coffee. We'll cool yours, Conway. No hot drinks for a day or so, for you. We'll have a coffee then get going, yeah?"

"Sounds good."

There was a knock. "Rowan can you get that?" Doc asked. He was packing up.

When Rowan opened the door for room service, he stooped and retrieved a piece of white paper from the floor. "Think this is for you," he said, handing me the paper without looking at it. Rowan poured the coffee and sat my cup in a bowl of ice. Inventive.

The flipside of the paper revealed another photograph.

Hawk and two girls going through security at an airport gate. There was a time stamp.

I handed it to Doc, found my cell phone and called Lee.

"Hawk's gone. He took two girls. What time is it?"

"After midnight," he replied.

"The photo is time-stamped, eleven-fifteen p.m."

"Someone took a photo of him leaving and delivered it to you?"

"Yep."

"Can you confirm the identity of the girls?"

I studied the picture, I was sure I knew who they were but even so, I compared it with the photographs we had on file. Better to be totally sure.

"Tasha Cravino and Samantha Rowe. He's gone, Lee."

"You coming in?"

"I'll be there soon." I hung up, drank my lukewarm coffee. He was gone with two kids. There was still one kid here somewhere. It didn't bode well for her.

Chapter Twenty-Four
Get Over It

Doc and I sat in the spacious office loaned to us by the area commander and listened to Lee's briefing. I showed him the latest photo. After close inspection, he agreed it was of Tasha Cravino and Samantha Rowe.

In another room, a psychologist spoke with one of the kids, the littlest one, Nicola. In yet another room the other child, Shannon Harris, sat with a female police officer and social workers. She wouldn't be going home to her mother. Police picked up her mother, Stephanie Harris, as she arrived home, minus her daughter, from the concert. She was being interviewed pending charges, in another part of the police station. Child, youth and family social workers were making necessary care arrangements for both of Stephanie Harris's children. They began with trying to locate other members of the family. The extended family is always the first step in emergency child placement.

Lee placed a file on the desk in front of me. "Medical report on Nicola's mother," he said, tapping the manila folder.

"What do we know?"

"It's not good. She had a full-on psychotic break and will be incommunicado for quite some time."

The psychologist tapped on our open door. "Agent Conway?"

"Come in."

"Nicola would like to talk to you."

"Excellent. How is she?"

"Resilient," he replied.

I went into see Nicola; I wanted to talk to her too. She smiled when I opened the door. "Ellie!"

"You all right?" I asked, sitting opposite her at the small table.

She nodded, her smile widened. "I'm okay."

"Can I ask you some questions?"

She nodded.

"Where did you meet John McClane?"

She was quick to answer, "Mom met him online."

This led me to ask, "How'd you find out about the Butterfly Foundation?"

"Mom. She said she found it and I should join."

"And the American address?"

She looked worried. I hastened to let her know she wasn't in any trouble. "It's okay. I'm interested, not mad or anything."

Nicola smiled. "A friend from another site – we play Bratz games online together – she said I could use her address."

"Okay. Do you know where your mom met McClane?"

"A chat room, I think." Nicola thought for a minute. "Yeah it was. She used to talk to him in a chat room and then on MSN."

"You have any idea what sort of chat room?"

"She used to go to a Grange one, don't know of any

others."

"Excuse me a minute?"

She nodded.

Outside the room I found Lee. "We need her mom's computer."

"I'll get Sean to get it."

I went back in.

"Did McClane come over to see your mom?"

"Yes, he said he was from Russia but he isn't. He has a funny accent, it's kind of like yours but more."

"If I show you a picture, can you tell me if you know who it is?"

I flipped through my phone pictures until I found the guy we thought was Hawk and showed it to Nicola.

"That's him. John McClane."

"Thanks Nicola."

She touched my arm. "You are her, aren't you?"

"Her?"

"Special Agent Ellie. It's you who started the Foundation?"

"It's me."

"Was your mom sick too?"

"Yes, yes she was."

"Mom was getting better and then Mr. McClane came and she got really sick," Nicola said. "He made her sicker."

"She is getting better now. She's in the hospital."

"Will he come back?"

"No."

"Good. I didn't like him." Quietly she added, "But Mom did."

"How come he brought you here?"

"To see the Grange concert. He said Mom signed something before he took her to the hospital. It said he was allowed to look after me."

Same old Hawk.

"Do you know your mom is here in Christchurch, in a hospital?"

She shook her head. "He didn't bring her here. It's too far."

"Maybe someone else brought her here." I watched her closely. "Did McClane have a friend?"

She shrugged. "I don't know."

"Would you like to see your mom?"

She nodded and smiled. "Who will take care of me until she gets better?"

"I'm pretty sure I can find someone to take care of you."

Someone better than a child trafficker. Perhaps a convicted felon or gang member. Maybe some kindly gentleman on death row.

"Am I in trouble?"

"No. You are not in trouble. We are happy we found you and I have a surprise, if that's okay?"

She smiled.

God, she was so young.

"I'll be right back."

I scraped my chair against the floor as I stood up. This

time I left the door open. I opened an adjacent door and beckoned to Rowan.

"Come and meet Nicola."

He smiled and walked toward me. The other three looked on. "You want them too?"

I grinned. Is he nuts? Who would ask such a question? "Don't suppose Tony has a guitar ... or even you?"

Rowan smiled and winked at me. "I love the way you said 'even you.' I do play you know."

"I know."

"Unfortunately we don't have a guitar but we do have CDs," Tony said.

"You're awesome."

Walking backward into the room, I shielded most of the hallway commotion from the curious Nicola. Quite honestly, I was surprised I could walk backward without falling.

"Well, young lady. I'd like you to meet some friends of mine," I said and turned around, then stepped aside. Rowan strode into the room behind me wearing a mile-wide grin. The band followed close behind. I watched Nicola's face, hoping it wasn't too much.

Her little face lit up. A strangled squeak escaped her lips.

Rowan held his hand out to her.

"Hello, I'm Rowan Grange."

Nicola blinked in an owl-like fashion and froze, mesmerized.

I leaned in and whispered to her, "You can shake his

hand."

She whispered in my ear, "He sounds sort of like Mr. McClane."

"It's okay Nicola. It really is Rowan Grange."

She hesitated, then thrust her small hand in his. Tony stepped up next to Rowan and handed Nicola a CD. She smiled.

I left them to their visit and went back to Lee.

My head ached, my eyes hurt and I could've sworn I was already asleep.

Lee had spent time interviewing Shannon Harris. Like Nicola, she didn't really know much. They were supposed to meet another man with another girl but never did.

The room with Shannon was next.

"Hi, how you doing?"

She looked up at me. "All right. Who are you?"

"Special Agent Ellie Conway."

She shrugged.

"Where's my mom?"

"She's being interviewed by police."

"She was going to sell me," Shannon said quietly. "Who does that?"

There was no way I was prepared to defend her mother's actions and no way to make it sound any better, so I moved on.

"What was with the concert?"

Shannon looked slightly surprised then smiled. "Supposed to be my birthday present ... but I didn't believe Mom would buy the tickets."

Smart kid. She didn't; someone gave them to her. Not something the kid needed to know.

"You liked Grange for long?"

"Yeah, my whole life."

Wow. That long.

"I have a few more questions and then a surprise for you. First – do you belong to the Grange fan club?"

She shook her head. "It's too expensive."

"Have you ever been to a Grange chat room online?"

"No. I don't use the internet much; it keeps being cut off. Mom says it breaks but it doesn't. She doesn't pay the bill."

"Does mom use the internet much?"

"At work, she talks about Facebook and stuff to me. I think she goes to some chat room where she talks to, you know, old people who like Grange."

I scrawled in my notebook to remind myself to look for links to Grange chat rooms on her mother's work computer.

"Thanks for that. Now for you, I have a surprise. Wait right here."

Rowan and the band were waiting in the hallway.

"You guys are really great for taking time to see these kids. The kid in there," I pointed to the door, "is Shannon. She's been a fan her whole life." I grinned. "Let me get into the viewing room then you can open that door."

I hurried into another room and sat facing a large window. I could see Shannon sitting at a table, with the door open. She shrieked as Rowan and Tony walked in and again, as the rest of the band followed.

Seeing her so excited, animated and full of life, did a lot to ameliorate the horror of the night.

She reminded me of Carla.

Chapter Twenty-Five
Damned

Sean drove us back to the hotel from the police station. It wasn't a long drive. The sun rose as we arrived, turning the sky a myriad of colors. Brilliant orange and pinks reflected in the huge glass hotel windows and I didn't have the energy to acknowledge the beauty of the summer sunrise on a dismal Friday morning.

There was no way I could suitably explain why but I desperately wanted to go home. My gut told me something bad was going to happen to Carla and I needed to be there. Hawk was gone with two kids, a third was still missing and all hope was fading. And the trail of death was getting old. As keen as police here were, working with them after the death of our liaison was difficult. She was killed because of us and I understood the stress that placed on everyone.

"I want to go home," I said. "Today."

Sean nodded. "I'll get you on a flight."

I was done with New Zealand and over having my chain jerked by Hawk.

No one commented. They exited the car in an uncharacteristically sullen silence. Sam opened the front passenger door for me.

"Thanks." He nodded.

Sean opted to come with us. On the way up to my room, I asked the concierge to have breakfast brought up.

I eased my body onto one of the couches, mindful that my head wasn't keen on me dropping like a stone. My eyes wanted to close but I knew that'd open a whole can of worms. A spinning can, at that.

Sam and Lee slid into the armchairs. Doc sat next to me. Sean called Air New Zealand from the room phone and booked us a flight home. We were leaving Christchurch in five hours.

"We need to pack," I said.

No one replied.

My cell phone rang. I checked the display, saw Rowan's name and let it go to voicemail. My phone rang again as room service set out our breakfast on the small table by the window. Again, I let it go to voicemail.

A few forkfuls of scrambled eggs and half a warm coffee later there was a knock at the door. Sam opened it. This time there was no flurry, no fanfare, no grinned greeting.

"Is she here?" Rowan asked, his manner unusually subdued.

"Yeah," Sam replied. "Come in."

I stood, let my brain catch up, then walked over to Rowan. Sam excused himself and went back to his breakfast.

"We're leaving today," I said.

"So are we," he replied. "We're not doing another gig here, not after what happened."

"Fair enough."

There was an opportunity to discuss chat rooms and I

grabbed it.

Work mode was more comfortable for me anyway. "Do you have an official chat room attached to your fan club website?"

"Yes. You want me to show you?"

"Please." I pointed to the couch. "Over there." My laptop sat on the coffee table.

He showed me the website, which was comprehensive. There were videos, photographs, forums, merchandise, ticket sales and a chat room. Rowan emailed someone. While he waited for a reply, we watched the conversation in the chat room.

"I found this ..." Rowan said when he heard an email alert. He clicked on a tab and opened the email page, then opened a chat site. Rowan logged in. There were thirty-five screen names in the room. Conversation was flying. I noted Rowan used a girl's name, not his own. He flicked back to the official chat. His name came up as Admin007.

A smile ventured across my lips. Double-oh-seven. Grange, Rowan Grange.

I leaned over and opened both screens at once.

"Hey, Lee."

"Chicky Babe, how can I help?"

"Any way we can download these conversations as they happen?"

He had a look at the screen, let out a low whistle, twisted his face, ran his hands through his hair and then reached for the laptop. "I think so."

Sam came over for a look. They conversed in short choppy sentences full of technical-sounding jargon but seemed to successfully finish each other's thoughts.

Rowan and I watched. I slid my hand through the air above my head, indicating the conversation was way above my head. He grinned and agreed.

Ten minutes later Lee and Sam announced they had achieved the goal and both chat rooms would spill their guts to a secure server under FBI control.

I pulled an FBI form from a manila folder on the coffee table then hunted for a pen. Mine was nowhere to be seen. Rowan pulled one from his pocket. I smiled at him, wrote quickly then handed it back.

"You can keep it," he said. "They're new and I was given two of them."

"Thanks. I need you to read and sign this." I passed him the paper, which said that he authorized the activity in the chat room and had full knowledge of the investigation. It was easier than getting a warrant.

It was better at this stage to keep this between Rowan, my team and me. Limit the sharing of knowledge.

Rowan gave me the pen and then stood up. "We're leaving in an hour. I'll call you when we're all home."

"Yeah, do that," I replied, walking him to the door.

Rowan gave me a hug. I hugged him back because it seemed like I should.

"I'll call you," he whispered and then he was gone. I didn't know if he would or wouldn't. If I were him, I'd run. I'd run and never look back. I was fairly certain I'd be on his management's black list – and his publicist's hit list – and they'd be working overtime to prevent me contacting him.

When the door shut, I leaned on it and looked at my team, hunched over laptops. "Hawk's hunting in the Grange chat room but I don't think it's the official one." My words floated across the room, carried by the music I heard in my head. Before I pushed the pen into my pocket, I had a proper look at it. Emblazoned on the side of the black, enameled barrel was the band's name and logo. Fancy.

Detective Jones called me as I finished my coffee. I walked quite steadily across the room with the phone. The new day sparkled beyond the window.

My words seemed cold as I launched into my leaving speech, "We're leaving New Zealand. It's been fun an' all but Hawk's gone. This was not as successful as I'd hoped. I'm sorry he managed to take two kids with him. We will carry on trying to find them from back home."

"That's partly why I'm calling," Jones said interrupting me. "Melanie Talbot never made it to Christchurch. We recovered her body three hours ago from Wellington harbor."

My heart sank, my fears confirmed. "Poor kid."

"Preliminary findings indicate she hit her head and toppled into the water right in front of the Interisland Ferry terminal."

"Trying to escape?"

"I'd say so. We'll have to wait for the autopsy. I have a

suspicion that she was already dead when they tried to snatch Emma. She was ..."

"The replacement," I added.

"It's pointing that way."

"That does explain the out-of-character attempt to take two kids known to each other."

"We confirmed the passport is a fake. It's expertly done but still a forgery."

"Excellent. Keep in touch, Faye. You have my email and contact numbers? I'll pass you over to Sean; he's going to carry on here."

"Let me know if you make any progress. Best of luck, Ellie."

"Thanks for all you did," I said. "Here's Sean."

I passed the phone to Sean. He'd agreed to continue working with her on any leads uncovered in New Zealand, as part of my team. I didn't voice my feeling that there wouldn't be any. Hawk didn't leave anything usable behind and I was damn sure he was gone with the two kids we didn't find, as the picture suggested. Tasha Cravino and Samantha Rowe would haunt me. They'd haunt me as much as Detective Faye Jones saying she knew Mac. One day when I felt stronger and the timing was right, I'd ask her about Mac. Wondering if that day would ever come could drive a person mad.

Packing took longer than I thought. Maybe it would've been quicker if I hadn't made such a god-awful mess since we'd arrived. My energy was lacking. Doc and I packed in silence. We moved around each other gathering clothing and checking drawers.

I managed a quiet word with Sean.

"I need a favor."

"Name it."

"Someone working for Delta has compromised our investigation. I knew it from the minute we found the dead cop, though I suspected it before we left Virginia."

"Want me to look into anyone in particular? Or Everyone?"

"Everyone." I didn't want to cast my shadow on his investigation.

"Might take awhile."

"I know."

"I'll call you with my findings."

No little girls squealed at Lee while we waited at the airport. That was a relief. We were in for a long flight, had short fuses and were all armed.

Once safely on board, I tried to decide the best way to pass the time. Lee and Sam talked in hushed tones in the middle section of the row. Doc sat next to me. There was nothing much to see out the window. Stretching out my legs, I closed my eyes hoping tiredness would bring sleep before the spinning and the nausea overtook me. I couldn't avoid it any more than I could avoid seeing a red mist and smelling blood every time my eyes closed. It felt like I hadn't slept in months. Before long images of our time in New Zealand danced through my tired mind. Drifting deeper into sleep, they persisted, twisting into movie scenes, slinging distant memories of explosions and horror into the mix until Doc woke me.

"Conway, hey, you're dreaming," he said, shaking my arm gently. "Who is Saleh?"

"A ghost," I replied drowsily. "I see dead people."

"From Wellington?"

"Another life." The secrets of the past are buried under tons of concrete.

"You really all right?" Doc whispered.

"Yep."

"I've read your medical records. You can talk to me. I know what happened before."

"Not necessary. It was just a dream."

"What are the chances of being in two explosions in the same foreign country?" Doc asked.

I closed my eyes. "Probably a lot higher in Afghanistan or Iraq than New Zealand."

The compartment spun wildly. I grabbed the armrests to steady myself.

"Conway?"

"Spinning," I said, as the movement slowed and a wave of nausea crashed over me.

"You don't look so good."

"Thanks."

He dropped a paper bag on my knee. "Something you should have mentioned earlier?"

"Nope."

"Why are you so damn contrary?"

"I'm not contrary."

"No?" He wasn't convinced. "Black."

"Yellow."

He smiled. "You're feeling better."

"I am. It doesn't last long." I breathed deeply, feeling much better. "I'm fine Doc."

"Gloria exploded: you were right there. I took bone fragments and a tooth from your scalp. You were completely covered in blood and debris."

I looked out the window but all I could see was Doc's reflection as he leaned toward me. I sighed. "I'm tired. And I want to go home."

Sleep beckoned. I heard Lee's voice talking to Sam. All at once, Lee was part of my dream ...

... Music hung from the ceiling in higgledy-piggledy clumps. One by one, notes fell screeching harshly before splashing into a huge pot below. Sixteenths and quarter notes landed on top of each other. Sharps, flats and treble clefs rose in the bubbling stew. Some notes rearranged, floating up into the air in recognizable pieces. Other notes gathered Mac's words, 'It's all about the music' and infused them with energy.

Beyond the window, a hawk swooped from the sky and plucked a small bird from the beach.

Hudson Hawk and John McClane were one and the same person. His real identity eluded me.

Another Hawk swooped from the clear blue sky and snatched a small rodent from the grass; as soon as it was out of sight, another one appeared and snatched another rodent.

Music meandered along the water's edge, passing people, swirling around couples and families out for evening strolls. Trapped in a twisted mind game, where all the players bore the names of Bruce Willis characters and the ringleader went by the name Hudson Hawk. Nothing was what it seemed.

With Lee by my side I turned toward a grassed area on the left of the marina, small hills, that appeared landscaped. Manmade hilly bumps, scattered with small trees and shrubs but mostly vast grassed areas.

Over a hillock or maybe it was a grassy knoll, I found myself looking down on a sandy bunker, such as you'd find on a golf course but on a huge scale. This wasn't a golf course and on the far side was a storage shed of some sort.

Chickens pecked and scratched in the gravelly sand outside the sheds. Bales of hay were stacked in small groups. Cows, sheep and lambs milled about, some chewing on hay, some eating the few tufts of green grass poking through the gravel.

"I see chickens," I said and lay down on my stomach at the top of the sandy cliff to watch them. Gazing at chickens soothes my soul.

We lay there on our stomachs, peering over the edge of the cliff enjoying the view. A troll-like creature appeared below us and dragged a lamb underground. Fresh grass distracted a ewe that tried to follow. Within minutes the lamb's place was lost as the animals milled about eating. What was gone, was now forgotten.

Was that why Hawk choose the children he took, because no one would look for long? And no would remember them once they were gone?

Chickens scratched and pecked.

Five men wearing jungle-green camouflage and carrying rifles rushed from the shed, one sighted his weapon in our direction.

Lee and I crawled backward fast, then jumped to our feet and took off running.

Gunfire erupted behind us. Chickens flapped and squawked. The other animals seemed oblivious to the disruption.

I was close to Lee as we crossed the grassed area and hit the graveled driveway that lead to the main hotel entrance. We passed two people carrying weapons. They watched us pass but made no move to shoot. We headed through the lobby only to watch a scene unfold that was straight from a movie. Pick a Bruce Willis movie and go with it like everyone else.

Die Hard sprung to mind.

Armed men and women took control of the lobby and its occupants. My mother argued with a bartender in the bar. Her voice rose in a crescendo of irritation over the lack of olives in her martini. She looked at me and shook her head her in utter disappointment.

She stabbed a bony finger in the air, punctuating her words as she fired them at me, "What have you done this time, Gabrielle?"

"Not the bartender, like you," I retorted.

Lee grabbed my hand and pulled me behind a large

leather sofa.

"Your mother off her meds again?" he hissed in my ear.

"I think so."

The soldiers looked straight through us, as if we were transparent. A swirl of multi-colored musical notes twisted around them.

"Are you armed?" he whispered.

"Nope," I replied.

Nothing made any sense ...

... My eyes opened. The dream contorted in my mind. Its inconsistencies caused ripples of discontent. We're FBI. We are always armed was the rational thought which, for an instant, overrode my dream. My mind jumped back to the stadium, I should've known something was up. Who'd have thought a woman would explode? Me, I should have. What's the point of knowing what others don't and having psycho-prophetic ability if I can't save a young life? Where was the song to warn me of that?

The airplane cabin stretched before me. I scanned quickly for sightings of my mother. I recalled my last visit to her graveside, just a few weeks before we left the country. The visits did not stem from a misplaced daughterly duty to the dead. I liked to make damn sure she stayed in the ground. Satisfied there was no sign of my mother on the plane, my fitful musical sleep resumed, bringing the dream back with it ...

... From behind the sofa, I watched a man walk past

carrying an M16. He stopped and turned toward us.

Mac.

Mac?

A warning siren sounded in my mind. He stood his ground. A smile drifted across his lips.

"Lee, can you see him?" I tugged on Lee's shirtsleeve.

"You mean Mac? Yeah, I can."

Mac lifted his weapon, pointing the muzzle skyward as his finger slid onto the trigger. He fired. A short burst of music flew into the air chased by the muzzle flash. He saluted and moved away.

"What the fuck is going on here? What's with the dead people? How does his gun fire music?"

"I don't think this is real, Ellie," Lee replied. Several musical notes fell from his mouth. He coughed and out tumbled more.

My booted foot tapped the floor. I wanted out and I wanted out now. I started to speak but choked. Something was stuck in my throat. I reached into my mouth and pulled out pictures. I handed them to Lee, one by one. The last picture was Carla tied to a gravestone with a man crouched in front of her. A scream grew and wiped out the last remnants of music.

It made no sense but I had to get home ...

"Conway!" Doc shook my arm. "Conway, do you want a drink of water?"

I opened my eyes slowly. In front of me was the back of an aircraft seat. I turned my head left: out the small window I saw nothing but sky and below us cloud. To the right, I saw Doc then Lee, with Sam leaning around him, all looking at me. I was sure there had been a person sitting on the other side of Doc, not an empty seat for them to lean all over.

"Chicky Babe, you with us?" Sam asked.

I nodded and said, "She would've died anyway. We weren't meant to save her and the bomb wasn't meant to kill me. I was supposed to find her."

"I thought you were asleep," Doc said.

"Me too," I replied. "We were pawns, marionettes; we were played like complete fuc'n morons."

Chapter Twenty-Six
Motherless Child

Home felt great. It was hard not picking up the phone and calling Dad as soon as I walked in. But I resisted. It was the middle of the night. I forced myself to sleep for a few hours and woke on my second consecutive Friday morning. The International Date Line is a freaky thing.

At seven in the morning, I grabbed the phone and called my dad. I knew he'd be up.

"I'm back. I need an adoption lawyer."

"Welcome home. I'm fine, thanks for asking."

"Good, sorry. I need an adoption lawyer," I said, dropping my bag in the laundry and shoving my clothes into the washing machine.

"This about Carla?"

"Yes."

"I'll look into it, Ellie."

"Thanks Dad." I paused trying to gauge what just happened. "I expected a lecture."

"Sweetheart – you know what you are doing. If you didn't you would've said ... this is what I want to do, am I doing the right thing? And you did not. When you know your own mind I have no need to lecture."

I smiled. "So it's true, you do know me better than I know myself."

"That I do. Now I'll find a lawyer who'll help you bring Carla home, where she belongs."

"Meanwhile, will you find out about getting me tempo-rary guardianship – I don't want her in foster care while we're trying to make this permanent."

"That'll be my priority today."

"Thanks, Dad."

"You're welcome."

I slid the phone back into its base and listened for the beep that told me it was charging. In my office, I dropped Grange's new album, *Nocturnal Drifter,* into the DVD/CD player of my desktop computer and chose 'Play All.' It was funny hearing Rowan's voice coming from my speak-ers, now that I'd met him.

The music followed me to the kitchen while I made a peanut butter and jelly sandwich and coffee. I text mes-saged Carla, knowing she'd be getting ready for school. I just wanted her to know that I was home and trying to get custody of her A-sap.

Back at my desk, it was time to update the readers on the Foundation site. My hand strayed to my desk drawer; I opened it before I realized what I was doing.

Looking for cigarettes.

Old habits die hard. I pulled my hand from the drawer, ate my sandwich and took my mind off smoking.

My Foundation blog was typically light-hearted and fun to write. The intent was always to make the young people of the Foundation feel like a part of my day with-out giving them any detail. I wrote:

There's no place like home. I'm back from a short trip. Dur-ing which I met a rock star and was offered an opportunity to write a few songs. Isn't that the coolest thing ever? When we make the formal announcement, I'll post it here. Until then, you'll all have to wait. You may speculate all you like.

It's something very different for me.

You all know the drill ... email me anytime. The moderators are here to help with any questions you have. (Don't ask them who the rock star is.)

Next time I shall tell you tales of my dumpster-diving days of fun.

Y'all take care now, ya hear.

SSA Ellie.

I switched off my desktop and picked up my work laptop from the desk.

The joy of mobility.

Out in the living room my intention was to lie on the sofa with the rest of my coffee and some mind-numbing TV, while I surfed the World Wide Web and checked work email.

The blast still affected my head a little, despite my pretending I was okay. I made a mental note to call my doctor first thing in the morning.

With my laptop open I began the arduous task of checking my email from various accounts.

Among the regular emails I expected to find at my work address, there was one from an unknown. Normally I'd delete it out of hand but this one had an interesting subject line.

Don't all viruses have interesting subject lines?

I ran the virus checker over it first before opening and reading the contents.

Welcome home SSA Conway,

I hear you know about the chat rooms. Aren't you clever? Of course, knowing about them and stopping me using them are two entirely different things. Wanna watch me work? You owe me. You owe me three pretty little girls. Give Carla a kiss from Uncle Hawk.

Yours with true appreciation,

Eddie Hawkins.

I called Caine. I needed to hear his voice and response, while I frantically tried not to panic.

Not good.

The second he answered, I started talking, "I'm putting my work laptop on a courier. I think there is some kind of spyware on it, maybe another keylogger." I felt like my voice was racing as fast as my heart.

"Hi Ellie," Caine said.

"This is old. I mean this grew old during the Son of Shakespeare's days ... now I have Hawk dropping in spyware. Are all criminals cut from the same drab piece of cloth?" His greeting sank in. I took a deep breath, exhaled, and said, "Hello, Caine." I never gave him time to reply. "This is fucked up beyond belief. He's saying he is hunting in the Grange chat rooms and we can't stop him! He mentioned Carla!"

"Ellie! I have no idea what you are talking about."

The red haze of anger lifted slightly. "A keylogger and

Hawk saying he's using chat rooms and he said 'Give Carla a kiss from Uncle Hawk.' How the hell did he drop a keylogger onto my work laptop?"

"Because every time we come up with a new way to protect our information, some little dick hacks it for fun."

I inhaled deeply and let it out slowly, releasing the final traces of anger.

"You got email from Hawk?" he asked in typical gruff fashion.

"Yes. I'll print it and attach a hard copy to the case file."

"For now Carla is as safe as we can make her without pulling her from school and hiding her in a bunker." Caine growled less and less the longer I knew him. This time his growl gave way to concern. "My experience tells me teenagers are best not stored in bunkers."

"Okay." I don't quite know how 'okay' fell from my mouth; it wasn't even close to the hysterical screaming I heard in my head.

"You're all right? With this new development, the email, I mean?" Caine asked.

Caine could read my voice like no one else and anyway, I'd ranted at him, which I suspect gave him a big clue as to how I felt.

"I think 'me' and 'all right' parted company the minute I opened the email."

"Sam, Lee, Kurt?"

"They have the next few days off; we're all a bit shattered after the trip."

"Is there any reason to suspect Hawk knows where you live?"

"Not at this stage; he seems to be content with following me in the virtual world and all around Christchurch, New Zealand."

Whoever has been watching Carla probably knows where I live.

"I'm not happy about this."

No fuc'n kidding?

"What's he going to do, knock on my door?" As the words left my mouth, I mentally slapped myself. Good one, Ellie!

Caine exhaled with force, then sharply sucked in air as he said, "Do I have to remind you how it all turned out when someone did that?"

No, that wasn't necessary at all. I still have the nightmares and the scars. My fingers ran along the scar under my bangs.

"Days off or not, either Lee, Sam or Kurt need to be shadowing you."

I agreed but only because if I didn't, Caine would call them direct or worse, send someone else to baby-sit in the meantime.

Back in my home office, I plugged the printer into the laptop and made three copies of the email. One for me. One for Caine. One for the file. Then I copied the URL that lead to all the transcripts from both chat rooms into an email and sent it to myself. Just because he said I couldn't stop him didn't mean I couldn't analyze the conversations.

I powered down my laptop and closed the lid, then shoved it into a courier bag and addressed it to Cyber Division. One copy of the email went into an envelope addressed to Caine. That would go with the courier too.

Someone had rifled through my personal files, either in person or by means of a nasty program created for such things. It was as bad as someone going through my drawers. If someone rifled through my files in person it had to happen while we were away. I took my work laptop with us.

The courier company had someone pick up the package and letter.

What was I missing apart from brain cells? Hawk was hunting kids, this time without the gory trail of bodies left by his previous employees. He was still killing, just not as prolifically.

As far as I could tell, he now did not use the Foundation.

What was with the involvement with Grange? Was it convenience, was it because they were one of the most famous bands currently touring? Was he using other band chat rooms too?

It was feeling personal but there was no way Hawk could have envisaged my meeting with Rowan Grange. If he did, then he had one amazing crystal ball.

I thought about how we arrived at the decision to go to New Zealand. Hawk misbehaved, we followed him. Although we weren't a hundred percent certain it was him, until we got to New Zealand. He led us to Christchurch. He led us to the Grange concert.

The nagging, chilling feeling I'd experienced, when I knew it was Hawk, returned. It was too easy finding those kids. And why leave such a mess of bodies?

How could he have known I would see the Russian at the Casino? My thoughts were pointing to a scary scenario. If he were watching me like the photographs suggested, he would've known Rowan and I were in a private dining room overlooking the casino floor. That explained why the Russian looked up that night.

And the references to Bruce Willis movies: what the fuck was that all about?

I owed him?

I owed him set of steel bracelets and a date with an electric chair.

Knowing I couldn't put off calling Lee any longer I picked up my cell phone. I decided to open with an apology.

"I'm sorry to do this to you." I hoped I sounded as sincere as I felt. "Caine thinks I maybe a target, all leave is cancelled. To make it fun, you're on bodyguard detail."

"Cancelled?"

"More relocated ... to my place."

Lee chuckled. "I got nothing planned, Chicky. I'm on my way."

"I'll let Sam off today, we'll pull him in tomorrow," I said. "I heard a whisper he has a girl, plus he's recovering from the blast."

"I heard he had a girl," Lee replied. "See you in an hour or two. Lock the doors. Call Kurt in."

"Yeah, yeah. Hey, bring that bug detector thing."

"You think something's in the house?"

"I dunno."

I hung up.

Doors. I was feeling decidedly antsy. I checked all the doors and windows. I checked upstairs, looking in all closets and under the beds. I even checked the showers.

It didn't help. Antsy was how it was going to be.

Violation does that to a person.

The comforting old creaks and groans of the house didn't alleviate the problem either. Usually I found them soothing, like a collection of songs written for me.

Not poems. No, not poems.

It was daytime but it didn't help. The trees were naked; I could see all the way across the yard and deep into the woods. It didn't help. I wandered up the stairs and into my bedroom. I opened the French doors that lead to a small balcony overlooking the backyard, and a cold wind hit me. The sun tricked me into thinking it was warm. It wasn't. Yet twenty-four hours ago, the wind was warm and the sun hot.

A bang from downstairs jolted me back to Virginia.

It sounded like a door. The front door hitting the doorstop.

I grabbed my badge from the top of my dresser and dropped the lanyard over my head. Without even thinking about it, I pushed my holster back onto my belt. My fingers wrapped around the grip of my Glock. A muffled thump at the bottom of the stairs made me pause. A thump, like someone dropping something. A bag maybe. An interior door opened. I peered over the banister and looked down the hall. Had I shut the office door?

If I did, it was now open. Either way, I needed an explanation for the shadows I saw moving across the floor through the open door.

It's the cat.

The smile faded as I heard the computer power up. Not even our cat was that smart. Then I remembered the cat was with my brother.

Walking down a few stairs, I was acutely aware there was no cover. The landing a few more steps away had a small bookcase and a phone. Mac and his love of phones; one upstairs in our room, one on the landing, one in the kitchen and another line into the office. A few more steps.

The shadow moved.

I snatched up the phone and pressed in Lee's number while I continued moving. Being caught on the stairs would be stupid. I could be dead before I turned around to run. I made it to the bottom before Lee answered.

"Hello?"

With the phone to my shoulder to muffle his voice, I moved into the living room. I'd left that door open. With three rooms between the office and me, I felt a little safer speaking.

"Someone's in the house," I said in a whisper, as I watched the doorway.

I heard the office door close and listened for footsteps. None. Whoever it was had shut themselves in the office.

"How many? Where? And where are you?"

"I don't know how many. Someone is in the office and has turned on my computer. I'm in the living room now."

"Get out," he said.

"It's my house, I won't."

"Get out, Ellie. I'm sending police."

Contrariness kicked in.

"It could be Aidan," I suggested, not believing it for a second.

"Get out. Aidan wouldn't sneak in, he'd yell out."

Would he? What if my dear brother was sneaking around looking for poems for another surprise poetry book? I considered that a possibility and therefore he deserved to be found by police.

I took a breath and crept into the hall. I had an urge to close my eyes and run for the front door. I didn't.

The door was shut. I shoved my gun into my holster and held the phone in my mouth. I needed two hands for the door: one to turn the handle and one to hold the edge of the frame so I could get my weight behind a decent lift-and-pull maneuver. The door had a habit of sticking. Mac never got around to fixing it.

Whoever opened the door, didn't know it would stick. That explained the bang as it flew open. I sighed as I closed it behind me. It wasn't Aidan. He knew about the door and complained about it often.

With the phone to my ear, I hurried behind Mac's

truck. From there I could get into the garage if the need arose. I could also see out to the street. My car was behind Mac's truck. The keys were in the office. Spare keys for Mac's truck were in the garage but there wasn't enough room to maneuver with my car and the house so close.

"Police?"

"On their way, Chicky. What can you see?"

"No car. It's probably parked farther up the road. Can't see anything inside the house."

"Keep your head down," Lee said.

I could hear traffic noise and a siren over the phone. "Who's coming?"

"Fairfax PD."

"Can you get hold of the attending officers?"

"Sure, why?"

"No lights and no sirens. I want this person caught without any fuss." Of more importance, I didn't want the person to escape.

"You got it." The noise over the phone stopped.

"You close enough to turn the noise off?" I asked. Thinking he was making incredible time.

"No, but traffic is lighter than usual, have my flashers on and people are getting out of my way for a change."

In the distance, I heard sirens and hoped they weren't heading for me.

He used the radio in the car to call the PD dispatch and relay my request. The sirens stopped. Guess that meant they were heading for me and had received the message.

My attention returned to the house. Something fluttered or shimmered near a back window.

"Unsub has moved to the kitchen."

"Line of vision?"

"Not close enough to the window for a good view of the driveway area."

"Head down, Chicky."

"I'll keep it firmly attached to my shoulders. I'm hanging up and going for a look."

"Bad idea!"

I hung up.

I could go to the kitchen window and look in. I put the phone down on the ground by the truck so it wouldn't ring and give me away, then snuck toward the garden that ran under the window along the back of the house to the kitchen. I saw a shape in the kitchen. I stood up for a better view and watched someone riffling through my drawers. Why would anyone go through kitchen drawers?

Is that how so many teaspoons disappear? Are they stolen?

Furious almost covered how I felt. I spied a bag on the kitchen table. That could've been what I heard drop onto the floor. There I stood, staring straight into my own kitchen watching some moron go through my stuff and he didn't even know I was there. I could just make out the sound of cars stopping quickly out on the road.

I pulled my gun from my waistband, held up my badge to the window and knocked with the barrel of my Glock. The guy jumped about four feet in the air. He grabbed the bag and took off. My guess was for the front door. The slow crunch of footsteps approached from the driveway. I shoved the gun back into its holster and crept toward the front door. I wanted to see his face when he found the cops waiting.

He hauled ass out my door, right into the path of four uniformed police. I made my presence known with an amused cough. A tall blond officer pushed a young man to the ground and cuffed him. Another officer stepped up. He looked at me with a huge grin plastered across the faded summer tan on his face.

"Agent Conway," said the familiar officer.

"What are the chances of you turning up on my call out, Josh?" I replied with a smile.

"Heard you were working the Butterfly Murders case again. I hope you get him."

"Me too," I replied. I hadn't seen Josh since Mac's death. Josh was inside the crime scene that night with Sam, Misha, Lee and me. "Find out what that little prick was doing in my house and on my computer. Don't let him out on bail. FBI will pick him up when you're done with your interrogation."

He was now a loose end. We knew what happened to loose ends: they tended to die unpleasantly.

"Will do."

I poked the man on the ground with the toe of my boot. "What's your name?"

He turned his head against the roughcast of the driveway; a bloodshot eye looked up at me. "Malcolm Crowe," he said.

A penny dropped. That name I did know.

"Sure it is," I growled. "Take Doctor Crowe away."

Anger fermented inside me. Another Willis character this time from *The Sixth Sense*. Surely, Hawk would eventually run out of movies or characters?

I see dead people.

A squeal down the street heralded Lee's impending presence. Moments later Lee strode up the driveway, looking pissed and flushed. He pointed behind him and muttered, "Damn kids! I don't look anything like him."

All I could do was smile.

His eyes smoldered under a deep frown. "You want me to leave you outside and get your home declared a crime scene?"

"Not so much." A lot of effort went into controlling the smirk that rose every time anyone squawked or squealed after Lee.

"Shall we do this?"

"Yes, let's."

I followed Lee into the hallway.

"Where do you know he went?" Lee asked.

"My office and the kitchen, for sure."

"Let's start in your office then."

Mac's computer was on. The screensaver spiraled photographs I hadn't seen in a year and a half across a black background. Lee moved the mouse and the pictures of Mac and me disappeared.

Nothing seemed to be missing from the room. Sitting

on our shared desk were two new digital cameras, two computers, a printer, an iPod, and untold music CDs.

I had a habit of taking jewelry off while I was at my desk. Behind my keyboard was a jumble of bracelets and rings, both gold and silver.

"Robbery wasn't his intent," I commented.

"No it wasn't, he could've made a few dollars with the stuff on your desk."

"What did he want?"

Lee was looking through the history on Mac's computer. There was recent activity, as the screensaver suggested. But he couldn't find anything in recent history. According to the computer, nothing was uploaded or opened. He hadn't even had a peek at Mac's Outlook. It seemed that all he'd done was turn on the computer.

"There's nothing here Ellie."

"Why would anyone break in and turn on a computer?"

Lee shook his head. He clicked on the start button then the 'turn off' icon. We watched as Mac's computer powered down. The webcam light went out then blinked back on.

"Did you see that?" I asked pointing to the now-active camera.

"Well, that's interesting. He did upload something. A little program that can turn webcams on while the computer is apparently off." Lee reached over and pulled the webcam's USB plug out of the computer. "That should solve that problem."

"I'm not convinced."

Lee pulled a silver rectangular object from his pocket and adjusted the thin aerial on it.

"This will only pick up active signals. But if that little dick planted something else it's probably active."

I scurried from room to room, turning off everything I could remember that was wireless and was back in the office with Lee fairly quickly. His toy beeped and burped and flashed it's way around the house. I thought it was going to burst into flames in his hand.

"I think it's got issues," I said, as it squealed like a pig on the stairs and would not shut up no matter what Lee did.

Lee persevered, sweeping each room and checking everything possible in the vicinity of the over-active machine's alarmist behavior.

Finally he shut the detector off. "Stupid thing. Think it's developed a fault."

"You think there is anything here?"

Lee gave me one of his serious looks. "I don't think he was in the house long enough to plant anything clever."

Good enough.

I toured the house again this time turning everything back on. We walked into the kitchen and both avoided the obvious display on the counter in the middle of the room. I checked all the kitchen drawers, looking for anything missing or out of place and found nothing. With a sigh I turned back to face the island counter. Lee and I stood shoulder to shoulder looking at photographs fanned out like playing cards.

"We are avoiding the obvious question," I said. "How did Dr. Crowe know where I live?"

"Because Hawk told him," Lee replied.

"And Hawk knows this how?"

Lee shrugged. "He knows altogether too much and I wish I knew how."

Then I suddenly felt like Gopher from Disney's *Winnie the Pooh* movie. "I'm not in the book you know." It wasn't as if I needed more proof that someone was feeding information to Hawk. But I certainly had it.

Like any self-respecting law enforcement officer, I kept latex gloves in the cabinet underneath the sink. We pulled them on. Lee disappeared then returned with his camera, he took several pictures of the display. When he was done, I lifted the photographs and looked through them.

I'd seen most of them before in Christchurch. I skimmed past the ones of Carla. They made my skin crawl. I handed the new pictures to Lee, one at a time.

"Nice shot of us boarding the plane," I said, as he looked at the first one in his hand. I passed another. "Don't you love how this person captured the essence of this scene?" The picture was of me arriving at the Christchurch police station with Doc, followed by Rowan and the band. "Hey, that's out of order."

Lee nodded. "Yeah, it is. I wonder why?"

I shrugged. The guy who set them out could be stupid, or it could be something. I looked at the next picture in my hand, Rowan disembarking an airplane. I looked again then showed it to Lee. It wasn't what it seemed.

"Someone watching Rowan, being photographed by our Unsub?"

"Who the hell is that person?" Lee asked, squinting at the corner of the picture. "Magnifying glass?"

I produced one from a kitchen drawer and thrust it into his hand.

"Look, Ellie," he said and pushed the photo and magnifying glass under my nose.

"He's under surveillance. Who?"

"I'll try for a clearer picture and run it through a few data bases," Lee muttered. He gathered the rest of the pictures and headed off to my office.

Tell me it's a nightmare.

Lee returned grim-faced and holding his notebook, some papers and a pen. "Maybe spooks or NCIS." He scribbled some notes in his notebook then handed me the pen. "Not sure how I got your Grange pen but it was in my pocket."

I put the pen in my jeans pocket. "You borrowed it at the airport this morning."

A light went on behind his eyes. He remembered. "I'm still struggling with the whole leaving New Zealand at night but arriving home in the wee small hours of the same day. We got home before we left New Zealand."

It was not easy dealing with International Date Lines. My mind turned back to NCIS, spooks and Rowan.

"This makes no sense, why would they be watching Rowan?"

"This must have something to do with the military connection to Hawk."

"How many flags went up when you ran the face?" I asked with much curiosity.

Lee grinned. "Three big red ones." He thrust the paper at me.

I read it, gave it back with a shrug and said, "Add it to the pile." We were collecting too many requests via military channels to keep out of the way. If this was a military operation, then someone needed to fill me in. Noel Gerrard needed to fill me the fuck in.

I called and left a message for NCIS Special Agent Noel Gerrard.

Chapter Twenty-Seven
Bounce

So many thoughts converged as I tried to sleep that my dreams twisted into truly hideous events and I gave up. I wasn't dealing with the dizziness when I lay down, or closed my eyes, terribly well either. A late night call from my father-in-law, to remind me of a family event the next day, bugged me. I begged off because of the case but he insisted I drop in for a few minutes.

It was Beatrice's birthday after all.

Celebrating my barmy mother-in-law's birthday wasn't high a high priority for me. I couldn't decide which was the worse fate, being in the same room as my brother-in-law or having my house broken into by a movie character.

Instead of sleeping, I used my personal laptop to read the conversations from the chat rooms. It made for interesting reading. I was pretty sure I'd narrowed Hawk down to one of two screen names. Dave Addison or Maddie Hayes. Both names from the 1980s television series *Moonlighting.* Of course, Bruce Willis played Dave Addison.

I broke the news to Lee after I'd made the morning coffee. He was about as happy as I was. While he was drinking his first coffee, I announced a brief stop at my in-laws on our way into the office. There was no way to soften the blow, so I just blurted it out.

"Bob wants me to drop by – it's Beatrice's birthday."

He almost spat his coffee across the counter. "It's never good when any of us go there."

We stopped at the nearest 7-Eleven on the way and picked up a box of chocolates for Beatrice. Turning up empty-handed would make the experience way worse.

The usual chaos associated with Mac's family awaited us, even at nine in the morning. Bob apologized in advance for anything Eddie might say – he'd overheard a conversation Bob had with my father the day before. My brother-in-law Eddie started in on me as soon as Lee and Bob fell into conversation in the kitchen.

He was expounding the virtues of family and how some people should never be parents. Actually, I thought he was talking about himself but then he astounded me by telling me I was one of those people. He'd heard that I was considering adopting a child and felt it was in my best interests to tell me that it was a bad idea.

I was in no mood to play along. He was huffing and puffing through tightly-pursed lips. I suspected his anal sphincter looked like that too, as it tightened around the broomstick manifestly residing up his bum.

His eyes squinted in a nasty fashion.

My left hand slipped into the back pocket of my jeans. With my fingers curled around the object, I pulled it out and let my hand fall by my side; my fingers opened the blade without the need of my eyes. I felt it lock into place.

Could he see what was in my hand now? If he could, he didn't react.

I waited.

His lips tightened.

Must be one hell of a straw he's sucking on.

I swapped the cold blade to my right hand. His eyes never left mine.

"You have no idea how much I detest you," I replied. "You are to never go near my child. Make sure you understand that, Eddie. Never." My hand tightened around the handle of the blade.

He huffed with pent-up rage.

"If you adopt that child, that will make her my niece," he said with glee. His eyes narrowed some more. It seemed impossible to me that he could see anything beyond his stumpy eyelashes and the fatty bags under his eyes.

"No, Eddie. She will never be your anything."

My honesty went unappreciated. He scowled and his eyes disappeared altogether.

"The court will never let you adopt if you are going to deny her a family." His words smacked of a thinly-veiled threat.

"I have family. Carla will have family. You are not part of it. You are not related to me, you moron."

"I was a deputy sheriff," he said, full of self-importance. "You can't talk to me like that."

"You were fired for being drunk on the job," I said. My strike was surgical in its delivery.

He balked. His face blanched. Spittle flew as he hissed, "I resigned."

If that hit a big nerve then my next statement would

damn near detonate his head. "You made up a mental illness to allow yourself an excuse for failure."

He stammered out, "It's real. I have it."

I let it go, no sense arguing with the wannabe insane. Eddie was the faux-relative no one wants and no one can get rid of.

I watched, calculating the time it would take for his gasket to blow. I started a countdown in my head.

Mac spun in his grave.

Ten, nine, eight.

A thick vein began to throb in Eddie's forehead.

Seven, six, five.

He turned a pretty shade of purple.

Four, three, two.

His right hand formed a tight fist, his body shook.

One.

My right hand slipped forward – I saw the sudden shocked look on his face – then I jabbed upward fast and hard. I twisted and pulled. I took a step back to watch what would happen next. He clutched his throat. Blood spilled between his fingers. He grabbed at his throat with his other hand.

As if that would help.

It was fascinating. He stared at me with those hateful, patronizing eyes. They didn't seem patronizing as the color drained from his face and poured over his shirt-front. I saw the gorgeous velvet red dripping off his elbows and onto the floor.

A hand clamped over my hand. The knife I held disappeared. Someone spun me around and grabbed me by both arms. An intense face met mine.

"What in the hell do you think you are doing?"

I watched his mouth move; the movement enthralled me. The sound seemed delayed, like a badly-dubbed spaghetti western.

"Ellie?"

"Lee?" I returned.

I turned my head slightly to better view the corpse; for an instant, it was the bloodied body of Gloria Rowe. I straightened up and looked at Lee: it didn't make sense.

"He's alive?" I couldn't believe my bad luck. Eddie was still alive.

He was still freaking talking.

Amazingly enough there wasn't a mark on him.

"What did you think?" Lee asked. His expression mimicked one I'd seen on Mac's face more times than I cared to remember. He was worried.

I'd crossed way over the line.

I opened my hand and stared at the pen Rowan had given me and then put it back in my pocket.

"Nothing," I said.

Lee turned to Eddie and said, "You should make yourself scarce."

Eddie's mouth flapped; words failed him at first then spilled out in an almighty rush, "She's a bitch! I don't know what my brother ever saw in her. She should not have a child in her care."

He postured, posed and pointed. "Mac had a lucky escape, dying like he did. I wouldn't be surprised if she was to blame."

Lee glanced at me as Eddie crumpled to the floor clutching his nose. Blood poured from between his fingers.

"Did you hurt your hand?" I asked.

"Not really," Lee replied.

I smiled and called out to Bob, "Eddie needs some ice for a broken nose ... and we're leaving."

Lee and I hurried out the back door. A blast of cold wind hit my face bringing something familiar with it.

I just couldn't place it.

Chapter Twenty-Eight
Learn To Be Still

We didn't go straight to work. I asked Lee to take me to Fairfax Inova hospital. The whole interlude with Eddie was alarming. I've always believed I had a predisposition to insanity and that seemed to be pointing right to it. Lee waited for me in the car while I hurried through the main entrance and up to my neurosurgeon's office. I managed to convince his nurse that I needed to see him immediately. She was all of twelve and still wore braces. Last time I saw her it ended in a *Doogie Howser* flashback. I fought it this time, with everything I had.

My long-suffering neurologist listened to my tale of woe from Christchurch, how I was really fine but just a bit dizzy at times. He sat in silent contemplation as I re-told the stabbing of Eddie. After a short neurological exam he suggested, pending an MRI, it was possibly BPPV or benign paroxysmal positional vertigo. The worse thing was the visual disturbance during the attack. It's a tad dangerous when I can't see properly. He also ran through the Epley maneuver and instructed me to do the same simple exercises twice a day for the next few days.

He also said no to driving. I convinced him BPPV was not a big enough deal to have me removed from the case. On the plus side, he declared Eddie deserved everything he got and my mental balance was not an issue. I was imaginative. Leon suggested if I ever retired, I should try my hand at writing.

There was a certain amount of guilt associated with my visit to Leon's office because I hadn't told Kurt what was going on.

It was early afternoon when we arrived at work. Lee was still apologizing about breaking Eddie's nose. I imagined he'd been going over the incident while waiting for me.

"Will you stop!" I said, walking next to him along the corridor that led to our offices.

"I shouldn't have done it, Ellie. He's not right in the head and I hit him."

Lee was going to beat himself up over the incident all afternoon. I grabbed his arm and stopped walking.

"Listen to me. Eddie is a lunatic but he knows what he's doing and that crack about me being responsible for Mac's death ... was designed to get him hit."

In all honesty, I didn't think Eddie was far off the mark.

"I shouldn't have done it. I know better than that."

"Yes, you do. So, don't do it again," I replied. "Consider yourself smacked across the knuckles SSA Davenport, and move on."

He smiled. "Is that official?"

"Abso-fuc'n-lutely." I hoped Eddie would not go spouting his poison at the courts; his special brand of bullshit would drag things on unnecessarily.

"All righty then."

Lee and I grinned at each other then moved on to my

office. My office wasn't only *my* office; I shared it with Lee and Sam. It was a sizable room and needed to be. Misha called with news: we had something to chase, not just chat room conversations. The photographs, the break-in – the web cam being turned on, the lovely email Hawk sent me, the last picture of someone watching Rowan – he was here all right. Hawk was playing his games, as he did before. He was determined to involve us as much as he could. Sending someone to my home ensured we'd stay actively involved. The thing I couldn't figure out was why he wanted it like that and why he wanted a camera in my office. Guess he couldn't get his rocks off any other way. Misha was heading out on Hawk's trail. I checked my watch.

"What time did Misha say he'd be in?"

"Just after midnight," Lee replied. "We meeting him? Or we sending a car?"

"Us, I think it should be us."

"Friendly faces and all that jazz," Lee replied with a nod of agreement.

Lee picked up a CD from my desk. I could see him turning it over in his hands and feel the questions brewing.

"Yes, it's Grange's new album and yes, it's from the *Drifter* tour that they're on now."

A pang of guilt drove through me as I remembered the concert. Not because we'd successfully ruined the evening for forty-eight thousand people, but because a life ended. And I couldn't stop it from happening.

Lee grinned. "Let's put it on then SSA, let's get this joint moving."

He slid the shiny disk into the stereo on the other side of the room. I carried on checking email, accompanied by Rowan Grange singing and feeling as if I could fall into his song.

I gathered emails and printed out a bunch. I liked keeping hard copies – our filing system also liked hard copies.

"Lee, grab a file will you, and drop these in it. Mark it 'New Zealand' and use the Butterfly case number with an amendment." The paperwork generated by the case was unbelievable. By the end of it, we'd have boxes of paper-work and evidence; everything imaginable had to be doc-umented and filed, because that's how we do it.

There were a few minutes for me to dash into my Foundation account and check my blog comments. Judg-ing by the amount of comments left welcoming me back, I'd been missed.

An uneasy thought crept in. Someone else used my laptop. I thought only my team had access – and it should've been only my team – but Rowan used it in Christchurch.

"Lee?"

"Yes," he replied without looking up.

"Rowan used my laptop in Christchurch. He probably had twenty minutes unsupervised time on it."

"You worried he could've planted that key logger?"

"Maybe."

"My gut tells me Rowan has nothing to do with this situation."

Mine too. Between bouts of doubt.

"I hope not."

Forensics would find out where the keylogger and whatever else was on my machine came from, or at least who wrote the program. There was a partial report on the Malcolm Crowe person who'd broken into my home. According to the preliminary interview with police, he was paid to break into my home by an unknown subject. The Unsub told him I was not home.

He was supposed to turn on a computer, upload a small file and remove all trace of his activity. According to police, he had no knowledge of what the program did. I found that a little hard to swallow, considering he knew how to erase his tracks. There was no mention of what he was doing in my kitchen nor was there mention of his real name. There was also no mention of how he knew there were two computers or which one to turn on.

Why didn't he tell the police he'd left photographs?

"Lee, what happened to the photographs?"

"I left copies at your place and have the originals here," he replied and pulled them from his bag.

"Great, thanks."

Lee wrote up the chain of evidence for the photographs.

Something I'd read was niggling me. "Hey Lee, Crowe was adamant that the Unsub told him I was *not* home. How the hell would anyone know I wasn't home?"

"You said yourself you feel like you are being watched."

"Yes, that's true. You think someone followed me home at some stage? You know my street; it's a cul-de-sac full of well-meaning nosy neighbors."

Lee grinned. "Cul-de-sac does sound better than dead end. And I know your neighbors. Any strange car would definitely have drawn the attention of that elderly neighbor of yours; she would've scurried over to report the intrusion."

"Scurry is an apt word; she's very mouse-like." It still bugged me that the Unsub told Crowe I was not home. How did he know?

The mountain of paperwork in front of me finally diminished. I even put in requests for reimbursement on the credit cards before we headed out across the bridge and back to Fairfax County, Virginia.

I turned my head too quickly to look at something and dizziness hit me with such force, I was glad Lee was driving. I'd engineered him to drive ever since the blast. It was bad enough I still carried a weapon and was still at work. Driving would be monumentally stupid: even I was not that crass. Before I could stop myself, I had my cell phone in my hand and was talking to Doc.

"It's Conway," I said when he answered.

"What do you need?"

A little voice in my head said 'tell him.' "Can you meet us at my place?"

"Sure. I'll be right over."

I hung up as my mind whirled through my setting up

of Eddie. The blast of wind that hit my face as I left my father-in-law's house. I smelt the wind.

Words tumbled in the air then bounced off the windscreen.

"Lee, I smelt the wind."

"It's not windy now, Ellie."

"No, in Christchurch at the stadium, I smelt the wind."

He glanced sideways at me. "That was a windy night."

He wasn't getting it. He wasn't getting it because wasn't making sense. "When I was waiting for backup in that tunnel ... I smelt cologne."

"We're talking about a stadium that contained forty thousand plus heaving bodies; cologne is the best thing you would've smelt."

He had a point. Most people smelt of booze, some of vomit and a few smelt truly repulsive.

"A cologne I've smelt before, Lee."

"All right I'll bite ... when?" He'd turned on his patient voice.

"When I was jacked heading for Tulley Gate, when we were after the Butterfly Murderer."

Lee pulled off the road minutes from my home.

"So you think whoever jacked you was in Christchurch?"

"Probably. Cologne smells different on different people; what I smelled there was exactly the same as in my car that day."

Lee looked at me.

"Exactly the same, Lee."

He didn't make a move to disregard my statement. Probably because my very acute sense of smell lead to the arrest of another Unsub. It was our secret weapon. I told no one outside the team how I knew the nurse attempting to administer a fatal drug to my dad, was the same person who'd killed most of the regulars from my chat room and cut my throat. Not much more than a scratch really. Hardly worth worrying about.

Lee knew. Lee was there when it all went down. Lee believed me now.

"The problem here is we caught both people involved in your hijacking/kidnapping," Lee said slowly.

"So we thought. Neither of them wore this cologne. Someone else must've been in the car."

"A third person." He looked at me for a beat. "You think the cologne is Hawk?"

Did I think that?

"I think we need to find out what cologne it is, it's the only lead we have."

"Sounds good. Guess we can hope it's a rare scent."

"I think it is. I've smelt it twice and I've come across a lot of people in between times."

He nodded.

Lee checked the mirrors and pulled out into the traffic for the short trip home.

Chapter Twenty-Nine
Beast Of Burden

I set my coffee cup on the kitchen counter, not bothering to rinse the last of the black dregs down the drain. Doc rinsed his cup and mine.

Lee sat at the kitchen table still nursing his mug and staring at the latest warning from the Defense Department and another sheet of paper containing more information on the man we'd identified watching Rowan. Every now and then, he doodled on a piece of the paper with my pen.

"A Military spook," he said under his breath. "Why would the Department of Defense and the CIA be interested in a rock star?"

I rubbed my temples with my fingers.

Doc sat down at the table. "You need something for a headache?"

"No, it'll be okay. I have no clue why the D.O.D. would be interested in a rock star," I replied before really thinking about the question. "Who was the guy?"

"CIA. Think they could be working joint ops with NCIS?"

"That wouldn't surprise me."

The CIA thing intrigued me. I knew we'd get zero information from them. With the CIA involved in military intelligence and criminal investigations, we'd get precious little information from anyone. Unless I talked to

Sean O'Hare to see what he could uncover.

"There are too many military connections in our case to make this a coincidence," Lee said.

He was right. From day one of our first tap dance with Hawk, there was a military connection but it started out Army and now it's Navy and spooks too. But why Rowan?

"Could the interest in Rowan be because of Rowan's connection to us and Hawk's connection to terrorism?" I was thinking aloud rather than expecting an answer.

Lee appeared deep in thought before he said, "Hawk's into making money by selling kids. That doesn't appear to have a connection warranting Naval Criminal Investigation, except we found a person of interest to them in New Zealand."

"I think we can assume they've been interested since we first discovered that woman using a Department of Defense computer to hack the Foundation, back during the killing spree phase of this investigation," I replied. "This feels like it's become some sort of joint forces super-spook investigation. We need to be read in – but I'm feeling that ain't gonna happen."

"Gerrard?"

"I'll try," I replied. I had a sneaking suspicion that he was avoiding me. My last call went to voicemail and wasn't returned.

Lee nodded. "Surveillance on Rowan makes no sense to me."

We knew he wasn't a person of interest. The circumstantial evidence however wasn't so kind. The chat rooms were dedicated to his band, he used my laptop, and the kids were all at his concert. I left another message for Agent Gerrard. There are a whole lot of people who will lead you nowhere if you let them.

"I'm hitting the hay," I said.

"Sleep well, Ellie. Doc and I will crash in the guest room if we get tired." Lee smiled. "It won't be the guest room for long. It'll be Carla's room soon."

"Here's hoping. You know where everything is, right?"

"Sure I do. Go on to bed," Lee replied with one of his bigger grins. "I'll wake you in time to get Misha."

"'Night," I said over my shoulder.

Before going upstairs, I checked the front door, back-door and the exterior door from my office. As I walked up the stairs, the disjointed floaty feeling of earlier returned with vengeance. I clutched the handrail and waited for a moment. My head spun in sickening circles. I took a deep breath and tried to steady myself.

After several breaths and with my hand firmly on the handrail I walked slowly up the stairs. The last thing I wanted was to fall and have Doc and Lee racing to my rescue. How embarrassing would that be?

A photo of Mac and me sat on the nightstand next to our bed. I fell into bed not bothering to remove anything except my jeans and boots. I hit the lamp base with my hand. As the light faded to black, my eyes rested on the picture.

"Save me a seat next to you," I whispered, then rolled over, letting cool darkness soothe my tired eyes and wash over my dizzy head.

Alone, I listened to the noises of the house settling, recognizing the creaks and groans of the old wooden house and hearing the tree branches softly scratching in the breeze. Comforting noises that meant I was home.

For an hour I lay there and then gave up and flicked the lamp back on. As a warm yellow glow filled the room, I saw my brand-new personal laptop snoozing on the chair in the corner. I tossed the covers back scrambled from my warm bed grabbed the laptop and scurried back under the covers. Holding the laptop, I recalled a pensive feeling regarding my work laptop from earlier that day.

Why did Rowan use my laptop? I answered that myself. To read my blog. It shouldn't be a big deal.

I fired up my laptop and sat staring at the web browser screen. I had no idea what I wanted to do, I just I knew I didn't want to think.

No one was online in the Butterfly Foundation chat room except two moderators. I snuck out again before anyone noticed me. Why I went into the room at all isn't quite the mystery it would seem. It was the same reason I logged into the MSN and Yahoo Messengers and checked the list of online contacts. I hoped for a miracle, prayed that *Galileo* would magically appear.

Dead men don't talk, nor do they sign into messenger services, or collect mail. When things got bad and life without him was just plain hard, I wrote emails to Mac at his *Galileo* account and sent them off. It made me feel better. I knew one day his email account would be full and the emails would start returning. That was some-thing I'd deal with when it happened.

With blurred vision, an aching head and what felt like the burden of my past pressing on my shoulders, I surfed for another hour. It was a struggle to remain semi-alert and even to read words on the screen. All day it felt like I'd missed half of everything that went on. The cologne issue vexed me.

I ran a Google search for high-end colognes from Germany or France hoping to find something helpful. I don't know what I was thinking. It's not as if you can smell them over the internet. I felt a smile wander across my face.

Imagine if you could smell everything you clicked on?

That's some weird shit.

A small blue window popped up from the bottom of my screen. It said, *Galileo signed in.*

Without a pause, I clicked on the little pop-up and opened a chat window.

Otherwisecat: *Mac?*

Galileo: *Babe, you okay?*

I clicked the request camera button. He accepted. He was right there in front of me.

Otherwisecat: *I'm always okay.*

Galileo: *Babe ... dead people don't use MSN. You're talking to me on MSN. Wanna do over?*

Otherwisecat: *Fuc'n smartass!*

Galileo: *You're not dizzy? Don't have a headache? You didn't get caught in a fuc'n explosion and get a concussion?*

You don't have BPPV?

Otherwisecat: *I am, I do and yes, I did. I do and again I do but I'm okay! Can we talk about you, and where you are?*

Galileo: *I'm right here watching you. I know this is a little whacky.*

Otherwisecat: *They're gonna fuc'n lock me up if anyone gets wind of this.*

Galileo: *Maybe…*

Otherwisecat: *Maybe's ass.*

Galileo: *LOL. No one's going to lock you up, Babe. I won't let them.*

Otherwisecat: *I'd like to see your incorporeal self try to stop them.*

He was right there. His eyes stared at me. His smile reminded me. My fingers traced over the picture on my screen. He smiled.

Galileo: *Ellie?*

Galileo: *He's a good man, Ellie. He is a good man.*

Otherwisecat: *Who is?*

The screen wobbled, wavy lines crossed my vision. I blinked slowly.

He was right there. His eyes smiled at me and his concerned brow reminded me of life and how it was to live.

Galileo: *Ellie??*

The screen vibrated. A buzzing noise emanated from the laptop. I felt it hit my head then pass right through.

A new message followed.

Galileo: *Don't give Kurt such a hard time. Ellie. This isn't about Rowan. Ask Lee, he'll tell you.*

Otherwisecat: *Ask Lee? Mac, is adopting Carla a good idea?*

I typed in slow motion or maybe it wasn't, maybe my connection was slow. I felt a smile drift across my face as I recalled a smartassed comment to Mac from a few years ago. 'Satellite, dude, it ain't slow, it's atmospheric.'

The computer buzzed on my knee again. When I looked at the screen, Mac was using all caps at me. Was it really necessary to raise his voice via capital letters?

My lamp flickered. I closed my eyes. Exhaustion? My eyes were too heavy to remain open. I needed sleep.

There was a buzz, then my light went out.

A voice came out of the soft light. A deeper voice than Mac's. It said several things before I heard anything I understood.

"Ellie?" Lee asked. He seemed awful close. "We have to go get Misha. Wake up."

"Ellie, come on."

Something vibrated through the quilt. I sat up and saw the laptop. The screen was closed but the buzzing continued.

Lee leaned over me and picked it up. "Do you mind?" he asked. I shrugged. He lifted the screen then sat heavily on the bed.

"Tell me you are awake," Lee said.

"I'm awake," I replied.

He turned the laptop to face me. "Explain?"

On the screen was an open Messenger window. A con-

390

versation between Otherwisecat and Galileo. The last thing typed was a message to Lee from Mac aka Galileo it read: *Lee, Don't let her work too hard. Something fucky is going on here. Tell her about the background check on Grange and that adopting Carla is the best idea she's ever had. She needs to talk to Kurt.*

"When was it sent?" I asked. My eyes wouldn't focus properly on the times on the screen.

"An hour and a half ago," he replied. "Who could have access to Mac's account?"

No one. Why would anyone do that? "It was Mac. Read the conversation," I replied, knowing my answer wouldn't fill Lee with confidence.

He scrolled up and read a little, then gave me a long questioning look.

"I'm not convinced," he said and brought up a track and trace program. "I'm going to trace this and I'm presuming it won't lead back to heaven."

"What if ..."

Lee held his finger to his lips. "We'll cross that bridge later. Meanwhile, whoever it is knows a lot about you. You feeling all right?"

"Yeah, Lee." I smiled and trotted out my usual answer, "I'm okay."

He grinned. "So Mac saying you have to talk to Kurt is fantasy?"

I shrugged.

"Nothing new there then. I'll be watching you."

"Nothing new there either," I retorted.

Seems everyone is watching me.

Lee dropped the subject and reminded me we had to go to the airport and pick up Misha.

"Get Sam too," I told him. "I'm feeling we'll be moving on Misha's information right away."

"Gear?"

"Bring a spare weapon for Misha; we don't know if he's carrying a sidearm. Make sure we each have cell phones, radios and laptops. Spare magazines, night vision equipment, bulletproof vests and ask Doc to check the medical kits are fully stocked."

As soon as that left my mouth, I remembered Mac lying in a pool of his own blood.

Lee nodded, his face contorted with what I guessed to be the same memory.

"Got that."

"Misha contacted us directly? No one in the office knows about this meeting tonight?"

"I'm not aware of anyone other than operational Delta A knowing he's even flying in."

"I don't want anyone contacting the office until this is over."

"I'll pass it on."

"Have I got time to shower?"

"Yeah, go for it. I'll put a call through to Sam and get our gear stowed." Lee picked up my laptop and left the room. He tapped the case. "I'll have a quick go at this too. The ping should be done shortly."

Great, that's both my work and my personal laptop

acting like bitchy teenagers, inviting strangers over and having a party at my expense.

Chapter Thirty
Have You Seen Your Mother Baby?

"How reliable is this information?" Lee asked from his position near my right arm.

We'd been lying on the cold ground for nearly an hour with no sign of anything or anyone. God I love stakeouts, especially in the wee small hours of a Sunday.

"As good as it can be, my friend," Misha replied with customary politeness.

He'd looked like seven kinds of hell when we picked him up at the airport. I didn't think he was doing a lot of sleeping.

"This is the place they're using, yes? They're holding kids here?" Sam asked from my left.

"My source says this is it. This is the dockyard. They ship the containers from here?"

"Yes, it is," I replied. I lifted my night-vision binoculars and scanned the area ahead of us. There were upward of forty containers, sitting in rows. These were outgoing, already cleared and sealed by customs. I saw nothing. I turned the binoculars and my eyes toward the gate, the only gate. The containers were due for loading and if they were going to stash people in them, it would have to be within the next hour.

"Conway, are you well enough to do this?" Doc asked.

"Yes." No, that's why you are here.

"We haven't had time to talk. Is there something I

should know?"

"BPPV," I replied. It was unnecessary to expand on it.

"I thought so. I'll stick with you, just in case."

An engine started.

"What's that?" Lee asked, peering into the darkness.

"Look up," Misha said.

A crane boom moved and we could see the small red lights along the boom. Bless night-vision binoculars.

"A gantry crane, over by the far fence," I said. "We may have something."

Lee used his binoculars. "They're moving a container out of this area."

"Could be swapping it out."

"Makes sense, these are cleared and sealed. It would be easier to swap a container than to traipse children through the port."

Welcome to the party.

I pulled my cell phone from my pocket and called in a request. Thermal imaging from a satellite. Sam tapped at keys on his laptop.

"You got the link yet?" I asked and shoved my phone back into my pocket.

"Almost."

"Can you make the container they're moving into the yard your focus?"

"Got it. We have heat signatures from the container." He stared at the screen. I watched his lips move as he counted. "Six."

"Any chance they're shipping livestock?" I asked. It

pays to check these things.

"Not from here. If that is what's going on, then Port Authority will take a dim view," Lee said.

"Call in for backup, and let's do it. Sam, you and Misha take the car and hit the crane. I want whoever is in that thing. Lee, Doc and I are going for the container."

Looking through my binoculars, I counted how many rows and containers we needed to pass to find the correct one. Once down there, we'd have no visual.

"Wireless. Stow the laptop in the trunk, let's do it."

I stood up, brushed dirt off my jacket and released my gun from my holster.

Lee and I moved several feet away from each other and both spoke into our microphones. "Sound check."

The other three voices came back loud and clear.

"Meet you on the other side," Sam said.

We took off running. Keeping low and moving fast wasn't that easy. We slid down the bank to the hurricane wire fence. Lee pulled wire cutters from a backpack.

"Let's hope this fence is off," he muttered glancing at the high voltage warning. He started cutting wire away from the bottom. We needed to peel back enough for us to slip through. I'd asked the company to cut the power to the fence. Still, in the back of my mind, I expected Lee to be twitching and peeing himself any second. It was a great relief that he wasn't, and hadn't.

He grabbed the cut section and lifted it back. I slid under first, followed by Doc.

It didn't take long to drop the section back, mark it,

and find ourselves lost in a dark maze of huge shipping containers. We ran and hoped it was the right direction. There was no chatter coming through from Sam or Misha.

"Sam, where are you? Over."

"At the crane. Over," he replied, his voice a steady calm whisper.

"Let Sam take him, Misha," I said. "This is our turf. Over."

"I am having his back. Over." Misha replied.

Lee chuckled.

"Thank you. Over," I whispered back.

I was running short of breath, our pace bordering on frenetic as we searched for the container. Somewhere east of us we heard sirens.

"How many rows Ellie?" Lee asked. In the dark, we couldn't see each other properly. I knew he'd turned back toward me, because his voice was clear.

"Fifteen. I think we were in line with the container when we came down the hill." I turned back hoping to see the small hill. All I saw was another looming dark shape that blocked the starlight.

Noise erupted in my ear. I stumbled bumping into Doc.

"Here, take my hand," he said. I could see something dark extended in my direction.

"Thanks. I'll be fine."

"Conway, take my hand."

I groaned inside, sucked up the urge to snap off his

397

head, and took his hand

"That wasn't so hard, was it?"

Don't push it.

The noise continued. Misha's voice, Sam's voice and two unknowns; machinery moving. Gunshots.

We hurried on, slightly slower but possibly more determined. Over my earpiece, I heard another voice, this time it was unexpected.

"Ellie. Have eyes on you. A hundred yards straight ahead then stop. Over."

"Roger, Caine. Over."

Lee began counting as we ran, using our strides to measure. I didn't expect Caine to turn up on this. I was glad to hear his voice, real glad to hear his voice. Misha and Sam acknowledged someone. I ignored them to concentrate on the container that materialized in front of us.

"This it?" I asked, hoping Caine would confirm, which he did.

Lee did a quick check around the container. He ran back and grabbed my arm.

"This way."

We were at the wrong end.

"Caine, any movement? Over." Lee asked.

"Affirmative," he replied. "One person is moving. Over."

"Let's hope they're not expecting us," I whispered. Lee inspected the lock. There was only one way to open it. He pulled a detonator from his belt.

"Fire in the hole," he whispered.

Doc threw his arm over me and pulled me aside. There was a small flash and loud noise. The lock blew apart.

Caine's voice interrupted my thoughts. "Six stationary signatures, one moving. I repeat you have seven heat signatures, one is moving. Over."

Doc took the left, I took the right. We trained our weapons on the doors.

Lee pulled open the doors, going with them out of the line of fire. I shone my flashlight into the darkness. Lee appeared beside me.

"Raise your hands," he called. "Walk toward us."

A lone figure moved into the beam of torch light. Nothing else moved. Lee grabbed the woman by her wrist and spun her to face the container door. The metal clanged as he pushed her against it. He hauled her hands behind her back and cuffed her without speaking.

I entered the container, shining the light up and down the interior. I spoke to Caine, "We need ambulances. There are six kids in here. Over."

"Copy that. Over."

Doc knelt beside one. "They're unconscious."

I looked around. In the far corner, I found a medical kit and an area obviously for the woman.

"Send up a flare Ellie, it'll help the paramedics locate you. Over," Caine said.

I trotted out of the container and hauled a flare from my belt. Lee stood over the woman. She was face down on the concrete. I broke the flare and threw it a few feet away. Within minutes, running feet sounded, heading toward us.

Misha's voice came from somewhere close by.

"The crane operator, he didn't make it," he said as he came into view.

"This was a good tip, Misha," I replied, shaking his hand.

"You have the children?"

"We have six and the escort."

"They are well?"

"It looks like it. Doc is with them now."

His face broke into a beaming grin. "We do good."

Doc's voice cut in over the microphone, "None of these girls are older than ten or eleven. Transporting them to hospital now. Over."

"Copy. Are you going with them? Over."

"As long as you are okay," he replied. "Over."

"Affirmative. Go. Conway out."

"Walk with me ..." I said, taking Misha's arm. I knew my team and Caine could hear us. "There is a strong military connection, including surveillance. What do you know?"

"We are focusing on the children, my friend. Let the military work on the rest."

He did know something. His façade of the cool FSB agent didn't fool me.

"Tell me!"

"You know he is a terrorist. This is a matter of international importance. Not our concern."

"It is our concern. Our people are caught in this ..."

"Our focus is the children," he replied with calm insistence.

"It is, but we seem to be caught in something military," I replied. "What do you know?"

"There is talk of weapons purchased from North Korea. There may be a link."

"Hawk?"

"He is using the funds from the sale of the children to purchase weapons."

"What sort of weapons?"

"Nuclear."

'Holy crap!' I heard the others whispering in my ear. I paraphrased and asked, "Who's working on this?"

He shook his head. I knew he could hear them too.

"Misha?"

He shrugged. "I cannot answer."

Chapter Thirty-One
Any Other Day

The dark start to Sunday left a bad taste in my mouth and the stitches annoyed me. Sitting at my desk at work didn't help the trouble I was having with the whole nuclear weapon thing. Not that I didn't think it was possible, because I knew it was. Misha's disclosure also made more sense of the spook aspect. If they were looking for missing nukes then surveillance in our operation was justified. Still, the polite thing to do would've been to read me in. I didn't quite understand what they expected to find by placing Rowan under surveillance.

Maybe someone had a crush.

What irked me was that Hawk had obviously taken a lot more kids than we knew about. To make the sort of money they needed, he must've been poaching kids from all over the world for a long time. So, why was Hawk so determined to engage us in his game? Was he trying to throw everyone off the nuclear trail?

Finding the kids alive and well was wonderful. This time I felt as though we'd pulled the rug out from under him. I believed he didn't expect us to find these kids.

It bothered me that Misha couldn't or wouldn't say who exactly was tracking Hawk.

I tried to take my mind off the previous night by checking my email.

A message from Rowan almost made me fall off my

chair; the chat room situation was obviously bothering him and he'd done some nosing about on his own.

He'd sent me a copied section from a chat room and an invitation to stop by and have a look for myself. Something did interest me about the conversation and I surmised it was what made Rowan pull it out. One of the participants appeared to be a young teenager and was desperate to talk to Rowan. She was jailbait and she was apparently freaking out over something that had happened to her. The conversation pointed more to a fan-type-fantasy scenario. She wanted an excuse to be rescued by one particular person. It didn't matter that Rowan was old enough to be her father. Maybe she didn't have a daddy. The more disturbing element was the reaction of a guest in the room, especially when the guest eventually logged out and came back as a supposed band member.

As Rowan pointed out in his email, the person who posed as Rowan, wasn't Rowan. I could clearly see Rowan sitting in the room sidebar, using the same girl's screen name he used when he first showed us the room. Sure, it's possible to be in a chat room as two different people, just use different browsers. I hoped Rowan didn't know that.

Despite the drama queen aspect of the room, and the look-at-me-I'm-so-needy thing the little girly had going, I detected something else, something far more sinister. I recalled the email from Hawk. This was a good hunting ground.

I emailed Rowan and said we were looking into it. Then called out to Lee and asked him to get someone from cyber to run some ping and trace software on the occupants of the chat room in question. Running a ping and trace would tell us if anyone logged into the chat room as two different screen names. It's easy to cheat and use different browsers but harder to use multiple ISPs. I also asked if they had someone who could sit in the room to gather intelligence. That made me smile. I'd seen precious little intelligence on display in the excerpt of the transcript I'd just read.

Seemed there was a whole lot of stupid going on. It wasn't like the conversations I had read the night before. They had a more defined adult tone; now I was sure Hawk had used either Maddie Hayes or Dave Addison as his screen names then. This time the predator used names of band members.

"What's so interesting?" Lee asked.

"Someone pretending to be a band member in a chat room with underage children; you do the math."

"Nice. You think this could have something to do with Hawk?"

"Judging by his email and considering what went down at the Christchurch concert, it could be. It could be but this feels wrong."

"Feels wrong?" Lee asked. "This is the same chat room he knows we are monitoring?"

"Yeah, but the kid is older than he usually likes. And he doesn't use band member names. Her profile says

404

she's fourteen," I said – acutely aware that Carla was about to turn fourteen and that Hawk had already suggested he was going to grab her.

Lee agreed. "That doesn't fit his profile; he's always liked them younger and twelve has been the oldest so far."

"Have Cyber check it out and if it's unrelated but sinister, they can hand it over to one of the dedicated Innocence Lost task forces," I told him. It's good to have a plan. The FBI Innocence Lost National Initiative was founded in 2003 and by October 2009 had recovered eight hundred and eight-six children.

"You think it's unrelated, don't you?"

"I do. Tell Cyber it looks sinister."

"I'll get Cyber in place A-sap."

"Thanks."

A question arose that could not be avoided. Did we have a list of all the venues the band played since Hawk came into our lives?

The answer was no, but I knew where to get one without tipping off anyone to my train of thought.

Wikipedia.

It was a simple matter of typing in the tour name and I found all the venues including the pre-tour shows. There was nothing in the DC area, or Virginia, in the period of the Butterfly Murders.

Hawk must've gathered victims solely from the Foundation, until we ran him out of town.

Too much heat.

Just as I thought the use of the Christchurch concert may have been a one-off, I came across a list of European concert venues and dates for the *Drifter* tour Grange were now on.

It was bad. Munich, Hamburg, Stuttgart and Frankfurt in Germany, Brussels in Belgium, Helsinki in Finland, Oslo in Norway, then Copenhagen in Denmark; from there the band flew to Australia and on to New Zealand.

There was a moment of disbelief as I scrabbled through the files until I found the information from Misha about missing kids in Europe. They matched.

Hawk was following the tour.

My phone rang. When I answered, I heard a familiar voice.

"You busy?"

"Not really, waiting on some feedback is all."

"Dinner?"

"Thought you were at home in New York."

"I am."

"And I'm in DC," I replied.

Obviously, dinner was out of the question.

"Do you think it's possible that someone is using the band's name to prey on kids?"

Ah, so that's why he rang.

"Anything's possible. I'm having it checked out. We'll find out what's going on within the next twenty-four hours." What was I going to do? Tell him over the phone?

"We really should have dinner. And soon," Rowan said. His voice injected a much-needed lightness into my world.

"You'd have to come here I'm afraid. I can't bug out in the middle of a case."

"Is that an invitation?"

"I think so."

I wasn't entirely sure that was wise, knowing what I knew. No, probably not wise at all. But Mac said he was a good guy. Let's listen to the dead.

My ability to see an overview of the situation was missing. So I called Carla.

"Hey kiddo. How's your weekend?"

"It's all right, kinda boring. We have a field trip coming up for history class."

"Awesome, do they let adults go?" I'm up for a field trip; for fun I could trick Lee into tagging along and enjoy the screaming and hysteria that'd follow.

"I have a permission slip and it has questions for parent-helpers to fill out. You have to agree to a police check."

We both laughed.

"I didn't know who to give the form to," Carla said.

"Hang on to it. I was planning on coming to take you to dinner tomorrow night." I hoped I'd have some idea of where I stood legally by then. Dad had hired the best lawyer in the District and he had already petitioned the court for interim custody. We were meeting the judge at ten on Monday morning. Due to the sensitive situation, the judge was hearing the case in the privacy of her chambers.

"Yay, dinner!"

"I don't want to freak you out but I need to ask, do you still feel like someone's watching you?"

"Yeah ... when I'm at school or going to school and back here again. It's worse on the sports fields."

"Okay, just do what the agents tell you. See you tomorrow. Be good!"

"I will."

It was wonderful hearing her voice. I loved the tinkling sound of her laughter. As wonderful as it was, I could still hear Mac's voice in my head, 'It's all about the music.'

Chapter Thirty-Two
Superman Tonight

Sam and I arrived back at my place in the dark. Sam, Lee and Doc had drawn straws. Sam won or lost, depending how you look at it. It was dark when I'd left and dark when I returned. I felt like I'd missed an entire day.

I called Noel Gerrard at NCIS intending to leave another message. Much to my surprise, my call didn't go to voicemail. He was at work on a Sunday.

"El?"

"I had a conversation with my husband."

"You recently married again or are we talking deceased husband?"

That was one of the things I liked about Agent Gerrard, he was a no-frills kind of guy and went straight to the crux of the matter.

"Dead."

"Did he want something?"

"Checking on me, so he said."

A patient silence flowed down the phone line. It blanketed the receiver in my hand and dripped over my body. A silvery glow embraced me.

"What do you want El?" Noel's voice sent the liquid silver scurrying out of sight.

"To know I'm not nuts. Either someone is pretending to be my dead husband, or he's not dead, 'cos dead folk don't use MSN."

"Either way, that creates issues."

"No kidding." I listened to his breathing for a second. "I know this isn't an NCIS problem, Noel. Lee has someone looking at my laptop as we speak. Could have an answer within a year."

He laughed. "Backlogged huh?"

"Oh hell, yes. Meanwhile I'm on my third laptop in as many days."

"You want me to look into something?"

"No. I just wanted to tell someone." I dropped my voice to a spooky whisper. "I talk to dead people."

"If my Great Aunt Ivy comes through, can you get her key lime pie recipe?"

"Smart ass."

"It scared you a bit, didn't it?"

"Just a smidgen. What if it is him?" It's not as if I don't talk to Mac all the time, but usually it's in my head or I whisper something. But twice now he's appeared in a messenger window and we've had actual conversations. Am I that insane?

"Some beyond-the-grave séance type communication, you mean?"

"Yeah."

"Then ..." He paused. "Then El, I think it's great that Mac can communicate and it's less scary than it being some prick messing with you."

"Yeah."

"And you can answer once and for all the debate regarding life after death."

"Don't you think that's a stupid expression? How the hell can there be life after death. Death implies lack of life."

"You know what I mean."

That was the most I'd ever heard Noel say at once. We edged ever nearer a to philosophical discussion and that scared the bejesus out of me. New depths. It was easier to think the Messenger conversation was a lapse in my sanity, or a glitch in the software, than consider actual messages from beyond the grave.

"I saw him, Noel."

"I think it's normal to think we see them."

Yeah, maybe someone who looks like him from behind in the distance on the street.

"In the Messenger window. We both used the web cam."

Silence.

"Noel?"

"I don't know enough about computers, El. Could be it's some kind of electronic memory?"

"A glitch that repeated an old conversation you mean?"

"Something like that."

"What do you suppose the odds are of that in a brand-new machine?" I mused aloud.

"Even I know that shouldn't happen. Do you think it was him?"

"Looked like him, a bit thinner in the face but yeah, I think it was Mac."

"You lead an interesting life, Agent Conway. You want

me to come hang out tonight?"

Inside me was a 'yes' but it wouldn't come out.

"Nah. Just wanted someone to know I'm seeing things." Someone I trust, someone who won't use it against me and try to derail my adoption plans. Someone who doesn't think I'm insane.

Then I heard him whisper, "I see dead people." He laughed for a moment. "How about I finish up here and swing by on my way home?"

"You moved?"

"Nope."

"You still live in Georgetown? Then you can hardly swing by Oakton on your way home from the Navy yard ..."

"I'll bring coffee ..."

"Sold. To the man with impeccable taste in coffee."

I hung up and found I was smiling. God, I'm a sucker for good coffee. There were way worse things than having the very attractive Noel Gerrard bring me coffee. One of those was the situation with Grange concerts and missing kids. As much as I didn't want to admit it, things were not looking good. Not only were they playing in Europe when seventeen kids disappeared, they arrived in New Zealand a day before the first kid went missing.

Could Hawk be an employee in Grange's tour? Is he using someone on the tour to snatch kids? How would they do that? What's the lure?

Memorabilia maybe? Backstage passes? Promises of meeting the band? I watched my theories swell uncontrollably in an enamel-baking dish. I poked them with a skewer. It came out sticky.

Hawk could be blowing large amounts of smoke up our asses and using Grange just as he used the Foundation. I stabbed the metaphoric skewer into my theories once more. It came out clean. I figured I was done cooking that batch.

Back to the recipe book in search of a new dish to create.

Gerrard didn't knock. He kicked. A booted foot tapped low on my front door. Upon opening it, I found Gerrard standing in front of me holding two coffees.

"Come on in."

He gave the door a shove behind him. "You okay, El?"

I took a coffee and led the way to the living room.

"Yes. I'm ..." I measured my response with care. "I'm awesome."

Gerrard smiled. "You are."

"You flatter me."

He sat in one of the armchairs; I sat opposite him.

"What's going on?" Noel picked his cup up and sipped at the contents.

I locked my eyes on his. "You avoiding me?"

"Nope," he replied, one corner of his mouth smiled.

"You sure?"

"Yep."

There was a bang in the hallway. I glanced at Noel; his hand was on his gun. Sam's head poked around the door. "Yo, Gerrard. Good to see you," he said, grinning.

"You too, Sam."

Sam shifted his line of vision to me. "Ellie – you've been getting a bunch of hang-ups."

"I have?" I didn't recall hearing the phone ring at all. That meant nothing. I can tune most things out or maybe it meant the machine picked it up every time.

"Same number has called and hung up four times this evening."

"Try calling it back."

"On it." Sam disappeared again. Two minutes later he hollered, "Ellie, we got trouble!"

Noel and I followed the sound of his voice to the kitchen.

"Trouble. What a surprise." Noel commented.

"It sure as hell is trouble," Sam replied and called the number again then handed me the phone. I felt the blood drain from my face as I listened.

A New Jersey accent spoke, 'She's a bit older than I ordinarily like but I'm sure I'll be able to get a good price for her. She's beautiful. Little blonde Carla with dark brown eyes. Bet she will taste divine."

"Yes, that's trouble." I wholeheartedly agreed with Sam's assessment and pressed re-dial then handed the phone to Noel, so he could hear it too. "I was talking to Carla a few hours ago."

"What'd she say?" Sam asked.

"We talked about a school trip and dinner tomorrow night; she also thinks someone is still watching her."

"She doesn't know about the photos?" Sam asked.

"Nope," I replied.

"I'm concerned," Sam said, his forehead creased in a way I'd never seen before. He was more than concerned.

"Find out who pays the bill on that number. I'll call police and get the patrols at school stepped up," I instructed.

Noel had something to say, "Make sure there is an escort following the car she's in at all times."

"Is it Hawk?" Sam asked. I gave him back the phone.

"That would be my guess. Record the message, please."

Back in the living room I made some more calls from my cell phone, leaving Noel with Sam.

Seventy-five percent of me wanted to bring Carla home, declare the spare room to be her room and never look back.

A chime from my replacement laptop made me jump. A Messenger window opened. Galileo signed in and typed a message.

Galileo: *Babe, you doing okay?*

Otherwisecat: *Maybe*

Galileo: *Maybe's ass. What's wrong?*

Otherwisecat: *You're dead, Carla is in protective custody and Hawk is threatening to grab her. What could be wrong? Oh by the way – your retard brother wants to stop the adoption.*

Galileo: *Still a smart ass I see.*

Otherwisecat: *Nothing gets past you.*

I called out to Noel and Sam, "Can you two come here

please?"

They didn't mess around. "What do you need?" Sam asked, bounding into the room. Noel walked in behind him. Noel did not bounce along like an overzealous puppy dog. He walked with purpose.

"Look at my screen and tell me what you see."

I moved the laptop over on the coffee table so they could sit on either side of me and view the screen.

Galileo: *That you Sam? Hey Noel! Good to see you man. Where are Lee and Kurt?*

If it were physically possible for Sam to go pale he would've. He exhaled sharply and shook his head. "This makes no sense."

"Tell me about it," I replied. "But I'm thinking the three of us aren't sharing the same hallucination, so something fucky is going on."

Noel said nothing.

Otherwisecat: *Lee is working with Misha. Kurt is at the hospital. I got the music thing. I get that this is about Grange. Now help me find Hawk.*

Galileo: *I'm dead, not magic.*

Otherwisecat: *I thought dead people knew everything. Can't you just ask around and find the fucker?*

Galileo: *He's going to grab Carla.*

The messenger window faded to grey and the message on the top of it said, Galileo has signed out. I tried to leave an off-line message but the Messenger service told me that Galileo didn't exist.

"Oh for fuck's sake, I know that already!" I turned to Sam. "I'm not nuts?"

He shook his head. "You're not nuts."

"What music thing?" Noel asked with restraint after re-reading the conversation.

"I kept hearing Mac's voice tell me, 'It's all about the music' – it started in New Zealand while we were …"

Sam interrupted, "While we were trying to figure out how Hawk convinced the kids to go with him or whoever grabbed them."

"Yeah. The lure – Grange concerts," I replied.

"Don't forget the Grange chat room, Hawk's new hunting ground," Sam added.

"Okay, I get the music thing now too," Noel said. "But I can tell you, without a doubt, that Rowan Grange and the rest of the band are not involved with Hawk's operation."

I smiled. "And you know this because you have them under surveillance?"

Half a smile twitched on his lips. "And you know that how?"

"A ghost didn't tell me, if that's what you think. Hawk did. He photographed Rowan being photographed – we ran it through facial recognition software."

"And you were told to back away …" Noel said but didn't offer any more insight into why we were told to back off.

"Yep."

"It seems to me that we have an interesting situation with your dead husband. Shame he couldn't give us more information. It's possible the voice on the phone was Hawk and he implied he was going to take Carla," Noel said, his voice quiet and thoughtful. "I'm heading off."

"Too spooky for you?" I asked as Noel reached the door.

"Nope. I wanna go tap some spooks on the shoulder and see what they know about ghosts, Hawk and Carla."

And with that he was gone.

Chapter Thirty-Three
Welcome To Where Ever You Are

Sam dropped me off. I hurried into the family court building at nine forty-five on Monday morning and found Dad waiting outside the judge's chambers with an expensively attired lawyer.

"Karl Mansfield," he said, thrusting his hand at me.

"Ellie Conway, nice to meet you."

A door opened. I recognized the woman who stepped out and smiled at me.

"I wondered if it was you when I saw Gabrielle Conway on my docket," Judge Hartwell said. She introduced herself to my father and acknowledged the lawyer, whom she knew.

"Is this a problem?" I asked.

She smiled. "No, not at all. This is not criminal court, this is family court – you're not on trial."

My heart thumped hard. My palms felt wet.

"Okay."

Judge Hartwell was kidnapped a few Christmases back by a disgruntled grandfather, after she declared him a pedophile and stopped all the access he had with his grandchildren. It was my case. I got to bring her home to her small son and Special Agent husband.

"Come on in Ellie, I know time is of the essence in this case. I've already spoken to the young lady in question this morning and a rather unfortunate man called Eddie

419

Connelly – he seemed to think he's a relative of yours."

"Brother-in-law," I replied. Soon to be deceased if he keeps up his interfering shit.

"So I gathered. I'm issuing a restraining order. He is not fit to be let loose on society in general, let alone a child. I trust you have no objection."

"None, whatsoever."

"Attached to Carla's file was a letter from Cassandra Smith. She stated that in her opinion as a senior social worker and as someone with firsthand knowledge of the relationship between you and Carla, that you are the ideal mother for the child."

A sneaky tear rolled down my face as I remembered Cassie telling me she'd written a letter.

Twenty minutes later, I walked out with a piece of paper stating I was now Carla's legal guardian, pending formal adoption. Easy money for Karl this time. He was going to handle the adoption papers and they were apparently very straightforward.

Dad walked with me out of the building. "I'm taking Carla out for dinner tonight, I'll tell her then," I said to him.

"You tell her Grandpa can't wait to spoil her rotten."

"Thanks, Dad," I said and gave him a hug. "I will."

Out on the street a car horn tooted. I looked over and saw Sam behind the wheel of a black SUV. He waved. I ran over.

"How'd it go?" he asked as he pushed the door open for me.

"What? The big-assed grin not enough of a hint for you?"

"That means I'm an uncle. But – I'm not uncool, so maybe we should change ..."

"Uncle to aunt?" I said with a chuckle.

Sam grinned. "You walking home?"

I shut the door and put on my seat belt. "Where is everyone?"

Sam looked slightly uncomfortable as he negotiated traffic and tried to avoid my question by ignoring it.

"Sam? Lee and Misha? Doc?"

"Lee wanted to go back to Fort Belvoir. Misha said he shouldn't, so he went with him."

Of course he did. "I can hardly wait for the explanation."

"Lee reckons we missed something. He was ranting about the Fort being pivotal to the case and he thought he could snoop around a bit."

"This won't end well."

"Probably not."

"Let's pretend I never heard that. Is Doc still at the hospital?"

"Nope, he's meeting us at your place."

It didn't take long before Sam and I were back at home. All the way home I felt eyes on me. Sam assured me no one had tailed us. What surprised me was that the feeling hung around once I was inside my home. I was used to feeling Mac around me watching, but the feeling I'd had since Cassie's death was sinister.

With my legs tucked up under me in my chair, I gazed out the window. Nothing looked back at me. My mind drifted along with the weak sunbeams and wintery woods. Before long, I found I was thinking more about painting Carla's room than the case.

"Is Doc coming over?" Sam asked, breaking the spell cast by the dormant trees. He looked up from his laptop.

"Yeah, should be here any minute."

"Did you hear from Rowan?"

"Was I supposed to?"

"He called, looking for you this morning."

"Can't be that important. He could've got me on my cell."

Sam shrugged. "Saying he called, is all."

I grinned at him and listened to footsteps outside on the driveway. "Doc's here."

"I got it," Sam said, hoisting himself to his feet and putting his laptop on the coffee table.

Doc followed him back into the room.

"Conway," he said before he sat down.

"Doc. How are the kids?"

"Being reunited with parents or family right about now."

"They from here?"

"No, mostly from New York and New Jersey."

I mulled that over for a few minutes. Cyber were investigating the chat room activity and had agents in the chat room posing as young girls while looking for anomalies. I wouldn't have any news for Rowan until they gave me their preliminary report, which I didn't expect until much later in the day. I had a feeling the new room activity was unrelated to Hawk but still hideous and malicious.

"Sam, any word on my laptops?"

"Not good news. Your original laptop picked up a key-logger. Your personal one seems to be hosting a ghost."

"No such thing."

"Tell cyber that. There was nothing to ping, Ellie. The whole conversation originated from your machine. No one can explain how ... all we know is it happened."

"Great." I hadn't expected them to find anything.

I reached for the phone on the table and called Rowan. It wasn't quite as easy as that; I had to use my cell phone contact list to find his number. I don't commit numbers to memory from one or two uses. Sometimes I wished my life was like a movie then maybe I could just pick up a phone and dial.

"Hey, got a minute?"

"Yep," he replied.

"You called me today?"

"I did. Thought maybe we could grab a coffee?"

"Is this like dinner yesterday?"

Hard to do from different states.

There were footsteps outside the window, coming up the path. I heard the same thing over the phone.

He wasn't in New York anymore.

"I take it you are about to knock on my door?"

He laughed.

"Thought I might."

There was a knock. Sam looked at me. "You okay to get that?" He was half out of his chair already with Doc close behind.

"I'm okay, guys," I told them. "I'll get it."

Rowan strolled in, carrying a leather jacket in one hand and greeted Sam and Doc. I stood by the door trying to figure out what had turned my blood cold.

"Have a seat Rowan," Sam said. "I'm making coffee, you in?"

"That'd be great." He dropped his jacket over the arm of the sofa and sat down.

The doorway felt vulnerable. The eyes of the room were upon me.

I sighed.

"What's wrong?" Doc made a move toward me. By the look on his face, I knew he was thinking I'd had a transient ischemic attack, or worse, a cerebral embolism. Hey, I would've too, faced with me freezing in a doorway, with what I suspected was my lip curled in a disgusted sneer.

"It's just ..." I started to explain and it sounded insane even in *my* head. "Fuck! Rowan, are you wearing new cologne?"

There I'd said it. Yet another comment that made me seem like a lunatic.

"Yes, I am. You like?"

"Yeah ... no ... not so much."

Way to go Ellie! What's he supposed to say now? How is a person supposed to react to that?

"Sorry," he replied, with much sincerity.

"What's it called?"

Sam was back at his computer poised to Google the name. Doc still scrutinized me.

"Late September."

Sam typed. I watched from the doorway.

"Is that as close as you're going to get?" Rowan asked.

"I'm sorry," I said, because I was and that was all I had.

"Point me to your bathroom ... mind if I take a shower?"

Forty million women screamed 'he's going to get naked in your bathroom' and I nodded like a dullard.

Sam hauled to his feet. "I'll show you," he said. "I'm on my way to make coffee anyway."

"Get some of Mac's clothes, they should fit," I said and slipped into Sam's seat as Rowan passed me. I found myself holding my breath.

"Should do," Sam replied. "You're about six foot, aren't you Rowan?"

"Close enough," Rowan replied.

Their voices continued but all meaning was lost as the walls of my home buffered their speech.

My phone rang. I grabbed it and flipped it open. "Speak to me," I said.

Lee said, "We've been kicked off the base. Someone pulled our authorization." 'Curmudgeonly' didn't capture his demeanor.

"Do you know who?" I wasn't surprised. We'd received

425

several warnings to leave the military aspects out of our investigation but I knew Lee.

"Nope. We were escorted off five minutes ago under armed guard."

"Head back to the office."

I closed my phone then, almost as an afterthought, rang the Director. I waited while her assistant transferred my call.

"Director, do you know why my men were escorted off Fort Belvoir?"

"I do. You're going to have to let the military connection go, Ellie. Work any other angle but not military."

"You can't be serious!"

"I'm very serious," she replied.

There was no mistaking the tone in her voice. If I pushed this, I could well find myself drowning in an ocean of trouble.

"Can you tell me why?"

"No. I cannot."

"Thank you, Director."

I tossed my phone onto the coffee table where it bounced and landed on the rug.

Damn!

"Problem?" Doc asked.

"Yes. We've been ordered off all military aspects of the case by O'Hare."

In keeping with the new instructions I went back to my search and followed the first link on the computer. It was to a perfumery house I'd never heard of, KS. As I read the company information, I discovered they were an American jewelry and clothing company with an exclusive perfumery house in Paris, France. I found the cologne listed as unavailable for purchase outside of France.

Odd.

Guessed that meant people would want it more. Smart marketing: nothing creates sales like exclusivity. Sam set a cup next to me, passed one to Doc and took a seat.

"What's up?" he asked.

"Lee and Misha were ordered off the base. Director O'Hare ordered us to keep away from any military connections to this case."

"Not good, Chicky."

Wished I knew what was so damn important about the Fort and why they didn't want us investigating possible leads. I was starting to wonder if Hawk was an asset, inspiring a sick feeling in my gut.

"Not at all." I changed the subject and inclined my head toward the door. "Rowan?"

"He's almost done," Sam replied, staring at the screen I was reading. "What did you find?"

I told him about the exclusive cologne. "Is it what Hawk wore?"

"Yeah. It has a different undertone on Rowan, but it's the same cologne."

"Interesting."

"Weird," I replied. "What are the odds, Sam? Same rare cologne as our man?"

Rowan knocked on the door, as he came in. He'd towel

dried his hair and he wore a grey button-down shirt of Mac's. A good fit.

"Nice," I said.

"Smell gone?" he asked, leaning down toward me. His face brushed my hair.

It took two attempts to say, "Yes."

Rowan grinned.

"There's a coffee for you," Sam said.

I smiled at Sam as Rowan moved toward the sofa. He grinned back and nodded.

"Have you done any concerts since you returned?"

"We played at Starland Ballroom in Trenton Saturday night."

"That wasn't on your tour schedule."

"It was a spur of the moment thing. We played with a couple of other bands."

New Jersey.

I excused myself and left the room. A sudden onslaught of dizziness made me feel sick as I headed to the kitchen for water. With a tall glass of cold water in my hand, I sat at the kitchen table. The water slipped easily down my throat.

Out the window, the woods called to me. The dogwood trees stood straggly, barren, desolate, yet holding their own in the wait for spring. I finished half the glass of water then tipped the rest away. I lingered for a moment at the window above the sink, looking for the first glimpse of daffodils poking through the cold earth under the trees. As much as I wanted to see the small green shoots,

I saw nothing but slushy grey snow. Movement caught my eye; fascinated, I watched a chicken peck its way across the yard. Unbelievable. I couldn't think where it'd come from. I didn't know anyone around us kept chickens. I'd certainly never heard any. It disappeared into the woods leaving nothing but dull slushy snow and bare branches to look at. The bird reminded me of the pet chicken I'd had once. Poor Abigail met with a shocking end. A tear escaped my eye. I wiped it away. Everything dies.

I threatened the sky beyond my reflection, "Don't fuck with me."

Doc's face appeared next to mine. "I wasn't intending to."

"Good to know because I'm over people fucking with me."

"Turn around."

He peered into my eyes as though if he tried hard enough he could see my thoughts. "What's going on in there?" Doc tapped an index finger on my head.

"Just trying to make sense of this mess."

"You feeling okay?"

"You gonna stop asking me anytime soon? It's starting to piss me off."

I went back into the living room. Doc didn't follow me right away.

"The cologne, Rowan, where'd you get it?"

"Are you all right?" he asked, pointing to his own face and suggesting with the action that I had something by my eye.

I wiped a finger under my eye and removed smudged mascara.

"I am," I said. "About the cologne?" I hoped I didn't sound too formal.

"We get gifts, products, from various companies. It was a gift."

"How did it arrive?"

"It was a gift basket from KS. I don't know exactly. Things like this go through our management company."

"Did you choose the cologne?"

"No, there were four and they were already named, supposedly matched to our personalities." Rowan grinned. "Guess someone didn't do their job right."

Fuc'n bingo. Someone did his or her job very well indeed. They knew he'd wear it to see me.

"You don't know who actually sent the basket do you?"

"No, management told me it came from KS. I don't get the details."

"Okay."

Sam called Lee and Misha to fill them in, then called the KS head office and asked for the publicity department.

After spending some time rolling his eyes, sipping coffee and being bounced from person to person, he learned the basket originated in France, from the Paris office, as well as the exact contents. Four different colognes, four handcrafted pendants on white gold chains, four different sets of male skincare products. Everything named and gift tagged for a particular band member.

I had a horrible feeling about the pendants.

"Rowan, you don't have a pendant on you?"

He smiled sheepishly. "No, I didn't like them. I'm not into big flashy pieces of jewelry."

That might prove to be really good news.

"I'm sending someone to pick up the basket and the contents. Has it been divided up yet?"

He shook his head. "I've seen it, but the others are taking breaks in various places."

"The cologne?"

"It's still with the basket; I stopped into the office and looked at the loot, tried it and came straight here."

It didn't matter how many times I rolled that around my head, it didn't work. New York to Virginia, he tried it on the way here?

"Clarify ... you didn't drive all this way to see me, did you?"

"I did."

Now that's interesting. I left it alone. I could feel Sam's thoughts on the subject building to a crescendo and didn't want to go there.

"Sam, tell me about KS."

"They're an American company founded by Kendra Masters, as in the K. She married Sasha Petrovovich and made him a full partner in the business. They changed the trading name to KS. What started as a predominantly jewelry manufacturing company grew into a multi-million dollar clothing, skin care and jewelry empire."

"Sasha isn't your run-of-the-mill American name, where's he from?" Doc asked.

"Russia, so it says in his bio, but he calls himself a child of the universe. He apparently went to boarding school in Germany, college in America then spent time in England, Switzerland and back in Russia."

"Oh good, because what we need another is Russian connection," I muttered. "Rowan, can I have the phone number for your management ... agent ... whoever handles this type of thing."

He handed me his cell phone with the contacts page open and a name and number highlighted.

I called the number from my phone and asked for the basket, any notes, or cards and all the contents for forensic testing. The management camp was defensive, immediately, with talk of warrants and lawyers.

Rowan slid the phone from my fingers as I pulled it away from my ear for a second to vent my irritation in the form of a disgruntled glare at Sam.

"Hand it over," he stated. "There is no way we want the sort of publicity that comes attached to this case." He paused and listened then countered with, "A warrant will generate publicity."

He gave the phone back.

"They'll do it."

Abracadabra: the woman was suddenly much friendlier and much more accommodating. I informed her someone from my team would pick up the basket within three hours.

A sudden and awful thought occurred to me.

The pendants. A woman's head exploded because of a barrette, which wasn't so very different from a pendant. A pendant bomb would make a nice-sized hole in someone's chest instead of head.

I grabbed my phone and called Lee. He answered on the twelfth ring. I counted each and every one.

"The pendants in the basket you're sequestering may be explosive devices."

"How would they get through customs?" he countered sensibly.

"Good point," I replied. "Okay, go ahead and pick 'em up."

"Hang on," he said. "Did someone bring the basket into the country or was it couriered or sent via the postal service?"

"No idea."

"On second thoughts, I'll ask for a bomb disposal team to meet us."

"Good thinking."

The cool blue of the leather armchair was comforting. My eyes closed. The room moved in gentle undulating circles within my head. Part of me felt soothed by the movement, the rest of me felt sick.

I opened my eyes and checked the time on my watch. A nagging feeling came over me. I logged into the fake Grange chat room and settled back to watch some stupid conversations.

Didn't take long before my mind wandered and I

looked over at Rowan. Another man dragged into a mess by means of my job.

"What brought you to Virginia? Shouldn't you be home before the next leg of the tour?"

"I was home," he replied, drinking his coffee.

"And now you're here."

"And now I'm here."

"Why?"

He smiled. "I wanted to see how the case was going."

"Phones are handy for that sort of enquiry."

"I rang and you weren't available."

"And common sense dictated you drive from New York to find out why?"

His smile never faded. "No, to be interrogated, of course."

Sam chuckled but didn't look up from his laptop.

"You're quite the smart ass, Mr. Grange."

"And you have a very nice ass, Agent Conway."

Sam and Doc roared with laughter.

"Thank you very much." I pulled my legs up under me, curling into the protective cocoon that was Mac's chair. The cold, pale-blue leather reminded me of graves and widows weeds.

I could see a light shining in the dark.

I had a smile on my face, I know I did. I liked Rowan. He made me laugh and let's face it he was easy on the eye, which sure didn't hurt.

"You don't make it easy ..."

"Make what easy?" I said, reading the screen in front

434

of me.

"Getting to know who you are," Rowan replied. "You know so much about me and I feel like I know nothing about you."

I held a finger up to stop him for a moment. "Hawk is up to something and it's not going to be good. He pulled out of New Zealand too fast ..."

Sam came over and crouched beside me. "Tell me, Chicky."

"Look at this chat room conversation."

The entire room was supposedly full of Grange fans but the tone felt wrong.

I started pulling words from the lines of text, letting my intuition guide me. Sam watched for a moment, then called Cyber Division and asked that they try to identify locations for all participants.

Words were stringing together almost without intervention. I didn't feel like I was typing them in a document – line by line – I copied parts of conversations I was drawn to. The screen names gave us the raw material; I just had to put it together to understand it. "Remember the eighties show *Moonlighting*?" I asked. Everyone nodded. "Let me introduce you to Dave Addison and Maddie Hayes."

Sam watched as I assembled the conversation.

DaveAddison: *Everything is in place.*

MaddieHayes: *All three?*

DaveAddison: *Yes. Day, time?*

MaddieHayes: *Thursday 6 p.m.*

DaveAddison: *Last sale?*

MaddieHayes: *Confirmed – shipping tomorrow.*

DaveAddison: *Fund Transfer?*

MaddieHayes: *Completed.*

"Sam do we have a location?"

"Cyber says MaddieHayes is inside the USA, narrowing location now. DaveAddison is in Syria."

"Hawk," I hissed. "So who is his friend? Male or female?"

"We got MaddieHayes – Virginia, Alexandria."

"Can we get an actual address?"

"They're still trying."

"Any idea what the first part of the message refers to?"

Sam shrugged. "Something that's set to happen at 6 p.m. on Thursday."

"Could be the end of the world, for all we know."

Both chat participants logged out. Leaving confusion in their wake in the chat room. Within minutes, the people left started playing a lyric game. Someone wrote a line of lyric, the others were supposed to guess what song it was. They mostly sucked. The occupants needed to listen to the songs with better ears.

"All three what are in place?" Doc muttered.

"No idea."

"What are they shipping?" Sam wondered aloud.

"Kids?" I said, and then had second thoughts. "Weapons?"

My eyes met Doc's. I could see his thoughts. "Nukes. It could be three nukes that are in place."

A *Moonlighting* episode played in my head. I was in the eighties, complete with shoulder pads and big hair. A drunken Dave Addison danced across a crowded bar singing 'Respect.' Even playing a drunk, Bruce was cute when he was young. I doubted Hawk was ever cute.

The mystery of Hawk's helper within the USA needed solving because that person meant Carla was in danger. My thoughts about Hawk and his friend were not exactly professional. Wishing them both a slow painful death seemed at odds with my training and moral code. Chanting, 'Die scum, die' wasn't very FBI. I kept the chanting to myself. I doubted it would please Doc if I let my freak flag fly too high.

"All this means is that they are using the chat room to communicate. I presume that means they think we can't understand the conversations."

"We couldn't, Chicky. You're the one who saw the pattern in the words. Lee and I would've moved on without seeing it."

I nodded my head. My fingernails tapped on the laptop case.

"Wish they'd said more. It feels like we got the end of a message."

"Maybe there is more. I'll start a search through the transcripts for their names, now I know what to look for in the conversations I might even find something," Sam said. "Feels like we don't have much time."

"Because we don't," I replied with a small laugh and a generous eye-roll. "Hey, the world's ending at 6 p.m. on

437

Thursday and it's Monday night already."

Sam smirked. Something twinged in my gut. I wasn't entirely sure I was joking about the world ending.

Rowan made his presence known. I'd forgotten he was there.

"Now what?"

"Sam's looking for more conversations, Lee and Misha are trying not to get blown up, Doc's waiting for me to fall over and I need to see a kid."

Sam grinned. "I'll tag along on that mission."

"Hoping you would, someone needs to drive and it can't be me right now," I replied.

Doc nodded, agreeing with my decision regarding driving. I experienced a sudden bout of friendliness towards him. "Want to come?"

"Sure," Doc said. "I get to meet Carla."

"Yep."

Rowan spoke. "Can I come, or this some kind of team-building exercise?"

"You can come," I replied.

"Where are we going?" he asked.

"To visit my daughter." I knew saying that was a bit premature but I wanted to try it. My daughter. Had a nice ring to it.

"You have a daughter?"

I nodded.

Sam smiled and grabbed his keys.

"I'm an uncle," he said, as we piled into his car.

"Thought we decided you were too cool to be an uncle,

438

Sam."

The smile on his face waivered, his eyes widened. "I'll be the coolest uncle around. I sure don't look like an auntie."

No, he sure didn't. He looked like he could save the world before breakfast without even breaking a sweat. My smart mouth just wouldn't shut. "Hang on!" I said. Raising my hand. "Just trying to imagine you in a dress. Well shit. Now I got LL Cool J in drag."

"You going there?"

"Trust me, it's not by choice. How the hell am I going to scrub that image outta my brain?"

"You're skating on thin ice, Chicky."

Laughter bubbled. "Let's ask Carla if she can live with having an Uncle Sam, shall we?"

He lunged for my phone but missed. I slipped the phone back into my pocket without texting Carla. "Watch the road," I warned.

Rowan spoke from the backseat. "How old is your daughter?"

"She'll be fourteen in a few weeks."

"You have a teenager?"

"Yes, I do."

"See what I mean about you being hard to know? I had no idea you had a child."

Sam pulled up a driveway. We waited for the agents to come out and clear us.

Two agents approached the car, weapons drawn. They checked our badges and photo ID. Rowan sat silently in the back of the car next to Doc until told we could go inside the house. One agent stayed with the car.

I knocked on the front door. Chrissy opened it quickly and ushered us in. The other agent disappeared from behind us. I looked back and saw him heading back down to our car.

"Carla is in the living room watching TV," Chrissy said. She smiled with flirtatious coyness at Sam.

Carla poked her head around a doorway. She smiled then squealed, "You're here!" She barreled across the hallway and wrapped her arms around me. I hugged her back.

"I'm here. I know we're supposed to do dinner – but will you settle for take-out pizza?"

"Okay," she replied, still hugging me.

I looked at Sam. "Would you and Chrissy go grab pizza?"

"You sure?" Sam asked, glancing around.

"I'm here with Doc and we have two agents outside – no one's getting in. Go ..."

He didn't need to be told twice. Chrissy had already pulled a jacket from a hall closet and put it on. Carla led me into the living room by the hand. Rowan followed along. I was waiting for the squeal when she realized who he was.

It didn't happen. She very calmly gave him a once-over and suggested he sit on the sofa. He smiled and obliged. Doc hovered in the doorway. He was back to wearing suits and looked every bit a Special Agent bodyguard.

Carla and I sat on another sofa.

"Carla, I have news ..." I said.

Her eyes widened. "Is it good?"

"Where's that parent help form for your trip?" I asked. "I'd better fill it in, if they require a police check."

Her mouth opened and closed, and then she squealed and threw herself at me. "Really? You're my mom?"

"I have interim custody of you; the adoption should be final by your birthday. Is that okay with you?"

She squealed again. "Yes! I have a mom. I don't have to live in foster homes anymore." She glanced at me as if looking for reassurance.

I nodded and smiled. "No more foster homes. As soon as we close this case you can come home."

"Home," she said. "Home! A real home!"

"Let's call my dad. He can't wait to start being a grandpa."

Carla nodded. "Can I?"

"Absolutely." I gave her my phone and watched as she called my father. They talked for a few minutes, she squealed a lot and laughed. A song filled my head, 'Testify' by Lorenza Ponce. As I listened to Lorenza singing, I realized I was living for love but a far different love than I'd ever imagined. For the love of a ghost and a child.

Rowan leaned back on the sofa and said nothing. He watched with a smile on his face. I surmised it would be very hard to watch Carla without smiling. She radiated joy in all directions.

Doc indicated that Sam and Chrissy had arrived back. I

smelt the pizza before I saw them. When the door opened, Carla jumped to her feet and ran to Sam.

"Did you know? I have a mom!"

Sam swung her around the room. "Yes, I know. You also have some uncles and a grandpa. You got yourself a whole family." He placed her back on her feet.

With the cheekiest smile, Carla said, "You're not un-cool, Auntie Sam. What pizza did you get?"

Sam's smile froze. Chrissy laughed. I high-fived Carla. She really did belong with us.

"Chicky?"

"I swear I didn't tell her!"

We ate, we talked, and it was just what I needed. It was hard leaving her there and heading home but, until Hawk was behind bars, she was safer where she was.

But there was still a nagging doubt.

Chapter Thirty-Four
Don't Lose Your Head

It was heading toward ten-thirty when we finally got home. Ten-thirty and a bitterly cold dark night. It felt like a Friday not a Monday. The four of us sat in the living room, simply because it was bigger than my home office. I started chasing things I had forgotten about, getting reports, to keep myself awake.

Doc kneeled beside my chair. "It wouldn't kill you to sleep."

"I will, when this is over. When I bring Carla home."

He sat back on the couch next to Rowan and picked up his laptop. "Plenty of time to sleep when we're dead."

A smile paused on my lips before I dove back into work.

"Anything about the Russian diplomat?" I asked Sam.

He was being held at Christchurch Central police station until the Russians could pick him up. Misha had a word with someone in Moscow and said diplomat was required to talk to FSB about his involvement in the Virginia murders and his involvement in child trafficking in New Zealand. I suspected the *talk* involved water, electricity, and things we didn't need to know about.

"Not yet. I'll chase that."

I picked up my cup from the table and took a gulp of coffee. Cold, yuck, coffee.

Rowan leaned over and took the cup from me.

"I'll make coffee. Sam, you?" he stood up.

"That'd be great," Sam said, handing up his cup. "You sure you know how to make coffee? Don't you have people who do that for you?"

Rowan grinned. "I make a half decent cup of coffee."

Rowan declined my offer of help. I let him go. Standing seemed like a lot of effort. Why was he here? Why my laptop? Why the pictures?

"Sam, you buying any of this?"

"This?"

"This ..." I said, waving a hand toward the kitchen.

"He's sweet on you, Chicky; any idiot can see it."

I'm obviously completely retarded.

I laughed. "I don't think so."

Sam shrugged. "Whatever."

I'm a married woman. Until death do us part. Mac didn't seem to grasp the concept of death leading to parting. For a dead guy he was dropping by an awful lot. It wasn't easy being the live partner in such circumstances. Not that I was doing much living.

"He's keen," Doc commented.

"No, he's just a friend," I retaliated.

"I think you're missing a few signals; probably blasted right out of your head."

"Sam, say it isn't so."

"Some guys, they like dangerous women."

Rowan came back in with the coffee in time to hear Sam's comment and derived a conclusion.

"He's right, some guys like dangerous women." He

paused and smiled, it was truly disarming. "I prefer intelligent blondes with knowing blue eyes and a kick-ass smile. A side of danger is not unwelcome."

"Oh please." My eyes rolled so hard my brain raced to keep up.

"It's so hard to believe?" He sank into the sofa.

What was that roaring I heard? Forty million women screaming, 'Pick me!' At least I think that's what they were saying.

"We'll talk, soon as this mess is cleared up."

Rowan grinned at Sam. "Is it ever good when a woman says, 'we'll talk'?"

"Not in my experience," Sam replied.

"Mine either," Doc added.

"Work," I said, with a well-placed glare in Sam's direction. "Thanks for the coffee, Rowan."

"You're welcome. Can I stay?" Rowan asked. "If you're going to work all night, I can make coffee."

Doc kicked my foot and winked at me. I glared at him then replied to Rowan, "Sure. If you don't mind being bored shitless."

"You don't mind?"

"Not at all." I like to keep my possible suspects close; just because a dead man and an NCIS agent said he wasn't involved didn't mean I wasn't going to be watching closely. Knowing he'd done an impromptu show in Sayreville and the missing kids we found in DC were from New Jersey and New York served to heighten my remaining suspicions.

"You always work from home?" he asked.

"No," I replied. "Not always."

Sam intervened, "Circumstances occasionally make Ellie's place more convenient as our base."

Rowan nodded. He turned his questions to Sam.

"Are you any closer to finding that guy you were after in New Zealand?"

"Just when we think we are, he throws a curve ball. Lee and Misha were chasing a lead but it fell through," Sam said. "They're on the way to New York for the pick up."

"We're chasing our fuc'n tails," I grumbled and thoughts emerged regarding the basket and gifts. "Rowan?"

"Yes."

"Have you had anything else, besides the basket, given to you recently?"

"A pen," he replied.

"Like a biro?"

"More like this ... I gave you one too," he said and dragged his jacket off the arm of the sofa, then rifled through the pockets until he handed me a very nice up-market refillable pen. I held it in my hand for a few minutes. It was black, with gold accents; on one side of the barrel was the band's logo, on the other side, 'Grange.' It was the same as the one he'd given me.

"Very nice," Sam commented. "You have one, Ellie?"

"Yeah, Rowan gave it to me before we left Christchurch. It's ..." I unfurled my legs and stood up then patted my jean pockets. I pulled the pen from my back pocket. "... here."

"Where'd they come from?" Doc asked.

"It's a prototype from the record company. They're having them made up as gifts for special events."

My turn. "Fancy, and it was delivered directly from the record company?"

"I was given them both in London, a courier delivered them to the tour manager."

I sat up straighter at the mention of a courier. I needed something clean to open the pen onto, so I reached for a magazine from the pile under the coffee table.

House and Garden. Mac's subscription still came. I opened the magazine out and found a sealed advertising envelope inside it. I removed the envelope, carefully opened all sides and spread it flat on the table. It would do to contain possible evidence without contamination. Then I unscrewed the barrel of Rowan's pen and tipped the components onto the envelope.

"Okay. One spring, one pen refill, the mechanism that retracts the ball point nib ... and extras." I peered at the spread out components.

"Extras?" Rowan said as he leaned forward.

"Seen anything like this before?"

Sam, Doc and Rowan nodded.

"That's like a tiny microphone, you had a clever version on your shirt in Christchurch," Rowan said pointing to a small metallic object. "But what's that?" He pointed to a small capsule.

"A GPS device," Sam muttered. "Fuck me seven ways on Sunday, you've been bugged and tracked."

I unscrewed the barrel of the pen Rowan had given me, and tipped the contents carefully onto the card.

"Rowan was bugged and so was I. Look!" I pointed to the small microphone from my pen and another small object the size of a vitamin capsule. "Don't that just suck? Whoever did this knows we know and knows where we are."

Sam left the room. When he came back, he had a small paper bag. He tipped all the pieces from the pens into the bag and sealed it with a good-sized piece of tape. Then he wrote his name across the seal.

"I'm picking they aren't all like this," I muttered. "This is not going well at all."

Sam removed the bag from the room.

"Where is it?"

"In the kitchen, I can't tell if its sending information, so best kept out of harm's way. I'll take it to the lab myself," Sam replied.

The pen. The break in. There wasn't anything wrong with Lee's bug detector after all. Lee had the stupid pen in his pocket while he was doing the sweep, no wonder it was having a fit.

"Lee and Misha?" I asked Sam.

"Whoever was listening knows they're headed to New York."

"Did we mention an address?"

"I texted it to him, Ellie. We never said it," Rowan

replied.

A rush of cold hit me.

"Phone, get me the phone!"

Doc handed me his, his eyes darkening as he tuned in to my wavelength.

I called Lee. My mind screamed 'Answer the damn phone!' If only he could hear it. Come on, answer it.

I pointed at Sam, "Try Misha – and Caine."

Sam used his cell phone and the landline.

My call flipped to voicemail. I left a message, "Lee, do not go for the basket. I repeat, abort the pickup. Send bomb squad alone."

"Misha's on voicemail too."

Caine's voice grumbled from the coffee table, "Hello!"

Sam threw the phone to me. "Lee and Misha could be walking into a trap. They've gone to retrieve evidence from New York. I have reason to believe a bomb may detonate when they pick up this evidence."

"Address?"

I threw the phone to Rowan, he told Caine the address then handed it back. "I'll close the building down and get the disposal guys in there, now."

Caine hung up. I dropped the phone into my lap. I took a breath. I needed more information from Rowan and he didn't look happy.

"You okay?" I asked.

"No," he replied with a shake of his head and downcast eyes.

"I'm sorry, my world sucks. I'm really sorry you fell

into it."

"I didn't fall in, Ellie," he said, with surprising conviction. His head came up and eyes leveled at mine, he held my gaze. "I stepped in, under my *own* steam."

My life is no place for good people. I shut my thoughts off; they left me feeling upside down anyway.

Things began to fall into place. "Rowan, did you get the pens before you toured Europe?"

"Yes. It was the night of our last London show."

"I don't suppose you still have the packaging?"

"I do. I emptied my bag in my study when I got home. The packaging will still be in the waste paper bin by my desk."

Smart man. It's not a good idea to leave identifiable rubbish in hotels or anywhere else where stalkers and the like can find it. Even if it means carrying packaging all the way around the world.

I looked at Sam. He already had his phone in his hand. He called Lee's phone and left a message, "If you don't explode, call home. Immediately."

My eyes closed for a second. A series of horrendous events were slotting into order creating a possible scenario of total terror.

"Conway, you okay?" Doc asked.

"Doc, they need to move Carla."

He looked at his watch. "It's just gone midnight, so it's officially Tuesday. When is the world going to end?"

"Twenty-twelve according to the Mayans," Rowan commented quietly.

"Thursday at 6 p.m.," I said. "She needs to go to a new safe house tonight."

"Yes, she does."

Rowan leaned back, his face clouded with worry. "You don't actually think the world will end do you?"

I crossed my fingers out of his sight. "Nah, we're just diffusing tension, having a bit of fun with the situation."

"Have I put you and Carla in danger?"

Sam jumped in immediately. "Hell no, we can take care of ourselves and Carla, nothing new in us being the targets of a fucktard." He jabbed his finger into the air. "Pity the fool that comes for us!" Mr. T would've been proud.

Sam was good. I doubted he was good enough, even with Doc backing him up. Rowan was no fool.

Sam was texting on his phone. Then my phone buzzed. Sure enough, it was a text from Sam. He wanted to know if Rowan knew about the break in on Friday. I texted a single word reply, 'No.' The next text asked if Rowan knew about the blast injury. I replied 'Kinda.' Sam raised an eyebrow at me after reading the message. I shrugged and attempted an innocent look.

Why did they always fail?

There was no sense in all of us sitting there drifting toward abject gloom but that's what was happening. All we could do was wait. Wait for a phone to ring and tell us what went down in New York. It was late; we were tired and weird things were revolving in my mind.

"Why don't you try getting a few hours sleep?" Doc

suggested.

"I'll be okay."

My reply drew conspiratorial smiles from everyone.

Chapter Thirty-Five
Last Cigarette

Tuesday crept up fast as Monday disappeared in a flurry of phone activity. There was a plan for while Carla was at school. They would move her gear to a new safe house out of the area, then pick her up after school and take her to the new house. Seemed better than hauling her out of bed in the middle of the night. Extra agents were on surveillance outside the house for the rest of the night. It took a lot of work to stop thinking about Carla and concentrate on trying to make some headway in the case.

"We've had special agents from cyber in the chat rooms and they've been tracing the ISPs." I smiled at Rowan's confused expression. "They were watching when 'Rowan' was trying to pull a fourteen-year-old in the unofficial room." I didn't want to tell him he was under surveillance by us. "We know it wasn't you." I secretly hoped the fourteen-year-old girl was a fifty-year-old inmate in a federal prison.

"As far as I can tell there is no untoward activity in the fan-club-controlled chat room."

He nodded. I guessed the look that crossed his face was relief, probably mixed with some ideas on damage control. Sooner or later, the existence of the other chat room and Hawk's involvement would touch the Grange Empire. It's a multi-million dollar corporation. He'd be stupid if he didn't think about damage control.

I couldn't decide if I'd scored a black mark against him because he appeared relieved the fan club room wasn't involved. Just for a second it amused me that I felt worthy to judge another human being.

What a fuc'n cheek. Who did I think I was, the Queen of England? I expected to hear the words "If it please your highness." I adjusted my imaginary tiara, and found Doc studying me intently. What to do? Feign embarrassment, shrug and smile, ignore my interlude and move on?

A light flickered behind Doc's eyes. Without so much as a smirk he said, "The tiara suits you."

My jaw sagged.

Doc's fingers reached out and gently closed my mouth.

"That was a tiara you repositioned on your head?"

Come on voice, work. "Yes."

He smiled. "It suits you."

"Get out of my head."

"But there are deep dark recesses in there that have never been explored," he replied, humming the theme music to *Star Trek*. "Conway's Mind – The Final Frontier."

" 'It's life, Jim – but not as we know it'," chimed in Sam.

The zany and ridiculous humor threatened to tip me on my ass.

"Out!" I exclaimed, as Kirk broke into my thoughts with a well placed 'Beam me up Scotty' and Spock declared the entire episode illogical.

Doc jumped to *The Next Generation* and launched into a

fine impersonation of Picard. Eventually silliness gave way to stillness. My breathing returned to normal. I hadn't laughed like that in a long time. It felt exhilarating. There was something life affirming about crazy, hyena laughing. For a few minutes there, my accompanying giant cloud of despair dissipated. Life was dynamic again. I liked it. Even the lack of control felt good.

"How'd you know about the tiara, then *Star Trek*?" I choked a giggle until it stopped struggling.

"I'm good at charades and I thought I heard the *Star Trek* intro."

Interesting and spooky all at once.

"No one has ever climbed into my head unprompted before."

"I found it dark, mysterious and hard to navigate."

"Keeps intruders out," I replied.

He laughed then pointed surreptitiously to Rowan.

Rowan sat in a cloud of serious gloom.

"Come on, Rowan. It'll be fine. Hey, this is what we do," I said. With a flap of my hand, I hoped to send the cloud packing.

"It's not that, not entirely anyway. It's you. It's being around you."

That was bound to happen.

"I'm not good for people. You should run ..."

"That's not what I mean ... You're so amazingly resilient and strong. It's easy to give up but to hold it together, when everyone would understand if you fell apart, that's true strength."

Speechless. He rendered me speechless.

Sam interceded, "He's right, Chicky Babe."

"Carla's a lucky girl," Rowan added.

"Stop now," I said. "It's all an illusion that rests precariously on my ability to remain sane."

Rowan stood up and took the cups to the kitchen. He said he wanted coffee, I knew he wanted a cigarette.

"You can smoke in the kitchen but do it by an open window … and don't talk because the bugs are in there!" I called after him.

His reply wafted down the hall on a plume of smoke, "Okay."

I inhaled deeply sucking the weak smoke into my lungs.

"Still want one?" Sam asked.

"Yep."

"That's what's different," Doc said with a grin. "You're not surrounded by a fog of smoke anymore."

I flipped him off.

My phone rang. I didn't want to look at the display but I did as I lifted it and flipped the screen open.

"Caine."

Sam stopped what he was doing, his attention focused on the phone and me.

Caine sounded relieved as he said, "They're okay. They cleared the office themselves before the Bomb Squad made it in. You were right, the pendants were explosive devices."

When I breathed out, I realized I'd been holding my

breath since picking up the phone. I smiled at Sam. He slumped back into the chair. Relief washed over his face.

"Send them to complete the pick up at Grange's home and have the bomb squad go too. Then tell them to come home."

"Will do."

I hung up and called out to Rowan, "You done? I need to talk to you."

"Coming," he called back.

When he was in the room, I kicked the door shut and told everyone about the necklaces. Rowan sat down. The expression on his face spoke volumes. He was one un-happy camper.

"Why?" he asked.

I sat down and took a few seconds to put together everything I'd learned about Hawk since our first dance seventeen months ago.

"Hawk has identified your band as a way of getting a great supply of pre-teen girls. He's a psychopath and needs high stakes to enjoy the game – so he engages law enforcement. Seems he had so much fun murdering my husband that he wanted to play with me again." I watched Rowan's face as I poured out truths as I saw them. "This guy, he's a financier ... he is very good at what he does. He buys, sells and trades, like a stock trad-er, except he's dealing in kids not pork bellies. His only purpose is to make as much money as he can as quickly as he can. Not for anyone investing their kid's college fund – he's doing it for a terrorist organization."

"What will they do with it?"

I crossed my fingers in my lap so he couldn't see them and adopted an uninformed tone, "We don't know; it seems likely they'll use the money for weapons."

"What does he get out of messing with you and me?"

I was glad he didn't say us.

He reached for his cigarette packet. I didn't stop him. My hand reached for his pack without my knowledge. Before I knew what I was doing, I had a cigarette in my mouth.

Rowan leaned forward and took the cigarette gently. He raised an eyebrow, put it in his own mouth and lit it, then handed it back.

I held it for a split second; the struggle to quit flew out the window and I took a long drag. The smoke filled my lungs and soothing nicotine slipped treacherously into my blood stream. I had a head rush of major proportions. Talk about a dizzy.

God it felt good.

Doc shook his head but kept his mouth shut.

Could I answer Rowan's question without scaring the hell out of him I wondered, as he lit another cigarette. Sam coughed and fanned his face as smoke headed right for him.

"Yeah right," I said, smoke rushed from my mouth.

Sam grinned and tugged his own pack from his pocket. "If we're smoking inside, we're smoking inside." He lit up. "Sorry Doc, you're outnumbered."

"I think I can handle it."

Every drag on my cigarette invoked waves of nausea but I knew I could push through it – it'd only last a few minutes.

"Let me try to explain how this sick son of a bitch works," I said and hoped I actually could. "He doesn't care about anything or anyone. This isn't because he's some religious zealot ready to blow himself up. He doesn't care about religion either. Doing what he does isn't very exciting for him. Kids are easy to manipulate, mostly; he can get as many as he wants, whenever he wants. No thrill."

Rowan nodded.

"Last time we encountered him, he hired a couple of killers to work with him. It upped the ante sufficiently to give him a buzz. He even toyed with us. He did his homework: he knew who would get landed with the case and tailored it to suit."

"You?"

"Yes." I stabbed the cigarette into the ashtray Sam pushed in my direction. "This time, he dragged us half-way across the world. He knew I'd go. He made sure of that by killing Mac ... did a few other things I'm not going into right now ... and has roped you into his game." I still wasn't one hundred percent sure the band weren't involved, so I held off mentioning Europe and the litter of bodies left in New Zealand.

"How does it end?"

"Badly probably." I could feel the smile on my face as I thought how I wanted it to end, with Hawk's death.

"I'd hate to go up against you," Rowan said. He stubbed out his cigarette butt.

"That's because you're not a psychopath," Doc replied. "No normal person wants Conway on their ass."

I smiled. That was an unexpectedly nice thing to say.

"What a vote of confidence," I said, unable to shake the smile. "At this point, Rowan, we don't know how it ends. I sincerely hope we can get him before he disappears again."

"Is there much danger he will?"

"There's nothing to say he won't."

"... and this doesn't drive you crazy?"

"It's what we do. We're a specialist unit – Psychopaths R Us."

Doc nodded in agreement.

Rowan finally smiled. It was weak but it was there.

Sam piped up, "And more often than not the Unsub attempts to make it personal. Seems they like or maybe need to taunt. Maybe it ensures the ever-present suggestion that they may eventually be caught."

"... and do you? Catch them I mean?"

"Not always," Sam replied.

"Often enough that our budget doesn't suffer and our SAC comes off looking good," I said.

"No wonder you write the poetry you do," Rowan said.

I feigned a wounded expression. "What? You don't like my love poems?"

He chuckled. "Man, they're few and far between."

His shoulders relaxed. I knew it would be okay. I knew

he'd be okay. I wanted to believe Mac was right about Rowan and wrong about Carla.

The strains of a country song drifted through my mind. I heard Tim McGraw singing 'Don't take the girl.' Mac loved that song but it always made me cry. Now I needed God to listen: Please, don't take the girl.

Rowan's voice penetrated the song. "Typically, how long do these cases take?"

Tim McGraw faded away.

"As long as it takes," I replied as half my mind wandered off with the song.

"Ball park?" With that, he broke my thoughts wide open.

"That was the ball park ..."

Sam interrupted, "We'll work it as long as we have leads."

"Where's it going now?"

I heard the question as the final installment of a horrible poem leapt into my head. I grabbed a pen and a piece of paper and wrote it down while Sam answered Rowan's questions regarding the case direction and explained forensic testing. Unlike television, forensic testing isn't instantaneous; we're not the only agents using the lab and waiting for results from priority cases.

Doc was watching me write but from where he was, he couldn't see what I was writing.

The poem was now complete. I even had a title. As I read it, I felt bile rising in my throat. Was that really what was on my mind? The words sliced into my psyche like a hot knife into butter.

Gone.

It culminated in the end
Dripping off the edge of life
The ooze that was primordial slime
Is all that's left at the end of time.
Full circle?
Does it matter?

Rain pounding
Mud squelching
One by one, they leave
Surrounded by flowers
Alone in the earth
The moments before, did they count?
What was special about the day?
Did you measure up in a universal way?

Cold seeping through the lid
No matter how a life is lived
Biodegradable flesh is how it will end
How long before it all caves in?
Sinking quietly into the murk
Was it worth it?
Did you live?

I folded the piece of paper and slipped it into my jeans' pocket. No one should ever see that. Doc should never see that.

Rowan watched me with one raised eyebrow. "Sam

said you found six kids; did the Hawk guy expect that?"

"I don't think so. The pen was here on the kitchen counter. So he wouldn't have had our signal closing in on the address or been able to listen in on the conversations."

And no one in the office knew about it.

"You sure?"

"Well no, but it wasn't easy to get the information and took a lot of our Russian counterparts working damn hard to get us that lead. It didn't drop from the sky. Misha was so worried about conveying the information that he brought it himself. We didn't discuss our movements that night, not downstairs anyway."

He nodded and seemed satisfied with the answer.

"How about bugging me?"

I sighed inwardly. He had a lot of questions but answering was keeping me awake, which I appreciated.

"You were definitely part of the game. Judging by the two pens, he was hoping you'd hand one on to someone. Could be that it was me was fortuitous for him, rather than orchestrated. He'd have to have one hell of a crystal ball to know we'd meet at any point."

Rowan nodded.

"I'm thinking he used the bugs on you to track the band and arrange his kidnappings accordingly." While he was so interested, I thought about taking the opportunity to share the photographs with him. The whole idea of telling him that someone was watching him and me turned my stomach upside down. I looked at Sam. He was engrossed in what he was doing. True to form, he felt my eyes on him and he looked over.

I indicated he should take Doc and go make coffee or something. He stood, stretched, and excused himself.

There was a danger that I'd chew through my lip as I searched for the best way to introduce the pictures and the complex issue they opened.

"What's the matter?" Rowan asked.

I held up a finger. It wavered in mid air as I tried to tell him. I could feel the weight of the words and the knowledge that his career could be at stake should the public ever know the origin of the pictures.

"Hey, Ellie ... whatever it is, it can't be that bad." He sank to his knees in front of me and I wanted to throw up. How could he be so wrong?

"Talk to me."

Did he think I didn't want to? I wanted the floor to open up and swallow me.

"Please."

Words don't fail me. I couldn't decide if I was going to choke, or trying not to gag.

"How much do you believe ... any publicity is good publicity?" I asked, knowing I was asking the question of one of the most private celebrities on the planet.

He didn't say a word, not one word.

"Hawk has left photographs. He started leaving them in Christchurch, stuck in the door of my hotel room. The last lot he had placed on my kitchen counter. You're in some of them."

Rowan never flinched; his eyes remained locked with mine.

"No one knows about the photographs except Delta team. We don't release sensitive case information to the media."

My tongue played with the stitches in my mouth while he weighed up my words.

Finally he spoke. "Thank you."

I blinked. "Thank you?"

"Yes, thank you. You don't have to worry. Even if they did leak out, I'm not going to be running screaming because our names are linked in the press."

"But having them linked by a child trafficking terrorist?"

He shrugged. "Not much difference between him and the paparazzi."

He had a valid point. The difference could come down to the semantics of predation.

Chapter Thirty-Six
Last Man Standing

It was still dark on Tuesday morning when Lee and Misha checked in to report they'd located the wrappers from the pens. Lee had something else to report, which seriously spooked me.

"Ellie, we found two photos stuck in the doorjamb at Rowan's place."

My eyes closed hoping there would be no spinning as I readied myself for the next part of his sentence.

"One of Rowan standing in your hallway, carrying coffee cups and one of Carla, sitting on a bed brushing her hair."

"That's not possible," I muttered. Except I knew the picture of Carla was possible. I knew the GPS in the pen would've sent our location to Hawk when I visited Carla with the freaking pen in my pocket. What if he planted something before we moved her? I wanted to smack my head into the wall. I couldn't be sure Carla was safe, all because of that stupid pen.

"He's walking toward the living room with four coffee cups, some kind of balancing act."

"How the hell is that possible?"

"My advice to you is ... check the hallway for a camera and get out of the house. Say nothing that could be overheard."

"All right, we'll see you soon," I replied and rapidly

tried to think of somewhere to meet, somewhere safe, somewhere unknown. "I'll text you in ten."

That seemed the best option and least chance of anyone eavesdropping.

We hung up. I tapped Sam on the shoulder and indicated his laptop. He handed it over. I opened the notepad and typed, '*We're being watched. Could be a camera in the hallway*', then showed the note to Doc, Rowan and Sam.

Sam nodded as he read it and after a few minutes of key tapping, he opened a window on his computer screen. I recognized it as a program we used to eavesdrop on electronic signals. A few minutes later a picture that looked exactly like my hallway flicked up on the screen. Doc and Rowan gathered around him and watched. I walked into the hallway then back, pretending to check the front door. The angle of the picture gave us a location so I knew roughly where the camera would be. Above the door was a clock, the camera had to be concealed near it. Whoever was watching saw us coming and going. I couldn't see anything without staring straight at it and that would've given too much away.

"Volume," I whispered to Sam. He turned it up.

"Good coffee Rowan," I said in my usual speaking voice. Before I'd finished, the sound streamed into the room via the laptop.

I nodded at Sam. He turned it off.

Dammit, the pen in Lee's pocket masked the signal from the freaking camera. Fuc'n pen.

On a piece of paper I wrote, 'Get your jackets, we are

out of here.' I slid the paper toward the men.

Rowan took the pen and wrote, '*Can't you take the camera down?*'

I replied, '*It's too late, he's seen and heard too much.*'

We grabbed everything we needed and left the house. Rowan's car was on the street so was Doc's. Sam's was behind mine in the driveway.

"Whose car?" Rowan asked.

"Not yours or Doc's, they've been sitting on the street ... this guy likes bombs and knows where Ellie lives," Sam replied.

Rowan blanched. I shook my head at Sam. He'd obviously forgotten Rowan was a civilian; bombs tend to scare normal folk. On the qt, they didn't do wonders for my sense of security either.

"Let's take Sam's," I replied with a reassuring smile.

I jumped into the front passenger seat and opened my laptop on my knee. Rowan climbed in the back. Sam drove. I called Lee as we approached the first intersection.

"Meet us at work," I said then hung up.

Sam smiled. "Good thing that's where I was headed."

"Looks like Crowe did more than upload a program to run Mac's webcam and leave pictures on my counter." I remembered what Noel told me about Crowe.

Someone told him I wasn't home. Our mole? I had the GPS pen. Hawk would've known where I was. But Lee borrowed the pen at the airport and didn't give it back until after the break-in. So Hawk wouldn't have known I was home until he heard Lee talking to me on the phone. What else did I do or say with that pen around?

I'd had the pen since we left New Zealand. He wasn't just one step ahead, he was all over us.

The email alert chimed as we pulled into the underground garage an hour later. I opened it to find it was a photograph. This time it was the guy we knew as Hawk waving from stairs that led to an airplane. The time and date stamp said it was only fifteen minutes earlier.

"He's leaving!"

I called Caine. "He's leaving, looks like Dulles International airport, the picture is fifteen minutes old."

"I'll make some calls," he replied.

I hung up.

"Come on, let's go," I said, willing my voice to remain calm. "Rowan, I'll show you where our office is."

There was nothing to say as we walked to the stairs and began the climb. Halfway up, Rowan asked how much further there was to go and why we didn't take the elevator.

Doc stepped in. "She has an illogical hatred of elevators."

Doc didn't mention that having BPPV made that hatred more pronounced because the movement unbalanced me. For that I was grateful.

Rowan laughed. Yay me, I live to amuse.

We climbed the rest of the stairs in silence. The knowledge of the photograph at the airport severely dampened my mood. I wanted this over. I wanted him caught.

Preferably, I wanted him dead. Eye for an eye. I wanted to rip his arms off and beat him with the soggy ends.

My phone rang as we walked the carpeted hallway to our offices. It was Caine.

"You're going to love this. No Hudson Hawk was on any passenger list, but a Harry S Stamper was."

"*Armageddon* … he's changed his name."

The song I'd heard in Christchurch came rushing back. Aerosmith, 'I don't want to miss a thing.' It meant more than I first thought. That was my first hint at Armageddon.

"Want to know where he's going?"

"Sure," I said.

"Syria."

The weight I'd felt lift when we found the kids, hit me so hard I struggled for breath. It crushed me.

I flung open my office door, smacking it back against the closest desk. I kicked the waste paper bin across the room so hard it dented the wall.

Sam sat on the edge of his desk. Doc plonked himself into Lee's chair and Rowan hovered in the doorway. I threw my chair into the wall behind my desk smashing a hole through to the next office.

"Fuck!"

Chapter Thirty-Seven
We Weren't Born To Follow

Tuesday had been a long day of wading through transcripts and evidence reports. The only good thing I could see in Hawk leaving was that Carla was safer. I didn't believe for one second that she was completely safe. I still hadn't uncovered the mole. My suspicions were my suspicions and I hadn't shared them. We knew from the chat room that the person using the screen name DaveAddison, was in the Middle East and the person using MaddieHayes, was in Virginia. It stood to reason that Addison was Hawk and he was gone. But who was Hayes? We were still waiting for some more evidence reports. Until they arrived and we truly had nothing more to follow, by way of leads, the Butterfly murders file was active. I pulled up a report from New Zealand police. The passport used by Weinberg was a fake, as we'd suspected. Police discovered a netbook in his hotel room and analyzed his activity. They found a link to a chat room. The same unofficial Grange chat room we'd been investigating. Stephanie Harris's work computer was also subject to the same forensic analysis. Again, they found a link to the chat room; evidence that suggested she was frequently in the room. She also belonged to the official site. That didn't please me.

A property owner found Abbey Jenkins's mother dead in an empty apartment. Police sent me the scene photographs. I could almost smell the chlorine in her hair through the paper. I was very glad I didn't have to visit that crime scene in person. I've seen enough of Hawk's handiwork to last a lifetime. The face told me it was Hawk's work. Peaceful. Drugged prior to death.

"Don't give me that look," I greeted Noel, as he sat in my office drinking FBI coffee. I was feeling more than a little cantankerous.

"What look?" Gerrard asked, inspecting the transcript from the unofficial Grange chat room that I handed him.

"That you-know-better smirk you are so famous for."

His eyebrows rose incredulously. "Have dinner with me tonight?"

"My father warned me about men like you."

He smiled. "Your father trained me."

"And you want to have dinner?"

He shrugged lightly. "The alternative this pretty boy pop-star?" He waggled a handful of pages at me but didn't wait for an answer. "Apart from riveting dinner companionship, what else can I do for you?"

"Let me talk to David Dunn and that jerk we picked up in Christchurch. The one who called himself Tom Mix. Harvey Bauer, wasn't that his name?"

"Why?"

My turn to give an incredulous eyebrow lift. "Because this is my case. I've lost Hawk. I need to know what they know."

He shook his head. "You think I'm withholding information?"

Did I think that? No. I thought the right questions weren't being asked but knowing how good Gerrard was at interrogation, maybe it wasn't my smartest thought.

I dropped my bomb. "There's a mole in the FBI."

"You're sure?"

"Someone told Dunn how to find me and possibly warned him I was about to arrive at Cassandra Smith's home. The only person who knew where I was that day was someone attached to Delta."

"Do you know who?"

"I think so. Proving it will be difficult now. But I think I know."

"Let me talk to Dunn again and see what I can find out in the light of this new information," Noel offered.

"Okay. Now tell me why Grange is so interesting to NCIS and the CIA."

"His name keeps coming up and we have ongoing Marine involvement in this case. It's a precaution. We're doing our jobs."

"I'm doing my job too." I leaned back in my chair. "So it's got nothing to do with nuclear weapons?"

He smiled, raised one eyebrow and said, "Dinner. You need to eat sometime." His immediate dodging of the question spoke volumes.

"I do. I'll take a rain check." I also needed to sleep but I wasn't about to do that either.

He nodded. "All right, you know how to reach me." On that note, the next best thing to Jethro Gibbs strode out of my office.

I stared down at the transcripts. What was I missing? I wondered where else in the World Wide Web he trolled for children. Disney sites? Barbie? Nah. He needed vulnerable victims, ones desperate and malleable. Band chat rooms were clever. Pose as someone they can't resist or better still as a mother figure or just a friend. Smart. Picking a Grange chat room might've been clever right up until we arrived.

Lee was at his desk writing up reports.

"Hey. We need to investigate this Grange chat room more thoroughly."

"What have you found?" he asked.

"I don't know exactly." I thumbed through the papers again. "At least one woman claims to know the person calling himself Dave Addison. And another seems convinced but doesn't claim to know him personally."

"You want to know how well they do know this person?"

"Yeah. Physical addresses of the most frequent members. I need to know if that woman has spoken with him on the telephone, met in person, webcammed or is this blind faith and only chat room and email?"

"Hawk used a woman before; could be doing so again."

"Could be. Last time she was a willing participant. Are these women, or are they idiots?"

"You heading down some sick, twisted curve ball road here Chicky Babe?"

"I think so."

I'd gone to the dark side. I stared at the papers on my

desk and allowed myself to visit the worst case scenario.

Someone tapped on the office door, then opened it. Doc walked in.

"How goes the fight?"

"Slow," I replied. "Grab a chair; tell us what we're missing."

Doc pulled up a chair next to my desk.

"I'm signing into that unofficial Grange chat room." Something twinged and prodded at me. "Do we still have agents in that room?"

"Nope. They were pulled when we lost Hawk; they turned over information to the Lost Innocence Initiative. You were right about a predator using the room and that it wasn't anything to do with Hawk."

I signed in as Otherwisecat. Lee grabbed his laptop and signed in as well. Sitting staring at the babble in the chat room wasn't exactly riveting stuff. It was akin to watching a *Days of Our Lives* episode. Two women declared they would kill for Rowan. Two planned to stalk him on the remainder of the *Drifter* tour. Several read fan-fiction on some site. They were eager to share the link with me. I opened it in another tab and discovered it was more like fan-porn. Nasty.

Doc seemed to enjoy it. "Imaginative stuff."

The conversation in the chat room turned to Facebook. I swear I could hear squealing as they typed using more exclamation points than anyone could ever need.

It didn't take more than a few questions to ascertain if any of the women had jobs capable of feeding their stalk-ing. I was curious. They weren't CEO material but it seemed that manufacturing plants paid quite well; they had money to burn when it came to the band, so why not belong to the official site?

I thought back to the infrequent concerts I'd attended in my life, while two woman discussed being in the first five rows at every concert in Europe. That was serious money. It was also a serious addiction. Then I realized they did belong to the official site as well as this fake one – they couldn't get tickets like that without being a fan club member. I wondered how far they would go to make sure they always had concert money on hand. David Addison's screen name popped up.

Lee typed quickly then said, "I'm running a ping and trace on his IP address, Ellie."

I waited with escalating impatience, while women fawned all over him. He started asking how many of them had children.

"He knows I'm here," I said. "He's recognized my screen name."

Lee agreed.

Two seconds later a private message box opened on my screen. "A message from *Addison*." I proceeded to read it out to Lee. "'*They're too easy.*'"

"Nice, are you going to reply?"

"Yep. This is my reply. '*I'm sorry don't think I know you.*'"

Lee laughed.

A reply came back very quickly. "He's annoyed. He says, '*Did Christchurch mean nothing to you?*'"

"You going to reply?"

"No. Where is he?"

"He's routed his signal through several proxy servers across Europe, it's almost resolved. He's in Syria."

"Look at the room!" I said. "He's trying to find out who has kids and who is going to a concert in Dubai next month."

"They have that much money?" Lee replied.

Not these women apparently, but four of them suggested friends from the United Kingdom who were going and taking their twelve- and thirteen-year-old daughters.

"We need to shut this guy down." I private messaged all the women in the chat room and told them I was an FBI agent and that they were talking to a predator. Lee was working on having the room closed by the owners of the chat platform. He'd left his laptop and was on the phone talking to someone about the chat room.

His email alert sounded. "I have IP addresses and real names for registered members of that chat room, who are in there now."

"Awesome."

An alert sounded. I looked at another private message on my screen.

'Pretty pretty Carla is going to be mine.'

"That's wrong. Tell me that's wrong."

Doc turned my laptop to face him.

"It's wrong. He's in Syria and Carla is in a new safehouse." He closed my laptop. "What we're going to do is go home and get some sleep."

"Sleep? He's going to take Carla." I could feel panic rising.

"He's in Syria," Doc repeated.

Lee stood up. "Doc's right. Let's go. This is just driving us nuts."

Outnumbered. I held them at bay for a moment and called Carla. While I talked I found myself being escorted down the hallway and then up the stairs.

"Hey, everything all right? The protection squad still with you?"

"Yes, Mom." She sounded groggy. "Everyone's here, everyone's fine."

"Just checking."

"It's ten o'clock. I was almost asleep."

"Sorry baby. This will be over soon and then you can come home."

"Yay. Goodnight, Mom."

"Goodnight Carla."

Chapter Thirty-Eight
I Won't Lose Faith

We arrived at the office early Wednesday morning and spent most of the morning going over everything we found the day before. It was nearly three in the afternoon when the world turned upside down.

Heavy footsteps pounded up the corridor outside our office. Suddenly Sam filled the doorway. "We have a problem SSA."

I turned from Lee to Sam who filled the doorway. "What's up?"

"This ..." He hauled Joey into view.

"Joey?" I stood up. "Let's take this to an interview room."

Sam nodded. He escorted Joey with a firm grip on his upper arm to one of the many interview rooms scattered along the corridor.

Once inside the sparsely furnished but comfortable room, I enquired what the problem was.

Sam prodded Joey. "Tell her."

Joey fidgeted. "It's Carla ..."

"And? I'm going to need more than that."

"She's gone."

"Gone? Gone how ...?"

She's under protection. Chrissy McQueen is with her. Carla can't have gone.

"I think taken." He dropped his head so far it almost

hit the table he sat at. "I didn't know who the guy was. He stopped me when I was leaving her house, a couple of weeks ago – the day you took me there."

"When did she disappear?"

"This afternoon."

I glanced at Sam. "Amber alert – how long ago do you think she disappeared Joey?"

Sam waited for Joey's reply.

"An hour and thirty minutes."

"I'm putting out the alert," Sam said, and left the room.

"What guy stopped you?" I thought back to that day. I took Joey to visit Carla and woke up the next day in a hunting cabin, prisoner of a Marine called David Dunn.

"Some creep, never said his name. Asked me all these questions about you. Stupid shit, like what you talked about in the class that day."

I flattened my hands on the table and leaned toward him. "What'd you tell him?"

He looked panicked. "Am I in trouble?"

"No. What did you tell him?"

"I told him about how you talked about poetry and movies and the FBI."

Movies. *Die Hard 4.0*. Bruce Willis.

"I'm going to show you a picture. Tell me if you've seen him before."

I flicked through the pictures in my phone and showed him the one a kid in New Zealand had identified as John McClane and that Misha thought was Hudson Hawk.

"Yeah, that's him."

"You're sure?"

He nodded.

"Stay here. I'll be back." I left Joey and ran back to my desk. Lee was still working on closing down the chat room and briefing Cyber on the latest attempts at procuring children via the chat room. He looked up as I slid into my chair and started going through files.

"Problem?"

"Joey thinks Carla was snatched. He identified Hawk as the man who asked him a ton of questions about me." But we had a picture of him getting on a plane. What the hell was going on? My head spun as I realized he'd somehow followed through with his threat. "I think I know where the Bruce Willis thing is coming from now."

Lee nodded. "Tell."

"My favorite movie?"

"*Live free or Die Hard*." Lee replied without thinking.

"Yep. That's what Joey told Hawk too."

"But he's been using Hawk since we first met him."

"Yeah ... he has. I think he's from here. I think he's from New Jersey," I said, typing quickly as flashes of insight fired in my brain; knowledge I couldn't explain to myself, let alone anyone else. "I think the Hawk thing was him being a smart ass. He looks foreign. He looks like we thought, of Russian and Arab descent but that doesn't mean he wasn't born here." I was looking for passenger manifests for airlines that flew into Dulles, matching the times and days we suspected Hawk to have re-entered the

United States after leaving New Zealand.

"Where was Hawk from, in the movie?"

"Hoboken," I replied. "What if his visits to the US coincided with more personal matters, even family commitments?"

"He left the country using the name Harry S Stamper and headed for Syria. That may be him in that chat room – he's accessing it from Syria," Lee said.

"Nicola saw him as John McClane and she said something about his accent." I scrabbled for my notebook and rifled through pages of notes. "He told her he was from Russia but his accent was like mine but more. Whatever the hell that means."

"She didn't react to Rowan's accent?"

I flipped pages and looked for my observations as she met the band. "She said he sounded more like McClane than I did."

New Jersey.

I started running Hoboken through all the airlines I could think of, hoping it would trigger something. It triggered something all right; who knew so many people from Hoboken traveled overseas? I began to apply filters to my search. Lee came around my side of the desk.

"Where's the jpeg of the picture of Hawk?" he asked, nudging me out of the way and double clicking on the electronic version of the case file. "Facial recognition software might pick something up."

"Good thinking."

He grinned and tapped his head. "Up here for thinking, down there for dancing."

"Can I leave you to it? I want to get back to Joey."

"Go. I'm fine here."

Chapter Thirty-Nine
Stick To Your Guns

"Joey, tell me why you think Carla has been taken."

"She didn't answer my latest text messages this afternoon."

Oh, come on.

"Joey – I need more than that."

"And that guy who questioned me, I think I saw him when we were hanging out yesterday."

"Hanging out. You and Carla? Where?"

"Yeah, me and her. We'd been to the movies and went for ice-cream after."

"Agent McQueen?"

"She was with us."

"Did you tell Agent McQueen you saw him?" He nodded his head. "She said I was imagining things."

Joey sounded beaten. He was dealing with weight-of-the-world stuff.

"We'll do our best to find her, Joey. You wanna hang out here with us?"

He nodded. "Is that man who asked me questions the guy who killed her mom?"

The truth burst forth from my mouth. "Yes. I think it is."

His tough shell crumbled. Tears sprang.

There was no escape. I was alone in the room with a distraught teenager and I was the cause.

"Hang on, Joey. Just hang on. I'll be right back; I need to talk to my team."

I sent five text messages. I sat down and waited. One by one everyone I'd messaged arrived.

"Joey, this is Special Agent Lee Davenport, Special Agent Kurt Henderson, Special Agent in Charge Caine Grafton. You know Sam." I waited. With a flourish of his long black leather coat Misha stepped into the room. "And this here is FSB officer Misha Praskovya." I clamped a lid on the Mills and Boon/Harlequin thing that happened whenever I saw Misha in his coat. Now was not the time for romance book covers to come to life. Bad enough I was dealing with Kevin Costner flashes every time Doc got too close. I surely didn't need Fabio as well.

I gave a briefing on everything we knew from Joey about Carla's disappearance. It wasn't much.

Sam put a BOLO out on Carla to supplement the Amber Alert. Misha spoke to Joey, "The day you were asked questions by Hawk ... we were under the impression that Hawk was en route to New Zealand. But he was here."

Christ! How did I miss that?

"He was here," I whispered.

Lee looked at me. "I'm on it. We were looking at the wrong days." He tapped on his laptop.

"How is he in two places at once?" I grumbled. "I fuc'n hate ghosts."

"Who saw him in New Zealand? We had an ID – yes?" Sam asked, more to find the information in his head than expecting an answer. "Nicola Gallagher, our nine-year-old. She went missing when?"

"Abbey Jenkins was the first kid to disappear. She was missing five days before we found her. Samantha Rowe was next, then Tasha Cravino. Nicola disappeared the day after we arrived," I replied. "Then Melanie Talbot went missing. They found her body – she died trying to escape. Samantha Rowe and Tasha Cravino have not been found."

"The day after we arrived," Lee repeated. "Look at this." He spun his laptop toward me. It was the passenger manifest for our flight to New Zealand. I saw it without having to be directed. Harold S Stamper was on our flight. "Seating plan?"

Lee pulled up the plan. "He was across the aisle. The whole fuc'n trip. Right there."

He pulled up his passport information.

Tears prickled in the back of my eyes.

"We need to find out who he really is. Misha told us Hawk flew to NZ as Eddie Hawkins, but we now think he flew to New York or DC. So maybe someone else flew as Hawkins – while Hawk came in here as Stamper. Two places at once. Two Unsubs."

Two. That changed everything. Or did it. Were there two Unsubs or one man with two identities? Did he find someone who looks enough like his passport photo to fool people?

Joey grabbed my arm. "You need to find Carla."

Yes I fuc'n know!

A wave of holy hell crashed over me. I could feel the

color drain from my face as the tide receded.

I clung to an image of Carla, as if it were my life preserver. I had to find her.

My cell phone buzzed. I checked the display.

Carla.

"It's from Carla," I said and opened the message to find it was a photo of a church. "It's a picture, anyone know where this is?"

Caine took my phone and passed it around. Moments later Lee had an answer. "I think its St. Paul's, Rock Creek." He entered the name into Google Earth and seconds later was zooming in on the church. "Am I good or what?"

"You're awesome. St. Paul's, Rock Creek – zoom out a bit." Damn. The old cemetery gave a lot of hiding places and a lot of ground to cover.

I hoped Carla still had her phone and it was on. I texted a reply. *I'm coming to get you.*

Caine paced the room talking on his cell phone. When he stopped, the room fell silent. "There was a shooting at a college campus in Northern Virginia," Caine said. His voice grated more than usual. "Our SWAT teams were deployed by Chrissy."

A lump in my throat threatened to choke me.

"We do this alone – without SWAT," I replied. I looked at Sam. "Gear up: meet us in the parking garage. Misha, go with him."

"Yes, SSA." He hustled from the room with Misha.

I hurried down to my office and took two spare magazines from my drawer. I pushed them into the magazine holder on my belt and tucked in my shirt. My phone rang. It was Sean. "It's her isn't it? Chrissy McQueen?"

"Yes. There is a large discrepancy between goods purchased and income."

"That could be explained by an inheritance or lotto win – or selling drugs?"

"I wouldn't rule out drugs … from what I can tell … she's been paid in cash by someone and it started about two years ago."

"Thank you." I hung up. From the closet, I took an FBI jacket. I pulled it on and turned around almost smacking straight into Doc.

"I saw how the color drained from your face."

"So would yours if it were your kid."

"Yes, it would."

He was starting to grow on me.

Doc and I hurried back to the meeting room.

Even he was unprepared for my next statement. "Arrest Special Agent Chrissy McQueen."

The entire room fell silent.

Caine almost dropped his phone. "Ellie?"

"Arrest her. At this stage she's an accessory to murder. She's the only one who could've passed information to Hawk and his minions." And one other thing. "Where the hell is she?"

"I'll find her," Caine replied. "You're sure?"

"I pulled in a favor and had us all put under the microscope. It's her."

Caine nodded. "Go, bring Carla home."

Joey jumped to his feet. "I'm coming."

We're here again with a teenager demanding to come and it went so well last time. I mentally slapped myself upside the head. Here we go again.

"Stay here, I'll get someone to keep you company," I said.

"No. You don't understand. I have to come."

"Fine." I glared at him and delivered a severe caution, "You stay in the goddamn car and you do as you are told, or so help me God I will cuff you to the nearest railing and leave you there." And he was wrong, I did understand.

"Okay." One corner of his mouth twitched upward.

Chapter Forty
Live Before You Die

I called DC Police as we drove and asked for help in searching for Carla in and around Rock Creek Park. I wanted to tell them how urgent it was, that the world may end tomorrow and I haven't had a chance to be her mom yet. But a warning voice in my head restrained me. It was Wednesday and we still didn't know what was going to happen at 6 p.m. tomorrow. I had Lee's laptop on my knee. The screen and the facial recognition software running made me feel sick, even though I missed most of the activity. I was hoping against hope that the picture we had of Hawk would turn up something. We'd run it through the system first time we came across him but had been limited by the software. Now we had a newer version. Another difference was confirmation that the man in the picture had definitely been involved in the kidnapping of children in New Zealand.

Joey fidgeted behind my seat. I turned my head to look at him.

"We'll find her," I said. "We will."

"We're five minutes out," Lee said.

An alarm sounded from the laptop saving Lee from a witty and possibly caustic reply.

"We have a match, actually we have two matches," I said.

Lee turned into the trade entrance of St Paul's, drove

to the old stone church and found a car park nearby.

Doc tapped my shoulder. "So tell us, Conway – name that scumbag."

"That would be scumbags, plural. Boris and Viktor Abbasi of Hoboken, New Jersey. Identical twins. Born March 19, 1965 in Hoboken."

I called Sam.

"We're looking for Boris or Viktor Abbasi. Our Hawk is a twin."

"A twin. So why did one go and one stay?"

"Won't know until we find him."

I hung up. Lee was talking to DC Police. He'd taken the laptop and emailed the photos and driver's license information for both twins.

Joey tried the door handle.

"Kiddy lock, Joey. You're not going anywhere," I told him.

"Can't I help?"

Last time I left a kid in a car, it didn't end well. Lee nodded ever so slightly.

"You're coming. But you stay with us. No running off; no stupid behavior. There are armed cops looking for Carla. Do not get in anyone's way. Do not become a target."

Sam and Misha pulled up beside us.

Lee pulled the trunk release. I climbed out of the car, opened Joey's door and instructed him to wait by the trunk with me. Lee's door shut with a bang. I took a bulletproof vest from the trunk and handed it to Joey. I threw my jacket in the trunk and I pulled my vest over one shoulder then fastened the Velcro closures on the other shoulder and down the side.

"See?" I asked.

He nodded and followed suit. I pulled my FBI jacket back on. The three of us stood next to the car wearing Kevlar vests and waterproof jackets, announcing us as FBI front and back. Across the road, soldiers lay in the cold ground in regimented rows at the Soldiers' Home National Cemetery. I wondered what they would make of this.

Bob Marley squeezed into my consciousness singing 'Buffalo Soldiers.'

A police cruiser pulled up beside our car, then another beside that. A blond cop leaped from the driver's seat and called out a greeting.

"Josh, you're joining us?" I called back with a smile.

"Sure am. This here is Philip, and those two in the next car are Jessica and Bronwyn."

All four officers joined us wearing Kevlar. Never trust the dead. They have a habit of coming back and scaring the living daylights out of a person. I'm not entirely sure they can't use weapons.

With a quick scan of the visible graves for materializations of the incorporeal kind, I stopped looking for ghostly activity and reminded myself that the Abbasi brother we were after was far more dangerous than a pissed-off ghost.

The cemetery covered a lot of ground and we were few.

"Let's do this. We'll divide the area into thirds from this point." I swept an arm along the street encompassing the churchyard and surrounding cemetery. Joey muttered something I didn't quite catch. I announced, "We'll take the middle third."

"We're looking for a girl, Carla Torres: blonde, brown eyes, about five feet tall," Lee said. "She may be in the company of a male with a New Jersey accent. He looks European. He's wanted for murder and kidnapping."

Josh nodded. "Let's go find the kid." He and Philip moved off to the left of us. Bronwyn and Jessica took the right, which meant they covered the circle with tombs that looked like little houses. I wasn't in the least unhappy about that, they were creepy and I didn't want to go in one. The cemetery reminded me of the late seventies horror movie *Phantasm*. I expected to see things scurrying amongst the graves. Vigilance was required to keep an eye out for the Tall Man.

The rector was a lovely woman who wanted to help. She gave us full access to all church buildings and assured us she hadn't seen Carla. Why is it that no one ever sees the creepy scary goings on in graveyards? Bet she hadn't seen the Tall Man either and couldn't understand how graves were being robbed.

Slowly we made our way through the church; I was reluctant to yell out in the building but did it anyway. Somehow yelling for Carla slammed the imaginary door on *Phantasm*. I was relieved to see the door didn't have a mirror. "Carla Torres!"

Joey and Lee echoed her name as we searched each pew and every inch of every room.

Nothing.

Sam's voice bounced off gravestones outside as he called Carla's name.

I called out to the Rector to let her know we were leaving her church in peace and exited the back of the building, looked right and saw the creepy little crypt houses and Jessica leaving one. An involuntary shudder caught me by surprise.

The five of us spread out across the middle section of the graveyard. Misha had Joey with him. We began to scour the gravesites. Calling out every few minutes. The calls from the other teams floated on the cold wind as we all moved deeper into the cemetery.

I heard a small noise. I listened carefully. It sounded like crunching.

Crunching plastic. Perhaps a food wrapper trampled underfoot.

"Did either of you hear that?"

Apparently only I did.

I listened again then pointed. "Over there, there is someone over there."

My hand rested lightly upon the butt of my Glock. We were all close, no longer spread across the graves. I whispered to Misha, "Keep Joey with you. I'm going to the right."

"I'll take Joey back a little," Misha said.

"Thank you."

Misha grabbed Joey by the arm and took him back behind a sturdy gravestone. Sam, Doc, Lee and I closed in on the place where I'd heard the crunching.

Behind a large, old and ornately carved gravestone, I caught a glimpse of red fabric. On the ground near my foot was a granola bar wrapper. Somewhere farther to the north, I heard heavy running feet. I could see no one.

With my gun drawn, I rounded the grave marker. A red sweater lay on the ground. I holstered my gun and lifted the sweater. I recognized it as the one I'd bought for her at Christmas. There was a cell phone in the pocket. I took the cell phone and gave Lee the sweater.

"No one here," I called to Misha. "Bring Joey over."

Again, I heard running footsteps, this time fading into the distance.

Joey looked at the sweater in Lee's hand. "That's hers."

My fingers held Carla's cell phone tightly, hoping it would tell me where she was and be the talisman that would get us to her in time.

"Someone was here, we have trash on the ground; whoever it was left running," Lee said.

Nothing is going to grab us and pull us down.

"Why leave her cell and sweater. It's cold out here," Joey asked.

"We don't know yet," I replied.

When I asked Misha to take him back to the church. Joey exploded with rage.

"I'm not leaving!" he screamed, waving his arms frantically.

Misha stepped behind him and pinned both his arms to his body. The boy fought and as he started to yell, Misha clamped a hand across his mouth and whispered in his ear. It took a few minutes for Misha to subdue him. We couldn't hear what he was saying as he spoke quietly into Joey's ear but within a minute or so, he'd averted a potentially nasty scene.

Somewhere in the distance, I heard a girl scream. Carla. The scream physically hurt me. Pain seared through my heart.

Joey struggled free. Misha lost his grip on him as he snaked out of his hands.

"Joey stay behind me!" I said curtly, brooking no argument.

"I can get her ..."

He tried to pass me – I ankle-tapped him. He crashed to the ground, grabbing at me on the way down. I shook him off and regained my balance.

Misha swooped in and dragged Joey out of the way.

"He's trying to throw us off," Sam said. "I doubt Carla left this stuff – he planted it."

I pulled my cell phone from my belt and called Josh. "Get hold of all police. Tell them to back off. Let us bring him in, there is child's life at stake," I instructed.

"How about the cops at the amphitheater and Rock Creek Park?" Josh asked.

"Stand them down, await further instructions."

"Take care."

I closed my phone and clipped it back on my belt.

"He uses bombs," I muttered, looking at Doc.

"I know. Let's do this." He adjusted one of the straps on his field kit.

"You think she's wired?" Lee whispered as we covered the open ground fast, heading in the direction of the scream.

Breathing hard I replied, "I don't know."

We were closer now.

Another scream. This time it was cut off. We edged slowly forward using trees and gravestones as cover. It was cautious going, which made it slow. Every now and then, I glimpsed Carla. The Unsub had her sitting with her back to a headstone. He circled around her. Looking out, keeping watch in all directions.

I was fighting flooding adrenaline. My body wanted me to hurry up but my mind knew better. Forcing slow deep breaths, we edged closer. Dropping to our bellies to prevent detection, we moved across the hard ground, littered with broken marble, stones, sticks and glass.

Agonizingly slow.

We maintained a steady forward movement, only stopping when the Unsub faced our direction.

My heart thumped hard against my rib cage. Each slow deep breath took extreme effort, slithering with handguns and in desperate need of our Hostage Rescue Team and their kick-ass snipers to take Abbasi out of the equation.

I sat back behind a broken headstone. Doc crawled up beside me. Abbasi was about sixteen yards away. I looked for the shot. A hand signal alerted me to Sam's position. He flashed two fingers twice and pointed. He and Lee had eyes on Carla.

I inhaled slowly and made a fist. Silently I scooted a few feet closer followed by Doc. He shucked off the backpack he carried. Another headstone provided better cover, I moved closer. The good thing about old graveyards is the abundance of ornate large headstones and trees.

Lee signaled telling me the Unsub was agitated. Not good.

Stay calm.

Breathe.

Doc was right next to me as I peered from my cover and saw a clear head shot. With my arm supported on a broken and eroded piece of marble, I aimed and squeezed the trigger. A shot rang out from beside me. Two other shots rang out. So close, I almost missed them.

He fell.

Carla screamed.

I scrambled to my feet and ran to her with Doc on my heels. The Unsub lay crumpled on the ground about three feet away. I reached out and placed two fingers on his carotid artery. Nothing. He had a tidy hole in the center of his forehead, and blood spreading from three bullet holes in his chest. Four wounds, four guns.

Doc spoke from beside me, "Nice."

I looked at Carla.

"Mom!" she shrieked struggling against the tape that

bound her to the stone.

"Right here, hush now." I holstered my weapon. My heart pounded. "Did he give you anything?"

"You mean pills?" she asked, as Sam cut through the tape. I could see her terror dissipating.

"No sweetie, a hair clip or anything?"

"Yeah, a really ugly barrette. I wouldn't wear it. He shoved it in my jeans' pocket."

"Lee, Sam, Doc ... back the fuck away," I said, maintaining eye contact with Carla. They took two steps back. "Move!"

"We're not going anywhere," Lee said.

No time to argue. I pulled latex gloves out of my pocket and put them on.

"Which pocket?"

"Right front." Panic crept into her voice. "What's wrong?"

I didn't answer her question. "I'm taking the clip out of your pocket now." I lifted the fabric away, opening her pocket. The clip shone as the light caught it.

I eased my fingers around the top and extracted it slowly.

As I lifted it free, I noted it was thicker than most hair clips. I saw a tiny light flash in the back. I needed somewhere to put it.

Sam ripped the last of the tape from Carla's waist and hauled her to her feet. With much care, I set the barrette down on the ground and took Carla's hand. Doc took her other hand.

"Now we run!"

We ran back the way we'd come. Lee and Sam were close on our heels. Doc pulled Carla and I behind an enormous ostentatious headstone. Sam and Lee hunkered down next to us.

All our cell phones rang at once. I answered mine.

A loud explosion made me jump. My head banged back onto a protruding piece of an angel's foot. Carla grabbed my arm and almost jumped into my lap. I hugged her and spoke into my cell phone. "Misha she's safe."

I hung up.

Lee and Sam were talking to various police teams, calling off the hunt once and for all.

"Carla, what was his name?" I asked.

"Hudson Hawk. Said he knew Mom." She shivered. I took my jacket off and wrapped her in it.

I'm sure he did, he may have been the one who killed her mom.

"Why was he so agitated before we got to you?"

She smiled. "Because of you. He kept saying he was late and you were ruining everything."

"Didn't say what I ruined?" If I was ruining something, I'd like to be able to take credit for it.

She smiled slightly. "He wasn't real chatty, ya know?"

Something in her mannerism told me she might have made a few comments to help his anxiety along.

"He has a brother and whatever he was late for, has something to do with him."

I looked up when I heard Joey's voice. He was running toward us, yelling, arms waving. Not a trace of the cool sullen kid from the classroom remained as he whooped and hollered with joy, barreling full tilt toward us, while dodging gravestones and jumping graves.

Carla hugged me and stood up. "Can I?"

"Go!" I smiled.

She ran to him; they almost collided. Sam and Lee laughed. Doc shuffled closer to me.

"You okay – you hit your head pretty hard?"

"Yeah, I'm okay. What could he have been late for?" I wondered aloud.

"His own death?"

"Nope, he kept that appointment," I replied.

"We may never know now."

"Maybe not. So why Carla?"

Lee had an answer. "To fuck with you, Chicky. It pissed him off you saved her last time. This time around, he could really twist the knife by grabbing her again. He's been tracking and listening to you since the day we left New Zealand. He knew exactly how to fuck with you."

"Something's not right, Lee. We're missing something vital," I replied. "We're missing something. Everything they've done to date has been carefully orchestrated; this feels unfinished. He doesn't leave loose ends ... what have we missed?"

He nodded. "You'll figure it out SSA. You always do." He grinned. "He's most definitely finished, that was one helluva shot."

You do what you have to do to save the ones you love. People should not fuck with my family.

"SSA Chicky Babe," Sam said to get my attention.

"Yes," I said, looking up at him.

"The medical examiner will be here soon."

"Good," I said.

We all watched Joey and Carla.

"Cute, huh?" Doc said nudging me.

"Yeah, cute."

Misha shepherded them toward us, wrapping his coat tightly about himself as he walked. His actions reminded me how very cold I was.

Chapter Forty-One
Let Me Be The One

"Go home Ellie," Caine said perching on my desk. "It's been a hell of a few weeks and an adrenaline-pumped Wednesday."

"Tell me again where you found her?"

"We found Agent McQueen in her car with her throat cut. The car was parked at Regan Airport."

"Loose end."

"Go home."

"Not until Joey has somewhere to stay," I replied. "And what the hell was Boris late for?"

Caine leaned closer to me. "Go home."

I moved a stack of papers. "Soon."

"Where's Carla?"

"She's at home with my dad."

"Go home to your kid, Ellie. She's needs to know you are there."

I read a report from Detective Jones in New Zealand. When I was done, I handed it to Caine. He glanced over it quickly.

"Two kids still missing," he replied, handing it back. "What do you suggest?"

"Interpol. They not in New Zealand. They left with Boris or Viktor, whichever brother took them."

Lee knocked on the doorframe then stuck his head into the room. "Rowan showed up at reception. I escorted him up here."

"Is he with you?"

Lee nodded. "Yes."

"I'm just winding up loose ends, he can come in." I dished out top marks for Rowan's persistence.

Lee and Rowan entered the room. Caine shook hands with them both and then turned to me. "Go home. You can finish the report in the morning."

We'd successfully cleared him and Grange of any wrongdoing or hint of involvement in the Hawk saga. It helped having Noel Gerrard let us in on some of his surveillance.

"Soon," I replied and shifted my attention to Rowan. "Pull up a chair. I have something to show you."

Lee and Caine blended into the background until they no longer existed. I placed a set of documents on my desk and pushed them toward him. Rowan pulled a chair closer, sat down and picked them up. "What is it?"

"That's what it looks like when we sign off on a line of investigation. That there ..." I tapped the paper. "That officially says you and Grange were never involved with Hudson Hawk – or as we now know them – the Abbasi brothers."

"I'm not a suspect?"

"Yep, that's what it means." I waited to see if he'd ask if I ever thought he was involved. He didn't.

"Do you know why they did what they did?" he asked.

"Nope but knowing that one Unsub is now identified and in the morgue is a good feeling."

I didn't imagine I'd ever know why the Abbasi brothers turned against their country of birth and did what they did. Boris's corpse didn't talk much. We did know that none of the family was left in New Jersey. Their father returned to Saudi Arabia after the death of his wife. She'd died of cancer eight months earlier. Viktor Abbasi remained at large and on our Most Wanted list.

"Where do we go from here?" Rowan passed the papers to me. Our fingers touched, sparks flew.

"I'm going home," I replied. "To my daughter."

Someone knocked on the door. I looked up to see Doc wearing a clean dark grey suit and white shirt. He didn't look as though he'd been crawling through a graveyard. I beckoned to him.

"Do you want me?"

He grinned. "There's a dangerous question."

"Only the answer could be dangerous."

"Just dropping in to see how you are."

"I'm okay, thanks."

Rowan stood up to leave. "Call me when you have time. I'd like to take you out to dinner."

He extended his hand to Doc, they shook. "Thanks for everything you did."

"My job," Doc replied.

Rowan turned to me. "Call me." He leaned over my desk and kissed my cheek.

A spontaneous madness came over me. "Hey, you wanna come and hang out with me and Carla?"

He smiled, one of those smiles that could melt the Larson ice-shelf. It no longer felt like the world was about to end.

"I'd love to."

"Y'all be good now, ya hear," Doc said, as I turned my computer off and slipped out from behind my desk. "Rowan, you'll have to drive. Conway is not driving for another few days."

"See you, Doc. Welcome to Delta A. I saw you requested to be permanent and I approved it," I said as I left.

Rowan took me home. For my first official night as a parent, Rowan, Carla and I hung out. We were like a regular family. I helped Carla with her homework then we played Play Station. Rowan sucked at *Guitar Hero*. Carla went off to bed at nine, tired and happy. Rowan and I waited until she was sleeping then tiptoed upstairs. We talked and watched a few movies. As he told me about his fabulous childhood, memories of my mom's less than stellar performance surfaced. Or maybe they surfaced because *I* now have a child to take care of. "What was your mother like?" Rowan asked as he looked at photos on my bookcase.

A ticking time bomb.

"On the outside, like anyone else's mother ..." I smiled. "She was good at appearing normal to the outside world, for short periods at least. But we didn't bring friends home." I want Carla to bring friends home, to laugh and to embrace life.

"This is your mom?" He pointed to a photo of mom and dad together. "She's very attractive. I can see her in you."

God, I hope not.

"Was attractive. Now worm food," I replied, trying to find a new subject before the memories flooded back. Mom's voice squawked in my head, 'He's not your husband, you hussy! What's he doing in your bedroom?'

I wanted to yell back, 'Takes one to know one.'

"Do you have any good memories of her at all?"

I fought a tide of bruises and pain in search of a happy memory. With half a smile on my face I said, "She made good scrambled eggs."

With her fuc'n scrambled brain.

The last breakfast with Mom emerged in a frightening, clear memory.

"Ellie, you okay?"

I took a moment to figure out where I was. The wallpaper was familiar but the voice threw me. I looked at him, surprised.

"Yeah."

Ding-dong the bitch is dead.

"There's something wrong, what gives?" His hand touched mine sending a sharp shock that made us both flinch.

"Nothing at all." Nothing I can explain to someone who hasn't lived my life. I have a daughter now. I cannot be my mother. I have to be better than that. It's now or never.

He didn't look as though he believed me but he was smart enough to know he wasn't getting another answer.

I looked at Rowan. He yawned behind his hand.

Then I noticed the legal pad resting on his knee and the pen in his hand.

"Were you writing?"

"Yes," he replied, with a lingerie melting smile.

Good to know.

Somewhere inside my mind things whirred, cogs clicked to the next position and the penny dropped.

"Holy fuck!" I read over his shoulder and the words sang right off the page. It was amazing.

"Beg your pardon?" Rowan looked a little surprised.

"You wrote a song about my life!"

He corrected me, "Your life so far. I have a feeling there is much more to come."

A noise outside distracted me before I could ask more about the song.

"Did you hear that?" I asked.

Rowan nodded.

I looked at my watch. It was five in the morning – another night without sleep was over. I couldn't explain why I was hearing car doors closing, out on my driveway.

Chapter Forty-Two
Mister Big Time

Two dark-suited figures approached the house. They weren't easy to see against the backdrop of pre-dawn. The security lights flicked on when they got within five feet of the door but they were out of my line of sight by then.

I clipped my holster to my belt, shoved my cell phone and wallet in one pocket and badge in another, then pulled a zip-fronted hoodie over my long-sleeved tee shirt. Someone knocked. I stamped my socked feet into my boots. At the doorway I turned to Rowan, he was sitting on the couch in my room with the legal pad on his knee.

"This isn't looking that good, dark suits at zero five hundred. I'll call you when I know what's going on." This was not how I expected Thursday to start. *Thursday.* I wondered if my visitors had anything to do with the end of the world.

"I'm waiting right here with Carla," he replied. "Be safe."

"The numbers for Doc, Sam, Lee and my dad are on the night stand, just in case. Tell Carla I'll be back as soon as I can. Can you drop her at school? Call my dad, tell him something's come up."

The knocking became more insistent. Rowan leaped off the couch and grabbed me. His kiss nearly stopped my heart. "I'll take Carla to school and call your dad."

"I'll call you," I said and bounded down the stairs as another loud knock resonated through the house.

Carla stumbled out of her room. "Someone's at the door," she mumbled, rubbing her eyes.

"It's okay baby, go back to bed. I'm going out for a bit. Can you handle Rowan dropping you at school?"

"No way!" Suddenly she was awake. "Everyone will freak!"

"Yes way. I'm sure they will. Go back to bed." With a kiss on her on the head, I sent her back into her room. "Grandpa will pick you up if I'm caught up in work."

Another loud knock.

I flung the door open taking both suits by surprise. The less shaken one spoke. "SSA Conway, we were asked to pick you up."

"And you are?"

A badge flashed in front of my face.

"Since when does the CIA run errands?"

"Please come with us, ma'am, there will be an explanation when we arrive at the location."

"And when will that be?" I asked as they escorted me to the black Ford Explorer at the end of my driveway.

"In approximately half an hour, ma'am."

One opened the backdoor for me. The Pentagon was just under half an hour away at five thirty in the morning. Langley wouldn't take much longer. Guess it'd all become apparent by the direction we went. I sifted through the Hawk case trying to determine if I'd overstepped the mark, if I hadn't pulled back quickly enough when instructed to back off the military aspect. Had that been the case I was sure Director O'Hare would've had a few words earlier. I'd filed the case 'Open but Inactive' and marked it 'Pending Forensic Examinations', which still weren't completed. The backlog in the forensic division was legendary. I had no hope of pushing anything through now the case was inactive. I had a body in the morgue and had to satisfy myself with that.

At the Pentagon, they took me to a tactics communications room. There I found Director O'Hare, along with the Director of NCIS, several of the top brass from Navy, Army and Air Force. It was a joint-force smorgasbord.

"SSA Conway, welcome to the party," said a tall, distinguished-looking gentleman wearing more medals than I'd ever seen in my life. He stepped forward and shook my hand. "You can call me Ted; they call me General Platt." He smiled. I liked him right away.

"Pleased to meet you. Can I ask?"

He seemed to ignore my question. The room was close; it seemed overly full of people in uniform.

"Sit down; we have something to show you."

Pressed into a seat in front of a large screen, I sat blinking in the dim light. There were rows of tiered seats; mine was right in front of the screen. To my left, across a small walkway, sat Director O'Hare, she smiled. I determined her smile meant I wasn't about to face hell.

"Sit back and relax, Ellie," she said.

At the sound of a familiar voice beside me, I turned my

head to the right. "Agent Conway."

"Special Agent Gerrard," I replied. "Has this anything to do with not returning my calls and not discussing business when you did?"

"Yes," he replied quietly. "Watch."

The only light now emanated from the huge screen in front of us. It looked to be a desert somewhere. I made out a road and a ramshackle building or two and very little else.

I expected a bowl of popcorn to appear at any second. The popcorn didn't come but coffee did. The lights dimmed as the screen in front of the room split suddenly into two different images. The desert road was on my left. On the right the screen was blank.

A man crouched in the aisle on my left, he leaned close and said, "I have a headset for you; a friend of yours will join us to say hello in about two minutes."

I took the wireless headset and put it on. The man continued talking in hushed whisper. "Your investigation turned up the same men we were also investigating. They took the money made from the sale of children and purchased nuclear weapons from North Korea."

Misha told me that much.

"You caught one by the name of Hudson Hawk and now we've found his partner in Syria. He's going by the name ..."

"Harry S Stamper," I said. I hated knowing that they used the characters from Bruce Willis movies to fuck with me.

"Precisely," he said. "Harry Stamper passed through a checkpoint about an hour ago, heading out into the Syrian desert. We are tracking him now." He pointed. "That truck you see, is him."

"They're not just partners. They're identical twins. Born of a Russian mother and Arab father, in Hoboken, New Jersey."

"You identified them." He seemed pleased.

"Yes. Boris and Viktor Abbasi. Fingerprints from the dead twin matched Boris Abbasi. So the truck contains Viktor." I was surprised they hadn't ID'd them but had to consider they had and hadn't seen fit to share the information.

A crackle erupted in the room from the speakers and into my ear via the headset. I knew the voice and answered without waiting for an invitation. "Misha?"

The right-hand screen filled. A cockpit camera showed someone wearing full flight gear giving the thumbs up.

"We never said goodbye, Ellie."

"Where are you?"

Was that him I could see?

He gave a thumbs up signal with one hand. "I'm in an air force jet; I just left an aircraft carrier in the Black sea."

It was him but I was no closer to understanding what was happening.

"Why?"

"Watch and you will see, my friend."

The image of the cockpit faded out. The entire screen became desert and a lone truck.

The room fell into silence, five minutes later an American voice filled the room, ten minutes after that an Israeli voice.

I watched in silence as the satellite images on the screen panned out to show nine planes flying in groups of three from three different directions, so low radar couldn't detect them. I'm sure they had some fancy term for flying that low. But I didn't know what it was and furthermore, I didn't care.

I watched as the planes converged on a single target on a road. Six planes dropped back. Three continued. It was like being at the movies and hard to believe what I was seeing was live.

Lyrics filled my head and I didn't know where they came from.

I knew the song but couldn't think of the name. I sat on my hands to fight the temptation to call Rowan and ask him what it was.

A command was issued in three languages and then Misha said, "For you, Mac."

We all watched in silence as missiles launched from the planes wound their way across the desert toward the target. The planes peeled off and disappeared from the screen.

Nothing seemed to happen then a huge explosion erupted, the screen flickered and there *was* nothing.

Misha's voice came back, "Target destroyed. Over."

A lump in my throat made it hard to speak. Several false starts happened before I managed, "Copy. *Dosvidani-*

ja. I owe you a bottle of vodka. Over." I handed the headset to the man on my left. "Thank you."

Director O'Hare stood when I did. "That's it, Ellie. The irony is inescapable; the threat from the man who changed his name to Harry Stamper has been nullified."

I gulped. "That much I figured."

"He planned to set off three nuclear devices, purchased with his ill-gotten gains. One in Tel Aviv, one in Moscow and one in Washington DC."

"How close did he get?"

"The weapons were on site and armed everywhere except Washington; he had the codes with him."

"Except Washington?"

"His partner," she said, then smiled and corrected herself. "His brother was to arm the weapon but you shot him before he could."

"Where is it now?" A horrible feeling crawled inside me as I considered the existence of a nuclear device stashed somewhere in the DC area.

"We have it, it's been disarmed."

"Where was it?"

"The amphitheater at Rock Creek Park."

"We were over that way looking for a ..." The words almost choked me. "Missing teenager, but located her in a nearby cemetery." Finding Carla where we did was not a coincidence. I wanted to go home and hug her.

I had an idea it would be a long while before all the information sank in. Something triggered a distant memory: Fort Belvoir and its importance. I looked at the General, and couldn't think of his name. "Sir, TEC are situated at Fort Belvoir?"

"Correct."

"That's why the connection to the base." I gave myself a mental head slap. It was all to do with nuclear weapons. More exactly the placement of nuclear weapons. The US Army Topographical Engineering Center was his prime objective inside the base.

"They'd been trying to access classified information, some of which was high-tech computer-satellite programs. That would've made the cell a vast amount of money ... and jeopardized not only our security but the security of our allies."

And suddenly hitting him with a missile, or three, didn't feel like overkill.

Cogs whirred and things slid into place. "It was never about child trafficking, not really. That was a very clever ruse to stop everyone looking at the cell for anything else and uncovering their real objective: the nuclear devices and simultaneous worldwide attacks." As it all began to make sense it was even more frightening than when I thought he was a child trafficker. "The orphanages in Russia? That's where they hid the plutonium and everything else they needed?"

"Yes."

"Taking the kids – kept us busy globally," I said.

"There is no doubt they did take children from across the world and sell them ... but the prime objective was a coordinated terror attack."

"Turned out they weren't as clever as they thought."

He nodded. "We're grateful for your work and diligence on this case." General What's-his-name held out his hand. "Without putting too fine a point on it, you helped save millions of lives." We shook. His name came to me.

"Ted, do I know any of this?"

He smiled slightly. "I'm afraid not, SSA."

I figured this was beyond almost everyone's pay grade. It would've been good to slap a 'Case Closed' stamp on the file but barring that, it was excellent to know we'd got him. It warmed me to know he was nothing but mist and his brother lay in the morgue awaiting burial.

"Can I go home?"

Two men stepped forward. I recognized them immediately.

Director O'Hare said, "Talley and Cole will see you get home." She touched my arm and whispered, "Congratulations on your custody petition, I hear Judge Hartwell is fast tracking the adoption. You'll officially be a mother by Carla's birthday. Also heard a rumor about a certain rock star …"

"Thank you, being a parent is exciting and being a first-time parent of a teenager looks set to be quite the amusement-park ride!" I replied with a grin. "And the other thing, it's not quite a rumor, but I'm taking it slow. Dunno if he'll measure up."

"Best you boys get her home," she said to my dark-suited escorts. "Life is waiting."

I looked around hoping to catch Noel. He was talking on his cell phone. I watched as he disappeared through the door without looking back. I shrugged internally. He probably had another case.

Something made me stop as Cole ushered me toward an exit sign. "What are your full names?"

"I'm Jeffrey Talley, and this is Jamison Cole."

Their names seemed very familiar. An internal screen fired up, showing me the Wikipedia page devoted to Bruce Willis's filmography. It scrolled, pausing long enough for me to see 1995 *Twelve Monkeys*, James Cole and 2005 *Hostage*, Jeff Talley.

"You know what? I need to catch Agent Gerrard. Thanks for the offer but I'll grab a ride with him."

I hurried away without looking back. With a hearty shove the door swung wide, light flooded over me. I spotted Gerrard stepping into the elevator. "Hey wait up!"

He looked back, grinned and held the elevator.

Survivor

Everyday
I think about dying.
About disease, starvation,
violence, terrorism, war,
the end of the world.

It helps
keep my mind off things.

ROGER McGOUGH
Holiday on Death Row. 1979

About the author:

Cat Connor is a prolific crime thriller author hailing from New Zealand. Her expertise in the genre is reflected in her engaging and suspenseful narratives, which have garnered a loyal following. Her work is known for its intricate plots, dynamic characters, and relentless pace, keeping readers on the edge of their seats until the very end. She has authored multiple books, including the popular "Byte" series, which follows the exploits of an FBI unit that investigates serial crime.

Cat's passion for crime and espionage is evident in her writing, as she strives to create a world that is both authentic and thrilling. Her meticulous attention to detail and extensive research have won her critical acclaim and accolades from readers and peers alike. In addition to writing, Cat enjoys speaking on topics related to writing and publishing. Her talks are known for their candidness, humour, and practical advice. With her unique blend of talent, expertise, and passion, Cat Connor has established herself as one of the most exciting and accomplished authors in the crime thriller genre.

Her other passions include music, reading, tequila, red wine, coffee, and chocolate. When she's not writing she can be found binge watching TV shows and spending time with her much adored animals; Diesel the mastador, Patrick the tuxedo cat, Dallas the tortie Birman, and Jimmy the thug.

You can follow and contact Cat at the following places:

Website: www.catconnor.com
Twitter: @catconnor
Facebook: @cat.connor
Instagram: @catconnorauthor
Bluesky: @catconnor.bsky.social
Threads: @catconnorauthor

Also by Cat Connor:

The Kiwi set Veronica Tracey Spy/PI series:
[Nothing happens here] -2020
[Lure the lie] - 2021
[Leave a message] - 2022
[Whiskey Tango Foxtrot] - 2023
[Foxtrot Mike Lima] - 2024

The FBI based Byte Series:
Killerbyte - 2009
Terrorbyte - 2010
Exacerbyte - 2011
Flashbyte - 2012
Soundbyte - 2013
Snakebyte - 2013 (novella)
Databyte - 2014
Eraserbyte - 2015
Psychobyte - 2016
Metabyte - 2017
Qubyte - 2018
Cryptobyte - 2019
Vaporbyte - 2020 (red)
Vaporbyte -2020 (purple)
Raidbyte - 2021 (collection of short bytes)

Whispers in the water - the poetry of SSA Conway and SA Connelly
Torrent - a collection of short bytes

If I were a carpenter - SSA Kurt Henderson's story (novella)

Array - a collection of short bytes